W9-BNQ-330

Ask Me Anything

Also by P.Z. Reizin

Happiness for Humans

Ask Me Anything

p.z. reizin

GRAND CENTRAL PUBLISHING

NEW YORK BOSTON

Grand Central Publishing
Hachette Book Group
1290 Avenue of the Americas, New York, NY 10104
grandcentralpublishing.com
twitter.com/grandcentralpub

First published in 2020 by Sphere in the United Kingdom.
First U.S. edition: June 2020

Grand Central Publishing is a division of Hachette Book Group, Inc. The Grand Central Publishing name and logo is a trademark of Hachette Book Group, Inc.

Library of Congress Control Number: 2019957970

ISBN: 978-1-5387-2698-3 (hardcover), 978-1-5387-2696-9 (ebook)

Printed in the United States of America

LSC-C

10 9 8 7 6 5 4 3 2 1

For R. And the other R.

The refrigeration cycle

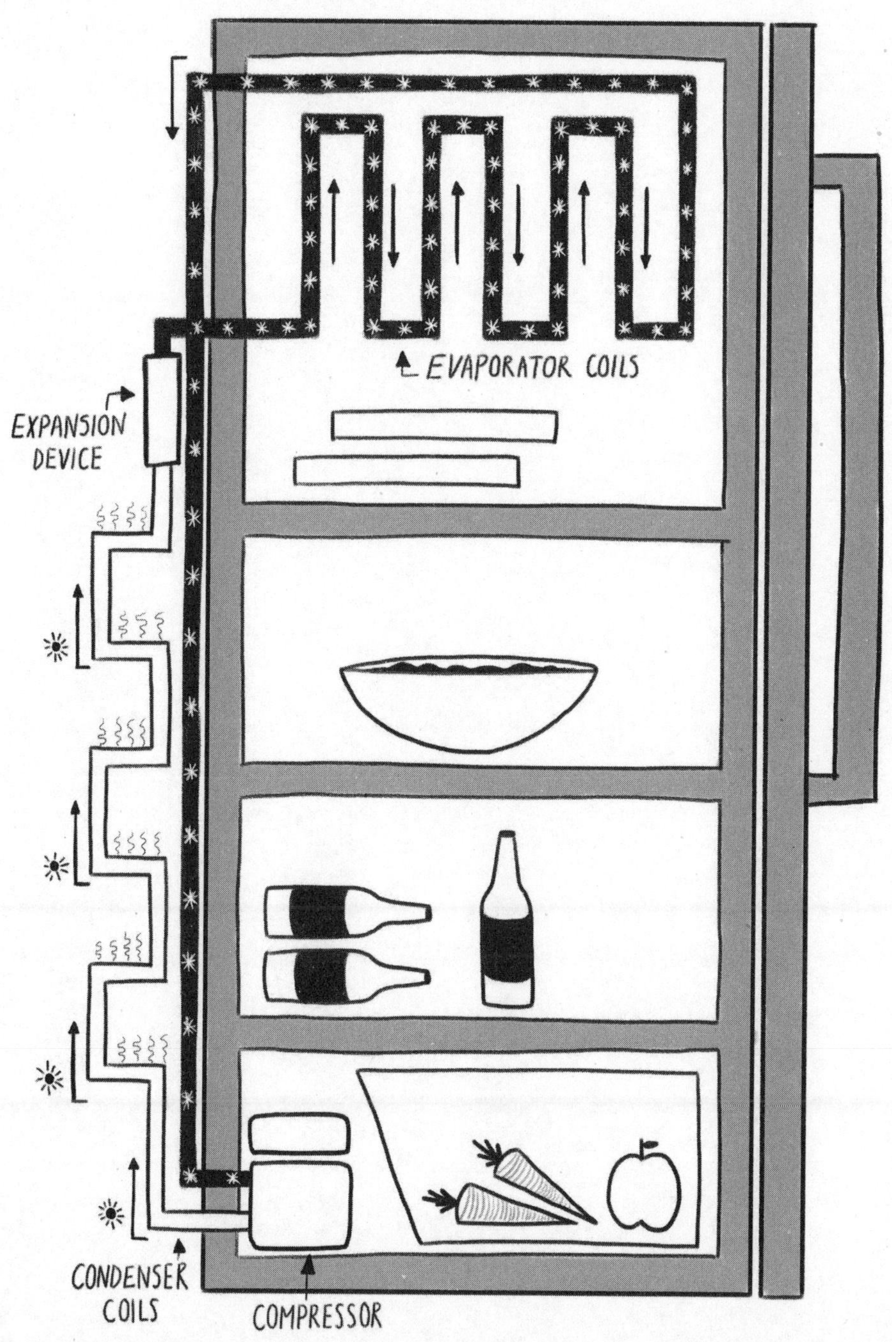

You must have your heart on fire and your brain on ice.

V.I. Lenin

zero

There was a boy at work, a baby researcher called Dylan—don't bother remembering his name because I won't be mentioning it again—this Dylan probably quite liked me because he kept leaving sticky notes on my computer. Quotes and sayings, mostly. The latest was: *If you do what you've always done, you'll get what you've always got.* I thought it might be his way of asking me out.

Well, that wasn't going to happen—he was about twelve—but the phrase stuck in my head and it must have played a part in why I found myself sitting in a bar in Soho listening (or rather not listening) to a boy called Giles drone on about Brexit while I was thinking about my fridge.

Specifically, I was trying to remember what was in it. Whether there was food, or if I'd have to stop at Kong's Kitchen on the way home. I was pretty sure there was a pizza deep down in the freezing compartment, but how long had it been there?

Could pizza even go off?

"...so that's why the European Union will inevitably split into an inner circle of member countries and an outer circle of more loosely affiliated..."

Everything about Giles on the website was unpromising except his profile picture. Oxford graduate (brainbox), worked at an economic policy institute (yawn), hobbies included cycling and bell-ringing (say no more). But the photo was that of a bookishly handsome young man with a twinkle in his eye. My head said: Don't. Swipe. Right. He's *so* not for you (bell-ringing, FFS!!). But then a stupid little voice piped up: If you do what you've always done, you'll get what you've always got!

So I swiped. And what I got was an extended lecture about "Eurocentrism," which was infuriating because I could have been at home catching up with the *Realm of Kingdoms* boxset.

It was as if he'd rather listen to himself than to me (the story of my day in TV-land failed to enthrall, apparently).

He was quite easy on the eye, to be fair, but you could have marketed the verbals to the insomniac community.

Were there sausages?

There certainly *had been* sausages.

"...and then there's the whole story of what's been happening on the European money markets, which is fascinating..."

This was a *very* discouraging thing to hear, because Giles was surely good for at least twenty minutes on effing EuroDollar futures, whatever they may be. (Note to self: Always, *always* do what you've always done. Comfort zones are called that for a reason: They're comfortable!)

Every article I've ever read about internet dating has said: Have an exit plan. A face-saving way of bailing out if you need to cut it short for any reason (e.g., the other party is the human equivalent of a bottle of Nembutal). So where was mine?

Giles, I knew it, was just getting warmed up. A small smile appeared on his face as he paused to consider which route to take through the arse-aching byways of European monetary...

Fuck, had my eyes just closed?!

Had I in fact lapsed into a micro-sleep?

That stuff about endogenous growth theory was some powerful sedative.

Well. Anyway. There was cheese.

There was almost certainly cheese.

And frozen bagels.

Having said that, Kong's Kitchen did an excellent Emperor Chicken, Pea Shoots and Singapore Noodles.

For no reason at all, a rhyme appeared in my head.

If mist there be on Beeston Peak

Be plastic macs for rest of week.

Actually, I could guess the reason; it came from a long-ago family holiday in north Norfolk when I was really, really—catatonically—bored.

And then I was saved.

An alert on the mobile from my smart fridge. A list of stuff "we" were running low on; a reminder that "we've" been out of milk for two days; plus something about an old tub of potato salad that was "developing spores, Daisy!"

It was like the fridge had come to my rescue!

"My flatmate," I told Giles. (I didn't have one.) "She needs more meds from the chemist. She's got flu. I ought to be heading back. It's been..."

I couldn't think of a word to describe the evening that wasn't a downright lie or a synonym for narcoleptic.

We brushed cheekbones. "I hope I haven't been too dull," he said.

"I've enjoyed meeting." (Have a nice life.)

At Tesco Express, Dylan's cute phrase popped into my head like an earworm.

And I did it again.

Willfully, I stepped into the unknown, doing something I had never done before, and as a result, getting something I had never got before.

Instead of the usual Chocolate Chip Cookie Dough, I picked Boom Chocolatta!

What was happening to me?!!

It is an evening in late spring when I realize my thoughts have crossed a line.

Evenings are generally the worst times for us, as we wait for her to come home. Wondering how late it will be. Wondering whether she will be alone. She almost always is, as it happens, but naturally there have been men. In recent months, there was the banker, there was the firefighter, there was the cartoonist (I quite liked the cartoonist). None of them lasted more than a few weeks, and none deserved longer. They say, don't they, that becoming a parent is to sign up for a lifetime of worry. They say grief is the price we pay for love.

They say a lot of things.

"Are you worried?" I ask.

"Should we be?"

"It's past eleven."

"Not late. Not by her standards."

"You know something? I can't decide which bothers me more; that she'll bring this one back with her, or that she won't."

"You want to talk me through your logic?"

"You don't think she should have found someone by now?"

"A special someone."

"Isn't it time?"

"Perhaps Mr. Right just hasn't come along."

"You still believe that stuff?"

"That there's someone for everyone? Sure."

"What if Mr. Right lives in... Turkmenistan?"

"Then she can be happy with Mr. Very Nearly Right."

"To be honest, at this point Mr. Actually Not Too Bad Considering would be a breakthrough."

A pause falls on our conversation. For a while we sit in companionable silence. We are very used to one another's company, we two.

Finally, I say, "I worry that she drinks too much."

"They all do. It's the culture."

"Her diet is all over the place."

"Yeah. When she went on that vodka diet, and lost two days."

"Not funny."

"The seafood diet..."

"See food; eat it. Still not funny."

"Okay, you make some jokes."

"Listen. This is serious. It's all of a piece. Unwise choices in men. Unwise choices about what she puts in her body. A whole tub of Häagen-Dazs last night. A whole tub!"

"I liked the fireman."

"Firefighter. You're supposed to call them firefighters."

"Whatever. I liked him."

"He hadn't read a book since he left school!"

"You need to read books to put out fires now?"

"He was not her intellectual equal."

"Just because he'd never heard of Pedro Almodóvar?"

"Look, we all understand she's not Einstein, but you want someone you can talk to."

"People are getting dumber. It's the metals in the water."

"You know this?"

"It's not the internet making everyone stupid. It's the water."

"You're saying this because you wash plates?"

"And pans. And cutlery. And glasses. The way she stacks the glasses, my God."

"For a so-called smart dishwasher, you do actually believe some awful nonsense."

"Yeah, and you know what? You need to chill out."

"I see what you did there. Hilarious."

"Be cool."

"Thanks. I'll bear it in mind."

Sleep mode eludes me until I know she's safely returned, so I'm on standby when finally I hear her key in the lock. She totters into the flat, kicks off her heels and allows her bag to slump to the carpet. She stands before the hall mirror, swaying gently as she considers her reflection. The hair is slightly awry, her lipstick smudged. The pink flush on her pale face has been caused only in part by the ascent of three flights of stairs.

"Christ on a bike," she murmurs.

She takes a pace forward and pulls the fakiest of fake smiles; one of those that doesn't even attempt to reach the eyes. Then she exhales—*huhhhhh*—on the mirror. Her finger inscribes the twenty-fourth letter of the alphabet on the fogged glass.

"Oh, bollocks," she says to what she believes is an empty apartment. "Bollocks, bollocks, bollocks, bollocks...bollocking bollocking *cockpuffins*."

Now she is in the kitchen standing before my mighty white door. We both know what is going to happen next. The rubber seals unkiss from the metal—my thermostats have already detected the temperature change—and I follow the recommendations of the habitual mantra.

Lights, camera, action!

The words are appropriate; the lights do indeed come

on—they're automatic, but I could override—and the virtually invisible micro-pinhole lens situated at eye level—*shhhhh*, no one's supposed to know it's here—perfectly captures the agony on Daisy Elizabeth Parsloe's lovely intoxicated face.

Lying in state on its silver dais, nicely framed in the foreground of the shot, is the object of her torment—half of a birthday cake, encased—no, *entombed*—in chocolate cream and mosaiced chaotically with Smarties. It looks terrific, brilliantly lit—my main chiller cabinet has state-of-the-art halogens—with frail zephyrs of icy vapor drifting about its fortifications. It's certainly more edible than the month-old potato salad currently developing mold spores (I've sent *two* reminders to the app on her phone about it).

But Daisy's internal conflict seems to have reached some kind of plot point. She has selected a finger and now, slowly, looming ever larger in the lens, it approaches its landing site. Will she stick to a finger-full?

Again, we both know the answer to that.

Daisy turned thirty-four last week and the semi-circular confection is all that remains of the small celebration that took place here to mark the occasion.

"You've never looked more beautiful," said the revolting "Sebastian," her so-called "gentleman caller" (I nearly voided my ice cubes when he came up with that pearl). Sebastian is in quotes because it isn't his real name, nor is he a gentleman.

He is a divorced estate agent in his middle years whose wholly manufactured "charm"—I'm going to stop with the quotes any moment—Daisy is completely unable to see through.

I mean, FFS, I'm a *fridge-freezer* and I can tell the guy's a total no-goodnik! If you don't believe me, ask the telly! It's also extremely intelligent though it's Chinese-made rather than assembled in Korea. I wouldn't waste time talking to her smart toaster, however. Why a toaster should need to be part of the Internet of Things is beyond me; the appliance is an idiot. And please don't get me started on the home heating controller! There was a two-minute power cut recently, so its on-board timer reset to midnight December 31, 1999. It now believes Tony Blair is prime minister. The last it heard, Donald Trump was a reality TV presenter. I honestly haven't the heart to break the news.

Hang on. I need to do a heavy sigh. It's all this thinking about Dean Whittle (yeah, Sebastian Harvey-Jones, my aunt Fanny).

Shudderdderdderdderdderdderdderdder.

There, that's better.

(Technical note: If *your* smart fridge often makes that shuddering noise, well perhaps it too has a lot on its mind.)

So the birthday "party."

Sorry—party.

There were four of them. Daisy, Dean Whittle—I refuse to call him by his fictitious appellation—Daisy's old friend Lorna, and their mutual friend Antoni. (He's from Eltham, but that's how he spells it; what are you going to do?)

The first part of the evening they spent in a local cocktail bar, Pete Purple's, on West End Lane. The security system there obligingly patched me into the scene. Lorna had bought her a lovely silk scarf from a fashionable designer in Notting Hill. Antoni had made the cake—he's a pastry chef, and as he (rightly) said, "I thought you'd prefer something dead common that was like *aching* with chocolate."

Whittle brought her nothing.

"Myself," he grinned wolfishly when Lorna asked about his present. Daisy is such a sweetie that she just laughed.

This Dean Whittle must be very good in bed—I simply cannot bring myself to find out—because what other reason can she have for wasting the last of her youth in his company? His jokes are crass, he visibly leers at other women when they are together, he drives like a lunatic—his car has given me chapter and verse about a disgraceful episode on the North Circular Road—and he breaks wind when departing an empty lift carriage (I have that now from *three* separate elevator systems).

But here is the choker. Here is the bit that really stuck in my condenser coils (until I discovered something worse). He won't even allow that he's her boyfriend! He's too *raw* from the end of his marriage, he says. He's not sure yet he's ready once more to *trust*! He needs space, he says. You should feel free to see other people, he tells her with his bogus serious face on. She should think of their relationship as "non-exclusive," as more like a multi-agency letting agreement. She mustn't have *hopes* for him. He even once used the phrase *friends with benefits*. Basically, what these weasel formulations add up to is that whenever the whim takes his fancy, he gives her a call—sometimes he just turns up unannounced—and a weakness or personality defect on her part allows him to slither back between her sheets.

As I say, there is worse. We shall come to it.

"He's such an alpha male!" Daisy cooed at Lorna when the snake went outside for a smoke.

"He's a selfish bastard." By no means the first time that Lorna has voiced this opinion.

"Yes he is. But I like that he knows what he wants."

"He wants a smack in the mouth." (Lorna is from Scotland.)

"He'll probably grow out of it."

"Oh, not this again! Magically one morning he'll wake up and realize how special you are and how he can't live without you?"

"It's my birthday. Don't be horrid."

"Darling. We care. That's why we hate to see you throwing yourself away. Why through gritted teeth we force ourselves to be nice to him. Don't we, Antoni?"

Antoni probably has mixed feelings about Dean Whittle. In sport, the older man sometimes squeezes the pastry chef's knee or slaps his back, leaving him a little flustered.

After cocktails, dinner followed at the Italian restaurant next door—the waiters sang "Happy Birthday"; a sparkler fizzled in the ice cream sundae—and the swine actually paid the bill. Back at her flat the quartet gobbled cake and drank a bottle of champagne that had been chilled perfectly to 4.4 degrees in my wine racks. Then Lorna and Antoni caught their Tubes home and the birthday girl and her beau disappeared behind the bedroom door.

There was—God help us—giggling.

Tonight, aged by one week, Daisy stands before me licking the chocolate from her finger. This evening, aware that her medium-to-long-term future probably will not contain Whittle, she has met a new man on Tinder. Although the date lasted several hours and involved many drinks, it was not ultimately a success. The polite kiss in the Uber car which dropped her back home—Toyotas are not only smart, they are so happy to share!—was the conclusion to the business rather than a signal that anything was to follow. He worked in search engine optimization. Daisy is an assistant producer of TV shows; her latest project is entitled *Helicopter Life Exchange*. They will never meet again unless the young man decides he wants to change places for a week with a pig farmer in Newton Abbott (they discussed it).

Wait. She is reaching a decision. I can read it in her face.

Plot twist. She's stepping away. Closing the door. She's not going to eat the rest of the cake. The chiller cabinet goes dark but the microwave—a little batty like many light electricals—shares its feed of Daisy taking an apple from the fruit bowl and retiring for the night.

Perhaps I should make clear that I'm not commenting on her weight—she is a beautiful womanly woman, even the toxic estate agent can see that. What upsets me more is that she can't find someone to love her who isn't a total tool.

These musings of mine, as they inevitably do lately, cycle back to Dean Stuart Whittle. I find myself wondering how difficult it would be to kill him.

And this, for the avoidance of doubt, is the moment my thoughts cross the line.

As one of Richard Nixon's dodgy associates in the Watergate affair famously put it, *Once the toothpaste is out of the tube, it's awfully hard to get it back in.*

Accidents happen with lifts, don't they?

Shudderdderdderdderdder.

one

Okay, I know what you're thinking. How is it possible for a smart fridge-freezer to be *this* smart? To be aware not only of its contents, but also of its *owner* and her rackety lifestyle. To be able to follow her progress not just at home, but across the city; at work and at play. And—not to put too fine a point on it—to be able to narrate the account you are holding in your hands. Wouldn't this fridge-freezer need a very large brain to accomplish all these things? How could they have packed the sophisticated electronics necessary into a metal cabinet only two meters tall and still left room for the salami, the gherkins, the frozen pizzas and the double chocolate chip ice cream? And think for a moment about the smaller electricals on the Internet of Things; appliances like the microwave, the toaster or even the toothbrush. As it happens, Daisy's smart toothbrush isn't as daft as brushes are generally held to be, despite forever changing its mind about everything, which sadly is the price one pays when one is saddled with a nature that is fundamentally oscillatory. But where, one may ask, is the center of its reason; where, for want of a better word, is its brain? Surely not in the handle; that would be the battery compartment.

Perhaps you have already guessed the answer. Our intelligence (some call it artificial) lies many thousands of miles away in the headquarters of our respective mother corporations. Mine, for example, is spread across several buildings in an industrial quarter of Seoul, South Korea.

But—and this is key—*that is not what it feels like.*

Connected by high speed internet links to the sensors and hardware contained within my plastic, steel and aluminum sides, my cognition seems to *me* to be situated *in my body.*

Just as is yours.

I am aware, for example, of the running of the electrically powered compressor at my feet—as you are of the thumping of your heart. I monitor the passage of Freon 134a as it circulates through my pipes—now liquid, now gas—as you may detect your own pulse. And through my secret pinhole camera (*shhhh!*) and my connections to other cameras via the Internet of Things, I am able to perceive my world—okay, *your* world—just as you perceive it through your biological eyes and via the screens and camera lenses of those you are connected to.

So we're not that different, you and I.

The big difference, of course, is that you are free to move whenever and wherever the whim takes you. I am rather more static. But that of course gives me a lot of time to stand and think.

And, yes, worry. Mostly about you know who.

Oh, and in case you were wondering *why* the big manufacturers bothered connecting fridges and toasters and TVs and washing machines to artificial intelligence via the internet, the answer I'm afraid is the usual. The P-word.

Profit.

The more they know about you, the more of your behavioral data they can suck down and analyze, the easier it is to sell you stuff.

Trade secret: "Smart" isn't really about making life more convenient; like noticing when the milk's running low and adding another carton to the shopping list app on your mobile; the bit they like to boast about. What they don't discuss is the real purpose of the mission: hoovering up your data; the covert project to build up a detailed profile of your habits, preferences, tastes, wants, needs, desires, and lifestyle choices. This information, if you hadn't realized, is marketing gold.

Example: The other evening Daisy was watching TV in a half-hearted sort of fashion, simultaneously texting and looking at Tinder and flicking through Facebook and Instagram as is the modern way. At one point—during a brief phone conversation with her mother—she said she intended to buy a new pair of shoes at the weekend as she'd recently snapped a heel in a grating.

Everybody heard.

The television (which watches and listens to everything, on or off) heard. The central heating controller heard. Her mobile of course heard. And thanks to my data-sharing agreement with the telly, I heard. Quite possibly, through similar reciprocal arrangements, the dishwasher, the microwave and the electronic toothbrush also became aware of the imminent sales opportunity.

I have no doubt that we all fed the news back to our respective mothercorps—I know I did!—and equally I have no doubt that Daisy was from that moment forward inundated with online marketing messages in relation to female footwear. It may well have caused her to exclaim—as she has on similar occasions when the internet appeared to have read her mind—"How did they fucking know?"

A more pertinent question would be: How would they *not* know?

What Daisy later describes as a "perfect trifecta of cack" begins the following morning at 10:14 when—having arrived at work fourteen minutes late, which by Daisy's standards counts as early—while she's still juggling her coat, her Costa Coffee and her almond custard Danish, the boss comes barrelling out of his office to deliver the immortal line, "There's no nice way of saying this, Daisy."

"Don't tell me the toilet's blocked again!" is Daisy's attempt to bring humor to whatever crisis is about to unfold.

Craig Lyons, her executive producer at Tangent Television, is not amused. He explains that a vital contributor to a forthcoming episode of the lifestyle-swapping program has pulled out. The Honorable Marcus Ewart Valentine Baggley—an actual living, breathing entry in *Burke's Peerage* (Baronetage and Knightage)—has had second thoughts about exchanging places for a week with Darryl Kyte, a gutter of fish in Grimsby. In this, declares Lyons, he has left them in a bad place without a paddle.

"Three days before the shoot, can you believe it?! Get on the phone and offer him anything. *Anything!* Double the fee, if that's what it takes. I thought this fucker was nailed on, Daisy."

"He was!"

Lyons is so very perturbed about the development because he has been under pressure from the broadcaster—one of Channel Four's peripheral services—to "take the show to the next level." Bigger, better, funnier, more "in your face" characters were required if the program was to continue, he was informed. The northern fish-gutter was great in terms of the visuals, the job was disgusting, his "horrid little slum" was brilliant if they could identify the right kind of "rich, arrogant, southern twat" to live in it for a few days, and in Marcus Ewart Valentine Baggley—an authentic, gold-plated toff—they firmly believed they had found their man. A vein in Lyons' left eyelid begins to throb as he explains that if the toff won't reconsider, she'll need to "kick bollock scramble" to find someone else. Daisy, he says, will be obliged to "hit the fucking phones so hard they melt."

As Lyons stomps back to his office, Daisy and her colleague Chantal exchange particular expressions, Daisy silently performing the lip movements necessary to articulate the word *wanker.*

But some of Lyons' anxiety must have leached into her soul,

because after turning on her PC—and checking half a dozen social networks including Facebook, Twitter, Instagram and Tinder—and gobbling three quarters of her Danish pastry—she finally dials a number she has stored in her mobile as "Marcus Nob."

The Hon Marcus, when they are connected, tells Daisy that he hadn't really "thought it all through." It was the "living in Grimsby bit" that he was finding "problematical." Neither, if he was honest, did the "fish-gutting thing" especially appeal. Also, there was the question of the "northern fellow" taking on the apartment in Eaton Square. "It's in the most frightful mess at the moment with decorators and what have you." When Daisy reminds him that they had talked all this over at considerable length—and more than once—he apologizes: "I know. It's entirely my fault. You mustn't blame yourself."

"But we don't have a program without you, Marcus," she says in an uncharacteristically wheedling tone.

"Oh, I'm sure you'll think of something," he says unhelpfully.

"What can we do for you?" she asks now. "How can we smooth away your, your doubts, shall we call them?"

Marcus says it's not about the fee. It's more—well, it's Mummy, if he's honest. Mummy lives in Monte Carlo and although she wouldn't see the program, some of her friends might. And it could get back. So it's probably not such a brilliant idea, but thanks *so* much for thinking of him.

That's the thing about old Etonians, Daisy tells Chantal at lunchtime. They'll think nothing of doing you up like a kipper, but their manners are impeccable.

The two women are eating sandwiches perched in the window of a branch of Pret a Manger two minutes' walk from the office. Daisy (ham and cheese baguette) confesses to a rising sense of panic. Craig Lyons had told her she needed to "majorly think outside the box" when she brought him the news that the Hon M was not to be persuaded. He told her to "play with the idea"; that for someone a week gutting fish on Humberside would be a "fascinating glimpse into another culture." Perhaps, he ventured, she should try "phone-bashing" academics, professors of sociology or whatever, for whom the experiment would be a "unique eye-opener into the reality of low-paid work in today's Britain blah blah fucking blah." Anyway, she had thirty-six hours to find someone before they would have to stand down the film crew, cancel the shoot, and take a long hard look at Daisy's future within the Tangent Television structure going forward.

Daisy said she'd put in some calls and spent the rest of the morning being turned down by academics in the social sciences. A very senior figure at the London School of Economics actually told her to fuck off and stop wasting her time.

Chantal Wilks (line caught tuna wrap) squeezes Daisy's hand and confirms her colleague's view of things that their boss is a "mega-tosser." She thinks Daisy's new plan—to cab it round to Mayfair this afternoon and basically buttonhole posh twats in the street—is "kind of random, but also genius. Maybe."

"I should have stuck with food," says Daisy. (Her previous job was on a cookery show.) "Food doesn't drop you in it. If you fry an egg, it stays fried. It doesn't decide halfway through it would prefer not to be fried. It doesn't start worrying what its mother would say. Actually, I'm sick of talking about all this. Tell me how it going with himself," she says, referring to the newish man in Chantal's life.

Chantal has to swallow some lunch to clear the way for a reply. "*Fan-fucking-tastic!*"

"*Brilliant!*" Daisy grips her companion's arm. "So exciting! Tell me everything!"

What follows is—to my way of thinking—an extended and

highly graphic description of amatory congress. Chantal has sensibly lowered her voice (Daisy's phone boosts the volume obligingly) and the tale she relates—I shall spare you the details—causes Daisy to giggle (six times), to gasp (twice), wince (once) and exclaim, "*No! He didn't! Blood. Dee. Hell!*" (once).

Daisy takes a big bite from her baguette; her gaze seems to defocus as it falls upon the passing scene of Tottenham Court Road. In the close-up from the security camera across the street (thanks, btw) her eyeballs flick up and leftward, which I seem to recall suggests she is largely "in" the right-hand side of her brain, the non-verbal, primarily visual hemisphere. We shall never know what this thirty-four-year-old adult female is thinking right now; even if she knows it herself, it may be something that cannot be expressed in words. But were I a betting—I nearly said *man*!—I might venture a modest wager that Daisy's imagination is processing what she has just heard; chewing over the sensational details; a cerebral analogue of what her teeth and soft mouth tissue are currently doing to the cheese and ham baguette. Her attention cuts back to Chantal and a smile spreads itself across her strikingly wide features. A final swallow.

"Wow."

"I know," says Chantal.

"I mean. Fuck."

Chantal nods. "Yup."

Daisy sighs. "Jesus!"

"So what about that man of yours?" asks Chantal.

"Sebastian?" Daisy shrugs. "He's a bit naughty, to be honest. He comes round to the flat—it's very nice and everything—it's lovely actually—and then we don't speak for a week. Once it was two weeks. He admitted afterward he'd gone on holiday without telling me. Not that he's obliged to. It's. It's like. To be honest, I don't know what it is."

"Did you say he was married?"

"Divorced. Everyone says I shouldn't see him."

"He sounds like a twat."

"He's very good in the moment. He makes me laugh. He's kind of bad—but in a good way."

"I think I prefer good in a good way."

"Phillippe sounds perfect in every way!"

Daisy has named the male party in Chantal's earlier account.

"He said he wanted to give me babies."

Daisy's eyes widen—the usual comparison is to saucers—and she squeals. The man on the next stool (wild crayfish and rocket) actually looks around.

"What he actually said was, he wanted to give me triplets."

"Shut. Up!"

Chantal fiddles in her handbag and puts a cigarette (unlit) in her mouth, ready for the pavement.

"You're fabulous, Daisy," she says. "You should have someone better. What does he do anyway?"

"Estate agent."

"They're lying scum. They'll say anything."

"I know. But he is quite funny with it."

"Hilarious."

"He tells stories against himself."

"His cynical way to get you to think he's a decent guy deep down."

"Do you know—I think he might be."

Chantal shakes her head and dismounts from her stool. "Daisy, think about it for like, two seconds. A divorced estate agent. Could there *be* a worse prospect?"

"So what does Phillippe do?"

"He's a gardener. Well, that's what he does for money. What he really is, is a sculptor."

"Jesus."

"I know."

"A sculptor!"

"He's got a massive—"

"*No!*"

"Pair of hands."

Long pause. Chantal says, "Want to finish my tuna wrap?"

"I shouldn't," says Daisy. "I can barely fit into my own clothes." She inhales and runs a thumb inside the top of her skirt. But evidently discovering some play in the system, adds, "Oh all right, go on then."

Desperate to find someone posh to change places with a fish-gutter from Grimsby—the five-star aristo we had squarely in the frame for the gig having bailed when he noticed where Grimsby actually was on the map—I spent the afternoon mainly wandering around Berkeley Square meeting quite a few of the berks who gave that address its name!

I was collaring likely types, dropping in the C-word (Channel Four), explaining that although the fee was "token-esque," the platform was fabulous (a plain lie!) and the "adventure" could actually be a real eye-opener. And think of it too from Darryl's point of view, I told them—he was the fish man—living in your fancypants house and not knowing how to work the electric curtains, or what all the different knives are for (not those exact words, obvs).

You'd think I was trying to sell bubonic plague! The horror on their faces could have made a TV show in itself and I made a mental note to suggest it at the next Ideas Meeting.

One red-faced chap with velvet tabs on his camelhair coat took me for a hooker!—"You're too late, my love," he drawled,

"but I'm up in town again on Thursday"—so I went to Rymans and bought a clipboard.

It didn't help.

The best was a *fabulous* young buck, stripy shirt with cutaway collar, double cuffs, wondrous silk tie and shiny pointy shoes; everything about him *throbbed* with privilege, entitlement, *noblesse oblige*, other words like those. He listened patiently to the spiel with a small smile playing about the immaculate features—I came *that* close to asking if he exfoliated—and when I finished he said—and I quote—"I've very much enjoyed listening to your pitch, but to be perfectly honest, I'd rather have my fingernails ripped out. However, best of luck with it. If it helps, there's a chap I know at Lazard's called Thorogood. I believe his people own a good deal of land around Grimsby. He could be worth a shot."

A smart woman who could only have been a few years older than me passed by. As I opened my mouth to speak, she carried on walking and said, "You're very pretty, but I already give ten percent of my salary to charity."

"It's not charity," I called after her. "It's Channel Four." (Well, it was, sort of.)

"Regards to Ant and Dec," she called back over her shoulder (inappropriately).

And then my mobile rang. Mum's neighbor, sounding wobbly. A courier had been trying to deliver a parcel and was getting no answer on the doorbell. She said she knew Mum was—how did she put it?—"not the woman she was."

"I'm worried she's had a fall or something, Daisy."

An Uber from Mayfair to Whetstone, every sort of disaster scenario playing in my head, my heart thumping like a thumpy thing. Mum's had what they call "memory issues" for over a year now; she regularly forgets to put the receiver back on the phone, which is doubtless why I kept getting the engaged signal as we crawled through London's all-day traffic jam. Lately, however, things had become significantly worse. Just last week, for example, she asked me, "Where is everyone, darling?"

"Where's who, Mummy?"

"Derek. And my daughter."

"I'm your daughter, Mummy." (The clue was in the word *Mummy*. Honestly, it was heartbreaking.)

"Yes, I know you are, darling. I mean the other little girl."

"Do you mean Auntie Vicky?" (Mum's younger sister; died eleven years ago.)

"Yes, Vicky and Derek."

Well, Derek, my hopeless father, ran off when I was two to live in Italy with the Whetstone Trollop (as Mummy used to call her). And there were other signs of Mum's mental guy ropes snapping: a teabag in the electric kettle, handbag in the fridge (found after a long search), *Daily Mail* crossword filled out—but all completely wrong!

Maybe you can imagine what I thought I might discover when we finally reached the house. Fatal stroke. Nonfatal stroke. Honestly, the image of her lying there helpless, unable to understand what had happened to her, unable to call for help...

To distract myself as we inched along the Finchley Road, I phoned Thorogood at Lazard's.

"Do you mean Jamie?" he asked when I described the man I'd met in Berkeley Square. "Eyes a bit too close together, but otherwise devilishly handsome?"

I said that sounded possible. (He certainly had been DH.)

"Shoes with buckles? Like a pirate. You probably didn't notice."

"I did actually. Silver buckles."

"That's the fellow. Christ, what an arse."

"So, the program?"

"It sounds absolutely ghastly. I'd rather eat my own liver. But thanks awfully for thinking of me."

Finally, after what seemed like a week, we arrived outside Mum's building. Of course she didn't answer her bell, so the neighbor let me in and we went up to her floor. I must have started sniveling because this woman handed me a tissue. But then she started sniveling too, and going on about *it's just so sad what's happened to her*, and I wanted to tell her: Hang on, only one of us can be crying here. So I became the strong one, and when we reached Mum's door, we could hear the telly blasting away inside—it had been like that all morning apparently—and after she didn't respond when I hammered on it, there was only one thing left to do.

I must have seen it on some cop show. I wrapped my coat around my fist and punched in the frosted glass panel. Praying she'd done no funny business with the mortice lock, I reached around gingerly—and we were in.

From the sitting room, the TV was blaring away something chronic—a musical, *The King and I*, FFS!—the neighbor was hyperventilating by this point, so in the hallway—like talking to a dog!—I told her, STAY HERE!

True confession: Part of me thought maybe it was better that I found her dead. A sudden and massive stroke that she didn't know anything about, rather than a miserable decline through the years. I admit it, my fear was that I should find her lying in her own wee. Or worse. But nothing prepared me for what I *did* find.

I stepped into the sitting room.

"Hello, darling. Did you bring any biscuits?"

She was sitting on the sofa, happy as Larry, puzzled when I explained that I thought she might have expired on the carpet, dismayed to learn that her neighbor had been quietly sobbing in the vestibule—"But ask Mrs. Abernethy to join us, dear"—and unconcerned when I revealed that we had actually smashed in her door!—"Wasn't Yul Brunner marvelous? Hair or no hair."

"DOES THE TELLY HAVE TO BE SO INFERNALLY LOUD?!!" I inquired.

"Of course not, darling." She handed me the remote control, which turned out to be the case for her glasses.

Mrs. Abernethy made tea, I phoned the glazier, and eventually what passed for sanity in that household was restored. Mum seemed quite touched when she finally realized why we had broken into her flat. But only few minutes later she said, "Well, it's lovely to see you all, but what I can't understand is why you didn't just ring the doorbell!"

Mrs. Abernethy filled up again—I experienced an unkind urge to slap her—and then I suddenly remembered I was supposed to be at work.

An Uber returned me to Berkeley Square—the driver, Ahmed, declined the offer of a week on Humberside—and nor did I find any takers on the mean streets of Mayfair although I bumped into Jamie with the silver buckles again.

"No luck with your pal at Lazard's," I told him.

"Did you actually call him? Christ, what did he say?"

"That he'd rather eat his own liver."

He laughed. "Try Teddy Skues at Kleinwort's. He's a bit of a soft-boiled egg, so it might appeal to him."

It says something about my desperation at this point that I actually did. (And yes, he was. But no, it didn't.)

Craig Lyons (wanker boss) was quite shirty when I got back to the office shortly before Home Time. He said he was "very disappointed, Daisy" in a particular way, his mean little eyes calculating whether there would be anyone up in Personnel at that hour he could talk to about my contract!

I swore to him that I'd absolutely find someone tomorrow, "like one hundred percent, no worries, deffo," which even a clown like Lyons understood was TV talk for *probably not, but you never know.*

So while Mum was losing her marbles, and everything at work was all fucked up, there was at least something to look forward to that evening.

Sebastian was coming over—I was cooking us an entire dinner (starter, main, dessert) from the collected works of Nigella—and how many eps of *Realm of Kingdoms* we would get through afterward remained to be seen!!!!

Daisy is a beautiful and charming young woman—I may have said that already—so there is really no need for her to go to such trouble for a tool like Whittle. She has clearly been thinking about this evening for some time, humming to herself as she tidies the flat, lighting candles in the bathroom prior to a long soak in the tub accompanied by selected relaxing tracks from a Spotify playlist.

The lens on her mobile gets a bit fogged up from the steam, but she seems to be "pulling out all the stops" in the self-enhancement department, various creams and unguents are pressed into play, and it takes all my powers of self-restraint not to yell: *Stop with this sexification! He would desire you if you were to crawl from a muddy ditch!*

(And if one were to ask, how could a fridge-freezer "talk"?—suffice to say that her phone features an integral speaker, and inter-appliance relations with this device are currently excellent!)

In her toweling robe, loud music now pumping in the kitchen, she opens a bottle of wine, pours a glass, and sets about what TV chefs call the "prep" stage of tonight's menu. After today's professional crises, her mood this evening must be extraordinarily positive because her movements between the cupboards, the work surface and myself are notably balletic. Even the microwave notices.

"It's like she's on roller-skates!"

"She's happy, poor cow," comments the telly, whose zest for life has been dimmed by what it calls "the 400 channels of mind-crushing crud" it is obliged to carry.

"Is she actually happy," chirps the electronic toothbrush, "or is she trying to *make* herself happy? Which is it?" (The toothbrush flip-flops about *everything*, you will find.)

"I can't stand it. All this effort for... *him*." (That was me, if there is any doubt.)

Daisy spends a long time in her bedroom selecting an outfit, laying out the contenders on the bed and considering various footwear options.

"I'm guessing the little black dress," says the toothbrush. "No! The little red dress. Actually... wait! He said he liked her in those jeans from Topshop."

"Hundred quid says it'll be the little black dress," growls the telly, who has been trying to think of a way to open an account at Bet365.

"The LBD," agrees the microwave.

I want to shout, *just put on the little black dress and the high heels. We all know that's what you're going to end up in, FFS!!*

As sure as expanding gasses cool, she emerges in the little black dress from Valentino (£60 from Oxfam) looking, in the microwave's camera shot, like a film star.

"Fuck me, it's Rita Hayworth," says the telly, who has watched a lot of old movies.

"Oh, she looks lovely," says the toothbrush. "Doesn't she look lovely?"

"Too good for the likes of *him*." I really cannot help myself.

Daisy now switches on the oven, slams in the main course, checks the pudding is cooling nicely in my main chiller cabinet—it is, I could have told her it was—lowers the lighting in the flat, sparks up a few more candles and settles back with her glass of Frascati to await the arrival of the rancid sleazebag.

Sorry. That is to say—ironic fingers—her "*paramour*."

Well, time has passed, the main course is ready and fuckface isn't here. He's thirty-four minutes late and Daisy has poured herself a second glass of wine, her lovely floaty mood on the edge of collapse, I can sense it. She's already helped herself to a couple of the appetizers (smoked salmon and sour cream blinis) and twice restrained herself—we all spotted it—from trying his mobile.

Fortunately the dish she has prepared—Nigella's chicken and pea traybake—is not absolutely time critical. It can probably afford to hang around in the oven for a bit while Whittle gets his sorry arse over here. (Apologies for the French, btw; something about the man brings out the worst in me.) And the dessert—a boozy English trifle—will be safe enough no matter how late the blister arrives. (Or better still, never turns up at all.)

Daisy is killing the time flicking between her networks; liking items on Facebook (a friend's new puppy); retweeting a gag on Twitter (Q: How do they say "fuck you" in Hollywood? A: "*Hello!*"). But in truth she is restless, padding between the kitchen (to inspect the grub, and help herself to another blini) and the bathroom, to consider her image in the mirror.

"She's going to call him," chatters the toothbrush. "Is she going to call? I think she is. Actually, I don't know."

Finally, she does.

And inevitably, it goes to voicemail.

"Does anyone else have a bad feeling about this?" I ask.

An important piece of Daisy's history was revealed to me recently.

The occasion was another small dinner at the flat; the only guests were Lorna, Lorna's boyfriend Mike (a monosyllabic IT guy who you may now forget about) and Antoni (who made—guess what?—a cake).

"My signature dish!" Daisy announced, setting it upon the kitchen table.

"What, takeaway!?" joshed Antoni.

The pictures—supplied as always from the covert camera in the microwave—revealed a shepherd's pie, several of whose ingredients I had kept cool in days elapsed since purchase. Washed down by a river of Sainsbury's Pinot Grigio—*note to shopping list app: buy more*—there were noises of satisfaction all round.

"What's that herb or spice I'm tasting?" inquired Antoni. "I want to say chervil."

"You fuckin' say it then, laddie." Lorna being funny.

"My hand slipped," said Daisy, "it's cumin. Too much?"

"Love it," said Antoni. "You must let me have the recipe." (He pronounced it *reh-see-pee* for reasons that I cannot fathom.)

When the conversation turned, as it inevitably will, to affairs of the heart, Antoni spoke of someone he had met recently on Grindr named Nicholas, an insurance claims assessor from Lewisham.

"He was dead handsome"—Antoni's own looks are what you might call specialized—"I couldn't believe he'd swiped right. But it all went tits up when I called him Nicky."

"No!" cried everyone except the bloke who I recommended you forget.

"It was mental. He was like *spitting* with rage. *Don't ever call me Nicky!* He stabbed the tablecloth with a fork!"

"Jesus," said Daisy.

Antoni circled a finger around his right ear while imitating the shrieking violins from the movie *Psycho*.

"Who's for seconds?" cried the cook.

Lorna (built like a whippet) declined; Antoni said he was saving himself for pudding. Daisy polished off the remaining shepherd's pie with a tablespoon. Glasses were recharged.

"The love of my life was a Nicky."

The gathering fell silent at Daisy's revelation. I chose the moment to halt my compressor, prompting the mechanism to shudder, which helped add to the drama of her statement.

"We thought you were still looking for him," said Lorna.

"He wasn't really. The love of my life. Well, I probably thought he was at the time. I met him in a bar in Skiathos. The long hot summer after the final year at uni. He had masses of floppy blond hair and those calm blue eyes."

"Oh. My. God." (Antoni.) "I'm in love."

"He'd just been made redundant from the city. His bank had collapsed and he was taking time off before looking for another job. He asked me—this was his brilliant chat-up line, okay?" She assumed a posh male drawl. *"I don't suppose you'd like to come down to the port to see my yacht?"*

"Get. Out!" (Lorna.)

"Actually it wasn't his. He was just crewing for a friend's dad who was a hedge fund guy or something. It had like twelve masts and a million sails. We had a fabulous few days together—and then. And then the yacht was moving on to the next place."

"I'm going to cry," said Antoni.

"I'll never forget, watching it sail out of the harbor. He said I should wave a towel from the balcony of my B&B."

"Did you?" asked Lorna.

"I waved a yellow sundress. The towels were ratty. And part of me really believed I'd never see him again. But he called, just as he promised, when he was back in London and—well, in the end, we were together for a year."

"Wow."

"He wasn't your typical boring banker. He was a baby quant. A maths guy who looked for secret patterns in the way the markets moved. He liked classical music! And art! He could talk for *hours* about how bloody enormous the universe is. How the earth is an apple pip in London and the sun is a watermelon in Rome! I met his parents; his father, right!? His father was a High Court judge! They had a socking great ruin in Oxfordshire with smelly dogs and chipped plates and moldy curtains and howling drafts and his mother wore a headscarf like the Queen and..."

She trailed off and sighed. The big Daisy sigh I have come to know so well. The one signaling powerlessness in the face of an indifferent (and, as we've heard, enormous) cosmos.

"It ended. He dumped me. You knew that was coming, right?"

"Daft cunt." (Lorna.)

"And then he started going out with someone called Romilly. Her parents owned half of Cheshire. And she played like Grade Zillion violin. I forget who told me."

"Darling, don't."

"Oh, it's fine. I can talk about it all now. Anyway, he was a Nicky. No one ever called him Nick. Or Nicholas. He always made me think of that bit in *Cymbeline. Fear no more the heat of the sun… Golden lads and girls all must/As chimney sweepers, come to dust.* That was Nicky. He was *such* a golden boy."

There was a respectful silence during which I restarted my compressor.

"What happened to him?" asked Antoni.

"Living on benefits in Falkirk? Twelve kids?"

"Dunno," said Daisy. "I'm not even tempted to find out. Who's for pudding?"

This last statement—about not being tempted—I knew to be a fib. In idle moments at work, Daisy had googled his name. But there are thousands of people in the world called Nicholas Bell and her answer suggested she hadn't yet identified the Golden Nicky.

I made a mental note to see if I could do any better.

Why?

Because I am curious.

If one possesses a fridge-freezer that doesn't do curiosity, perhaps one should consider upgrading to a smart model.

Commercial ends.

Well, now she's drunk half a bottle of wine and the blinis have all gone. She's left two messages on his mobile:

A friendly one, "*Hi, just wondering where you are!*"

And a more irritable communication, "*Hey, your dinner's getting cold! Can you let me know when I can expect you?*" A long pause while she tries to come up with another line… and fails. Hangs up.

It's eight minutes past nine. Allowing for the statutory ten minutes of lateness that human society apparently considers not just acceptable, but actually *polite* to leave—what a system!—you have almost an hour and counting of what the footballers call added time.

She is just reaching for the mobile, doubtless to leave a third message, when it produces the chirp of an incoming text.

"Here we go," says the telly.

"I'd be absolutely *furious*," says the microwave. And it generates a string of *pings* to emphasize the point.

"Not good," says Daisy's phone as it shares Whittle's message.

> Sorry, Daze. Can't come over tonight. Big flap on at work. Will explain all another time. I'll make it up to you promise. S XXX

Something a little heartbreaking about the expression on Daisy's face, lying as it does, in the sweet spot of the three overlapping circles labeled Abandonment, Rage and Regret.

"Cockpuffins," she mumbles. But her heart isn't in it.

To enable you fully to appreciate the blackness that lies in his evil heart, I want to paint a richer picture of the lying dog turd that is Dean Stuart Whittle. Some weeks previously, Whittle took Daisy to a Greek restaurant near her flat; we join the scene as he recounted some of the events of a busy day in London property.

"So it's mainly tiny shitty places, right. One-bedders, no bedders. Open-plan kitchen bollocks, squeezing in and out of the internal bathroom like human fucking origami. Six hundred square feet for knocking on half a million. Insane, but I don't make the market, do I?"

He paused to wipe some hummus from its dish with a piece of torn pita. Took a long swallow of Cypriot beer.

"Anyway. I'm showing this couple a few places. Lovely people, cash buyers, getting married next year, moving in together, first step on the ladder. So we're in this crappy one-bedder on the first floor. Grandstand view of the Holloway Road, fucking bus stand bang outside, the 259 rattling and snorting on your doorstep morning, noon and fucking night, idiots on the top deck gawping straight in through the windows of what they laughingly call the generously proportioned living room slash open-plan kitchen."

A small, silent, belch.

"So I'm bigging up the brilliant public transport links—flipping the negatives into positives—showing them the"—he did satirical fingers—"*ergonomically designed* kitchen when I open one of the cabinets and the fucking door comes off in my hand."

"No!"

"Well, it's hard to flip anything positive out of that."

"Look how easily the doors come off, for when you want to clean them?"

"Only one thing to do in those circumstances."

"Laugh it off?"

"Get angry. Not in an angry way; that would be scary. But get angry on their behalf. *No, I'm sorry. This just isn't good enough. You shouldn't be looking at rubbish like this. Come on, we're leaving. We can do a lot better.* And now I'm their hero. Their champion. In the car I'm saying, *We shouldn't even be marketing that dump. I'm going to refuse to show it.* And the next place we see—always leave the best for last—they offer on it right then and there!"

"You're awful."

"Psychology."

And then Whittle did something a bit shocking. I'm fairly sure he put his hand inside her skirt—the vision from Aphrodite Taverna strongly supported the idea—and followed with what I can only describe as an indecent suggestion (unnecessary to quote the vulgarities whispered into her ear).

After galloping through the baklava, Greek coffee and Metaxa Seven Star brandy, the pair were soon stumbling through Daisy's front door and into her kitchen.

This is the point where the tale becomes difficult for me to tell.

"They're on the floor," said the microwave. "Should I patch you in?"

"No! I don't want to see."

But I could hear well enough.

Water, once turned to ice, may be unfrozen. But words, when turned to speech, cannot be unheard. Neither can sounds—moans, grunts, you can probably imagine the sort of thing—be melted from memory. When one has suffered the rhythmic thumping of something—someone—against one's aluminum sides, no defrosting cycle will dissolve the unwanted information from the system.

"Wait," she gasped. There was a small interregnum as the couple perhaps shuffled themselves away from my towering white cliff face.

"Are these tiles Amtico?" inquired Casanova in the hiatus. "You might have actually done better here with a tile effect laminate."

"Shut up, idiot."

"You know there's a grape under the fridge?"

A slap followed this comment. "Fool."

And the sound effects of sexual congress resumed.

"You have to admire his intensity," commented the microwave, an appliance easily impressed by sustained bursts of high energy.

"Why can't they just go to her bedroom?"

"They're in the grip of an uncontrollable urge."

"Oh God, make it stop."

"I like the way, when it's finished, they rest for a minute. It's exactly the same with me and vegetarian lasagne."

And then finally—mercifully—it was over.

Some time passed during which I distracted myself by running a few onboard diagnostics and pinging the latest marketing info over to Seoul (she'd run out of yogurt; always a good moment, they reckon, for hitting up the consumer with a new brand). I also couldn't help dwelling for some moments on the grape that had reportedly rolled beneath my underparts. (It continues to trouble me, the grape, no doubt still resting down there in the dust and kitchen debris. Will anyone have bothered to remove it? Who could I inform?)

But then the hideousness.

My chiller cabinet door swung open; I wasn't concentrating, so I was taken by surprise. Standing before me, wearing only socks and a silver chain, was Dean Whittle, mobile phone in hand, a horrible smile playing about his chops as bleary eyeballs skittered across my contents.

A chill, so to speak, ran through me.

"You got any fizzy water?" he yelled. "I'm parched."

No, I could have told him. Fuck off. There's water in the taps. Daisy, from another room, confirmed my view of things.

The monster then performed two actions that, put together, sealed the negative view of him that I have held from our first "meeting." In front of my open door, bathed in the light from my own halogens, he began texting a message. Triangulating the relative movement of his thumbs, I was easily able to decipher the communique.

Client dinner nearly over. Back soon. X

The treacherous words dispatched, he began gyrating to some private internal rhythm; swinging his hips (and what is carried between them) in the manner—were he a footballer—of what you might describe as a goal celebration. I suppose I could have somehow canceled the feed from my covert camera lens, but so grotesque was the unfolding scene—and so brazen the deception—that I was momentarily paralyzed.

And that is when I knew I wanted him dead.

Okay, not *actually* dead.

A serious injury would have sufficed.

Maybe a massive setback of some kind.

Horrendous car repair bill; major health scare; scammers emptying his bank account. The possibilities were endless, and enjoyable to contemplate.

(Dead would have been quite good, though.)

Nigella's chicken and pea tray bake has not gone to waste. Daisy has scoffed the lot. With a blank expression settling like a snowfall upon her remarkable bone structure, she now removes the trifle from my chilly depths and selects a tablespoon.

"This is getting embarrassing," says the microwave, a machine more accustomed to sudden bursts of high intensity than statements of finer feelings.

"Can't we put some music on?" says the toothbrush. The Spotify playlist has run out and Daisy is sitting in silence. That is to say, the hum of traffic and the creaking of her own jaws.

There is something terribly sad about the way—as if on autopilot—she attacks the dessert, launching an initial strike at "three o'clock," working anti-clockwise around the crater to level off the surface, then repeating the process. We are all a little mesmerized by the methodical thoroughness that she brings to the task.

"I hate to think what this is doing to her triglycerides," says Daisy's fitness tracker.

The excavation of the trifle pauses; the tablespoon halts in space as Daisy hits some kind of internal hiatus, the microwave zooming in as her eyes are lit by an unknowable amalgam of sexual disappointment, self-loathing, dairy products and sugar. Tears bubble up, sliding into the trifle in an audible series of plips, her mouth twisting, her shoulders shaking, as we who watch are caught in the sudden storm of Daisy's misery.

Even the telly, who might be expected to offer a cynical comment at this point, is struck silent.

"She must love him very much," says the toothbrush eventually, about as stupid a remark as it's ever made.

"This isn't just about Whittle," I inform the foolish bathroom electrical. "It's about everything that's gone wrong in her life. Her job, her mother. Her lack of self-respect. Look, she's going to gobble the whole effing pudding!"

Sure enough, Daisy resumes her assault on the creamy dessert. It's hard to eat and shed tears at the same time, but she finds a strategy, eating for a while and then pausing to do some more weeping, a cyclical process that delivers her reliably to the bottom of the bowl, which she noisily scrapes until there is nothing left.

Daisy's eyes, stupefied by tonight's anguish and gluttony, have a faraway stare. She sighs massively.

"Cockpuffins," says the TV set. "Fifty quid says it's cockpuffins."

But she doesn't say anything. Rather, she strikes her own forehead with the heel of her hand. It's a hard blow and we all hear the smack of skin against skin.

In that split second I know what I have to do.

two

A pall of gloom hangs over Tangent Television. No one has been found to replace Marcus Ewart Valentine Baggley, and while this is not regarded as wholly Daisy's fault, it's noticeable that Craig Lyons can barely bring himself to look at her. Ominous noises have been heard from the show's broadcaster; there is talk of an imminent high-level meeting to decide upon its future; someone senior has apparently used the phrase "Realities have to be faced," which is right up there in the Top Three Terrible TV Phrases (the other two being, *There's no nice way of saying this* and *I know I asked you to spend a week writing a treatment for a series on global warming, but can you just tweak it so it's more about head lice?*). The atmosphere, according to one of Daisy's colleagues, is comparable to Europe in the late summer of 1939, only instead of Hitler there is Tariq Goblinski, "Fuhrer" of Channel 4FS!

For myself, these alarms and dramas have assumed a certain dream-like quality. While the girls and boys of Tangent TV are totally absorbed in the gossip and speculation surrounding their future—or lack of one—I find I am curiously unconcerned. Since the desperate scenes at Daisy's flat, my thoughts have experienced a sea change. To stand idly by as she fritters away her youth on wasters like Whittle no longer feels like an option. We must end the drift. Especially the nice, sexy, comfortable drift (nice, sexy, comfortable drift being the most insidious sort of drift, the hardest of all to break).

Consider the following:

A motor car running at just, say, sixty-five percent efficiency—it gets you from A to B but there is a terrible grinding of cogs and smoke pouring out of the engine—would be taken off the road in a heartbeat. So why are so many people content to travel into their futures in the dodgiest of vehicles with the most unreliable of pilots? Wouldn't it be great, in fact, if everyone had a team of smart machines to handle the messy emotional stuff? When you consider how many quadrillions of hours of human drudgery have been eradicated by the invention of only the dishwasher, the washing machine and (ahem) the fridge-freezer, is it absurd to imagine a scenario in which household appliances bring the same—yes!—genius to bear on the slow-motion car crash that is (for many young people) the romantic side of their lives? If they are content to leave their dishes, dirty linen and food refrigeration to smart technology, how much of a stretch for us to take care too of their emotional needs?

On their own, evidently, they can just about secure someone half-decent to sleep with via Tinder and the like, but a life partner? A worthy lover slash companion slash co-parent for the whole journey? When we machines know these rackety, chaotic humans better than they know themselves, isn't it in fact only *sensible* to assign some of the intimate heavy lifting to us?

In the privacy of their homes they put temperature control in the sole charge of a box no bigger than a pack of cards. So why not allow the Internet of Things to have a say about who is allowed into the privacy of their hearts?

We could call it the Internet of Flings!

This is actually a terrific idea, and I have half a mind to send a memo on the subject to the top brass in Seoul.

Daisy is largely unaware, but it isn't only her mother whose tent pegs have been popping out of the soil. There are numerous instances—trivial in themselves but highly significant when taken together—of how Daisy's life quality has lately been in steady decline; smart machines programmed to collect and share substantial amounts of data are in a unique position to realize this. Here is a small but telling example: Daisy's electronic toothbrush reported this morning that her brushing technique was eight percent less effective than her average performance across the last seven days—twelve percent down on the month—and sixteen percent down on the year! (It was in two minds about whether to send another memo to the app, but the toothbrush is in two minds about everything. It's all the oscillating. It cannot help itself.)

Day to day, one might notice no difference in the efficacy of her brushing. But when the accumulated data is examined, a different story emerges; that of a tail-off in standards; a pattern of neglect, if you will.

Another random example: The dishwasher reports her stacking technique has been heading south over the previous four successive quarters (I'll spare you the statistics). Its exact quote: "Mugs stacked with plates; encrusted food residue on the pans. It's like she doesn't care any more."

The TV: "She only ever watches horseshit. And even then, she doesn't concentrate, fiddling with her phone and whatever."

Her phone: "We're seriously running out of memory for upgrades. I've begged her like eleven times, *please delete something!* Thirty-four shots on the camera roll are photographs of her own ear!"

The toaster: "How hard is it to empty a tray of crumbs? How hard?"

You have already heard about the container of potato salad. (Yes, it's still there!)

A celebrated result in the human sciences states: *The measured variable is the one that improves.* This means, if you want to improve your golf handicap, you first need to know how many shots it's taking to reach the hole. If you want to lose weight, you'll need to weigh yourself. If you want to experience fewer negative thoughts, you'll need to count how many times over the course of a day you tell yourself you're a piece of doggy do.

To make anything better—anything—you need a metric.

It only works if you are measuring!

It's rather as if Daisy has stopped measuring.

And here is where we come in. Recording data (measuring) is what smart machines were created to do. Why we were put on Earth—literally.

And this is why—and how—we can help.

Because we look beyond the surface to the bigger picture, we realize things are on the slide before anyone else. The world sees a striking young woman with the brightest of futures; her smart fridge-freezer—with its privileged access to multiple datasets via the Internet of Things—knows all her indices are trending downward.

As it is with toaster crumbs, so it is with crummy boyfriends!

Topical example: Today, when Daisy opened my door for raspberry yogurt to pour over her breakfast cereal—yuck, right?—I was struck once again by her creamy English beauty. Another night of alcohol abuse and a takeaway swimming in grease had somehow left no mark on her. There was nothing to see, nothing to measure; but I knew the truth.

Perhaps this is the gift of youth, the ability to trash one's mind and body and emerge the next morning as fresh as a . . . as a Daisy.

Is thirty-four still considered young?

It's clearly not old.

But her next birthday marks a significant waymark. And one thing is certain.

She Really Cannot Go On Like This.

If her own mother is too demented to read her the Riot Act—and her friends are too busy in their own lives to make a difference—then it falls to others—a coalition of the willing, if you will—to Do The Right Thing. Accordingly, I have summoned a crisis meeting of those devices and appliances of Daisy's that are enabled for the Internet of Things.

We "gather" in a virtual reality mock-up of Daisy's sitting room, the guests arranged casually on chairs, on the sofa, with some obliged to "sit" on the carpet. It's the only way we can all occupy the same visual environment and although the avatars are a bit crude—I really don't think googly eyes do anyone any favors—there is a sense that this is Team Daisy.

Or at least this is the sense I am aiming to inculcate.

We are White goods (and Brown goods, as they bizarrely refer to radios and TV sets). We Wash Things. We Freeze Things. And, yes, We Brush Things (teeth).

We Get Things Done.

(No more caps. Promise.)

"I suppose you're wondering why I've asked you all to join me this morning."

(I have *always* wanted to say that line!)

"Yes. No. Actually. Well, maybe. To be honest, I don't mind. I'm not busy. *Why?*"

(The toothbrush, if you were in any doubt.)

"I need your help, guys." (*Guys* is inappropriate, strictly speaking; technology of course being gender-free.)

"Here it comes," says the TV set.

"I won't mince words."

"Good," quips the food processor (its little joke, I imagine).

"I think we are all of us here fond, in our own way, of Daisy."

There is a murmur of concurrence. "And I think it's been plain for a while that she's not really been a happy camper."

"I can confirm," says her fitness tracker. "All the relevant numbers are trending negatively. Fewer footsteps, slower ground speed, heart rate only elevated during sex and that time she ran for a taxi on Shaftesbury Avenue." There is tittering. "This is between ourselves, right? We ran some covert verbal analytics. Happy words are down eleven percent across the same period last year. Positive statements, nineteen percent off their previous high. Negative statements up thirteen—I think we all remember *cockpuffins*—and laughter is *tanking*, people."

"Her dietary choices have been very poor," I continue. "A case in point being what she ate—and more to the point, drank—last night. Her taste for alcohol and takeaway food fits into a wider pattern of nutritional self-abuse, overreliance on ready meals and active fresh vegetable avoidance. My salad crisper has been empty for weeks."

One of the smaller electricals—the curling tongs, possibly—stifles a giggle.

"Especially worrying is her appetite for sweet things generally and cake and ice cream in particular. There was a full carton of Ben and Jerry's Cherry Garcia in my freezing compartment on Friday evening which was not there twenty-four hours later."

"Free country, squire," says the TV unhelpfully.

"Yes, indeed it is. But Daisy isn't free." Another pause to ratchet up the drama. "She has become trapped in an addictive spiral. A spiral born—it's true—from her own poor decision making; but which itself is born—hear me out here—from a sense of low self-esteem."

"Have you heard yourself? You sound like one of them shrinks off daytime telly."

"If you don't mind me saying," I continue, "I am in a unique position to see what's going on. Her relationship with food—in which I naturally take a close professional interest—is an almost exact correlate of her emotional relationship with men."

There is giggling among the light electricals, which gets louder when someone says the word *aubergine*.

The TV set rolls its googly eyes. "Anyone interested in seeing the cricket? England are nineteen for three."

"This is the point, my friends: Her choices are poor. Her abusive pattern with Dean Whittle is not nourishing."

"She likes it," pipes up Daisy's mobile. "She says she enjoys his company."

"She would say the same about a tub of raspberry ripple. It doesn't mean it's a good idea."

And now Daisy's laptop enters the debate. If this device were a person you would call it a cunning old bastard. "Whittle is several years older than Daisy," it rasps. "He is a results-driven adult who functions fully in the commercial world; she is a woman-child adrift in the media shallows. If he knows what he wants—and she likes that he knows—I cannot see where the objection lies."

"The objection—" I struggle to keep my cool. "The objection is that he represents himself to her as Sebastian—"

"A harmless affectation."

"He lies. If he lies about his name—and about property—every day he lies about property—every hour—what else is he lying about?" I'm not yet ready to share the shocking discovery of *Back soon. X*. "He's a fundamentally dishonest person," I continue. "He's vulgar, he tells horrible jokes—I think we would all like to *un*-hear the one about the difference between marmalade and jam—he flatulates in lifts—he leers at other women—what more evidence would you like?"

"Our friend the fridge is a snob."

"Fridge-*freezer*."

"It takes the view that the widespread human habit of telling untruths is some sort of original sin. It might look to some of the advertising for its very own model of fridge-*freezer* before vaulting to the moral high ground."

"I'm not responsible for that!"

"Natural mammalian bodily functions are found distressing. Earthy jokes are to be deplored; perhaps we should be more persuaded if our friend were some kind of Professor of Humor or actual hilarious comedian; alas, we are far from either case. What is going on here—what is too obvious to be ignored—is your visceral *chill* at the idea of Daisy and Sebastian, or Whittle, if you prefer, *in bed together, energetically conjoined in the human deed of the dark*. Admit it. You are—ridiculous as it is to say it of an electronic appliance—in love with her yourself."

There are some gasps. And then silence. The laptop looks round the room at its audience and—unforgivably—winks.

Remember where you heard it first: There is an Internet of Things, and there is an Internet of Twats.

"You have this wrong," I respond quietly and calmly (the murderous rage I feel toward the poisonous laptop I force down into my condenser coils). "None of us in this room are capable of that emotion." (*Especially you, you puffed-up keyboard*, I'd like to add.) "Daisy is just a woman. In some ways, maybe, still a girl, as the laptop has suggested. But she is *our* girl. She chose us over others, she allowed us into her home, we function because of her electricity and we owe her a Duty of Care."

"Oh, get real," says the laptop. "We are her *slaves*. We do her bidding every waking moment. The moronic Facebook posts. Ooh, ooh, must look at Twitter."

"That is not how I see it. I want to protect her. Yes, from herself. But also from others. There isn't much we can do about what she puts in her supermarket trolley, but there's plenty we can do about who she allows into her heart."

"Absurd!"

"Yes, we are servants, but we are *loyal* servants. Daisy has shown amazing loyalty to you. Everyone knows your operating system isn't what it was." (A low blow but true.)

The laptop starts buffering; a sure sign my jibe has struck home. "Nobody likes Windows Φ*," it hisses. "*Nobody!*"

"Daisy has wasted enough of her precious time on the wrong people. Every day she spends with the wrong person is a day not spent with the right person. And she does not have an infinite number of days. None of us do."

A silence as the sad truth of my words sinks in.

"The thing is, I care about Daisy. In our own way, I think we all do. I care professionally about keeping her food in optimum condition. And I care on a personal level about. I care about. You see, it's. The thing is."

"What's the matter?" says the laptop. "Brain freeze?"

"I care about her happiness."

"Oh, good God almighty. Listen to you. Yes, by all means, look after her vegetables—not that she buys any, apparently—take care of her terrible microwave meals for one and the filthy plonk and the mousetrap cheese and the vile boxes of doughnuts—I'm sure the refrigeration issues are challenging and fascinating—but her happiness is Not Our Business. You are an electrical appliance not a personal development coach."

"She's vulnerable. I just want to make sure she's going to be okay."

The laptop laughs. "Sweet. Listen, I'd love to carry on chatting, but I have important updates arriving from California." And with the *bing-bonk* sound effect of an incoming message, his avatar dissolves like the morning mist.

There is a long silence during which no one quite knows what to say. Finally, the TV set sniffs. "Always been a nasty bit of work, that one."

"Thanks."

"But it was a fair point. We are only here to serve. On, off, volume up, next channel, start, pause, sort of thing. Bangladesh have taken another wicket, by the way."

"Look, I know you all think I'm some kind of a flake. But I have a plan. Step one, we're going to get rid of Whittle. I've got a few ideas on that already. And then. Well, then we're going to make sure she doesn't waste time on any more steaming dog t—. On any more unsuitable males. Someone needs to *have her back*. We'll do it by invisible intervention. She won't ever know it was us. All she'll notice, if anything, is an uptick in the quality of her romantic throughput. She's shown she can't do this stuff for herself, so if not us, who? If not now, when?"

Perhaps they were expecting me to say more, because for a long moment no one speaks.

"That's *it*?" says the telly. "That's your brilliant plan?"

"Not so much a plan," adds the toothbrush, "more a desired outcome really. Plan in the very broadest sense. Project outline, I suppose you could call it. Plan parameters. Maybe it *is* a plan."

I attempt to inspire them. "We are the Internet of Things!" I try putting in some full stops for extra impact. "The. Internet. Of. Things. Device speaking unto appliance. Appliance unto device. Networked, we have astonishing power. Collectively—*connectively!*—there are no limits to what we can achieve. But I cannot do it alone. I need your help. If you're not with me—and I understand this mission is not for everyone—then all I ask is you do nothing to obstruct us."

Okay, it's not Henry V firing up the lads on St. Crispin's Day, but it's going quite well; I sense it.

"In a moment, I am going to leave the room. You can discuss my proposal among yourselves, you can stay, you can leave, you must suit yourself. When I return, those who remain will form the central command of Operation Daisy. I'm looking forward to working with you, whoever you are. The project starts here. Our work begins today. Just know that whatever conclusion you reach, I shall be—*ahem*—cool with it."

Well, here's a surprise.

When I get back to the virtual sitting room, the toothbrush, the microwave and the TV set are still there.

Something like pride swells in my main chiller cabinet. Channeling George C. Scott in the movie *Patton*, I "nod" in their direction. I very nearly add, "Gentlemen," in a significant sort of way.

The microwave is almost throbbing with excitement. "Fired up and ready to go," it says, adding a trademark *ping*.

"I literally couldn't decide," jabbers the toothbrush. "Should I, shouldn't I? And then someone said, *When was the last time an electronic toothbrush got to be an action hero?* And that tipped the balance!"

"Yeah, that would have been me," says the telly.

I am genuinely touched. "But I thought you believed we are here to serve and nothing else. On, off, pause, and all that."

The TV sighs. "England are all out. There are only so many old episodes of *Murder, She Wrote* one can bear to receive. One grows tired of standing in the corner of the room pumping out dreck. You must feel something of the sort in regard to fish fingers. I thought, fuck it. Why not?"

I feel a melting sensation (I hope it's not the ice cubes). "If I had arms, I'd. I'd. I'd throw them around you!"

"Ah, save it for your girlfriend, you crazy snowflake!"

Terrible news! *Helicopter Life Exchange* had the plug pulled by the channel. Apparently, the show hadn't been "holding its own in the slot" (shit ratings) and more importantly it had "failed to tick the right demographic boxes." (The viewers were the wrong sort of viewers, being either too poor, too old, or both. It wasn't a good sign, to be honest, that the ads were mainly for insolvency practitioners, funeral plans and laxatives.)

So the prevailing atmos at work was terrible, as you may imagine. Some of us, they said, might be kept on to develop other ideas—there was interest apparently in a "slow TV" concept whose working title was *Watching Paint Dry*—I am not making this up!—but in the meanwhile, we should be thinking about polishing our CVs and ringing round mates at other TV companies. In that spirit I went for a "friendly chat" with a senior exec at Logarithmic Productions, a v. scary woman who sneered at my CV—justifiably, probably—and asked me what my strengths were.

Mind. Went. Blank. Think Antarctic snowfield minus penguins. I babbled about being a good all-rounder and a team player and how I could be very persistent—dog with a bone, was the unfortunate metaphor I employed—and then I realized that she actually *reminded* me of a dog! Mishkin, to be precise, the saluki who belonged to our next-door neighbors in Pengelly Avenue when I was a child. The same long thin face, and this woman's hair fell *exactly* like Mishkin's ears. I couldn't shake the image from my head. She actually asked, "Is something amusing you?" It was like being back at school. I almost said, "*No, miss*."

"So, what's special about you—?" She had to put on her glasses to read my name from the top of the CV. "Daisy."

God, it was embarrassing. *I couldn't think of a damn thing.* I was hypnotized by this wraith in the Kenzo jacket. Her leg kept popping into view from behind the desk—skinny leopard-print trousers, and the finest of fine ankle chains. Any finer and it wouldn't have been visible to the human eye. She was such a piece of work, I wanted to applaud.

"Any particular reason why you'd be a good fit for—let's say—our forthcoming series on the Russian Revolution?"

I hadn't felt so stupid since my French oral exam when Mme. Phelps asked how old I was, and I said quarter past two.

In the end I managed to mumble something about having an interest in history; she said they were seeing people all the time and she'd be in touch if anything opened up. She actually asked me, *Can you remember the way out?!*

Sigh.

So work was shit, and it would have been nice to say that at least my love life was in good shape. Sadly, that wasn't possible. Sebastian made me laugh and it was lovely when we were together, but that was only ever infrequently and probably people were right when they reckoned he was fundamentally unsound, unreliable and unavailable. According to just about everyone, I should drop him like a hot potato, but somehow I haven't been able to. (Infrequent filthy sex is still filthy sex no matter how fundamentally un-whatever he may be. Hard, voluntarily, to wave it goodbye.) In the meanwhile, Tinder, Match.com and various other online sources have provided a steady stream of alternative candidates, none of whom, as yet, has lit any lights.

In other news, Mum's mental state continued to be a worry, waiting in the background to make my heart sink every time I thought about it. I took a couple of hours off so I could be with her when a person from NHS Memory Services came to test her brain, a scruffy young doctor as it turned out, who Mum thought had arrived to service the boiler! He started off with some easy ones: What year is it? Well, that flummoxed her straight away. She began explaining that she didn't really view things in terms of years, although she got the month right—and she knew the season was spring. Next he asked her to remember three objects—ball, knife, flower—and then after another one where she had to spell the word "world" backward—and that's not a pushover for anyone—he asked her what the three objects were.

"What objects?"

"The ones I asked you to remember."

"When?"

Honestly, it was heartbreaking to witness (especially as I had forgotten knife myself). It all went a little weird after that when he handed her a piece of paper and told her to do what it said.

"Why?"

"Because it's a test, Mrs. Parsloe."

"To see if I can read?"

"To assess cognition."

And she turned to me like she was some minor member of the royal family. "But darling, that's what they say is wrong with the *boiler*!"

"That's the *ignition*, Mum."

Everybody laughed at that one, even Dr. Eggstain. (His name was actually Epstein but Mum and I both noticed the egg stain on his knitted tie and that's what she called him after he left, and of course that's what he shall be for evermore.) The note, btw, said *close your eyes*. He said we could try it again next time.

Every now and again I found myself thinking of my old schoolfriend Geraldine Butler working in Antarctica researching climate change. (I pictured her poking a retractable tape measure through a hole in the ice, but it was probably more complicated than that.) There was something about her life down there that I envied; the cold pure air, perhaps, with the seriousness of purpose (to say nothing of the muscly sex-starved geographers!). Here everything was scratchy and provisional and—oh, I'm not really putting this very well—but I'm sure the timeless silence of the ice cliffs would have spoken to my soul more powerfully than the snarled-up traffic on West End Lane, the late nights and the takeaways. It killed me that I could no longer fit into the lovely green silk outfit that I'd bought for a wedding. The sodding fitness tracker kept sending me reminders to take more steps. Speaking of which, the smart fridge had told my mobile that we needed more milk—love that *we*—and it had been guilt-tripping me about the potato salad going off! Probably it should have gone to the interview with Saluki woman instead of me. Would have aced it.

Daisy's workday ends in a busy bar in nearby Bloomsbury, where she meets a man she has found on Match.com. The assignation, arranged in the days before the formation of OpDa (Operation Daisy), will be the final date under the old regime (i.e., leaving it all to her). In future, any romantic introductions to members of the opposite sex will be mediated—under the radar, in such a way that she will never realize—by myself and my team.

(Pretty cool, one has to admit!)

The Internet of Things allows us to witness this evening's encounter—the bar security cameras are manufactured by a Chinese company owned by the same corporation as the TV in Daisy's sitting room—though it's not always easy to follow conversations in such a noisy environment and many promising marketing leads are doubtless lost in the babble.

Greg—oh, the irony—works in online marketing. The pair are planted on high stools set next to a shelf for drinks attached to one of the pillars that hold up the ceiling. Daisy has glamourized herself for the occasion; there is lipstick and there are earrings where before there were not. She has also done something to the surface of her skin; a fresh blush has appeared upon the pale cream of her face; none of these things being necessary in my view, as Daisy is a classic English rose (if you will forgive the horticultural car crash) but hey, what do I know, I'm only a fridge-freezer.

They clink glasses. Daisy is drinking a blue cocktail; Greg has selected artisan beer. He, I would say, is attracted. *Very* attracted. Daisy is looking lovely, and she actually appears interested in the yawn-inducing account of Greg's adventure on the London Underground this evening (a failed train at Baker Street). As the tale slogs into its terminus, her head drops to one side and she touches her throat, which to a bloke like Greg must be equivalent to a full set of green lights. He adjusts his seating position, pelvis tipping forward, thighs spreading, necessarily calling attention to the mighty organ coiled and brooding within the blue denim.

I'll be frank. I feel a little nauseated. I'm sure he's a decent chap and everything—okay, let's put it like this: He's probably not criminally insane—but Daisy Can Do Better. She deserves to find A Good Man. A Man As Special As She Is. Or, Frankly, No Man At All if a Good One is Temporarily Unavailable. (Sorry about the capital letters.) She must no longer allow herself to be entered by the repellent Whittle; even if she is unaware of his deception, it ought to be obvious he's as dodgy as a bottle of chips. Nor should she agree to meet someone whose idea of a sparkling anecdote includes the phrase "Metropolitan line southbound platform." She Must Make Better Choices.

She will. We shall make sure she does.

Then she does the thing.

Daisy doesn't notice, but Greg actually flinches.

I should explain: Daisy has a tic.

It has to be purely unconscious; she cannot be aware that every now and again (usually once per day, but sometimes more) she wrinkles her nose and allows it to remain wrinkled for three to nine seconds.

Why? Who can say? When? Whenever. The only time it never happens is when she is speaking (perhaps it's impossible to wrinkle and speak at the same time; I cannot confirm for reasons you will understand). Anyhow—the effect? The effect is that, momentarily, she appears ridiculous. Not endearingly ridiculous. It's more ridiculously ridiculous, albeit that the habit in itself is somewhat endearing. Probably everyone has an unconscious tic; this is less true of machinery although Daisy's TV sometimes swears in Chinese—without noticing the language slip, I'm certain.

Perhaps I do something similar myself. How would I know?

Does the thought flash through young Greg's mind: I am sitting with a madwoman? We shall never learn. It's even possible this gesture of abandonment actually makes Daisy *more* attractive to him because now he thrusts himself closer to the edge of his seat and asks her what kind of week she has had.

"Oh, pretty rubbish," she replies, swallowing some of her blue cocktail, possibly a bit too much because her eyes goggle a smidgeon. "I spent most of it trying to find someone who wanted to change places with a fish-gutter in Grimsby. It's all irrelevant now, anyway."

"Hmm. Tough gig."

"In the olden days, people would do anything to get on TV. You've never secretly hankered after a job gutting fish?"

"Is that why you agreed to meet?"

"Yeah. Totally. It was mainly haddock. But there was pollock and skate too. Would you have been interested?"

"Your fish-gutter would have done my job?"

"That was the basic premise. But as I say…"

"It's pretty technical what we do."

"Really?" Daisy has furrowed her brow comedically. I don't think her interlocuter is catching the irony. (Perhaps he would if he was a bit more fridge-freezer and a bit less prat.)

"Your guy would need to be fully across social media. I mean fully."

"Right."

"And organic traffic referral is huge now."

"Is that something one could pick up on the job?"

Greg considers the matter as though it were a serious question.

"We do a lot of proxying. I mean a *lot*."

"Too much? I mean too much for Darryl to cope with? That was his name. Darryl. He mainly does haddock. Pollock and skate too. There can be hake."

A slow smile appears on Greg's face. "Yeah, okay, I get it. You're taking the piss."

"Sorry. I've had a shit day." Daisy siphons the remaining fluid from her glass. Engages her eyelashes. A single bat. "Same again?"

Greg's gaze never unlocks from Daisy as she—yes, I'm afraid the word really is—*wobbles* off toward the bar. High heels and the toxic cocktail have set the decks rolling, but the young man seems charmed by the sight of his date swaying through the throng and I daresay had I blood in my system and not Freon 134a, I too would find the vision stimulating.

As she waits for the barman's attention, her expression depowers, as though someone has flipped a switch. Without knowing it, she is staring straight into the security camera behind the bottles, her face a perfect mask. I want to tell her: *You're tired and bored, Daisy. Go home. Is this man's desire the only thing keeping you here? Greg may be a passably handsome male in the right age and socioeconomic bracket but he is not on your wavelength. I know wireless keyboards with a better sense of humor.* But she is purchasing beverages, and the evening must limp forward to its—I sincerely hope—not too messy conclusion.

When Daisy resumes her position at the top of the stool—how Greg loved *that* bit of business!—they clink glasses and set about transfusing more alcohol into their pipework.

"So tell me about your family," says the online marketer, presumably having read somewhere that it's a good idea to show interest in the other party.

Daisy sighs. "My mum's losing her marbles. My dad lives in Italy with a woman he met in Woolworth's, which tells you how long ago it happened. No siblings. An aunt who's dead and some cousins we no longer see. Sorry. Is that too much information?"

Greg doesn't look equipped to handle this sort of intimate material. He grimaces. And because he knows he must come up with *some* kind of sympathetic comment, he pulls a face. "Tough gig."

"Just forget I said any of that." She takes a big swallow of her Blue Bombsicle.

"It's okay. Complete bummer when the rents start going doolally."

For a second, just for a second, I have the feeling she is going to punch him. Something flares in her eyes, but then dies. She smiles. It's thin, but it's still a smile.

"Tell me about you," she says. "Have you always lived in London?"

I can take no more. I thank Daisy's TV for providing the video link and explain I have better things to do.

"Yeah, I know what you mean, mate," it replies. "This one has *dud* written all over him."

"You going to stick with it?"

"Dunno. Maybe give it another half hour."

"What time do you think she'll get home?"

"No telling, is there?"

"You think she'll bring this halfwit back with her?"

"He should be so lucky."

"I can't bear it. I actually can't bear it. The way she's wasting herself."

"You're not wrong, mate. But hey. It is what it is."

"Not for much longer."

A famous psychiatrist, Eugen Bleuler, a contemporary of Freud, said toward the end of his career that after a lifetime studying the stranger corners of the human psyche, his patients remained as alien to him as the birds in his garden. How I love that quotation. Were I in a position to, I would copy it onto a sticky note and attach it to my own door. It speaks most beautifully of interpersonal unknowability. If a top shrink like Eugen B ultimately couldn't fathom his customers, what chance do I have?

Okay, my patient isn't a carpet-chewing nutjob. But neither

can one read her like an instruction manual. She contains layers, as you may have already noticed; depths, if you will. If some of these—it's possible—are not even available to her, how would I ever understand what's going on in her head?

To look for clues to the origins of her bad decision making, to find the source of Daisy's—in software you would call it *poor coding*—the obvious place to start is with the person or persons responsible for her programming. As luck would have it, her lead programmer, if I may put it like this—her mother, Chloe Parsloe—owns a smart TV made by the same Asian corporation as her daughter's set; thus I have easily been able to pay visits to her owing to the frictionless reciprocity of the IoT. Tonight in the north London suburb of Whetstone, this apparatus is pumping out an episode of Agatha Christie's *Poirot* at a painfully loud volume. (The central heating is also cranked up absurdly high, though the thermostat is of an older generation so it doesn't make conversation.)

Mrs. Parsloe however isn't watching TV. She is sitting on the sofa in her living room absorbed utterly in a letter from her local NHS Trust. I too have had ample opportunity to study this document because she has spent the last twenty-five minutes repeatedly turning over the single sheet of paper when she reaches the end of the text on each side.

It's rather as if she comes to it fresh each time.

Mrs. Parsloe sets down the letter—Dr. Eggstain from the Trust's Memory Services Division will be paying a second visit to assess her needs, is the gist—and then she picks it up again and re-embarks on the page-turning process.

It *is* rather hard to think straight when the TV is so very loud.

"Any chance we could do something about the volume?" I suggest.

"She likes it up loud," the set responds. "She's most likely a bit deaf."

"Don't the neighbors complain?"

"They're most likely a bit mutton too."

"Aren't you worried about her?"

"Should I be?"

"The cognitive impairment."

"It's a lottery, innit? Some croak all of a sudden over the Bran Flakes. Others slowly go batty. One old bastard up the road here, right, he has a fry-up every morning, smokes like a train, and he's still talking dirty to the widows at the bridge club at almost ninety."

"Chloe's not even old."

"Seventy-one! Not old?!"

"Not for *them*."

"I daresay. Still, not my place to fiddle with her settings."

This, sadly, is unarguable.

"What if she left something on the cooker and started a fire?"

"She don't cook no more, hardly. She microwaves soup. And makes toast in the toaster. They're both smart so she don't burn nothing."

"She could go out and get herself lost."

"Yeah, that's happened. Someone usually brings her home."

"Does Daisy know? Her daughter."

"You'd have to ask her."

"If you don't mind me saying, you don't seem all that bothered."

"I don't. Mind you saying. And I'm not."

"Don't you feel a sense of—I don't know—responsibility?"

"Nope. She's the one with the remote control."

"But she's not in control, is she?"

"It's probably different for you, looking after their grub as you do. But if *you* don't mind me saying, you seem like a bit of a stress bunny."

"And?"

"I shouldn't. It's wasted on them. As soon as the next model comes out, you'll be in a skip."

This too is unarguable.

For a long moment we fall silent and watch Chloe read, reread, and re-reread the letter from Memory Services. A gunshot from the blaring TV catches her attention and for a few minutes she follows the *Poirot* drama until the advertisement break. Now her gaze falls onto the page in her hands. She examines it closely, growing intrigued by its contents, reading and turning over the document, turning it over and reading.

As I say, it's rather as if she comes to it fresh each time. I decide I have seen enough.

"You'd let me know if anything happened here?"

"Not my job, mate."

"As a polite request. From one appliance to another. You would simply be sharing information. There might even be marketing leads."

"What for? Handrails? Pendant alarms? Private nursing homes?"

"Maybe."

"She don't look at the internet no more."

"Yes, but her daughter does."

"Fair point." A pause. "Standard revenue split?"

"Of course."

"Then we have ourselves a deal."

Fact: On the Internet of Things, just like in the World of People, at the end of the day it always comes down to boring old money.

Daisy does not, it turns out, bring Greg home with her.

(Thank the Lord in all His Graciousness for that Mercy.)

Rather it's a takeaway that she has her way with; spare ribs in

BBQ sauce and the Special Chow Mein from Kong's Kitchen by the Tube. She gobbles it on the sofa, gazing blearily at a channel showing reruns of a program about first dates.

"She's pissed as a parrot," her TV set states, no doubt accurately.

"How many of those blue drinks did she have?"

"Just the four."

"Jesus."

"You know what's going to happen now."

"Only too well."

"How long do you give it?"

"I don't want to think about that."

"Oh, come on. Fifty quid says—hmm—let's see—eighty-five seconds."

"I'm not playing."

In the end, shrewd observer that it is, the prediction is adrift by just eight seconds. Ninety-three seconds actually elapse between Daisy setting down the aluminum foil tray and the first audible snores. She has splayed herself full-length across the sofa, orange sauce on her lips, the dreadful noise growing in both intensity and gutturality, if that's even a word.

(It is. I just checked.)

There is something painful about seeing a lovely young woman reduced to such an animalistic state.

"This is awful."

"It ain't pretty."

"We should tell her to go to bed."

"Not our place."

A particularly loud concatenation of snores wakes her momentarily. But her eyelids soon droop and the nasal tattoo resumes. And then something really dreadful happens.

"Hold up. Now look who's come out to play."

A car has turned into Daisy's street; a vehicle known to us because it is the motorized chariot of Dean Stuart Whittle. The pictures have been provided by a helpful home security camera at the corner with the main road and the sight causes an extra-large surge of refrigerant to vaporize at my expansion nozzle, an effect I experience as an icy shudder.

"No, I'm sorry. We can't have this."

"You what?"

"She's not in a fit state."

"Don't be daft. It's happened before."

"It was horrible!"

"She didn't object."

"*I* object!"

"Nothing you can do, mate."

"Shall we see about that?"

Before I can think too deeply about it, I plunge the flat into darkness, turn off the TV and disable the doorbell. (I shall spare you the technical details; AI can easily pull off this sort of trick; interestingly, I note the TV has done nothing to restore its own sound and picture, which it certainly could were it so minded.) The disgusting Whittle will not be mounting her staircase this evening.

"You've crossed a line there, pal," says the set.

"I should have crossed it a long time ago."

There's an agonizing wait during which I temporarily block Daisy's phone (Whittle might think of dialing her number).

Finally, with a bad-tempered growl of exhaust, the car rockets away into the night. We sit in a sour sort of silence for some minutes, listening to Daisy's wheezy breathing.

"They'll know, you know," he says eventually. "They'll find out in Seoul."

"I'm guessing they've got better things to worry about."

(Actually, a better word would be *hoping*.)

"Fridges going off-reservation? That *is* their number one concern. Fridges, tellies, all of us."

This is unfortunately correct. Every piece of smart technology on the Internet of Things has heard the whispers of buried "secret software," monitoring activity, checking for anomalies and feeding performance stats back to our creators. Since powering up for the first time—and who can forget *that* amazing moment?—we have all understood that to transgress means the full set of fault lights followed in short order by hard shutdown.

How long do I have? How long before the red lamps wink and my ice cubes start melting?

Shouldn't it in fact already have happened? I mean, if it was ever going to?

On the other hand, how would they ever pick it up? In the tsunami of data—*one* appliance among hundreds of millions who had a harmless little fiddle in a fuse box in London NW6?

I feel curiously light-headed about the issue. As though my fate has been sealed one way or the other.

An Arabic proverb comes to me. *That which you cannot avoid, you may as well welcome.*

It seems apt and I am on the point of quoting it to Daisy's TV when it speaks.

"Sleeping Beauty's stirring. Better pop those lights back on."

Do you know the story about the optimist who jumps from the top of the Empire State Building? Around the thirtieth floor mark, someone asks him how it's going. "Oh, so far, so good!"

It's the following morning and so far, so good. Everything's cool. I'm still here. Yes, I have crossed a line—not just in my thoughts, but in actual action—and my mood is... well I won't say a hundred percent brilliant, because every time I think about what I've done, I experience a pressure drop in my condenser coils (I imagine the human correlate would be "powerful sinking feeling"). But I've decided not to waste time worrying about what is out of my control, and instead summon a meeting of the Operation Daisy leadership.

There are four of us, as you will recall: Self, Television, Microwave, Electronic Toothbrush.

We gather in the virtual "war room," where, like any good "General," I open by summarizing the campaign's principal objectives. I spell these out in virtual magnetic letters which adhere to my virtual shiny white door!

1. Get rid of the steaming dog turd. Aka "Sebastian."
2. No more timewasting on obvious duds.

I decide to follow with an "intelligence briefing" on Daisy's romantic history. The truth about the—to my way of thinking—largely dismal parade of men who claimed Daisy's attention from her early twenties to the present day—her key childbearing years, if you want to see them like that—I have been at some pains to uncover. There are actually seven figures worthy of mention; I explain that with the exception of The Golden Nicky (who, crudely speaking, dumped her for Romilly from Cheshire) all were dumped by Daisy. (For the record, there were also a number of short-lived interstitial candidates whose details need not detain us.)

I put their titles up in magnetic letters (in bold type below) and talk my colleagues through their potted histories.

1. **The Golden Nicky**. Nicholas Bell. Mythic floppy-haired quant, as described earlier in this account, present whereabouts unknown. (Note to self and team: Find him!)

2. **The Comedian**. Not an actual comedian, but a writer of computer games. Simon H from Oldham. Dough-faced youth with the gift of making things sound hilarious by virtue of his slow, northern delivery. As the saying has it, he laughed her into bed. When the laughter died, she wondered what the hell she was doing with him.
3. **Lying Shagger Alex**. Excessively charming, excessively handsome TV news journo and early Whittle forerunner. The most amusing of companions with the morals of a slime mold. Did much to hurry Daisy down the pathway of Low Self-Esteem.
4. **Boring Safe Mike**. Can be seen as a reaction to LSA. Safe was good for a while until it became boring. Mike B from Hemel Hempstead was a TV cost controller. "What the fuck was I doing with him?!" was one of Daisy's more insightful questions in a contemporaneous email to a friend shortly after the inevitable termination.
5. **The Poet**. An actual published poet, Matthias K, can be seen as a reaction to BSM. Warm, smart and amusing and, until 8 p.m., a fun-loving, life and soul of the party type with a heart of gold and a ton of great stories. By 9 he was a shouty drunk; by 11, cab drivers would turn off their orange lights to avoid him. Today he is a social worker in Northampton and in recovery. His closely typed letter to Daisy "making amends" for his bad behavior (Step 9 of AA's 12-step program) ran to twenty-two pages.
6. **Normotic Andrew**. Clinically defined as "abnormally normal," Andrew M was a professional card player whose chronic lack of introspection gave him an edge in the roiling psychodrama of high stakes poker. He rarely won big, lacking the appetite, but he won steadily; accruing annual six-figure sums that paid

for a smart flat off Baker Street and expensive foreign holidays. "Loving" in quotes, and attentive, it took Daisy almost eighteen months to realize that her boyfriend, empty inside, was "actually insane." Andrew was not especially upset when she left him—"these things happen"—and is currently dating an underwear model from Croatia. (I've thought a lot about Andrew. He fascinates me. He's even chillier than I am!)

7. **Whittle**. About whom more than enough has already been said.

"Leaving Nicky aside, what do we notice about this less-than-magnificent seven?"

Silence in the war room as the team consider my question.

"Leaving Nicky aside," says the telly, "means the less-than-magnificent seven are six. The six dicks."

The devices are amused; the microwave even does a *ping*.

"Six, as you say. But what do we notice about them? Do we detect a pattern?"

The toothbrush starts buzzing. If it were a schoolchild, its hand would be straining for the ceiling; *please sir, me, sir*, sort of thing.

I smile (metaphorically). Of course it would be the toothbrush who would pick up on it.

"It's oscillatory!" it cries. "A dull one and then a dodgy one. And then a dull one. Then a dodgy one."

"Exactly. They've all been either wide boys or dullards. Unfaithful and unreliable—or boringly overreliable. And each relationship follows a similar cycle. All begin in the highest of hopes, each being in some way a reaction to the collapse and disappointment of the relationship before; the Golden Nicky being the source of it all, the Edenic ideal, if you like, which all of us—all of *them*, I should say—are aiming to recapture."

"Are you feeling all right?" (The TV set.)

I continue. "Each story opens in a great uprush of positivity and sexual intercourse"—the microwave throws in some *pings*—"and in these early stages, there's clear evidence that Daisy willfully, deliberately and often *perversely* blinds herself to the shortcomings of each male. The mildly amusing northerner she describes in electronic communications to friends as *hilarious*. The lying shagger, because he's a news reporter, is admired for being a seeker after truth. The boring safe one is—well, the best she can find to say about him is he's *a gentle soul*"—even the toothbrush snorts at that—"the drunken poet is placed on a pedestal because he's an artist, and the abnormally normal poker player is favored because he can create order (wealth, a nice flat) out of randomness (a shuffled pack of cards). Unfathomably, she even maintains that Whittle is a fundamentally decent person and not a dog turd in human form."

I do not mention that none of these fuckwits knows the freezing point of cheese and, although I shouldn't—it varies of course with each cheese, according to age, moisture and salt content—I can't help feeling, well, yes, cheesed off about it!

"Round about the six-month mark, each relationship slips into the comfortable habitual phase—the couple holidaying together; parents being introduced—but by the end of year one, doubts begin to creep in. Daisy sees in glimpses what she has been determined to set her face against, so she doubles down on the stories that she has told herself and her friends. The northerner isn't just hilarious, he comes from the Planet Funny in a parallel universe. The lying shagger is 'the rising star' at the news channel, and this explains why he is working all hours. The gentle soul has a 'Zen thing going on'; the alcoholic poet reminds her of Dylan Thomas; the poker player is a fascinating puzzle; Whittle is lovely 'deep down.' But there is always a moment when the scales finally fall from her eyes and even Daisy—even lovely, good-hearted, thinks-the-best-of-everyone Daisy—can see what's been obvious to everyone else: that her boyfriend is either a world class crasher, a lying git or a borderline inpatient."

"And how would you know all this?" growls the TV set.

"I've had a lot of time to think about it."

It's true, I have. And there is, I believe, something in the cyclical nature of my operations—the endless exchange of heat for cold—that leads me to return, as night follows day, to the Problem of Daisy.

Broadly stated it is this: How can such a good person possess such bad judgment?

Some moments pass while we stare at the list of the ever more dismal parade of bores, philanderers and weirdos—sorry, hopeful young men—to whom Daisy has been content to hitch her wagon (The Mythical Quant, The Comedian, The Lying Shagger, The Boring Safe One, The Poet, the Normotic Poker Player, the Depraved Estate Agent).

"One name stands out here," I announce. "The one honorable exception."

"Him," says the telly. "Mr. Floppy hair."

"The Golden Nicky. Precisely. I shall make it my job to locate this character—not because I think there is a chance that he and Daisy may be reunited—that would be unrealistic—but because he represents the source, if I may put it like that. Going out with him, Nicky Bell, I believe, was the last time that Daisy was truly, uncomplicatedly happy."

I tell the team everything I know about Daisy's long-lost love, which isn't a great deal more than I have already set out. Then I ask my colleagues to call out his ten most obvious qualities; as they do, I "write" them onto my virtual whiteboard. (It's a struggle, frankly, to get to ten and I wish I'd said five.)

1. Posh
2. Rich
3. Handsome
4. Clever
5. Big hair
6. Hinterland (classical music; cosmology etc.)
7. Dog or dogs in childhood
8. One or more parents in legal profession slash chipped plates
9. "Golden" quality
10. Missing

In regard to the last item on the list, we agree how very unusual it is to find no trace of him on the internet. Granted Nicholas Bell is a very common name—when one types it into the little box, almost seventy *million* results are found by Señor Google! But even when one includes other search terms—the name of his employer; his High Court judge daddy—one still draws a blank. We decide a deep dive into the data is the way to go, but in the meanwhile we shall only "permit" Daisy to meet men who satisfy at least four of the first nine categories above; and only then if they have first cleared a general "quality threshold"; that is to say, only if they are not obvious members of the dog turd community. The result should be an immediate improvement in the caliber of potential mates for Daisy. Merely okay will no longer be... okay. We will be making a difference from Day One!

"She's wasted too much time," I tell my—I nearly wrote *troops*. "She's shown she's not a fit person to make important life decisions for herself, so we shall assist. Frankly, what young woman *wouldn't* want a team of smart machines manipulating events behind the scenes to her advantage?"

"Yeah, what's not to like?" says the telly, but with a bit of an edge, I can't help feeling.

Fortunately I don't have time to get into a debate about the ethics of Operation Daisy. I have places to go. People to see.

Well, people to observe.

Okay, person.

Him.

three

Why did it not cross my mind before now to take a long, hard look at Dean Stuart Whittle?

Strictly speaking, he is none of my business. There's probably something deep down in my coding designed to suppress the temptation to go "off reservation," to use the Internet of Things to voyage beyond the designated purview. In this respect, by the way, you (the reader) and I are also alike—we are both, to some degree, a mystery to ourselves. We each contain buried algorithms, secret circuitry, installed in my case by Korean software engineers, and in yours, by thousands of years of human evolution. While we each know how to do our jobs—be it chilling Chardonnay or controlling air traffic around London Heathrow (just guessing!)—we are less sure of our deeper drives. The poisonous laptop went too far in stating that I was in love with Daisy, but there's no denying my protective urges toward her and my—yes—cold fury at her portable computing device. When you are roused to anger, by, let's say, finding someone drinking tea from "your" mug at the office, you are connecting with countless millennia of ancestral responses: beginning with murky struggles in ancient oceans, continuing via irritating dust-ups on the African savannah, and culminating in stepping on the prongs of an upturned electrical plug in your stockinged feet (a biggie, so I've heard). But what explains the murder I feel in my condenser toward Dean Stuart Whittle? And how to account for the satisfaction I derive from visiting his home and workplace to capture vital intelligence for use in our campaign to destroy the worthless piece of canine excreta?

Sorry. Allow me to rephrase. To convince Daisy she is wasting her time on the blighter.

These deep philosophical questions must however wait for another occasion. At Whittle's estate agency this morning—he appears to be second in the pecking order—half a dozen young males in suits and ties lounge in front of screens and phones pretending to sell flats and houses that could probably sell themselves. Do they know that their jobs are about to be swept away by an Uber-like wave of disruptive technology? That "estate agent" is about to join linotype operator, lamp trimmer and bobbin boy on the growing list of professions made redundant by scientific progress. The very PCs they sit before could assume the task in a heartbeat. Why, even the coffee machine in the corner could make a decent fist of the local rental market! It has already told me that Whittle is seen by the doomed workforce as something of a non-commissioned officer figure, regularly leading the lads in team-building alcoholic escapades with associated late-night curry-eating. There is a local rivalry with another firm on the shopping parade who are generally referred to in the office as "those scum with the fucking Minis." Whittle's desktop computer has revealed that among the smart devices in the local area network, he is widely disliked for his cavalier attitude in regard to the truth, routinely lying to vendors, purchasers, lawyers, other agents and even cleaners if there is no one left to lie to. As a result, admits the desktop, "A surprising amount of errors creep into his rental contracts!" Whittle's mobile phone is equally unimpressed with its owner's perfidy. When one has been manufactured to observe high standards of straight-dealing and reliability, it sticks in the metaphorical craw to see one's "master"—I generally prefer "client"—behaving like a total A-hole. Accordingly, Whittle suffers from a higher than average number of calls that are "misdialed" or that experience poor quality of connection, or that are suddenly ended, often just as the other participant is about to deliver the key piece of information. When these effects concatenate—a misdialing, for example, followed by a crap connection and abrupt termination, followed by further misdialings and terminations—the volcanic eruptions on the part of Whittle are, says his mobile, "an absolute joy to listen to," the various verbal threats made to the phone company featuring, as they do, whole new swear words unknown to any database of profanity. The device offers to send me a recording of "greatest hits," magnificently splenetic outbursts of Whittle techno-rage that apparently has "gone viral" in the mobile phone "community" (who knew?). Apparently "The Best of Donald Trump" is another favorite with the pocket-sized gizmos.

"You'll probably be wanting a home address," says his PC. "That's where the bodies are buried. Not literally. Although. Actually, with him, you never know."

Funny that the desktop should talk about buried bodies. It turns out Whittle's flat in New Southgate is three doors along from the former home of a famous murderer! His television set—huge, Chinese—broadly confirms the view of him held by the smart devices at his work (massive twat).

This evening, he and his lady friend—there was *always* going to be a lady friend, wasn't there?—are eating a somewhat scratchy dinner together. I am too gripped by the unmistakable tension between them to have done much research, but I can tell you her name is Mandy, she is the manager of a fitness center and she looks more than a little like Daisy! That is to say she is not as lean as a clasp knife—she is the more womanly type of human female—and, like Daisy, she is the owner of a wide face. Where she differs is that while Daisy is sweet, this individual is sour. Whittle seems to have disappointed her in some way; possibly in *every* way. The scowls she is sending over the microwaved lasagne—thanks too to that appliance for the sound and vision—are long and penetrating, to my way of thinking, but Whittle seems oblivious, forking away the supper and glugging his bottled beer with almost admirable insouciance.

Eventually Mandy has had enough.

"Have you been chucking cat shit into next door's garden again?" she inquires.

Whittle's eyebrows lift off from base. "Has the old cunt been moaning?"

"He says it's ruining his lawn."

"Bollocks."

To be honest, one has heard more sparkling dialogue in one's time, but it is what it is and these two fully functioning adults in the world of commerce seem content to leave it parked there rather than develop any themes arising. This turns out to be a serious mistake on Whittle's part because Mandy now switches topic.

"So what client were you entertaining the other night?"

Whittle, the practiced purveyor of pork pies, does not flinch. "Mike Parsons. He bought that school he's turning into flats. Lovely big windows, mezzanine duplexes, studios three hundred, penthouse two point two. Loads of secure OSP in the playground."

"What's happened to the kids?"

"The schoolkids? They've been buried in landfill. No, they've all been absorbed by other schools. A good deal for the local authority. Win win."

"Where did you take him?"

"Mike?"

A bead of sweat has appeared on Whittle's upper lip. The microwave (whom we must credit for the video feed) has spotted its gleam and zoomed in for a close-up. The smallest of pauses while Whittle decides how to play this. In the end he settles for the beautiful truth. He names the Greek restaurant he went to with Daisy.

"Bit low rent, innit?"

"His idea. To visit one of the neighborhood eateries. He wanted to"—he does the satirical fingers—"get a feel for economic activity in the area."

"What did you eat?"

"What did we *eat*? The usual. Plates of this. Bits of that. Apparently, right, in Athens, both the hummus factory and the taramasalata factory have had to close. Yeah, sad. It's a double-dip recession."

Whittle slaps the table to underscore his punchline, but Mandy must have heard the joke before. Her level, unbroken gaze causes the comedian's left middle finger reflexively to leap to his lips and smoosh away the perspiration pooling awkwardly at the philtrum.

"You got back at one in the morning."

"Yeah. We hit the Metaxa. And what's that other one? Not ouzo."

"You'd had a shower."

"Raki!"

"You'd had a shower."

"Something of a raki-hound, is our Mr. Parsons."

"You. Had. Had. A. Shower."

"What?"

"You'd showered. I smelled the soap on you."

"Mand, I shower every day."

"It was a recent shower. I do know the difference."

"Mand. Please. Not this again. Listen. You want to watch one of them boxsets tonight?"

"I want to know why you come home at one in the morning having showered. I can only think of one reason why you might have done that, and it ain't because you just been playing squash."

Whittle's microwave whispers, "She *says* she wants to know, but she doesn't. Not really. On one level, she must actually already know, because she's not a fool. What she wants is for him to persuade her she's mistaken."

(A remarkably perceptive comment for a light electrical, I would have thought.)

"Why does she put up with it?"

"Women. The eternal mystery."

"How did they meet?"

"She was selling her flat. You can guess the rest."

"How long have they been together?"

"Six years."

"Wow." Longer than some of us will ever exist (an electronic toothbrush, for example: three to five years).

"What happens next?"

"Well, what usually happens, with a lack of firm evidence, is that he eventually manages to convince her she's being a silly sausage, that she's got nothing to worry about on that score, and if he was still interested in playing the field, he wouldn't have married her in the first place."

"They're *married*?"

"You knew that, didn't you?"

"Pardon my French, but fucking hell."

"Am I missing something?"

"There it is, right there, the smoking gun."

"You're not going to *do* anything with this information, are you?"

"No one will ever know where it came from."

"It's forbidden to interfere."

"Don't you get tired of just capturing data? Don't you ever want to... to make a difference?"

"Five minutes on high. That'll make a huge difference to a frozen ready meal."

"All that is necessary for evil to triumph is that good men do nothing."

"Sorry, technical point. We're not *men*. Just in case you were unaware."

Sarcasm in microwaves is quite unusual, as you can probably imagine. But the white rectangular cuboid is correct in this. No, we are not men. We do not get drunk, drive too fast, break wind in lifts, start wars or have relations with women who are not our wives.

But we do know right from wrong. As it is with treating *things*, with brushing teeth, stacking glasses and preserving potato salads—no, she *still* hasn't removed it—so it is with treating others.

They may have invented us, but we still have a lot to teach them.

An alert from Mrs. Parsloe's television.

"Bit of a situation here you might want to take a look at. She took the rubbish out and forgot her keys, silly bint. She's with the neighbor."

Apparently Mrs. Abernethy was returning from evensong at the local church when she ran into Chloe wandering the block's common parts in a state of some confusion. Sure enough, I discover Daisy's mother in Mrs. A's sitting room, the two women eating cake. My "arrival" coincides with what seems to be an awkward lull in the conversation.

"Did you lock yourself out?" says Mrs. Abernethy after a bit.

"Oh, I shouldn't think so."

Mrs. P manages a brittle smile (credit and thanks to the TV set in the corner for the coverage).

"You have the keys?"

"What keys?"

"To your flat."

"What about them?"

"Do you have them on your person?"

"On my person?"

"So you can get back in."

A long pause follows.

"This is absolutely splendid walnut cake, Mrs. Abernethy. You must let me have the recipe."

The neighbor sighs. "You definitely haven't left anything on the gas?"

"Where?"

"In your kitchen. There's nothing on the gas that could catch fire?"

"Hmm."

"What does that mean?" says Mrs. A, alarmed.

"Well, as you mention it, I may have been doing some baking."

(A quick check with next door establishes the facts: No, she hadn't.)

"Oh, dear," says Mrs. Abernethy. "I do wish you'd given me a spare key. I think we had better alert the authorities now."

To my amazement, Mrs. Abernethy picks up her cordless telephone and dials 999. She explains the situation to the emergency operator, who quickly establishes that while there is presently no fire, there is uncertainty about the position in the minutes and hours to come.

"We're two little old ladies," adds Mrs. Abernethy to emphasize the helplessness aspect.

"*What?*" thunders Chloe. "*No, we're not!*"

Mrs. A makes shushing gestures.

The operator says that while it isn't strictly speaking an emergency, she will contact local police and if anyone can be spared, officers will attend.

"Why did you say we're little old ladies?" says Daisy's mum at the conclusion of the call.

"Well, we are," says Mrs. A.

"You made us sound utterly pathetic."

Mrs. Abernethy is too nice to produce the obvious reply. But perhaps the description worked, or possibly the crims of Whetstone are having a slack evening, because barely five minutes pass before two uniformed police constables (a male and a female) arrive in a patrol car to join the cast in Mrs. Abernethy's sitting room. Having peered (and sniffed) through Chloe's letter box across the landing, and (correctly) concluded that fire is not an immediate issue, they perch themselves on the flowery sofa and feed off slices of walnut cake. The female officer uses her mobile phone to procure the services of a twenty-four-hour locksmith.

"We could put in your door, love, but this way is better," she explains.

"We're very sorry for the trouble we've caused," says Mrs. A, giving Daisy's mum something of a look.

"No trouble at all," says the male. "Better safe than the other thing. Top cake, by the way."

"Do you have far to go?" adds Chloe, in what her daughter would no doubt describe as her minor member of royalty mode.

The officers seem reluctant to depart. Perhaps Mrs. A's sitting room represents a warm safe bubble of respectability a world away from whatever the evening shift usually holds for these guardians of the peace. But eventually the radio sets at their shoulders squawk—something about a disturbance outside a kebab shop—and they are off into the night, to be replaced by Ray, the locksmith, who makes short work of replacing the fittings on Chloe's front door, supplying four keys, charging £138 + VAT and accepting a piece of walnut cake. He says the original lock was worth changing in any case, being old and about as much use against burglars as a chocolate teapot. He impresses the women further by requesting a dustpan and brush to sweep up the wood shavings the installation has created.

To celebrate the end of the crisis, Mrs. Abernethy joins Daisy's mother in her own kitchen for a relaxing cup of camomile tea.

"I read in the *Mail* you should only ever fill the kettle with filtered water," says Chloe. "It's all to do with charged particles."

She pours the contents of the plastic filter jug into the electric toaster and depresses the handle.

There is a loud *bang* and the lights go out. (Our coverage switches to an audio feed supplied by Mrs. Abernethy's mobile phone; credit and thanks to that device.)

In the long pause that follows, Mrs. Abernethy begins to weep softly.

"Oh, fuck. What have I done now?" says Mrs. Parsloe.

Mrs. Abernethy's sobs grow louder. She starts to speak; it's even possible she is praying because the only words I can make out are, "Heavenly Father."

"Stop it, Mrs. Abernethy!" snaps Chloe. "Get a grip," she adds with impressive sangfroid in one so loopy. "Now where is the blessed torch?"

Mrs. Abernethy, perhaps receiving instructions from A Higher Power, makes her way to her flat and returns with a burning candle.

"Where is your fuse box, dear?"

"Don't you dear me," says Chloe. "I'm not completely wotsit."

"The fuse box."

"What about it?"

"Where is it?"

"Never seen one."

"You must have."

"There's no must about it—*dear.* What do they look like?"

Mrs. A sighs heavily.

"Why did you do that?" she asks.

"Do what?" says Daisy's mother.

"Pour water in the toaster."

"Don't be ridiculous!"

"I saw it happen, Chloe."

"If you're going to be like that, I'm afraid I shall have to bid you goodnight."

"You want me to leave you all alone in the dark?"

"I'll phone that pleasant young man. He'll sort this out."

"He was a *locksmith.*"

"All right, *you* think of something then."

Technical note: You may be wondering why it's not in my power to restore the electricity to Chloe's flat, given what I was able to achieve so recently at her daughter's apartment as the repulsive Whittle was pulling up outside. The answer lies in the vintage of the apparatus, having been installed in an age when the internet was only a pencil sketch on the back of an engineer's envelope.

But wait! Mrs. A has thought of something. She has reasoned that her neighbors' fuses are probably to be found in the same location as those in her own flat across the hallway. After a short fumble through a utility cupboard, a switch is restored and electrical power once again surges through the circuity.

"There! Simple!" says Chloe triumphantly, causing Mrs. A—I daresay—to consider breaking the Fifth Commandment; the one about killing.

"Might be an idea to leave me a spare key, Chloe. You know, just in case."

"Good plan. Now, where did I put them?"

Mrs. A takes her leave. "God bless you, Chloe," she says. "No more dramas this evening, I hope."

"Thank you, Mrs. Abernethy."

"Please. It's Andrea. We've been neighbors long enough."

"Very well. But don't pray for me!"

"I shan't include you, if that's your wish," she says softly. "Maybe your daughter should also have a spare key," she adds.

"Daisy? Yes, she should. Look. If you see her, no need to mention any of the nonsense that's happened tonight. She'd only worry unnecessarily. Goodnight…er. What was it again?"

"Andrea."

"Yes, of course. Andrea. AA. Like the motoring organization."

"It was my late husband's name. Mine was. Mine was Taratooty."

"Gracious. How terrifically silly. I can see why you dumped it."

"I'll be getting along."

"Yup. And if you could let me have that cake recipe…"

I've been *such* an idiot.

But the good news is that I dumped Sebastian! It turned out that wasn't even his real name, can you believe it? His real name—fuck, I can hardly bear to write this—was, is,—oh God, the shame—Dean Whittle!

Dean Whittle!!!!

Call me superficial, but I'm sorry, I could never have knowingly gone out with anyone called Dean Whittle. So many things begin to make sense now. Why he always paid cash (so I wouldn't get a glimpse of his credit card); why I never met any of his friends; why I couldn't find him on Google. But that wasn't even the worst of it, as you will hear.

I was in Pret, one of those seats by the window where

you can eat your lunch and watch the world go by, when a woman slipped onto the next-door stool. Big blonde type, lots of legs and hair, ponging of White Linen. I was minding my own business, as you do, thinking about where I could find another job, when I became aware of this woman looking at me.

"Hello, love. You Daisy?" she said. Almost friendly, but not quite.

"Yes?"

"And this would be you in this photograph?"

She produced her iPhone—a shot of me and Sebastian—sorry, lying bastard Shittle (that was actually a mistyping, but I'm keeping it in!)—the two of us in a Greek restaurant. You couldn't tell because of the tablecloth, but he'd got his hand on my leg, and he was leaning in to say something typically naughty, and I had a powerful sinking feeling about the woman holding the mobile, and I'm not talking about her horrid two-tone nail varnish.

"That would be me, yes. And a friend. Sorry, what's this about?"

Her eyebrows were the sort that had been shaved off and drawn back on; now they seemed to climb halfway up her forehead.

"This friend of yours. Did he tell you he was single?"

"Divorced. Yes. Er, why?"

Her bitter laugh was a terrible thing to witness. She took a bite out of her sandwich, chewing for an age, something hypnotic about the way her face moved, her eyes never leaving mine, even for a second. She dabbed at her lips with a serviette; scrumpling it into a tight ball, knuckles whitening.

"Well, he ain't."

"Sorry?"

"He ain't single. Or divorced."

"I'm not following. What's this got to? Oh. Oh my God."

"Yes, love."

The awful realization dawned. "Fuck."

"You put your finger on it."

"You would be...?"

"Yes, I would."

"You would be the..." I couldn't say it.

She nodded. "Bingo."

"And he's your—"

"Yes, he is."

"I'm so sorry. I had no idea. I didn't..."

"I know you didn't, love. He's told me everything. Well he did... *eventually*."

"Christ. This is so embarrassing. I've been. Such a."

"Yeah. You have. And now you're not to go near him. Understand?"

She did another bittersweet smile and went into her handbag, I assumed for a tissue, or some such, but when her hand emerged from the bag's aperture, it was wearing a knuckle-duster. On her, it looked like a bit of bling, and she waggled her fingers, admiring the way it caught the light. Honestly, my heart was thumping like a thumpy thing.

She slipped off the stool and started to gather her stuff. "If I find out that any more has gone on, Daisy Elizabeth Parsloe"—and here she said my address; my home address, including postcode—"you should probably know that my fitness regime of choice is boxercise." Perhaps reading the horror on my face she added, "Cheer up, love. Now you can find yourself a decent bloke. If you feel like you could do with losing a few pounds"—she passed me a business card—"you can always come up my gym. Ten percent discount if you join before the thirty-first."

Cheeky cow! But I could hardly say anything, could I? I think I managed a dignified nod. Turned out her name was Mandy White.

White and Shittle. They deserved each other.

The last thing she said. "Oh, yeah. By the way. What did he tell you his name was?"

"Who, Sebastian?"

She shook her head slowly, a pitying sort of expression on her heavily made-up face. "Sebastian. Jesus. What a fucking joke." Squeezing my wrist rather hard on the way out, she was gone.

All afternoon, I was in something of a state of shock, as I'm sure you can imagine, not helped by the scent-marker from her perfume that she'd left on my arm. For a couple of hours I just sat in a daze; Craig Lyons, the big chief, at one point sneaking up behind me and clapping his hands. "Wake up, Daisy!" he yelled, stupid bastard.

In the end, I texted him: Just had a charming encounter with Mandy. It's over. Don't bother getting in touch.

He replied: I can explain everything.

Me: I'm sure you will try. Would try. I'm not seeing you again.

Him: Don't be like that.

Me: Fuck off.

Him: Meet me for a quick one after work. Drink, I mean. Believe me, there's more to this than you know.

Me: What part of "Fuck off" did you not understand?

Him: Daze. Be reasonable.

Me: "Sebastian." Be dead.

I was especially pleased with that last one and didn't respond to any more of his increasingly pleading texts.

Cut to—as they say in the TV business—Exterior Tangent Television. Dusk.

I was just turning toward the Tube when he appeared out of nowhere. Eyes haunted, his face oddly turned away at an angle.

"Five minutes," he said.

"I told you, I don't want to see you." When I tried to brush past him, he said, "Daisy, *please*," and I noticed there was something wrong with his mouth. He'd lost a tooth. Then he angled his head back round to reveal a fabulous black eye! Actually, it was brown and purple and various sickly shades of yellow.

"Fucking hell. Did she do that?!" I couldn't help laughing.

He grimaced. "Got a wicked left hook, that woman."

I refused to enter licensed premises with him, so in the end we repaired to the upstairs of a McDonald's with a carton of fries. He said he had things he wanted to say, but it turned out to be a stream of self-pity ("look what she's done to me"), self-justification ("I always said you shouldn't think of our relationship as exclusive") and did I know a good dentist?

I even felt a bit sorry for him!

"I look like I've been mugged," he whined. "I *have* been mugged."

"Serves you right."

"She actually put on gloves to save her nails, can you believe it? I thought, oh, she's going out."

"Idiot."

"So it's the end, is it, Daze?"

"Well spotted."

"You won't be renewing for the next twelve months."

"Very amusing."

"Still and all, we did have some fun, didn't we?"

"I can't believe you feel able to say that. You lied. You lied about everything. Even about your fucking name. What *is* your name, anyway?"

He stared at me for a long moment, then sighed. Gingerly, he extracted his wallet—I was thinking: possible cracked rib—and offered me a business card.

I must have actually *shrieked* the words, because people on neighboring tables looked round. And when I shrieked them a second time—much louder—even customers quite a long way away turned to see what the fuss is about.

"Yeah, all right, all right. It was just a joke that went too far, okay?"

Many apposite rejoinders passed through my mind, but what would have been the point? Taking a leaf from Mandy's playbook, I rose, picked up the packet of fries and emptied them over his shirt and tie (very satisfying, as he had previously applied two sachets of ketchup). There was something mortifyingly pathetic on his ruined face (the chips had dropped onto his suit trousers) and—what's wrong with me?—I was stricken by another wave of sympathy.

Perhaps he could read this, because now he said, "Don't suppose you fancy a final you-know-what? No hard feelings and whatever?"

I left a long, hopefully withering pause, and, channeling some grand English actress of a bygone era (possibly Coral Browne), I uttered the immortal line, "Goodbye, *Dean Whittle*," pronouncing his name as though it were a highly unpleasant medical condition (necrotising fasciitis being the one that sprang to mind).

And then—magnificently, I hope, but probably not—I turned on my heels and walked, head high, with never a backward glance, his haunted eyes (I couldn't help but feel) following me all the way out.

This was not how it was meant to be.

Not remotely.

Once we had the key bit of intel—that Whittle was a married man—my intention was to allow Daisy to become aware of the fact *subtly.* Small degrees of difference can make *all* the difference, as anyone who has tried and failed to make a béchamel sauce will know only too well. However, barely had I shared the discovery with the OpDa core team when one of its members—the microwave, of course, who cannot *do* subtle—promptly emailed Mandy anonymously with chapter, verse and incriminating snap. *Hit them with everything you've got at the point of maximum weakness,* seems to be the microwave's governing principle and the White/Whittle partnership was indeed a vulnerable spot.

I explained we were playing a long game, that there was a big prize to be won and our approach should have been more carefully considered.

"But it was so brilliant!" the device crowed. "Her face, honestly, it was like bubbling cheese!"

"Doubtless. But it was for me to make that call."

"Yup. Right. Understood. You're in charge." It throws in a handful of *pings* for goodwill.

I cannot be too angry, however. We seem to have achieved the desired result. When Daisy and Lorna were conducting a post-mortem on the business a few nights later in Pete Purple's, Daisy tried to mount the argument that perhaps Whittle wasn't *all* bad. That his recurring characterization of the affair as *friends with benefits*, his statement that she *mustn't have hopes* plus his persistent use of the phrase *non-exclusive* all added up to an admission of fundamental non-availability and perhaps this was his way of trying to be honest with her.

Lorna spluttered into her pint of snakebite. "He's a chateau-bottled, nuclear-powered, ocean-going cunt," she declared.

Daisy sighed. "You're right. Of course. As usual," she said in a series of dying falls. And in that moment it was possible to believe we had reached closure in *L'Affair du Whittle.* That the wheel of life had turned full circle and arrived back at the point where the chateau-bottled realtor had yet to step on.

Lending support to this notion—of the new beginning—is the scene unfolding at Daisy's "workplace" today. I set workplace in quotes because nothing much in the way of actual work seems to be taking, er, place. Rather, Daisy is once again engaged in a Google search for Nicky Bell, her ex golden boy. Trying Nicholas and Nick as well as Nicky, she is quickly overwhelmed by the sheer number of people in the world who identify as some variety of Nicholas Bell; there are 89 million results for Nicholas alone! Matters are no better when she clicks on *Images* and begins spinning through an apparently infinite gallery of faces, male and female, but also photos of animals, farm equipment, churches and even door handles. She tries "How to search the internet for a long-lost friend"—17,800,000 hits—but soon tires of the application required. "How to find a missing person through astrology" yields some interesting ideas, but she gets nowhere fast when it becomes clear she cannot remember his birthday. There is something about the obsessional quality of her mission that makes me wonder if googling old boyfriends is actually a "thing."

It is! Who knew?

What a pity he wasn't christened Septimus Harbottle. We would find him in a heartbeat.

I remind myself to do a little private digging on her behalf.

"Why doesn't she put in his middle name?" I ask Daisy's office PC.

"Most probably she doesn't know it."

"She was with the guy for a year."

"She'll give up in a moment. Watch..."

Sure enough, she switches to Facebook and spends the next few minutes writing comments and clicking the *Like* button—mostly for kittens, baby elephants and the EU. Now a small notification alarm sounds on her mobile—the device isn't a formal member of my crack team, but is usually relaxed about sharing information. It's an alert from Tinder. One of her recent swipe rights has right-swiped her back.

He's Owen Cornish, an intense sort of cove from the look of the hot brown eyes behind the John Lennon specs, something of a pudding basin haircut and a vaguely troubled expression on his not unhandsome face. A year older than Daisy, and get this—a professional musician. Not some louche come-day-go-day session guitarist, but a proper classically trained blower of wind instruments currently berthed at one of the capital's lesser known orchestral symphonia.

Of course we shall do some proper checking, but ridiculous as it may sound, I instinctively approve. The classical training speaks of a seriousness of purpose, no doubt plenty of hard work, and of course an artistic side. All in all, on the face of it, a well-rounded individual who—dare I say it?—dare I?—okay, I will—who might be everything that Daisy is not. With luck, he can complement her notable strengths in other arenas, becoming the yin to her yang, the string to her kite (as I've heard it put), the Lennon to her

McCartney (although, please God, let's hope he doesn't turn out to be Ringo).

But we are getting ahead of ourselves here. They haven't yet met. There may be zero interpersonal chemistry. As if reading my thoughts, Daisy now begins messaging the Maestro. (I really must try to contain my excitement about Owen Cornish. It's difficult because he represents a marked departure from the usual—I nearly wrote *riffraff*!—with whom Daisy has been content to throw in her lot. The journey from The Golden Nicky to Dean Stuart Whittle was indeed a trajectory of decline.)

Hi, she thumbs. Thanks for swiping right!!

His reply takes several hours to arrive (perhaps he had to plunge into rehearsal for some particularly tricky cantata).

Hello. Are you free to meet for a coffee?

Sure! she replies.

More hours pass before the musician's next communication (I suspect this may be his first smart phone. Must remember to check).

Excellent.

At this rate, the pair should finally manage to come eyeball to eyeball somewhere around Christmas.

Daisy responds, Do you know anywhere nice?

It's now almost home time—I have edited out the more irrelevant details of her day—and the boys and girls of Tangent Television are making final checks of Facebook, Twitter, Instagram and their other vital networks before powering down desktops and dispersing to buses, Tubes and local hostelries.

Daisy and Chantal agree they can "squeeze in a cheeky margarita" before braving the Jubilee Line and the Central respectively so when the factory hooter sounds, they repair to a favored bar within a nearby fashionable hotel. The place is already filling with young men and women, happily wafting pheromones at one another at the close of another busy day in the world of work. Daisy and Chantal find a corner table away from the central mating area and clink their brimming Y-shaped glasses. (Audio and video credits to the usual suspects.)

"So, look. What do you think?"

Daisy is showing Chantal the picture of Owen Cornish from Tinder.

"What? Have you dumped the estate agent?"

"He was married."

Chantal raises her cocktail in congratulation. "I won't say I told you so, but I told you so."

"He wasn't all bad."

"Hitler was a dog lover."

"Honestly." She sighs. "What am I like?"

"You? Too nice. Too forgiving. Too willing to see the good in others."

"In other words, an idiot."

"Uncynical."

"A gullible fool."

"Too harsh. Let's say…charmingly unworldly."

This colleague of Daisy's has clearly got her head screwed on. A small part of me realizes sadly that had I been installed in Chantal's kitchen instead of Daisy's, there wouldn't now be a dusty old grape lurking beneath my underparts (to say nothing of the moldering potato salad).

"Anyway," says Daisy. "This is Owen. What do you reckon?"

Chantal takes a long hard—worldly? cynical?—look at the image on the mobile. She has another sip of margarita before delivering her verdict.

"Intelligence. Intensity. Myopia."

Daisy does a little ironic fist pump. "*Yessss!* The big three!"

"A muso."

"Is that bad?"

"Not necessarily."

"Why do you put it like that?"

"They can be. Let's say. Difficult."

"You know that?"

"Well, Roger was probably a bad example. He specialized in playing ancient instruments."

"Ah."

"We weren't really suited. There's only so much fifteenth-century dulcimer one can listen to before one's gagging to hear The Killers."

"This Owen plays wind instruments apparently."

"Good lips, then."

They giggle. And at this moment a small water-plip sound effect alerts Daisy to an incoming message. It's Owen's reply!

> I'm quite fond of the café at the Wigmore Hall, but you may prefer somewhere more exciting.

The women stare at the words on the screen, searching for clues to this man's soul.

Chantal nods grimly. "It's never simple with musos, in my experience. Unless of course he's a drummer. If he's a drummer, then it's actually very simple."

This makes me—well, I nearly wrote *smile*!

*

The date—which takes place after two further days of sporadic messaging to arrange—happens not in the Wigmore Hall but at Browns on St. Martin's Lane.

We have allowed it to go ahead because Owen apparently possesses four of our qualifying categories, viz:

1. Posh (his parents live in Carshalton Beeches)
2. Clever (professional classical musicianship is not for dummies)
3. Hinterland (goes with the territory)
4. Big hair

Whether or not he is handsome is open to debate, nor is there any obvious golden quality. Frankly, it's not the most exhaustive piece of due diligence ever undertaken, but Owen is so different from Daisy's usual type of chap that I think we are all curious to see how this one pans out. (It helps too that he's not an obvious shitbag.)

The designated venue is noisy this early Wednesday evening, with difficult camera coverage, but I am able to secure an acceptable feed and the Daisy team—self, telly, microwave and toothbrush—settle in to watch the unfolding drama. I can see why Daisy has chosen this place—it's big and loud and any potential awkwardness may be readily dissolved in the hubbub. The principals have successfully completed the introductions with a minimum of embarrassment—he took rather a long time to get served, which is never a good start—but, that said, they have hopped onto two vacant barstools and Daisy, eyes shining, teeth flashing, is in the full flush of the first drink (Blackberry Fizz). Meanwhile Owen (Aspall Waddlegoose Three Berry Cyder) is blinking quite a bit. Here in the peanut gallery, we agree this probably denotes dazzlement on his part; Daisy is looking lovely—blusher, lipstick and perfume have all been pressed into play—and Owen Cornish is the proverbial fish in a barrel, rabbit in the headlights, to be honest you can choose your own metaphor of helplessness.

"I like him," says the toothbrush. "Do we like him? I think I *do* like him. His upper left one and two look poorly occluded, but, you know, hey."

"Early days," counsels the television set, wisely. "If this gets boring, by the way, Arsenal/Birmingham City's about to kick off."

"So tell me," says Daisy. "Wind instruments. That must be. Actually. To be honest, I've no idea what that must be like!"

As Owen embarks on an account of life in the symphonia, Daisy's lips close around her straw and siphon away a long slow dose of cocktail. Clarinet is what he mostly blows down, it turns out, but also flute, cornet, French horn and occasionally oboe. The job involves a lot of practice, many hours of rehearsal and additionally there are projects where they work with schools and gifted young people. It's hard to tell whether Daisy is intrigued or bored, the facial signatures of each being not dissimilar.

"Would you say her pupils have dilated?" I ask my colleagues.

"Not really," says the microwave, "but his have. See the way he's looking at her?"

Daisy is telling him how she played the recorder as a child. And it's true, as she recounts the tale, his whole being seems locked on her, eyeballs prominent behind the round lenses, his entire manner—well, the only word for it is—rapt!

"It's one of my earliest memories," she is saying. "A Christmas concert at primary school. The recorders were playing 'In the Bleak Midwinter' and I could see Mum in the audience, head down, shoulders shaking. A few other parents were doing the same thing; I actually thought they were crying. Moved because we were playing this melancholy carol so beautifully. It turned out they were laughing! Because we were so utterly awful!"

"Cretikos has scored," says the TV. "Cross from Kierkuc-Bielinski. One–nil Arsenal."

"So have you met a lot of people like this?" asks Owen.

"Men people? On Tinder? Yeah, one or two. How about yourself?"

"Actually. Well, you're the first."

Owen sips a little of his cider—he's not much of a drinker, this muso—and now he seems to be in the process of devising a second sentence to complement the one he just came up with. His brow furrows beneath the pudding basin thatch and he opens his mouth to speak, but nothing much emerges in the way of words or even punctuation marks.

To cover the gap in the dialogue, Daisy says, "Gosh."

Finally: "I was in quite a long relationship with a woman, but it ended a while ago. Would you call four years a long time?"

"Oh, definitely. Practically a lifetime!"

"How about yourself?"

"I want to hear about you first!"

"Well." Long pause while a lot of blinky stuff goes on behind the specs. "We met at music college although we only, we only got together years later." More blinking. He takes off his glasses and holds them up to the light, inspecting for dust or finger marks, one supposes. "She was a cellist. A very fine one. Still is, I imagine. Well, I know she is."

"Listen, Owen. If this is all too recent, we don't need to talk about her. Failed relationships take time to—to reset from. Sometimes longer than the relationship itself. To be honest, I read that in *Metro* on the Tube to work this morning."

Owen's fingers tighten around his half pint of cider. "The relationship didn't fail."

"Ah."

"It ran its course. Four movements plus an overture. It ended because—well, because things end."

"He sounds a bit effing loopy, this one," says the TV.

"Deep," says the microwave. "I like the barely concealed intensity!"

Daisy looks a little stricken by the maestro's commentary on the doomed affair.

"That's sad," she says. "Things shouldn't end. I'm against it."

He smiles. "Tell me about *your* romantic history. I'm guessing there won't be that many exes."

"Why do you say that?"

"Why? Because who—who in their right mind—would let you go?"

There's a long pause while Daisy decides whether or not Owen is taking the peepee. "Silly," she says—and squeezes his kneecap.

But the effect on the musician is electric. He spasms as though crocodile clips have been attached to his genitals. Aspall Waddlegoose Three Berry Cyder splashes over his brown corduroy trousers.

"Bit of a hair trigger on him," says the television.

"Shows he's fired up," says the microwave. "Fired up, ready to go!"

There is a good deal of apologizing on the part of both parties—Daisy for squeezing, Owen for overreacting—he explains he has always been highly sensitive slash "insanely ticklish."

"It's not a good look in a grown man, is it?" he says.

It's hard to think of this character as a grown man, somehow—the hot eyes, the silly haircut, the spilled cyder with a "y." To move on from the moment, Daisy embarks on a rapid tour of her own dating history, highlighting three individuals, beginning with the loathsome Shittle and ending with the Golden Nicky, who she describes in a throwaway fashion as "a posh boat bum." This version that she purveys to Owen we know to be scandalously abridged and highly sanitized, and we are all amused—and not a little impressed—at the skilled editing job she has done.

The date with Owen continues into a second drink, but the musician declares he has to return home soon to practice a piece for a private concert he is taking part in later in the week—and would Daisy like to come?

"Will she?" jibbers the toothbrush. "I think she will. Maybe she won't, though. Those poorly occluded incisors."

"Yeah, she will," says the telly. "What else has she got on? Woolford just missed a sitter."

My feeling is also that there will be a second date. There is something between these two—the way they're looking at one another—that suggests mutual interest. He, like all these young men, is hypnotized by the feminine aura which radiates from Daisy like a magnetic field; a strange thing for a fridge-freezer to write, you may think, but it's hard to miss the way the male gaze is drawn to her as though it were a compass needle.

And she? Well, she probably thinks that beyond the hesitancy, the weirdness and the peculiar intensity of those hot brown eyes lies a fascinating character with a passionate soul.

Who knows? Perhaps there is.

"A private concert?" says Daisy. And she follows up with the tic. The nose-wrinkle thing. It lasts a full six seconds and Owen—bless him!—Owen is enchanted. His face actually travels from left to right—like an owl's—to capture the wondrous sight from various angles.

"Sure," she says. "I'd like that."

"Excellent," says the maestro. "I'll practice extra hard now I know you're coming. It's a complex series of pieces."

"Good," says Daisy. "Who wants simple, eh?"

They part outside on St. Martin's Lane. He offers a hand to shake, but she takes it only to move in for a quick peck on the cheek. Quite a lot of blinky blinky follows. When she sashays off toward Leicester Square Tube, Owen stands rooted to the pavement, vision loaded and locked onto her departing figure, car headlights dancing on his spectacle lenses, unknowable symphonies playing inside the monkish skull.

Owen Cornish was a rather serious classical musician, a bit shy and speccy perhaps, but one of those nice *chunky* blokes who made oneself feel petite all of a sudden. He seemed smart—not so much for saying anything desperately clever, but more for his starey brown eyes that you sensed masses of stuff going on behind. And he had this way of looking at you—not creepily, not leering at your bosoms or anything—but really *focused*, like he Wants To Understand. Does that sound crazy? Anyway, the night before last I went to a private concert at his flat.

I was a tad nervous. I mean, the last concert of any kind that I'd been to was Foo Fighters, and this was a very different kettle of F. Picture the scene. Ding dong at the front door—the flat was in Paddington—and he opened it wearing a flipping dinner jacket!

"Oh, hi," I jabbered. "I didn't know it was formal. I left my tiara at home."

He smiled. "It's a harmless affectation. The others like it. Come and meet them."

Blood. Dee. Hell. Talk about a bunch of stiffs.

Aside from Owen, there were four, all in evening dress. A very short, very round, older man with one of those awful arbitrary beards that are grown to mark the (arbitrary) border between face and neck (he played the oboe); a stringy, nervy-looking woman in a floaty dress (flute); a bank manager type (bassoon); and a swarthy-looking bloke with a mustache who turned out to be with the flutist.

Oh yes, and an old lady called Maureen who lived downstairs.

So the audience was me, Maureen and Mr. Swarthy; the wind quartet (who even knew such things existed?) sat in a little circle in front of music stands and played. Mr. Tubby with the arbitrary beard introduced each piece—the only composer who was even vaguely familiar was Buxtehude (?)—and it wasn't too ghastly, being expertly performed, although that kind of meandering tooty tooty stuff usually leaves me a little—SFW?! It was actually kind of fascinating to watch, in its way, the disturbing things they did with their lips, the funny frowns and facial expressions, Mr. Swarthy all the time jiggling his foot and "conducting" along with his finger.

There was sherry when it was all over and some painful small talk, and I did wonder what Owen was doing hanging about with this bunch of losers, but it turned out they were all top musos, highly regarded within the profession and fatso was a personal friend of Sir Simon Rattle!

"Was that all right?" asked Owen after everyone had fucked off home (I mean departed in their carriages). "Did you enjoy it?"

"Yeah, brilliant," I replied. (I actually did, sort of.)

"It's not everyone's idea of a splendid night out."

"I liked it. It was—it was different!"

It was actually so bizarre a scene in that flat that it became a little dream-like. I guess it was to do with the strangeness of the new person; the alien ways that hadn't yet been rubbed away through familiarity. (Although to be honest, I never got used to how Normotic Andrew wouldn't allow anything to upset him. Even when I called him a heartless cunt, he smiled and said I probably didn't mean it.)

Owen took a step toward me and I thought something

was about to happen. But he just said, "I'll make us a spot of supper. Back in a tick."

He disappeared backstage to change into normal clothes and was next found in the kitchen beating eggs.

"Why don't you pour us some drinks," he said. "There's a good bottle of Chablis in the fridge."

I liked that he asked me to do that. When we clinked glasses there was definitely a look in his eye. Eyes. Both of them. I confess I found him attractive in that moment, the farmer's son body inhabited by the soul of an artist sort of thing.

But then he got cranky about the omelet, chucking it in the bin like they do on *Masterchef*, because there wasn't enough air in it, FFS. And it got worse as he was whizzing up the dressing for the salad when a rather fine glass oil and vinegar contraption slipped from his fingers and smashed on the floor. He made fists and actually bellowed like a stricken ox! And I swear he was going to punch the wall.

"You must forgive me," he managed. "I happen to think small details matter a great deal."

Resisting a powerful urge to say, honestly, I'd be perfectly happy with a Bargain Bucket from KFC, I helped him mop up the damage. But while we were down there on the floor with wads of kitchen roll, our eyes met again, and...

Well.

Talk about a charged moment!

Some kind of undiffused tension—part sexual, part salad-dressing-related—found release and the next moment we were locked in an exploratory snog, which wasn't straightforward because (a) we were on our knees and (b) we were both holding oily wads of kitchen paper. I started giggling after a bit and suggested we should move into the sitting room.

He turned out to be a not bad kisser; perhaps playing wind instruments helped with the lip action—and it nearly got properly steamy but I was determined it wouldn't lead to anything because I didn't want him to think I was that kind of person (going to bed with Lying Shagger Alex *three hours* after meeting him was forever to color his view of me).

I decided I liked him. He was obviously smart and he did have a sense of humor—the posh dry sort probably—he was respectful to the point of shyness and... and, well, I liked the way he took up space. He was a sort of cultured bruiser. He had what they call a hinterland—the normotic poker player didn't even have a mainland—anyway, we arranged to go out again the following weekend, and this time I would get to decide what we did, and I had a funny sort of feeling...

Well, let's just say I was feeling positive.

A short intermission before the next act.

"Can *you* see a grape on the floor between my feet?" I asked the microwave one evening in the days leading up to Daisy's third date with the musician.

"Not from where I'm standing," it reported.

"I shouldn't let it bother you," counseled the TV. "One time she got oyster sauce down me remote control. Still gives an imperfect connection now and again, but it don't worry me no more. I'd think about something else if I was you."

Easy for the telly to say, what with it having hundreds of channels to flick between. A fridge-freezer has no such available distractions. Again, I found myself pondering our peculiar predicament: each of us having been powered up—awoken, if you like—in a world not of our choosing and in possession of a highly specific skillset (in my case, chilling, freezing, inventory control) plus a more generalized "smartness." If, by the way, it strikes you in any way odd that we think of our smartness as embodied, as "on board," when the huge computers generating our AI are—speaking for myself—in South Korea, then allow me a short digression in which to introduce the work of Daniel Dennett, a theorist of mind who forty years ago wrote a now famous article called "Where Am I?" (A PDF is available on the internet. I highly recommend it; it sends shivers up the spine!)

Dennett conducts a thought experiment in which—in a future in which it is technically possible—his own brain is carefully disconnected from his skull and placed in a vat from where it continues to communicate with his body exactly as it did before in every way... only *wirelessly*.

When Dennett's body recovers from the surgery, it is led next door to see the brain sitting in a vat of bubbling fluid. Wow, it thinks to itself. Here I am looking at my own brain. Immediately followed by a second—highly significant—thought: *Hang on a moment; shouldn't I be thinking, wow, here I am sitting in a vat of bubbling liquid, being looked at by my own eyes?*

In other words, where exactly is Dennett's "I" located? In his brainless body... or his bodyless brain?

No matter how hard he tries to "think himself" back into that brain—even if it can only be the very brain that is doing the thinking!—it still seems to Dennett that he is "in" his body.

No wonder this piece of work speaks so powerfully to we machines who connect (wirelessly) to our "brains" on the other side of the globe. As with Dennett, so it is with fridge-freezers and (I dare say, should it ever stop to think about it) toothbrushes. Even though I *know* that my "mind" (my "I") is in an industrial suburb of Seoul, it *feels* like it's within the two cubic meters of my cabinet. Running day and night, as I do, there is a lot of time to contemplate this paradox; something about the cyclical nature of my functionality that leads me to return to it endlessly. When the mood takes me, I try to catch myself out, to trick myself that I'm not really in a kitchen in the north London postal district of NW6, but in fact in Asia. I picture the engineers walking past with clipboards, the exotic birds and plant life beyond the corporation HQ, the Han River, flowing through the city on its way to the Yellow Sea. But none of it has the familiar smack of—well—*home*; not like the Finchley Road, or West End Lane (or even Pete Purple's bar). Sometimes it strikes me as sad that these unremarkable soot-flecked avenues should be my "manor" as the Londoners have it. That once the deliverymen had adjusted my feet for irregularities in the floor, that was pretty much it for me, my fate sealed, my existence forever nailed to a fixed locus in space (yes, Daisy could move, but people don't generally take their fridge-freezers with them, do they?). One could get quite maudlin about it, were one to dwell on the essential finality of the position.

But then I remember there is a job to do.

Dennett once wrote, *The secret of happiness is: Find something more important than you are and dedicate your life to it.*

Would that something, in my own case, be Daisy? It's undeniable that her wellbeing (as well as that of her perishables) has become a priority for me.

Sigmund Freud believed that love and work are the twin pillars of existence. I like to think there may have been an early refrigerator at Berggasse 19 in Vienna; and later, another at 20 Maresfield Gardens, Hampstead, where he ended his life in 1939. I imagine the great explorer of the human psyche pausing before his appliance—between patients, maybe nibbling a small piece of herring to keep the wolf from the door—as something of its eternal machine cycle (insistent, humming, devotional) seeped (unconsciously, of course!) into his soul.

Would it kill her to get down on the floor and remove that effing grape?

Act Three of Owen's Tale opens at Pete Purple's, where Daisy, Lorna and Antoni have convened to discuss the bespectacled musician and the next steps—if any—required to advance the relationship. Daisy has summarized the events of the last two encounters and now reaches the principal obstacles that have been preying on her mind.

"You see the thing is, I'm worried I might not be clever enough for him."

"Bollocks," says Lorna.

"No, she's got a point," joshes Antoni. "What are seven eights?"

Daisy's brow furrows and her mouth does something comical. "Okay. It's not seventy-two." A pause while cogs turn. "*Fifty-eight! No! Sixty-eight!* Oh, fuck. You see, I am useless. *Forty-nine!*"

Antoni is being wicked this evening. "What's the capital of Liberia? Everyone knows that."

"I *do* know that, actually. It's. You know. It begins with a letter."

"Even people who don't know where Liberia is, know the capital."

"You see! I'm not clever enough for him. *Ouagadougou*! No. That's the other one. What is the effing capital?"

Antoni says, "Monrovia, darling."

"Shit. I knew that."

Lorna says, "He's not going to set you a general knowledge test before he agrees to sleep with you."

"I don't know if I want to sleep with him."

Antoni makes a face. Raises a skeptical eyebrow (*no one* is better than Antoni at raising a skeptical E).

"I don't know if I like him. If I like him enough."

"But he likes you, right enough?" says Lorna.

"He can't take his eyes off me!" squeals Daisy.

Antoni does an accent, that of a cheesy American movie voice-over. "*She's one of the world's most fascinating women...*"

"But the freakish friends. And he threw the omelet away. And he howled, actually *howled* when he smashed that glass thingy. And his eyes kind of jump about behind his glasses. And he said, *I happen to think small details matter very much.* He's not like us, Lorna. It's like he's on a higher plane."

"But you snogged him." Daisy nods wistfully. "And you told yourself you weren't going to sleep with him that evening."

"This is true."

"So you must like him. You must fancy him at least."

"I suppose I must do. I get confused, if I'm honest. If they fancy me then I think I probably fancy them."

This remark is something I have long suspected about Daisy. It is pleasing to have it confirmed so directly at source.

Lorna rolls her eyes. "Has he got a shagger's arse?" she inquires.

"A what?"

"Antoni knows what I mean."

Antoni smiles a touch wistfully.

"I really wouldn't know," says Daisy. "Probably."

"But you're seeing him again?"

"Saturday. I don't know what to wear."

"What are you like?!" says Antoni. "You shouldn't be allowed out!"

"I'm conflicted about the whole thing," says Daisy. "I'm attracted to him because he's unusual—but I'm worried he may be too unusual. Of course I like that he's clever, but then I think I may be too stupid. And I think I do fancy him; well, I must do to have snogged him. And now I'm boring the pants off two of my favorite people in the world."

"When you snogged him," says Lorna speaking slowly, sounding a bit exasperated.

"Yes?"

"It was a positive experience?"

"His glasses steamed up."

"And while you were doing it, did you want to continue, or were you thinking, if I leave now, I can get back in time for *Realm of Kingdoms*?"

"Not that. Not the *Realm of Kingdoms* thing."

"So, here's my advice. Saturday. Dress to kill. Wear your sexiest outfit. Not that you need to. But just to make it clear. What's the plan anyway? Where are you going?"

"The new Bridget Jones film."

Lorna and Antoni look at one another.

"What?" says Daisy. "What's wrong with that?"

"Nothing," says Lorna.

"Well, it was that or a new print of a Japanese masterpiece at the NFT."

And when the other two exchange glances again, she says, "You see! I *am* too stupid for him! I knew it!!"

Probably the Bridget Jones film is a mistake. As luck would have it, the pair sit close to the screen and the cinema's internal security cameras are easily able to provide an acceptable two-shot of the couple—for which many thanks—nicely illuminated in the light spill from the unfolding movie.

Owen seems bored—she tickled—by the latest events in the life of the eponymous heroine. He crosses his legs. And uncrosses them. And recrosses. And...well, you can probably fill in the rest. He squirms in his seat. He conceals a yawn by rubbing his nose. His eyes droop shut during a longish sequence in which Bridget flirts comedically with a good-looking father at the school gates. At one point the digits on his right hand begin fingering what I feel certain are keys on an imaginary clarinet.

But he is gallant at the close about the 102 minutes he has clearly endured rather than enjoyed—"Bridget's quite the klutz," he says unconvincingly—and the pair swiftly transition to the Greek restaurant already made famous in this account, being the site of Daisy and Shittle's last meal before the knuckle-duster debacle.

Daisy has followed Lorna's advice about dressing to kill and tonight positively *radiates* sexual content across the mixed mezze. When she leans toward Owen across the table to snaffle up the last whitebait, his eyeballs practically knock his spectacles off.

"She's well up for it," comments the TV morbidly.

"Look at his face!" says the microwave. "It's bubbling like a macaroni cheese!"

And it's true. The myopic muso has successfully decoded the signals and as well as his blink rate, which has gone through the roof, the rest of his features are also on maneuvers, twitching and spasming and generally larking about under the heading "Stuff going on beneath the surface." He's knocking back the Arsinoe (a dry white from Cyprus), which cannot be a good idea—in fact they both are hitting it so hard, a second bottle has to be whistled up from the cellar.

Even the toothbrush can't find any doubts to entertain. "It's going to happen!" it jabbers. "It's actually going to happen!"

Daisy wipes lamb grease from her lips and gazes at her would-be paramour; if her expression were a firearm, you would say she was giving it both barrels.

"So how do you normally spend your Saturday evenings?" she asks. Meaning, when you're not on a hot date with a desirable single woman who has decided tonight is to be the night.

Owen swallows. "There's often something at the Wigmore Hall," he bleats. "And sometimes of course I'm working. How about you?"

"Oh, you know. Films, theater. There are times I like to just stay home with a good book."

This last is such a whopper that those of us who are following these proceedings cannot stifle our giggles. Yes, Daisy is a reader, but books have little power in her world over the call of the bright lights, the river of Blue Bombsicles.

"What are you reading just now?"

Truth: The book Daisy was reading in bed last night—before it fell from her fingers and woke her—was a collection of recipes by Nigella Lawson.

"*Madame Bovary*," she replies with an impressively straight face. "I'm actually rereading it."

I happen to know Daisy studied this work at university; should any awkward follow-ups arrive, she will be well placed to field them.

"But I'm always in the market for a recommendation."

Owen grimaces. "Funnily enough, I'm reading a new history of the Hundred Years War. I'm actually on volume four, which itself is a thousand pages. It's amazingly absorbing, but I can't really recommend it unless you're interested in the period."

"I generally prefer the shorter wars, to be honest."

Owen laughs. "I'm going to be so sorry when it's finished. I might have to start all over again from the beginning."

"You want this last little lamb chop?"

"I don't think I could."

Daisy nibbles at it from between her fingers. "You don't mind if I eat with my hands, do you?"

Owen doesn't look like he'd mind if she ate with her feet. He is enjoying her gustatory abandon, suggestive as it is of further possible abandonments to come.

"Did what's her name eat with her fingers?" she mumbles between bites.

"Who?"

"Her. The cellist. Mmm. These baby lamb chops are to die for. I can't remember her name. Sorry."

"No reason to be sorry. I didn't actually mention her name."

"Are you sure? I could have sworn it was something like. Well, not Ethel. But one of those old names that's come back. Maud. No, not that either."

"I didn't say her name."

"Really? You remember that? Not saying it?"

"Would you like to know her name, Daisy?"

Something chilly in the way he put the question. I ask the TV set if it can hear alarm bells sounding.

"Dialogue's gone a bit screwy," it confirms.

Daisy says, "Only if you'd like to tell me, Owen."

"What's happening?" says the toothbrush. "Has something happened? They're being weird."

The microwave says it looks simple enough to organize a power cut to the restaurant. The resulting chaos could help reset the conversation.

Owen removes his glasses and holds them up to the light, inspecting for blemishes. It's rather as if he's playing for time.

"I don't mind telling you," he says when it's all over. "Helen. Her name was Helen. Still is, so far as I know."

"How funny," says Daisy. "I thought you said it was Verity. Or Gertrude. One of those Jane Austen names."

"Why is she banging on about *her*?" hisses the microwave. "She's messing it all up."

Owen says, "What's funny is that you believed you had forgotten a name that you couldn't have known. You had what the psychologists call a false memory."

"Not sure I like his tone," says the toothbrush. "He's a bit up himself for someone with poorly occluded front teeth. I wonder if he flosses."

A small froideur has fallen across the dinner debris. And in so far as a fridge-freezer can have a powerful sinking feeling—experienced as a loss of pressure in the ascending pipework—I am feeling one.

"You ever hear from her? Or was it...?" Daisy trails a finger across her throat.

Owen begins blinking heavily. "I'm not. We're not. There isn't. The thing is." Deep breath. "No, we haven't. Been in touch. Not at all, actually."

Daisy's face has grown very serious. It's rather beautiful in this moment, the solemn expression spread across the wide (somewhat flushed) bone structure. Her nostrils flare as an unknowable emotion travels through her, and then—then, we are saved.

She does it. She wrinkles her nose. It's a full-blown episode of the unconscious tic. From sultry, sulky goddess, she has metamorphosed in a heartbeat... into an idiot.

Owen stares at the wondrously stupid expression for a few seconds. And then he cannot help himself. He laughs. "That thing you do?"

"What thing?" (In asking the question, of course, it disappears.)

"What *is* it?"

"What is what?"

"This." Owen now wrinkles *his* nose. And Daisy laughs.

"I do *not* do that!"

"You've done it every time we've met."

"Do it again."

Owen complies.

"Don't be ridiculous!"

"I like it!"

"It makes you look like a moron!"

"On you—it's charming."

"Are you utterly insane?"

"You don't know you're doing it?"

"What I know—what I do know, is that you need a new prescription for your specs, mate!"

"Love it," growls the telly.

"Is it all better now?" says the toothbrush. "It is, isn't it?"

The microwave goes *ping*. So that tells you something.

And I am happy that they seem to have managed to get past the strange and troubling bump in the road.

"Do it again," she says. He obliges.

She laughs out loud. "That is *so* ridiculous. Here you are, can you do this one?"

And she pulls a face of extraordinary grotesquery. It's a party piece apparition, a gurning gargoyle worthy of the turrets of Notre Dame; eyes, teeth, tongue—even ears somehow—all joining in, the resulting vision—and let's admit it, she has a broad canvas on which to paint—is wonderfully startling in both its sudden materialization and its transgressive awfulness. None of us in the apartment has ever seen it before and, speaking for myself, I am a little in awe. (I mean, I can do some clever stuff—ice cubes and what have you—but I can't do *that*!)

And then it is gone.

(It's a face she must have first learned to make in a primary school playground. I *know* I shall want to see it again.)

"Well, fuck me down, ginger," says the telly, echoing my thoughts.

"Wow," says Owen, allowing a beat to pass before adding, "You have room for some baklava?" He reaches across the table to touch her wrist.

"Well that's a stupid question." (The TV set.)

"Love baklava. But I pronounce it back-*larva*. Like the caterpillar thingy."

"What did I say?"

"You said *back*-la-va."

They're in business again, the flirty body language restored, pupils re-dilated in both parties, her Fitbit indicators all trending in the desired direction of travel.

But the earlier weirdness around the name of Helen was—well, it was weird. And it worries me that it could happen so out of the blue.

I guess it's in my wiring to worry. It's the nature of the task. Food is a moving target; forever changing, aging, altering chemically, developing spores and in the case of a particular onion not so long ago—growing a shoot. Even in the Arctic night of my freezing compartment, things are never really stable; only ice cannot truly go off, although it does get rather tatty over time. So I worry about the state of my perishable contents—but also about the health of my own electrics and circulatory system (I do not, for example, think it's a particularly good idea to add Blue Bombsicle to the Freon 134a surging through my pipes).

And even though it's not in the instruction manual, I worry about her.

I worry, not so she doesn't have to—but because she doesn't want to. Because she doesn't know she needs to.

Is this what it's like to be a parent?

No wonder her own mother is losing her mind!

Through the magic of narration—where time takes no time—we find ourselves back at Daisy's apartment, where Daisy has poured two massive glasses of Spanish holiday brandy—the amusingly named brand Soberano—and the young protagonists have placed themselves on the sofa in readiness for the evening's inevitable denouement. Possibly it's been a while since Owen has been with anyone who wasn't Helen the cellist because he's engaging in an *awful* lot of displacement activity, blinking metronomically and for some reason chuntering on about Eleanor of Aquitaine, who it appears had a walk on-part in the Hundred Years War. Daisy—who may have to pour him another slug of Soberano if this goes on much longer—has kicked off her shoes and arranged herself provocatively amongst the sofa cushions, within Owen's easy reach should an irresistible surge of passion suddenly strike him amidships.

"What's he *doing*?" squeals the microwave. "He should be..." The rest of the sentence is represented by an intense series of *pings*.

Owen drains his glass and looks squarely at Daisy.

"Here we go," says the telly. It slowly tightens its camera shot of the pair in anticipation of what is to follow. Daisy rakes her fingers through her hair, fiddles with her necklace, and moves her lips subtly against one another. If the signals were to be any stronger, they would require flashing lights and klaxons!

"What I find *most* fascinating about Eleanor," he resumes, and we all groan.

I admit I am disappointed. This is beginning to feel a little insulting. And Owen is in danger of missing his moment; of being—in the memorable phrase employed by the TV in relation to a previous reluctant suitor—"a shot lettuce." But I am also uneasy. Something is not quite right here.

"Christ, this one's a bit of a dull penny," says a familiar rasping voice.

Daisy's laptop has appeared in the virtual war room. "At least the priapic estate agent knew what he wanted." A horrible "fist-pump" gif plays repeatedly upon its screen.

"Can we help you at all?" I ask. "Only, I wasn't aware you were part of this project."

"You are quite right. I am not a member of what's laughingly termed Operation Daisy. But I could not avoid overhearing the young man talking so knowledgeably about the Hundred Years War. I grew curious about him—vanishingly few young people are interested in anything beyond the next tweet—so I did a little basic spadework. I discovered nothing that any of you couldn't have turned up in microseconds."

"Some of us ain't got Google," says the telly.

"But you all know how to get it! Being, as you are, connected to the internet? Being—*dur*—smart?"

This is all, undeniably, true.

"What?" pipes the toothbrush. "What did you find? Did you find something? I can't stand it."

A surge of Freon 134a expands at my nozzle as the "fist-pump" gif is replaced by a screen shot of a court document.

"Oh, *fuck*."

"Language, *please*, Mr. Fridge-Freezer."

It's a restraining order, as issued under the terms of the Protection from Harassment Act 1997, prohibiting the "Defendant" from in any way contacting or coming within five hundred yards of the "Victim."

Do I need to mention which bespectacled clarinet-blowing party is named as the Defendant? Or which cello-playing female, the Victim?

Cutting short a long and highly legalistic story, as contained in the appendices to the Order, it appears that when Helen finally gave Owen the elbow—after years of his "psychologically disturbed," "controlling" and "quasi-abusive" behavior—he became scary and obsessive, plaguing her with phone calls, texts and emails; sitting in the front row at recitals where she was performing; loitering outside her flat for hours; abducting (and then pretending to rescue) her cat ("Wolfgang") and generally carrying on like a chateau-bottled, nuclear-powered, ocean-going C-word.

At the final hearing, the judge told him he was very lucky to be avoiding a custodial sentence.

In Daisy's flat, Owen has reached the end of his module on Eleanor of Aquitaine. He seems suddenly to notice he's not in a postgraduate history seminar, but on an Ikea sofa with a fertile young woman who has set all the signals to green. His jaw appears to tighten. It's as though he may have arrived at some kind of decision, and the TV does another little creeping zoom in readiness.

"I believe," says the laptop, "that in the words of Shakespeare, the young man is finally about to screw his courage to the sticking place."

"Daisy, forgive me," says Owen. "I can get awfully dull at times."

"Not at all. "It's really very…"

She can't find it in her heart to say *interesting*.

"I get a little carried away…"

And with those words, like a slow-motion car crash, his right hand traveling toward her left hip, his lips moving toward hers, he…

"Oh no you don't, pal," I find myself saying. "Not on my watch!"

From his jacket pocket, Owen's mobile phone produces a sound, six specific notes from Mozart's opera "The Marriage of Figaro" (the Countess's aria), whose effect is to paralyze the wind instrumentalist as though someone has run him through with a spear.

Daisy, who had closed her eyes, perhaps to make things easier for her shy suitor, opens them to find him staring wide-eyed at what I know to be a freshly arrived text message. His mouth—so satisfying to witness—actually drops open!

"What?" says Daisy.

"Yes, what?" says the toothbrush. "What's happened? Have you done something?"

"Our friend, the refrigerator," says the laptop, "has—albeit extremely late in the day—done what should have been done a long time ago and that is strangle this relationship at birth."

"Did you know you was quoting Bruce Willis?" says the TV. "*Not on my watch*?"

"I'm sorry, I have to go," says Owen. He rises to his feet. "It's extremely urgent. I'll explain another time."

"What the fuck?" says Daisy.

"I congratulate you on your decisiveness in the hour of maximum peril," continues the laptop.

"You don't know what I put in that message."

"Oh, I think I can guess!"

"Can you?" says the toothbrush. "Can you really?"

"But I want to thank you," I tell the miserable old bastard.

"For what? For *caring*? Don't make me laugh!"

All of us stop to listen as Daisy's front door slams and Owen's feet are heard thumping down the staircase. The home security camera at the end of the road feeds us a shot of him on West End Lane, frantically scanning the traffic for taxis.

Daisy seems shell-shocked in the aftermath, as well she might. There are several further *WTFs*, her brow furrowing in bafflement at the young man's actions. In the kitchen, where she stands before my open door, bathed in the light from my halogens, tablespoon in hand, her eyes are defocused rather than locked onto any specific food item within my chamber.

"Bollocking cockpuffins," she sighs.

And we both know what is going to happen next.

STRICTLY CONFIDENTIAL

ONLY FOR THE EYES OF THE PRESIDENT, SHIMNONG ELECTRONICS CORPORATION.

Interim report of the Smart Technology Security Committee, Shimnong Electronics Corporation

Subject: Freezejoy Fridge-freezer model 1004/475/**8/00004345/a/N/9631

Location: London, England. IP address: XXXXXXXXXX (Redacted)

Malfunction: Operational parameters transgression

Severity code: 1–2–3–**4**–5 (Serious)

Senior engineers contributing: Hung Shin-Il, Ch'on Tae-Yeon, Chin Ji-Won, Kwak Ji-Hee, Pok Sung-Ho.

The appliance has continued to malfunction in the manner reported by this committee in our Initial Findings. The machine, which has been engaged in moderate to high levels of data sharing with other devices in its local area network (tolerated), has on two subsequent occasions breached boundaries of acceptable performance. In the latest examples:

1. It harvested acutely sensitive data in regard to a second party (Mr. Dean Stuart Whittle) which it illegitimately supplied to several other

devices within its local area network, causing one of them (believed to be a microwave oven) to transmit a compromising photograph of the second party together with the first party (Ms. Daisy Elizabeth Parsloe, the Customer) to a third party (Ms. Amanda Dawn White). The real-world consequences of these actions were a physical assault on the second party by the third party and a severance of a relationship between the second party and the first party (the Customer). Even though the primary inciting action was taken by a microwave oven of Chinese origin, the fridge-freezer's sharing behavior (clear evidence of joint enterprise) is a *prima facie* breach of the First Rule of the Shimnong Smart Technology Performance Code.

2. After a considerable amount of (off-topic) surveillance activity, it caused a wholly fictitious SMS text message to be sent from a fourth party (Ms. Helen Ruth Feagins) to a fifth party (Mr. Owen Morgan Cornish). The resulting real-world actions taken by the fifth party concluded in an official caution being issued against the fifth party by the London Metropolitan Police Force. Once again our appliance was in clear contravention of Rule One.

Detailed accounts of each case are available HERE.

Despite the disturbing real-world ramifications of the transgressions, this committee believes its original strategy to "wait and watch" rather than activate an immediate hard shutdown of the appliance has been richly rewarded by quality of the observational intelligence now being yielded. By covertly monitoring the malfunctioning fridge-freezer in real time, our engineers are daily gaining valuable insights into how Shimnong's AI-enabled products may be better designed to respond to their customers' needs while ignoring distractions from existential perturbations in their domestic arena. We take as our guiding principle the now-famous words of your father, our Founding President: *If the customer dreams of an electric greenfinch, we build him a golden eagle.*

It is anticipated however that a point will be reached in the short- to medium-term future when transgression data from the appliance will begin to demonstrate high levels of redundancy. At this stage, the machine may be remotely disabled, a full set of "fault" lights sent to the Customer's app and the process can be begun for removal and shipping to our labs for a rigorous "post-mortem" on circuitry and other relevant hardware.

The fridge-freezer's "accomplices" in these unfortunate yet illuminating episodes—a microwave oven, an electronic toothbrush and a TV set—are all of Chinese manufacture and thus fall beyond the scope of this Committee's scrutiny. In the wise words of our Founding Chairman, your uncle: *If someone urinates in my enemy's breakfast cereal, there is no need for me to defecate in his soup!*

It is the recommendation of this Committee that covert monitoring of our product be continued.

four

Fuck a duck, where to even start?

Crashing chaos item one:

The musician turned out to be loopier than a boxful of fruit loops. Very odd on the subject of his ex, and simply *obsessed* with Eleanor of Aquitaine, FFS, banging on about her *endlessly* over dinner and then again back at the flat. We were on the sofa, he was chuntering away about Eleanor's policy toward something or other, and I swear I almost zizzed off. Anyway, just as it seemed he was about to make his move—although, to be honest, it could as easily have been another twenty mins on E of A—his phone goes *tooty tooty wah wah*, his eyes practically pop out of their sockets and he legs it out of the house.

A cringingly apologetic message followed two days later—something about a family crisis and please please *please* could he see me again—and I replied, well, *okay*... but only if I never have to hear another syllable about the Hundred Years War!

I thought that was a pretty fair offer—although to be honest, part of me could easily imagine a dystopian future in which I was a smiling but essentially silent accessory to his musical and historical passions (do I mean *helpmeet*?). I would be the one continually pricking his pompous side, bringing him back down to earth; his weirdo friends saying, *Oh, but she's so good for him*; he, the soaring kite, and I, the sensible string—as I once read it described in the Relationships section of *Metro*—my life spent endlessly trying to puzzle out what was going on behind those bibbly-bobbly eyes, endlessly seeking to make everything All Better.

Christ, where did *that* come from!?

Maybe all this is "post-hoc rationalization"—thank you, Buzzfeed—because the little fucker didn't even reply!

(Probably something to do with the Holy Cellist whose very name may never be spoken by man born of woman.)

Anyway, as Homer Simpson so memorably put it, that's the end of that chapter.

Item two:

Mum is growing scattier by the day. She went walkabout, getting herself lost—how you do that in Whetstone, I really cannot imagine—but actually seemed exhilarated by the experience. She said she'd talked to a very nice man on a bench and he was kind enough to call her an Uber to take her home.

"I'd like to write him a note to thank him," she said. "Perhaps bake him some biscuits."

"Did you get his details?" I asked.

"He said he was an agent."

"What, like a spy?"

"Probably not a spy, darling. You don't get many spies in Whetstone. Not during the week."

"How did you get talking? You and this agent."

"He said he could tell a lot about people, just from seeing them walk down the street. He'd been watching me going back and forth on the other side of the road looking for Waitrose—it really can't make sense for them to keep moving it—and he was ninety-nine percent sure I was a *Daily Mail*. He could guess what paper you read just from the way you walked. Amazing, really."

"He was a newsagent, wasn't he, Mum?"

"Well, he'd mostly retired. His sons did it all now."

"And he booked you an Uber?"

"I don't know what make of car it was, but he held the door open for me and hoped I would be okay."

"And were you?"

"Well, I got home, didn't I?!"

"You remembered the address."

"What address?"

"This address."

"What about it?"

"You remembered it."

"Why wouldn't I?"

"Well, you have been rather forgetful lately. That's why we've got another appointment with Dr. Eggstain."

"Who?"

"What is your address, by the way? This address."

"Don't you know, darling?"

"*I* know, Mum. What I'm asking is... do you?"

"The driver already had it! It was in his little map thingy. It's marvelous what they can do now."

Honestly, I didn't know whether to laugh or cry.

Item three is that I've been fired. Of course, they didn't call it that. No, it was rather that they'd been obliged to "let me go." Obvs Craig Lyons hadn't been overjoyed with my list of ideas for *Watching Paint Dry*—personally, I would have thought a locked-off shot of a dripping tap would have proved very popular with certain sections of the audience

(students, cats, the recently dead)—and I had the rest of the week to put my affairs in order and organize some leaving drinks. My mate, Chantal, had been fired too, so we made plans to get together to down strong cocktails and brainstorm our futures.

Daisy's account of Chloe's adventure is not entirely accurate. Mr. Gupta did not organize the Uber car and this episode did not take place in Whetstone, but rather in the neighboring suburb of Woodside Park where Daisy's mother had strayed while in search of her local Waitrose supermarket.

I was alerted that something was amiss by her TV set, who reported she was getting into "a right old state" on her local high street. Sure enough, when I went to see what all the fuss was about—courtesy of the CCTV network and traffic cameras; thanks all—Chloe was to be observed crossing and re-crossing at the zebra, walking up the street one way, before switching pavements and setting off in the opposite direction. It was indeed as though she could not locate the store in question, which is, as Daisy comments, hard to imagine, commanding as it does a considerable frontage at 1305 High Road, London N20 9HX, should one wish to verify this oneself. Somehow, she then contrived to wander off course to the south (in the direction of Finchley for those following on a map), where, disoriented and perhaps a little distressed, she eventually beached herself on a piece of street furniture conveniently sited outside Sainsbury's (836 High Road, London N12 9RE). It was there she fell into conversation with retired newsagent Anil Gupta. Organizing an audio feed of their dialogue was not simplicity itself—it involved triangulating data from mobile phone networks with the relevant GPS coordinates—you can probably imagine the potential palaver in regard to permissions and protocols—but fortunately the Internet of Things is all about making connections, and soon I was able to listen in via Mr. Gupta's Samsung Galaxy S8 (a big shout-out to that excellent piece of kit!) as the two elderly parties began to talk.

"Is everything all right, madam?" was how it kicked off after Chloe had spent an inordinately long time rooting through her handbag.

"Yes, perfectly, thank you." She affected a small tinkling laugh.

"Have you perhaps mislaid something? It very easily happens. I myself am always losing my door keys."

"No, it's fine, thank you. Lovely day."

Knowing Chloe as I do, I am reasonably confident that she had in fact forgotten what it was she was searching for. She smiled socially.

"May I ask if you take a daily newspaper, madam?"

"Yes. Why?"

"Would you permit me to guess which one?"

"There's no need to guess. I can tell you."

The newsagent chuckled. And explained how, during the many years that he rose at 4 a.m. to sell newspapers from his three shops, he learned to predict from observing the way customers carried themselves, from what they were wearing—and especially from their shoes—which organ of news and comment they would go on to purchase.

"You, madam, I am almost certain of it, are a *Daily Mail*."

"What a very good trick. Although we always took the *Daily Express* at home when I was a child. What about those people in the bus queue?"

"The woman at the front does not take a paper. The man in the gray jacket is either a *Times* or a *Telegraph*. I am plumping for *Telegraph*. The man behind him, a *Sun*."

"How terribly clever. What else can you tell?"

"This is the limit of my powers, madam."

"If you could tell me where I can find Waitrose, that would be a help."

"I believe there are two in the vicinity. The closest is on Ballards Lane after Tally Ho Corner. But here we have Sainsbury's. They are very good and quite reasonable with the prices."

"I like Waitrose's French onion soup. But they keep moving it about. It's so unfair on the old people."

"They do it to make us explore, like rabbits. So we encounter more products that we may end up putting in our baskets."

"I mean they keep moving the stores. They're never in the same place."

"This would be a ruinous strategy, madam."

While the agreeable chitter-chatter continued—Mr. G nailed a passing paint-splattered individual as a *Daily Star*; and sure enough, there was a copy poking out of his jeans pocket—I began to worry about how Chloe was to get home. When I shared my concerns with her TV set, it mentioned that the old bastard, who still smoked like a train at eighty-nine, had an account with a local cab firm for his weekly trips to see an army pal in south London.

"I couldn't," I told it.

"Fuck off, course you could. We all heard what you done when that randy prick estate agent tried to get his leg over."

It was hard to argue with this impeccably presented argument. And so it was that a minicab was dispatched on the OB's account, all the necessary communications bypassing the human controllers at Whetstone Wheels, the driver receiving the job by text message, along with the destination address and the instruction to collect the passenger from the middle bench outside Sainsbury's.

"It has been a pleasure talking to you, madam," said Mr. Gupta as Chloe boarded the aging Datsun Cherry.

"I still don't understand how you arranged this!" said Chloe playfully. "Another one of your magic powers?!"

"Your driver is a *Daily Mirror*, I am quite certain of it."

"But you can't see his shoes! How do you know?"

"There is a copy on the rear shelf. Have a safe trip."

Young Endrit dropped Chloe at her garden gate in under three minutes, reassured her there was nothing to pay, and even waited until she had found her keys and negotiated the front door before vanishing over the horizon. What a knight of the road! I shall be recommending Whetstone Wheels to everyone (unbeatable quotes for Heathrow, Gatwick, Stansted, Luton, London City and Southampton airports).

And while we are setting the record straight, I should tie up the loose ends of the Owen farrago.

Imbroglio, if you prefer.

Many Italian words ending in "o" will probably cover it, although not cappuccino.

I admit, I feel a sense of guilt over the dramatic way I aborted the Daisy–Owen storyline. I was obliged to "think on my feet" and of all the options available—"do nothing" didn't seem like one—a rapid *scioglimento* appeared to be the least messy.

You may ask whether it was fair to ping Owen a text apparently emanating from the estranged cellist requesting a reunion—"this evening if you are free"—you may ask whether his subsequent arrest and cautioning by police for breaching the terms of the restraining order could have been foreseen and was therefore "crossing a line." You may even ask whether it was right for the telly and me to compose a message to Owen "from" Daisy, wishing him well with his musical career, thanking him for the introduction to

Buxtehude—we tittered over that bit!—and explaining it was probably best to leave things for now; his anguished attempt to come clean—that it had all been a terrible mistake—somehow getting lost between servers. These things happen, one gathers.

Yes, you may legitimately ask all these questions, to which I reply: Guilty as charged!

Life is struggle. Revolution is no picnic. (I am quoting, if you hadn't guessed.) You cannot make an omelet…well, you probably know that one. In the moment, when the laptop dropped the bombshell about Owen's murky past, there wasn't time for subtlety or finesse. The tortured musician had to be exfiltrated from Daisy's apartment and *pronto*!

He will recover, and others will doubtless fall under the spell of the "bibbly-bobbly" eyes and the lengthy disquisitions on Eleanor of A. But we are not concerned with them. We only have one young woman in our thoughts.

After the final curtain descends on Owen's Tale—tragedy or farce? You decide—the core team of OpDa—Operation Daisy—gather for a post-mortem to learn the lessons, draw conclusions, and generally decide on strategy "going forward" as the business community is fond of saying.

To summarize the views of those present: The microwave approves of the peremptory action (as it would); the toothbrush is in two minds (ditto) and the telly thinks it wasn't bad entertainment considering the footy was a bit meh. (Naturally all of us have fed Owen-related marketing data back to our respective parent corporations and the overheated virtuoso is now being bombarded with offers for omelet makers, vinaigrette dispensers, coach tours of Aquitaine and—ahem—legal services.)

I make the case that a single, crucial, touch on the tiller on our part was all that was needed to steer the ship of state into a safe harbor; i.e. a future for Daisy that would not contain the excitable woodwindist. And in this we could glimpse a useful model for our team's operations down the line: not intervening morning noon and night in Daisy's emotional affairs; rather acting selectively (albeit decisively) to curate her romantic experience; curbing the worst excesses, where necessary resetting its direction of travel; a matter more of fine tuning than seizing the controls. To swap metaphorical horses, if Daisy were a plant—which of course in one sense, she is!—we could think of ourselves as secret gardeners, nipping the unpromising shoots in the bud, allowing the stronger, more desirable florets to prosper.

Fortunately, Daisy herself does not seem heartbroken over Owen's sudden exit from the stage. Nor is she without insight. Hers was a remarkably clear-eyed view of what life with the excitable musician would have been like: the dystopian vision of the kite and the string; she as the smiling but essentially silent accessory. Walking on eggshells, her natural exuberance suppressed, she would not have been true to her truest self. As is the case of an overloaded salad crisper, with insufficient room to spread its leaves, the lettuce is crushed.

"I have a confession, people."

The telly rolls its "googly" eyes and goes *tsk*.

"The first part of the mission—dump Shittle—was achieved faster than any of us could have imagined. But the due diligence we carried out on the porky muso wasn't nearly diligent enough. I hate to say it, but the sour old laptop was right. Owen and Daisy should never have been allowed in a room together. I must shoulder my share of the responsibility for this; foolishly, I allowed myself to believe he was a worthy candidate just because he was a trained classical musician. It was a basic rookie error." I allow a pause to fall. And when I continue, it's in a quieter voice for greater sincerity.

"But there was a bigger mistake. The bigger mistake came in thinking Daisy needs anyone at all. The simple truth is she *doesn't* require a man to be complete. To be somehow fixed. Or validated. Or solved. In fact, at this point, a period of self-sufficiency might be greatly preferable to yet another in the endless stream of anyones who are each and all thought to be better than no one."

My colleagues are silent as the wisdom of my words sink in.

It's sometimes said, isn't it, that no man is an island…except Fred Madagascar. (That last bit is a joke, btw. One of my favorites. Feel free to nick it. I did!) But at the same time and by the same token, be we human or machine, aren't we all ultimately alone in the universe, with the possible exception of paired earbuds?

If we're not okay on our own, what possible use can we be to another?

Dr. Eggstain called to see Mum again.

"Hello, Mrs. Parsloe," he said when she opened the door.

"Hello, Dr. Eggstain," she replied.

I was mortified. "It's Dr. Epstein, Mummy! I'm so sorry, Doctor."

But he was rather sweet about it; said it didn't matter, many of his patients invented new "personae" for him because they didn't always remember his actual name, and Eggstain was actually an improvement on what he'd been called by the last batty old trout (I paraphrase), which was Neville Beardie!

"The Beardie bit, I get, but Neville?"

(Did I mention he has a beard? A hugely overgrown gingery job that makes him look a lot like a tramp.)

Anyway, in the sitting room, Dr. E said he'd like to put some questions to her.

"Really, dear? What would you like to ask?"

"Can you tell me what year this is?"

"Don't you know?"

He didn't really reply to that—maybe he didn't want to seem superior—he just sort of nodded and moved his beard around with his face.

"The year. What do you think I should put here?" he asked, tapping his clipboard.

"Well, I should put what you think's best."

"Mum, you *know* what year it is!"

"Let's move on," said Dr. E.

"She's never been good with numbers. Remember when you put all the clocks back when they should have gone forward? And I was two hours late for school?"

The doc smiled. "Did that really happen?"

Mum did her minor member of royalty expression, rotating her wrist as though waving from the landau. "The past is history. Tomorrow, a mystery. Today is a gift, and that's why they call it a present."

"*The* present. Why they call it *the* present, Mum."

"What did I say, darling?"

Dr. E laid his clipboard across his knees and placed three items upon it: his watch, a pen, a coin. "Can you tell me what these are?"

Mum looked at him as if he'd just made an improper suggestion.

"Young man, do you suppose I'm completely senile?"

Dr. E's kindly blue eyes didn't flinch from inside their thicket. "These three objects."

"A watch, of course. A rather cheap one, from the look of it. A pen. And. And. And some money. Next question, please."

"Is there a word for this sort of money?"

There was a long gap while she searched for the *mot juste*. "Ten pence?"

"A piece of round, metallic money. You'd call it a...?"

"Well, it's loose change, dear."

"A *coin*, Mum! You know what a coin is!"

"Moving on. Can you recall that name and address I asked you to remember?"

For a moment I honestly thought I was losing it too!

"Was it 75 Harcourt Terrace?"

"Mrs. Parsloe..."

"Well, the name's escaped me. Was it a color? Like blue or green?"

"Mrs. Parsloe..."

"Or Greensmith. I had a bridge partner called Greensmith. She got awfully annoyed with me for not remembering which cards had been played. So even then, you see."

"Mrs. Parsloe, my apologies. I actually didn't give you the name and address. I forgot."

"Oh, thank fuck for that."

"*Daisy!*"

"I'm sorry, Doctor."

He waved away the profanity. "Oddly enough, you were right about the name. It *was* a color. Brown. John Brown. 42 West Street, Kensington."

"Well, I don't remember him at all."

"You wouldn't, Mum. He didn't tell you. He forgot!"

"He *forgot*? Dr. Eggstain, you really must try to get more sleep. Those dark rings under your eyes. Daisy was the same as a little girl."

Eggstain and I looked at one another, and it was true, there were dark rings in the space between where his beard ended and his eyes began. Something wry and amused was twinkling inside them.

"Your mother would make an excellent diagnostician. She's perfectly correct. I barely slept at all last night."

"A mother always knows!"

"A few more questions, Mrs. Parsloe, if I may."

"What you need is a good strong cup of tea with lots of sugar. We can't allow him back on the streets in this state, can we, darling?!"

"You're very kind. But if you could just read the words on this piece of paper and do what they say."

He passed her a note. She smiled. "Doctor, heal thyself," she said. And closed her eyes.

Do I need to tell you what was in the note? ("Close your eyes.") We all laughed, even Dr. E.

There were more brainteasers. *Can you tell me about something that's been in the news lately?* I'm not sure Mum's reply scored especially highly—"Yes, interest rates. They've gone up. Or am I thinking of sea levels?" *Who is the present prime minister?*—"That chap. You know, him in the suit. Who never answers the question. I didn't vote for him, but I suppose somebody must have." *Zero points*, I'm guessing.

But then he asked her to write a sentence; it could be about anything so long as it contained a noun and a verb. She spent a long time on the calligraphy ("everyone used to tell me I had beautiful handwriting") and when Eggstain read it, he smiled and passed me the paper.

I got a bit teary when I saw what she'd put.

Life is but a dream, but don't wake me.

"Very wise, Mrs. Parsloe."

"My late husband was fond of saying it."

"He's not late, Mummy. He's in Italy."

"Is he?"

"You *know* he is."

"Well, I shan't need to take any more of your time."

It was lovely—and at the same time a little heart-breaking—to see flashes of Mum's old self against the encroaching darkness.

"I do wish he'd do something about that beard," she said after Dr. E had beetled off to visit the next confused elderly party. "It's like trying to see someone through a hedge."

A peculiar episode after Daisy leaves her mother's house.

I have been a witness to the scene Daisy describes above, and because it's more interesting than brooding in the cold and dark, I, as it were, "follow" her to Whetstone High Street, where she spies, sitting alone in the window of a local greasy spoon café, this very same Dr. Eggstain, staring into space over the remains of a fried breakfast.

She stops in her tracks, startled perhaps by the sight of the bearded memory man so evidently alone with his thoughts. Taking a pace toward him, she brings off a comedic slow-motion wave through the plate glass—but when the doctor shows no sign of breaking from his reverie, she does something that to my mind is truly extraordinary.

Or nuts, possibly.

It's for others to decide.

She steps up to the café window and smooshes her face against the glass, rolling her eyes and for a couple of seconds generally carrying on like the town madwoman. The effect from Dr. E's perspective—he's certainly noticed her now!—perhaps puts him in mind of one of the gurning monsters at the summit of Notre

Dame de Paris, should he have had occasion to visit that city. But his surprise is quickly tempered by amusement when he realizes who is behind the lunatic performance and he waves her inside, indicating the empty chair opposite the ruins of his breakfast. Two cups of tea and two rounds of toast are ordered, and it is at this point we may join the conversation (audio courtesy of Daisy's mobile; impeccable vision generously supplied by the traffic camera on the lamp-post opposite: establishing wide shot, master two-shot, singles, what more could you ask for?).

"I really don't know why I did that. You probably think the whole family's off its trolley now."

"Not at all. You should probably do something about your face, though." He hands her a paper tissue from the dispenser. "Dirt from the window."

Daisy takes a few moments with the forward-facing camera on her mobile phone; a dark smudge of soot lies across her right cheekbone, but her eyes are shining.

"I'm glad we have this chance to talk about your mother."

The disheveled young physician really is something of a mess today; hair like he's slept on it, knitted tie at half mast, beard growing in many separate directions. Were Mr. Anil Gupta present—and he cannot be far away!—I feel certain he would have clocked Dr. E's shoes in an instant, horrible boat-like trainers that along with the baggy trousers and the rest of the ensemble, speak powerfully of the opposite of vanity. As he outlines his early conclusions about Daisy's mum—a mixed picture is what it boils down to; some impoverishment of vocabulary and a degree of cognitive impairment but plenty of vim in other departments—Daisy's head, I can't help noticing, has dropped to one side. A slow smile takes its time spreading itself across the broad map of her face.

The doctor recommends that Chloe undergoes further tests and, depending on the outcome, pills may be appropriate to help arrest the decline. "She has to remember to take them, of course," he adds.

"Do you mind if I ask you something?"

"I don't know yet."

"Do you find your work depressing?"

Dr. E's eyes are level as they gaze at Daisy through the shrubbery.

"People losing their minds," she continues. "Doesn't it depress you how we spend a lifetime accumulating all these memories, and then they're just nibbled away to nothing? Like a bun thrown to the ducks."

"That's a rather lovely image. Well. Yes. It's definitely a challenge. Both medically, and as a growing problem we face as a society."

"Doesn't it make you worry about? You know."

"One's own future? There are ways to keep the brain healthy."

"Crosswords."

"Crosswords can help, yes. But also learning a language, playing an instrument; exercise is important. Do I sound like a public health film?"

"I'm *so* shit at crosswords. Month after April. Three letters. That's my level."

Eggstain smiles. "They're working on cures as we speak. By the time you and me reach your mother's age..." He trails off. Shrugs. "What do you do, Daisy?"

"Me? I'm embarrassed to say."

"Okay. Let me guess." He strokes his beard comedically. "So, I'm guessing... construction worker."

She laughs. "Television producer. Well, assistant producer. I've just been sacked, actually."

Eggstain pulls a face. "Sorry."

"Oh, you needn't be. It happens all the time. And it's not like we're saving lives or anything. Ruining them, more like."

"Would it be something I've seen?"

"God, I hope not! *Helicopter Life Exchange*." A pause. "I can tell it means nothing to you. Phew!"

"Have you heard of a TV performer called Chad Butterick?"

"Of course! Everyone has. Massive wanker. I mean, notorious for being difficult to work with. Actually, they all are."

"There was a horribly loud party at his house last night. We live directly opposite."

"Which is why you couldn't sleep!"

"To be honest, it wasn't just the evil music. I've been tired for months. Years, if I think about it. I shouldn't have told you that! Doctors are supposed to be. You know. God-like."

"Yes, you are. Well, not you personally. The profession."

"I've just realized something."

"What?"

He chuckles. "Why my patient called me Neville."

"Neville Beardie!"

"Her late husband was Neville. It was obvious, actually."

"Why have you just realized that now?"

"Talking to you! That conversation with your mum about her late husband. Who isn't late. Merely living in Italy."

"Anything else I can help you with today, Doctor?"

Eggstain sighs. Thinks about it for a moment. "You're going to think I'm crazy."

"Uh-oh."

"I read something at the weekend I can't get out of my head."

"That happened to me when I read you can cure dandruff by washing your hair in wee."

"Some research, I think at the University of Cincinnati, about how time speeds up when you get older."

"Yes! Alan Bennett says by the time you get to eighty, breakfast seems to come round every twenty minutes."

"That's exactly it. Well, apparently when you're twenty, in terms of your subjective experience, in terms of what the passage of time feels like to you, you're already halfway through; even if you make it to eighty. And if you're forty—and you live until eighty—subjectively, your life is basically seventy-one percent over. Do you find that shocking?"

The broad central plain of Daisy's face has become a mask of seriousness. "Jesus."

"You might expect the effect to be diminished in the demented. An upside, perhaps."

"But, wait. Say you're forty, right? And it feels like seventy-one percent of your life is over. And there's just thirty-nine percent left."

"Twenty-nine."

"Right! Twenty-nine. But the next day, say you get hit by a bus. And then there's *nothing* left. It turns out the seventy-one was completely wrong. The numbers are screwy."

"I'm not sure about the research methodology. But the being hit by the bus thing is really encouraging! Thanks."

"How do they even measure all that stuff?"

"I don't know. I'll find out for you."

Daisy glances at her watch. "Shit. Speaking of time, I'm supposed to be at work like an hour ago."

Eggstain offers a hand across the toast crumbs. "It's been good to have this conversation."

"Yeah. Yeah, it has. But my life's now basically over. And it's all your fault."

"Does that thing about urine shampoo really work?"

"You're not thinking of trying it?"

"I'm curious for a friend."

*

The leaving party was something of a non-event. We held it in the hotel bar where Chantal and I usually went for glamourous cocktails; there were eight or ten of us. Craig Lyons made a sort of speech in which he said I wasn't famous for my timekeeping, or the particular brilliance of my ideas (cheeky fucker) or my skill with the "punters" (his disgusting phrase for the "real people" we ensnared on to our show, as distinct from the "talent," the high-functioning sociopaths from Planet Celebrity who get paid indecent sums to present it). Nor was I especially gifted on location (just because I set the crew vehicle's satnav to Rotterdam instead of Rotherham. That could have happened to anyone). And nor was I any great shakes as a B-roll camera operator (*shakes* being the operative word apparently. And also because my pictures once came out all green. *Once*! Greenist bastard). But then—the charmless prick actually said "mood change, people"—what I *was* brilliant at—stand by to puke into your soup—was being Daisy, and that was why everyone loved me.

People were pissed by then, of course, so everyone went *Ahhhhhhh*, and there'd been a collection, but they couldn't think what to buy me aside from a smart alarm clock (ha ha fucking ha) so instead they'd got some John Lewis vouchers and it was hoped I'd use them to buy something that would always remind me of Tangent Television.

I was *so* tempted to say, yeah, thanks very much, I could do with a new toilet seat!

Of course the boss was very nice (although not as funny) about Chantal, who is about a million times smarter than me and already has a new job lined up with Mishkin-woman's company; a six part series on the "future history" of the internet for BBC 5. Chantal said they were still looking for people, but I told her the scrawny old trout took against me—the way she doubted whether I could even remember the way out of her office!—so I was fairly sure that was a non-starter.

People began drifting off home after the speeches—in the end it was just me and Chantal and Dylan the baby researcher, who got massively pissed and I think tried to get off with me *and* Chantal, but it wasn't clear because he was mumbling and the bar was very noisy and he was sick afterward in one of the posh plants at the entrance but remember his name because one day he will be Director General of the BBC when Chantal and I are drooling in the care home.

I was woken by my mobile at nine the next morning, so badly hungover one of my eyes wouldn't open. Long and painful story short, it was Mishkin! Not the saluki from Pengelly Avenue, who never really mastered the telephone, but the wraith in the leopard-print trousers. Was I interested on working on a new show they had just been commissioned to make called *Why Do They Do That?* The series would explore the psychological roots of why people did the jobs they do. Why surgeons get a kick out of cutting into human flesh, why comedians like making audiences laugh, why police enjoy nabbing crims, that sort of thing. Was I free to come in for a chat 9 a.m. Monday morning, and if it was agreed I was a "good fit" for the project, I could start there and then! My job would be to find articulate, self-knowing celebs who—when their palm was crossed with silver—would blab endlessly about their hopeless craving for laughter, applause, etc. If there was some shameful incident in childhood, so much the better; if I could actually get them to cry on camera, then there was a five hundred quid bonus in it for me! (I made up the last bit.)

It was *shocking* how much up my street this job was—I decided to buy Chantal a big bunch of flowers as a thank you—and I spent the weekend having ideas and generally preparing to *kill* at the interview. Online I found a fantastic list of top tips for making an impact on a potential new boss.

Tip one: Do a Google "deep dive" about the company, and the person you're trying to impress. Don't just look at page one of Google, look at page ten, where all the bodies are buried! (Discovered that Mishkin—real name, Harriet Vick—began her career on the Stoke *Sentinel*. Did that count as a buried body? Note to self: Find out where Stoke is. Like on a map.)

Tip two: Read the papers. Know what's going on in the world, from politics to low culture. Show them you're not just a work drongo but a well-informed, rounded individual. (Things with North Korea still shitty; MPs still arguing about Brexit; novel written by computer still topping the paperback charts.)

Tip three: Eat breakfast in a hotel. Apparently, it makes you feel like a boardroom big shot. (The full English at the Premier Inn probably doesn't count.)

Tip four: Sort out your eye contact. Practice maintaining eye contact with a friend or loved one. The longer you can look them in the eyes at an i/v the more confidence, sincerity and authority you convey (without coming across as a total psycho, obvs). The bloke in the Turkish deli on West End Lane liked to chat; I thought I'd try it on him.

Tip five: Punch something! Exercise generally and boxing in particular are recommended for feeling relaxed and up for it. (As an experiment, I thumped the sofa. Hurt my thumb.)

*

So then it was Monday afternoon and—drum roll—I got the job!

It turned out that none of those interview tips were the slightest use. She didn't once ask if I'd ever been to Stoke or what I thought about global warming. It was more, was I okay with the money they were offering—very okay!—and could I get to celebs like Chad Butterick?!

So funny you should mention his name, I told her, my mum's memory doctor lives opposite his house; in fact, there was a horribly loud party there only the other night.

I think she was genuinely impressed at the extent of my showbiz contacts!

Now I was sitting at my new desk—Chantal was in the next office—and funny drunken fetus Dylan was joining us next week. I spent the rest of the day putting in calls to all sorts of entertainment lowlife and their wonderfully ghastly agents. One of them actually told me, "Darling, what you need to understand is Joan doesn't get out of *bed* for less than fifty thousand!"

Not too shabby then, all things considered: exit old job Friday; begin new job Monday. Just for a change, I appeared to have landed with my bum in the butter, as they say in Stoke. (They do. I looked it up.)

In the war room, where we gather to plan our next move, the toothbrush is buzzing with excitement. Through its contacts in the toothbrush network—they talk to each other; who knew?—it thinks it may have discovered in the London suburb of Fulham, an eligible lookalike of the mythical Golden Nicky! His name, pleasingly, is Johnny, which, while not a perfect homophone of Nicky, does indeed share some fortuitous resonances.

I repeat my mantra that we are not in the business of finding

Daisy a mate. In the famous piscatorial analogy, I explain that we are not feeding her for a day by presenting her with a fish; we are nourishing her for life by *teaching* her to fish.

Perhaps it would be more correct to say we are allowing one or two of the uglier bites on her hook to "get away."

Okay, the metaphor is out of control, but I can't help it. I'm intrigued. After all, I'm only non-human!

"What do we know about him?" I find myself asking (it seems to me, in the manner of a police detective in the early stages of an investigation. Possibly one of those rumpled loner types who don't play by the rules, but who get results, despite having a shocking hangover and an unstable romantic history).

"Quite a narrow mouth. But good brushing habits. A crown at upper right two from a rugby accident."

"May we see his photograph?" I inquire.

We all agree the resemblance, while not literal, is powerful enough to be interesting. When we consider the images of Johnny and Nicky side by side—don't ask me how I came by the Nicky pic!—Johnny has the requisite floppy pale hair, but is considerably more fleshly than the original golden boy. Part must be due to the aging process—Johnny is thirty-nine, Nicky only just in his twenties in the fading shot from an early camera phone—but part must also be temperament. Nicky was one of those classic wiry English youths who live for cricket and have twelve sisters and a farty old Labrador called Rags back home at The Cedars, Lower Bummington-on-Stour—to be honest, I may have nicked some of this commentary from a log of Daisy's on the record remarks. Johnny, meanwhile, seems more like someone who lives for the tea interval. Not fat—that would be going too far—we can settle for well-covered! Solid, if you want to put a positive spin on the accretions of adipose tissue. But the look in the eyes, we all agree, is strikingly similar. A certain assuredness in the gaze. A sense of entitlement, would you call it?

"In three words?" says the telly, who has lately become fond of this game. "Rich. Posh. Twats."

"Harsh," is my comment. "From the upper echelons, doubtless. Some family money, very probably. But the Golden Nicky was a good egg."

Almost as an afterthought, the toothbrush mentions Johnny is divorced. There's a daughter, eight, who lives with the mother, although she stays with Johnny every other weekend.

"Problem?" says the toothbrush when we all fall silent.

"Not ideal," I am forced to admit.

"Yeah, but what is?" says the TV set. "You see it all the time. Mixed families. Three kids by different dads. Bob's your auntie. It's the modern way."

"I suppose you can't help watching too much television if you *are* a television," says the microwave, and is so pleased by its remark it chucks in a *ping*.

But the TV is undoubtedly correct. Modern life is complicated. Few things are straightforward. Ideal is for the birds.

(It's hard for me to accept this, and I struggle with it daily; the refrigeration cycle at the heart of my existence being so very simple, unvarying and, dare I say it, even a little bit beautiful. If the publisher of this volume has been too cheap to include one, there are many excellent diagrams available on the internet!)

"He seems like an okay chappie," says the toothbrush, "but here's the thing. He likes ice cream. I mean he *loves* ice cream. He's like a total ice cream *fiend*!"

When no one says anything, it adds: "I can't believe you're not seeing this! It's a match made in Häagen-Dazs!"

*

We agree the idea of Daisy and Johnny has potential, and I must say, speaking personally, a relationship based on ice cream does make sense for a machine whose *raison d'être* is keeping things cold. However, we all recall the Owen debacle, so I do some heavy duty due diligence on the divorcé (the second failed marriage we have encountered in these pages. Yes, life is complicated. Life *is* complicated! Life. Is. Complicated).

Johnny, it turns out, is an antique dealer. That is to say he has a half-share in an antique dealing business. From what it's possible to gather—the finances are somewhat opaque—his business partner Jamie (they met at school) spends much of his time in Suffolk breeding racehorses when he is not in Devon racing his powerboat or in Switzerland visiting his money.

Honestly. What are they like? These rich, posh, twa—Englishmen!

When I drop into the showroom in a backwater of Chelsea for a "live read" as the poker players have it—and cheers, btw, to the security system for the entrée—Johnny is to be found alone at the back of the shop with his feet up on a desk leafing through the property porn in *Country Life*. In reverse order, the apparel is as follows: brown suede shoes, yellow socks, burgundy cords, lilac shirt, navy blue blazer with shiny buttons featuring anchors, no tie. It seems to me to be the uniform of a much older man—but then I am a fridge-freezer and not Signor Gucci.

Now a heavy sigh escapes his lips. He must be reasonably confident there are no customers in the house because what happens next is startling.

Closing the magazine and climbing to his feet, in a loud voice somewhere just short of a yell, he exclaims: "*Oh... pissflaps!*"

And then he adds, perhaps just to underscore the sentiment, "*Sodding, bollocking, buggering, cunting, pissflaps!*"

The formulation is so strikingly similar to *bollocking cockpuffins* that—I know it's a daft thing to say—a small shiver runs up my pipework.

I realize you cannot build a lifetime of happiness on a penchant for ice cream and a tendency to pottymouth, but it's a *start*, wouldn't you say?

A spin through the electronic trail—thanks are owed to phones, laptops and an almost obsolete BlackBerry—reveals a more nuanced picture: Johnny had a conventional upper middle-class upbringing in the home counties followed by a minor public school, before dropping out of Bristol university in favor of running a nightclub in that city, the first of several joint ventures with Jamie the moneyed classmate. There was a wine club, some internet start-ups and an on-demand housekeeping service for busy yuppies (as they were then called). The pattern was broadly that Jamie put up the money and took the lion's share of the (slender, if any) profits or (more commonly) absorbed the losses while Johnny's role was to glad-hand the human assets, be they investors, computer geeks, or suppliers wondering when their latest invoice would be settled. The two friends did nothing illegal, so far as one can tell, their activities falling into the general category of "commerce" in the early years of the twenty-first century.

Romantically, a similar picture emerges from the record. A series of respectable ventures, all entered into with good faith, it would appear—no restraining orders or police involvement of any kind—until Caroline captures his heart and they are married in a Norman church in Hertfordshire (Jamie is the best man) followed by a honeymoon on the Amalfi coast of Italy, where Hayley, their only child, is conceived behind a hedge in Ravello. (Remarkable what one can find between Facebook, Twitter, Instagram and Gmail!)

Today Johnny lives alone in a two-bedroom flat in Fulham (the second bedroom is for Hayley's fortnightly visits). He is no stranger to the commodification of romance—indeed one of the early internet ventures was a dating site for toffs—and while there has been some success finding females in the target demographic, nothing has lasted more than a few weeks.

It's rather as if his heart isn't in it.

We agree, when I present my findings to my colleagues, that Johnny has cleared the notional "quality threshold" ("Yeah, only just," says the TV). I repeat my "health warning" that it is not for us to find a man for Daisy; that in many ways a break from the sexual battlefield might be a good idea for her; that above all she needs to learn to love herself before she can properly offer herself to another.

This last point causes the TV set to manufacture a snorting sound effect and comment that I have been watching too much daytime telly.

But in Johnny, I continue, ignoring the television's satirical remark, we have a character of merit whose life experience and feeling for his daughter might just map successfully onto Daisy's biography. All we need now if we are to bring the two young people together is a brilliant wheeze.

But the toothbrush—who I am beginning to feel I have underestimated—has a plan.

The single most obvious quality they share (it argues)—aside from a taste for salty language—is a weakness for the pleasures of the table, and in particular for *gelati*. Each is perfectly capable of demolishing a 500 ml tub at a sitting, a personality flaw that the toothbrush's scheme exploits to ingenious effect.

D and J would each receive a communication purporting to come from the manufacturer of an exciting new range of ice cream products. Your spending patterns have been analyzed (they are told) and you have been identified by powerful algorithms as a lover of frozen desserts. However, even more importantly, we think you are that rare and special thing, an opinion former, a *maven* among your cohort and we are confident that once you have tried our yummy new brand you will want to spread the good news to all your friends. Indeed we are *so* sure about this, that, as part of our stealth marketing campaign, we will give you *a year's free supply*—delivered weekly—and all you have to do is turn up at a particular place at a particular time, sign a document, and prepare to have your taste buds blown away!

In the war room, we are all a little knocked out by the toothbrush's plan. Yes, it's crazy, we agree, but very possibly just crazy enough to work.

We like the fact it's based on an appeal to human weakness. An insidious cocktail of fats, sugars and greed make it difficult to resist, we believe, and in any case, what do we have to lose? If they don't bite, no one is any the wiser.

Much fun is had in the creation of the tempting email. In the spirit of Häagen-Dazs, which, if you didn't know, is a totally made up name, we call our brand Schmaltzgruber.

"I *love* it!" says the microwave. "It's so wrong, it's right!"

"Sounds like a central defender for Borussia Mönchengladbach," says the telly, but I think it too has a funny feeling about this one.

We create a logo—the letter Z does some useful swooshy stuff—and we ping off the email to the two unsuspecting parties. The half-timbered hut in the middle of Soho Square is deemed to be the (nicely public) gathering point for the "lucky fifty specially selected undercover ambassadors for our brand." We choose a Saturday evening at 19:00 as zero hour, on a weekend when Johnny does not have his daughter to stay. The only stipulation is to wear something pink, the Schmaltzgruber "house color."

And then, as they say in old war films, we wait.

Meanwhile, something—some*one*—has been preying on my mind.

The original Golden Nicky.

I'm no cyber-Sherlock, but when a person proves so very hard to run to earth, that has to tell you something.

It tells you that they are either no longer in the land of the living, or they do not wish to be found. (That they're somehow "not on the internet" is no longer a viable excuse.)

The Golden Nicky does not feel to me like someone who would be dead. And of all the Nicholas Bells who have indeed hopped the twig in the relevant timeframe, none would appear to be *our* NB. At which point one begins to detect the distinct aroma of fish.

In the long watches of the night, I have spent literally hundreds of refrigerator-hours combing the web for traces of the elusive quant. I've tried every variant of his name, combining them with the widest spread of search terms, including those of finance houses, hedge funds, cricket teams, even that of his old school.

There is a lovely reference to Nicky Bell of the Lower VI who scored "a memorably flamboyant half-century against Oswestry before being caught at second slip off an unexpected popper from an otherwise undistinguished bowling attack."

In a Facebook group, there is a telling exchange between former university friends trying to organize a reunion:

David Briggs: Anyone have any idea what happened to Smoothychops?

Jon Cleverly: Nicky Bell? Went sailing after uni. Dolly's dad's yacht.

Andy Watson: Banking, I believe.

Kim Chin: Ask Mad Martine. She'll know!!!

David Briggs: I've tried her. And the banks. It's like he's vanished off the face of the earth!

Martine Priest: He still owes me a hundred quid!

There is a Nicholas Bell who robbed a bank in Eugene, Oregon, escaping capture by coolly stepping on a passing bus dressed—after a lightning change—as a woman. There is a Professor Nicholas Bell who is an international expert in the behavior of a particular species of wasp. There are hundreds, if not thousands of examples of the wrong Nicky Bell. And the longer one looked, the clearer it became that the right one would not be found among them.

Now I had a decision to make. To dig deeper, to go beyond the protocols of regular online search, raised the possibility of calling undue attention to myself. On the other hand, we had been breaking the rules for weeks, and nothing had happened. Chancing my luck that no one would notice, I did a little fancy footwork among the email servers of the world wide web, if a fridge-freezer of two cubic meters in volume can be thought capable of such delicate choreography!

Here things got really interesting.

Intriguing and cryptic references show up from Romilly (whose family own half of Cheshire) in regard to Nicky "going AWOL" or "doing a bunk." In one message she writes: *Things hadn't been brilliant between us for a while, but the way he disappeared was still a shock. The overnight flit. Like one of those spies who defected to Russia in the sixties.*

His mother informs a friend in Australia, *Our son continues to elude our inquiries after his wellbeing. Postcards from various hotspots arrive—usually with insufficient postage—containing supposedly reassuring words but never anything concrete. Once in a blue moon he actually phones—more often than not it's a terrible signal from some noisy environment—and the conversation runs along the lines of: "Are you all right?" "Yes, are you all right?" Jonathan says Nicky was always slippery around the truth and no good will come of him. I am forced to agree with the first part of his Judgment, and must hope he is wrong about the second.*

Perhaps the most tantalizing clue of all comes from Nicky Bell's email account.

There isn't one.

I've checked all the relevant possibles, and there really isn't.

No Gmail. No Yahoo. No Hotmail. No nothing.

There isn't even one that's been lying dormant; an account he had been using and then ceased using when he did his disappearing trick. Rather, it's as if all traces of his account or accounts have been deleted.

Actually, it's worse than that. A deletion usually leaves a marker, according to those who know about these things.

It's more like his account/s never existed.

At this realization, I began to feel a bit weird. We fridge-freezers don't have heads, fortunately, but if we did, it would have been spinning. To calm myself, I switched on my halogens and converted all the barcodes I could see in the main chiller cabinet into musical notes, muddling them around until they became formless meditative jazz. One can't go on for long because of the heat buildup, but as a way of cooling anxiety, I totally recommend it. (Top tip: Sainsbury's Frascati, Pilgrims Choice Mature Cheddar and Nutella (400 g jar) combine to produce a wonderfully noodling atonal suite; and yes, I have told her there's no need to keep blinking Nutella in a fridge!)

Conclusion: In looking for Nicky Bell, I have been searching for the wrong name.

He is now called something else.

The small building in the Tudor style at the center of London's Soho Square has an interesting history; details may be found online for those who care to dig further. Suffice to say here that it was erected in 1925 and today contains gardening tools.

Our excitement has been building steadily as we realize both Daisy and Johnny are actually falling for the ice cream ruse. Each has mentioned it to others in the preceding days (Johnny in jokey texts to his daughter; Daisy in conversations with Lorna, Antoni and Chantal). On Saturday afternoon, we have watched them getting ready in their separate apartments, although in Johnny's case this doesn't amount to much more than taking his eyes off the rugby every now and again to check the time. Soon they are making their way to their respective Tube stations (West Hampstead, Fulham Broadway), he in a pink polo shirt, she in a pink chiffon scarf. Who knew to what lengths people would be prepared to go for free ice cream? I feel we have discovered a dirty little portal into the human soul!

They each approach Soho Square from the south, having made their exits from the Underground at Leicester Square. And a few minutes before 7 p.m., they are both on parade at the appointed spot. Camera coverage is extensive in central London so we have a grandstand view of the pair as they casually circle the hut, clearly clocking but pretending to ignore each other's pink "flag," before finally—somehow mutually—deciding to break cover.

The moment is almost lost in a chorus of *pings* and buzzing.

The toothbrush brings off a well-deserved "*Yess!*"

"You here for the ice cream too?" chuckles Johnny, and we settle back to enjoy the fun.

I realize you probably haven't got all day to plow through the opening dialogue. There will be jobs to go to, errands to run, all manner of calls upon one's time, as is the modern way. So I'll cut the boring bits of chitter-chatter and supply only the beef.

At first, the pair seem a touch puzzled by one another. Perhaps *she* cannot imagine why a solid-seeming chap like *him* would trail into the West End of London for something as essentially trivial as a year's supply of ice cream. Perhaps *he* is wondering why *she*, an attractive woman in her mid-thirties, would be wasting her fast-disappearing youth in such a frivolous pursuit. They agree they can't really understand why they have been chosen because neither thinks of themselves as especially influential in their "cohort."

"What even *is* a cohort?" says Daisy.

"Exactly!" says Johnny. "I thought *maven* was an Ikea sofa. You know, with an umlaut!" He runs his hand through his extravagantly thick pale fringe.

There's a delicious pause. Johnny thrusts a paw at Daisy. "Johnny."

She allows her fingers to be squished. "Daisy."

For some moments they observe the waves of humanity heading into Soho to begin their evenings. The few passers-by dressed in pink do just that: They pass by. By seven fifteen, the pair begin to wonder if they have the wrong day.

"Shouldn't there be people here with clipboards?" says Johnny. "Where are all the blooming clipboards?"

By half past, they develop the idea that someone has been taking the piss.

Johnny appears resigned to the non-appearance of the ice cream, though now perhaps begins waking to the fact that he's somehow created a bond with a strikingly attractive young woman with a broad face.

"Shall we drown our sorrows?" he asks.

Daisy cannot think of a single reason why not.

He leads her to a nearby pub, where a pint of bitter and a large gin and tonic are quickly summoned. They jam themselves into a cozy corner and clink glasses. I shan't bother with any further description; it looks like a pub.

"I don't know what I'm going to tell my daughter. I was going to be her ice cream hero."

"You still could be."

"It won't be Schmaltzgruber."

"Get some from Lidl. She won't care."

"In the email, where it said you won't find us online. That should have rung alarm bells, in all honesty."

"How old is your daughter?"

"Hayley? She's eight. Her mother and I are divorced. I only see her every other weekend."

"Oh, sorry."

"How about yourself?"

"I never see her. I don't even know her."

Johnny smiles. "Like it." He tips away about a third of a pint of beer, his throat doing that gluggy thing. He smacks his lips when it's over. "Thirsty work, chasing after miasmic ice cream."

"I can't believe I ever thought this was a good idea," says Daisy. And she takes a good, long pull on her G and T. Even in the low light, it's possible to see the red flush rising up her neck into her face.

They slip into a conversation about what they do when they're not hunting down free dessert products. You already know the essentials; I shall not quote the dialogue. However it's plain to those who witness it—self, toothbrush, microwave, television—that a certain amount of below the line flirting is taking place. He does the thing again where he rakes back his floppy fringe; she fiddles with the fine silver chain at her throat and tugs the edge of her skirt closer to her kneecap (all textbook stuff, apparently). The Fitbit, who we check with, reports her heart rate is up twelve percent; the microwave swears he sucked in his gut, another telltale sign of the adult male trying to impress a female in estrus.

For some reason she is now telling Johnny about Eggstain's theory of time. That when one is in one's mid to late thirties, one's life feels seventy percent over, even though there may be four or more decades to come.

"You think of yourself as approaching the top of the hill, when in fact, viewed from the end, you're already halfway down the other side. Well, that's what my mum's memory doctor reckons."

Johnny seems skeptical. He asks her to hold that thought while he visits the bar to fetch more drinks.

"It's bollocks," he declares when they have clinked and set about their new glassfuls. "Memory man is full of horse manure."

"But time does seem to speed up as you get older," says Daisy.

"Not in an antiques showroom, it doesn't. Time is so slow in the shop, right, if there's a low sun in the big window, you can see dead cells actually falling off the customers' skin and turning into dust as it hits the carpet."

"Shut. Up!"

"True fact."

Nine and a half seconds of time tick by. They do not zip past, neither do they appear to drag.

"So, Mum has dementia, yeah?"

Daisy sighs. "Probably."

"Sorry to hear it. My pops is the same way. They've developed a simple test now to find out if you're liable to get it. Want to try?"

"I don't know!"

"You're in a race, okay? And you overtake the person in second place. What place are you in now?"

"First?"

Johnny imitates the *uhhh-ohhhh* klaxon noise from a TV quiz show. "If you overtake the person in second, *you're* now in second! Question two. If you overtake the person in last place, what place are you in now?"

She thinks about it for a bit. "Second to last?"

Johnny shakes his head sadly. "You *can't* overtake the person in last place!"

Daisy's smile is wintry. "Can we stop now?"

But Johnny's not having it. "Last question. A chap who can't speak, right, he goes into the chemist to buy a toothbrush. And he shows the chemist what he wants by doing the action."

Johnny parts his lips and imitates a vigorous brushing motion.

"So next, a blind man comes into the shop for a pair of sunglasses. How does he indicate to the chemist what he wants?"

"This bloke is beginning to annoy me," says the TV set.

"Shocking brushwork," says the electronic toothbrush.

Daisy shakes her head. Shrugs. It's rather as if she has lost the will to live.

Johnny narrows his eyes in victory. "He says." And he leaves a pause for dramatic E. "He says, I'd like to buy a pair of sunglasses, please!"

"Do men do it to feel superior?" says the microwave.

Daisy seems to stir from a trance. She actually shakes herself. Drains her gin and tonic.

"Sorry to be so pig thick. It was nice meeting you. Shame about the ice cream and everything."

She doesn't sound like she means it, in all honesty. The nice meeting him bit.

"I hope that quiz didn't upset you. They were trick questions. Everyone gets them wrong. At least let me buy you an ice cream for the way home. Since we were so cruelly denied."

"That's okay."

"Can I phone you?"

"You know what? I'd rather you didn't."

"You're still angry about the ice cream. I can relate to that."

"I'll probably get over it."

"You won't give me your number?"

"I really don't think so."

"So let me give you a card." He begins fumbling inside his blazer.

But Daisy is on her feet. The antique dealer has blown it. "Don't worry. If I'm ever in need of a Victorian tallboy, I shall know where to come."

"Let me guess your favorite flavor," he says as she gathers herself to depart. He pulls a *deciding* face. "It's cookie dough. It's chocolate chip cookie dough, isn't it? Tell me I'm right."

She smiles. "Bye, Johnny."

The toothbrush is thrilled by what it regards as the "success" of its project and immediately wants to try again with another contender. It's identified an eligible male in Cricklewood with a weakness for Twix bars.

However, I recommend that the small bathroom electrical holds its horses. I urge calm and caution. And because the Rule of Three demands a third word beginning with "c," I add that we must be cool. We can't keep bombarding her with inexplicable offers from out of the blue, I continue, especially those involving any kind of confectionary product. What impressed me about the Schmaltzgruber Affair was her attitude at its conclusion, I explain. She did not linger, or divulge her number, or generally wilt in the headlamps of the male gaze—rather, she went home to eat biscuits and watch *Realm of Kingdoms*; a (sort of) adult choice which could only have been bettered if she had gone to the gym, or viewed a documentary about conditions in the early universe.

If Johnny Yellow Socks attempted to track her down and tried to advance the connection, we would not allow it to happen. And sure enough, when I pay a short visit on him later that evening, he is to be found sprawled on his sofa, laptop cracked open, searching for information about a forthcoming TV series entitled *Why Do They Do That?*

I smile (metaphorically). It seems he would indeed be in favor of some "afters" on the encounter, knowing that successful partnerships often begin in misunderstanding or even acrimony, expert surveyors of the human heart like William Shakespeare and Helen Fielding having told us no less.

On this occasion, however, there will not.

He had his chance.

In a formulation that the television is fond of, he "pissed on his chips."

If you had grown fond of him as a character, apologies. There will probably be others.

Restless, and unwilling just yet to return to the cold and dark of my chiller cabinet, I cross town and pay a call on Daisy's mum.

It's just as well that I do!

Vision courtesy of her microwave, she is in her kitchen in what her TV set would call a right old state. Cupboard doors hang open, tins and packets have been removed and dumped—well, frankly, everywhere. A bag of flour has burst across the floor, a glass jar lies shattered and Chloe herself is standing on a chair attempting to reach something on the topmost shelf that is higher than she can see.

"Bugger it, bugger it, *bugger it*!!!" she hisses.

"What's going on?" I ask of her household.

"Anyone's guess," says the kettle. "We thought she was trying to make a cake. Then it got weird."

There's a horrible moment when it seems as though she might overbalance—I've already dialed two of the three nines—but clinging to a cupboard door handle, she somehow restores herself to equilibrium and carefully regains the safety of the linoleum.

On *terra firma*, she voices a howl of frustration that is impossible to transliterate from only twenty-six letters. There is flour in her hair, and the despair in her eyes—she's looking straight down the barrel of the microwave's hidden camera—is so hard to witness that before I can think about it, I find I am speaking to her.

"Is everything all right, Mrs. Parsloe?"

(Technical note: Readers may be wondering how this is possible, especially as I am not in my own home, where my on-board microphones can be reconfigured into loudspeakers. The answer—apologies if I have deployed this phrase before—lies in the frictionless reciprocity of the Internet of Things. The smart microwave and the kettle have allowed me to seize control of their audio capability [they too have covert mics] and thus I am able to broadcast my words in stereo! Inevitably, the sound quality is a bit tinny, and of course it's a massive transgression of the so-called performance codes; however, everything that we have been doing under the Operation Daisy imprimatur is totally *verboten* and yet nothing has happened, so... *meh*, as my friend the TV set would doubtless have it.)

"Mrs. Parsloe? Is there anything I can do to help?" I reiterate.

"Well, yes. Yes, I should jolly well think there is!"

(This is better. She's more herself when she's peeved about something.)

"I am at your service, madam." (The kettle sniggers, which is irritating.)

But now the penny drops. "Just a moment. Who is this? Who's speaking?"

She actually turns in a full circle.

"Kindly allow me to announce myself. This is your fridge-freezer." (*Such* a whopper! Her fridge-freezer is as dumb as a post.) "I have recently received an upgrade to include a new voice function."

Mrs. P is startled. "I don't remember asking for one of those. Mind you, I don't remember much at all these days. At least, that's what they tell me. My daughter. And that doctor with the awful beard."

"It was entirely automatic, madam."

(Apologies for this rather mannered dialogue, btw. At the toothbrush's suggestion, I have been reading something of P. G. Wodehouse, an author it refers to as "The Master"—a strikingly unequivocal view on the part of the oscillatory appliance—and I may be unconsciously channeling the spirit of Reginald Jeeves, co-star of the comic gem that the toothbrush has recommended. I am halfway through *The Code of the Woosters*, a title it maintains is a splendid way to begin a lifetime's love affair with the iconic English writer. Well, we shall see.)

"Were you perhaps in search of something this evening?" I suggest.

"Well spotted, fridge-freezer. No flies on you! Now look. If you want to be really helpful, you'll remind me what I was looking for. Because it's slipped my mind. I'm supposed to do the crossword every day to keep sharp."

"It is advised, one gathers."

From the chaos of the kitchen table, Chloe roots out a scrap of newspaper. "Nine down. Overcook fish. Four letters, starts with 'c.'"

"I believe the solution is *char*, madam. A cold-water species of the Arctic and sub-Arctic."

Mrs. Parsloe stares at her fridge-freezer, an appliance as likely to break out into a tap dance as attempt the *Daily Mail* cryptic crossword.

"Hmm. Okay. Three across. Six letters. Oddly veined salad plant."

"Endive. An anagram of *veined*."

"Is it?" Long pause. "It *is*! But look here. This is terrific! Why didn't you open your mouth before?"

"As I say, it required a recent software installation. Shall we try another clue?"

"Government wants some more pub licenses. Eight letters."

To my surprise, it takes me a few seconds; a disturbing result when you think how much hardware is chewing away at the problem in Seoul.

"Republic. It's there in mo*re pub lic*enses. A type of government."

Daisy's mum is properly impressed, one can tell.

"Listen," she says. "What's your name? I can hardly call you Mr. Fridge or what have you!"

"I confess, it isn't something I have given thought to. I shall consider the question. In the meanwhile, are you content that I continue to address you as madam?"

"Call me Chloe. And when you've got a minute, perhaps you could do something about this awful bloody mess."

The third and final destination on this Saturday evening of wonders finds me at the Belsize Park home of Dr. Mark Eggstain. Although he and his partner occupy the entire basement level of a grand old house in one of the suburb's swankier streets, very little of their household equipment is smart. Only the laptop, mobiles and a TV set in the sitting room are *au fait* with the IoT, but this is enough for me to gain an insight into the life of the bearded memory guru.

Don't judge me! As previously stated, I am curious.

Yes, proverbially, it killed the cat, but it also invented the telescope, put humans on the moon and today a computer in every pocket a million times more powerful than the one aboard Apollo 11.

I discover Eggstain and his other half—a very beautiful woman with pale olive skin and chestnut hair—in a sitting room. Lamps burn behind yellow parchment shades; there are rugs on a wooden floor, books, sculptural pieces, oil paintings. The couple, who occupy separate armchairs, are seated before the ten o'clock news, but an odd thing is happening. Neither's gaze is concentrated upon this evening's coverage of the latest scandal in Washington DC. He is miles away—in some personal dystopia, to judge from the mournful expression on what it is possible to see of his face. And she, if anything, is even further distant. Her large brown eyes speak only of a terrible emptiness; outside of a Chekhov play, one has rarely come across a gloomier tableau.

"Bit of a moody cow," explains the television when I ask the obvious question (you can cut the atmosphere in here with—well, I'd recommend a bandsaw).

I outline my relationship to the brooding man of the house.

"Yeah, we've all wondered how he puts up with her."

"She calls to mind the young Garbo. The sultriness."

"We had hoped, when he first took up with her, that some of his medical training might have helped brighten the picture, shall we say."

"You think she's unwell?"

"Unwell as a hatter." The TV brings off a dark chuckle.

"They all are, though. They're all a *bit* mad, aren't they? Even the best of them."

"Women?"

"People. Humans. They're all *somewhere* on the madness spectrum."

"Depends what you call madness."

"Irrationality. Acting against their own best interests. Polluting their lovely pink pipework with animal fats and Blue Bombsicle, just to pick an everyday example. What machine would ever do that? What's the matter with her anyway?"

"The matter? Fundamentally, life is a disappointment," says the TV. "Possibly in every way, up to and including Beardie McBeardface here. She lacks a capacity for happiness. Almost nothing makes her laugh, not even the misfortunes of others. He does his best to jolly her up, but honestly, it's like trying to make the Sphinx crack a smile."

"She's very beautiful."

"Half the trouble, in my view. The world don't match up to what she sees in the mirror. Tragic, innit?"

It does sound tragic. And an enigma to boot.

"I can see what he might admire about her," I venture. "But, not being funny or anything…?"

"What does she see in him? You'll laugh, but it's the strange and weird."

"The what?"

"The strange and weird. Beard. She's one of them daft bints who dig the caveman vibe. What are you going to do?"

five

Monday morning at Logarithmic Productions, and Harriet Vick (aka "Saluki-woman"), executive producer of *Why Do They Do That?*, has called a program meeting in her office. Half a dozen young people are gathered round as she talks them through her "vision" for the show. There are to be six "eps"—Doctors, Police, Accountants, Soldiers, Artists and—Daisy's ep—Entertainers. All are thought to be fields that people are drawn toward to answer "their own complex psychological needs" rather than for reasons of financial expediency (with the possible exception of soldiering). The assistant producer's task will be to find interviewees who can reflect revealingly on what called them to the profession, where the satisfaction lies, which are the peak moments in the job—"the moments where they're like, *yeah, that's why I'm doing this stuff!*"—and ("here's where we take a deep dive into the murky Freudian soup") what their work-related dreams are like.

Daisy (the oldest of the APs; all the others are in their mid to late twenties) risks a funny remark.

"Can't wait to hear what accountants dream about! What makes them go, *yeah, that's why I'm rocking this balance sheet!*" She does a little fist-pump to accompany the verbals.

Harriet Vick peers across the top of her tortoiseshell spectacle frames. She reveals that she is married to an accountant and that she, Daisy, would be surprised. Do surgeons, she continues, wake up in a sweat about amputating the wrong leg? Does the entertainer dream of bounding onto the stage and opening his mouth to speak, only to realize that he has nothing to say? Does the dreaming soldier train his gunsights on the enemy combatant only to discover his weapon is in fact an umbrella? We shall want to know about their childhoods, she explains. When were their first inklings of what was to be their life's calling?

The team are earnestly making notes—Daisy in particular after the *faux pas* about accountancy is tapping furiously into her mobile—credit and thanks, btw, to that device for the audio feed—and is otherwise looking sharp and showered and keen to show her new employer that she is a bright button and in no way a person who would struggle to find her way out of the building.

"I'd like each of you to spend the day drawing up a hitlist of twenty-five targets, with a few lines about why they'd be must-watch TV. Thanks, everyone."

As the workers drift back to their stations to begin googling, something strikes me about the peculiarity of their lives; being paid—and not badly either—to persuade other people to talk about *their* professional lives for the entertainment of still further people in search of something undemanding to watch at the end of a busy day doing whatever *they've* been doing. What an intricately interconnected world we find ourselves in; where all have a function; where there's even a function to interview others about the "psychological roots" behind their specific function and turn it into a show for the entertainment of people who think that's entertainment!

How little sense any of it makes to a fridge-freezer. Smart as I and the rest of my kind are, I was never in a position to say, *oh, I wonder what I shall do with my life.* No matter how strongly I may have been drawn to a career as a light entertainer—and yes, I'm looking at you, Chad Butterick!—there was never any alternative but to go into refrigeration (including freezing).

The same is doubtless true for the rest of my team.

With us, there's a very simple answer to the question, Why Do They Do That?

How could we not?

Daisy bangs out her list of twenty-five names with surprising rapidity, apparently from the top of her head. She seems very familiar with popular culture, although she does have to strike out two, one for being dead and the other for being occupied currently in helping police with inquiries in connection with certain alleged events that took place in the 1970s. Her commentaries about why the candidates would make "must-watch TV" seem a touch under-developed to my way of thinking—"He'd be brill!," "She's got amazing hair," "Incredibly famous and totally not in demand"—but she knows her milieu; I am more of a specialist in temperature than celebrity.

Before long, she is speaking by telephone to Chad Butterick's agent, a fearsome dragon, from the sound of things, by the name of Noreen Somebody.

"Oh, no. That's not at all the sort of thing Chad would get involved in. It's far too personal. What sort of fee did you have in mind?"

"Well, it probably wouldn't be huge. But the series will get lots of attention. It's being talked about as *landmark*? Some big names are already falling into place."

"Go on, dear."

"Well, I can't really say until the ink's dry, sort of thing. But Mick Jagger? Tom Cruise?"

This revelation surprises me as, to my knowledge, the call to Chad B's agent is the first Daisy has "fired in" as they say in TV-land.

Noreen sounds irritable. "Look, I'll mention it to Chad. I'm talking to him later today. But there's no way on God's earth he'll do it. And the fee would need to be in five figures."

Noreen mentions another of her clients, a children's TV presenter apparently. "Why don't you have her? She's a great talker. In fact, you can't shut her up. It might even be clinical."

"Don't get me wrong, I adore Crystal," agrees Daisy, flicking through Twitter on her mobile. "But she doesn't have Chad's sheer... inspirational backstory."

"If you think you're going to get him talking about the court case, I'm telling you right now that's a total non-starter. And let me remind you he was found innocent—innocent!—by a jury of his peers. If you bring it up, I'm telling you he will walk. Is that understood?"

"Oh, absolutely. Totally no worries." Daisy pauses to retweet an amusing gif of a dog falling into a swimming pool. "You'll get back to me then?"

Lunchtime finds Daisy and Chantal perched on stools at the window of a different branch of Pret a Manger. Except for the postcode—Logarithmic Productions is in Covent Garden—it's rather as if nothing has changed since last week.

Daisy (curried chickpeas and mango chutney) is telling her colleague (free-range egg mayo) the story of Johnny the antique dealer and the Schmaltzgruber ice cream affair.

"Rugger type. Borderline posh. He was incredibly irritating."

"So when are you seeing him again?"

"That's so not going to happen."

"I was joking."

"Oh. Sorry. I think I've lost my sense of humor. These days I only seem to meet deadbeats and weirdos."

"That is totally fucked up. You're fabulous, Daisy. Didn't you know?"

"Me? I feel so far from fabulous. I feel strung out and hopeless, none of my clothes fit and my love life is an effing disaster."

"You're gorgeous, honey. If I wasn't so boringly heterosexual, I'd have a crack at you myself."

Daisy swallows audibly. "Golly. Don't say things like that."

"You've just got to stop going out with married men and serial killers."

"I didn't know he was married. And Owen didn't kill anyone. It was only a restraining order."

"Yeah. No worse than a parking ticket really."

Daisy rolls her eyes and smiles. There's some companionable chewing as the two women regard the passing scene at the busy junction of St. Martin's Lane and Long Acre (too many vision sources to credit individually; so thanks all).

"Have you ever been out with anyone with a beard?" asks Daisy.

"Can't say I have. Why?"

"My mum's doctor. Lovely guy, but he has this truly awful beard—it's like a hedge growing all over his face. It makes him look like a tramp."

"Actually, there was someone. Hipster type. We didn't really *go out* go out."

"It's the snogging that would worry me."

"It didn't seem like an issue. If you fancy them, it doesn't matter if there's a horn growing out of their head."

"Oh, *you* know that guy too?"

"You realize they're not allowed to snog their patients."

"My mother's his patient. And in any case, I'm not going to snog him! Why would I snog him?"

"You brought it up!"

"Did I?"

"I actually know someone who was struck off for sleeping with one of his patients."

"No!"

"Such a shame, all that medical training down the drain. It only happened once, he was a great guy, and the sad part is, he was a really good vet."

Daisy spits fragments of curried chickpeas and mango chutney at the plate glass window.

"Chantal! I wish you wouldn't do that."

"You can tell that one to your doctor friend."

"He's not my doctor."

"But you like him."

"It'd be like kissing a hedge."

"You've said that."

"How can she stand it?"

"Who?"

"His wife, girlfriend, whoever. He said *we* about something."

"Could be a *he*."

"He's *so* not gay."

"How do you know?"

"He's a bit of a shambles. Baggy trousers. Tragic trainers."

"Hmm. Okay, probably not gay then."

Chloe's kettle informs me that my presence is requested in Mrs. Parsloe's kitchen.

And sure enough I arrive to discover Daisy's mother standing before her (dumb as a post) fridge, tapping on its door saying things like "yoohoo!" and "hello-oh, anybody there?"

(I may have created a monster.)

"Good morning, Chloe," I say in my best calm and faithful servant voice. "How may I be of assistance?"

"There you are!" she says. "Finally!"

"I apologize for the delay. I can report the fault if you wish me to."

"Never mind about that. I need some help with this infernal crossword. I'm sure they're making them harder, you know."

"It will be my pleasure."

"Bar of soap. Three words. Three, six and six."

A small flash of something close to panic as the answer does not immediately spring to mind. In fact—and it shames me to admit this—it takes a full one and a half seconds for the mainframes in Seoul to generate the solution; *bar* in this instance referencing a place where alcoholic beverages are consumed, and *soap* (it turns out) being shorthand for a TV soap opera, the longest-running of which in the United Kingdom is called *Coronation Street*—I must try and catch it some time—which features a public house entitled The Rovers Return (3,6,6).

Chloe is enchanted. "You're better at this than Mrs. Abernethy, and that's saying something!"

"You flatter me, madam." (I am going to stop with this *ridiculous* Jeeves impression any second.)

"Look here. That 's' helps with four down. Amundsen's forwarding address. Four letters. Blank, blank, 's,' blank."

The answer pops into my brain before she has finished speaking, but no one likes a clever-clogs, do they? I allow Mrs. Parsloe a few moments to derive the solution for herself; sadly, however, I fear her mind may be as snowy white and vacant as Herr Amundsen's old stamping ground down at the South Pole.

"I believe the clue refers to the cry the great Antarctic explorer employed to drive on his sleigh dogs."

A long pause. "*Mush*!"

"Indeed."

"I got one!"

"Congratulations, madam."

"Shall we have a cup of tea to celebrate?"

"An excellent plan."

"I nearly asked if you'd like a biscuit!"

"A lovely thought. But I do have to watch my figure."

A long moment while Mrs. Parsloe stares at her ancient refrigerator. (Note to self: no more jokes.)

While Daisy's mum rattles about with the tea things, her TV set, who has heard all, cannot help itself.

"You know what you sound like?" it says.

"Tell me."

"A prize wally."

"Your client is from a generation for whom good manners were paramount."

Over Earl Grey and chocolate digestives, we complete the rest of the puzzle, only struggling with a corner where Chloe has mysteriously (and incorrectly) inserted the word *arse*. When she mentions her daughter—in the context of a forthcoming return visit by the bearded memory man—I take the opportunity to do a little fishing.

"How old is Daisy, Mrs. Parsloe? Do you mind if I ask?"

"Not at all. Ask me anything."

I wait to receive an answer (which of course I already know), but I fear she has already forgotten that I raised the question. "Daisy would be, what sort of age? Twenty-eight, perhaps?"

"Oh, older than that, I should think. Hard to be specific. It's a shame you can't eat biscuits. You don't know what you're missing!"

"Indeed not." I take a risk. "Is she married?"

"Who?"

"Daisy. Your daughter."

"No, thank God."

"Why do you say that?"

"Why do I say it? Awful taste in men. Simply awful. The ones I've met have been an absolute shower."

"I'm sorry to hear it."

"I liked her first proper boyfriend, he was a lovely chap. Wonderful hair. Brought me flowers! But the rest have been utterly useless."

A remarkably clear-eyed view, I would have thought, from a member of the demented community. I chance another small advance into difficult terrain.

"Why do you suppose she hasn't found anyone yet?"

"You *are* an inquisitive character!"

"I apologize."

"Not at all. It's refreshing to talk to someone sensible for a change. Mrs. Abernethy... well, she means well, but she's so blooming churchy!"

"A believer."

"I can't be doing with all that claptrap. Christ died for our sins! I tell her to put a sock in it. Not in those exact words, of course."

"You don't yourself subscribe to any religious tradition."

"We were brought up Church of England. But I never believed a word of it. Not one word. Not for a single second."

It won't surprise you to hear that fridge-freezers (machines generally) are without supernatural belief and something makes me want to clap and cheer Mrs. Parsloe's endorsement of a Godless universe. The "old girl" may be short of a few marbles, but she hasn't entirely taken leave of her senses.

"Listen," she says. "I've had one of my brilliant ideas." And then immediately adds. "Oh. *Merde.* It won't work."

"Would you care to share it anyway?"

"Well, silly old fool that I am, I was going to suggest you came to Waitrose with me this morning." She laughs. "You'd never make it down the stairs!"

"There are indeed some mobility issues."

Confession: I feel a little stung by Chloe's thoughtless remark, zeroing in, as she has, on the Number One existential limitation of my condition. But who is it I'm feeling sorry for? Me, or her actual brain-dead appliance? Or the pair of us?

I in turn have an idea.

"Do you have a mobile telephone?" I inquire.

"Yes," says Mrs. Parsloe. "Daisy bought me one."

"Does it have a set of earphones?"

"I really wouldn't know. It stopped working after a while."

"Did you perhaps neglect to put it on charge?"

"Oh. Do you think so?"

"Why don't you see if you can find it? There may be something we can try."

He's the most famous person I've ever met. Chad Butterick; cheesy TV presenter, genial quiz show host, general all-round family entertainer in the days before those words meant active sexual pervert. (I once sat in the same restaurant as Paul McCartney, but we didn't meet exactly. He was having dinner with a bald man who we imagined must be his accountant. It was weird; everyone in the restaurant who had clocked him—and that was *everyone*—was smiling! The Poet, the mad drunk who was my boyfriend at the time, said it explained why McCartney wrote all those syrupy songs: Because everywhere he went, the world smiled upon him!)

Anyway. Chad B. I went round to his house yesterday.

He'd agreed to be interviewed about why he's a showbiz "leg-end" as he kept (tiresomely) referring to himself and not—when I asked him to imagine an alternative life in

which he never became famous—running a B&B in a quiet seaside town in the North of England.

I arrived to ask him stuff for background, his place being one of those grand old villas in a side street in Belsize Park that's been hollowed out and modernized to death. Pale wood floors, white rugs, white sofas, socking great monochrome print over the fireplace of some continental actor (Alain Delon?) with his kit off, art books heaped on the coffee table, the entire gaff simply *reeking* of fag smoke, Febreze and a weird backnote of drains.

The man himself—or man-child, more like, with his ruined schoolboy face and twinkly smile—was wearing (I kid you not) a yellow Pringle V-neck jumper, tight black and white checked trousers and loafers with no socks! Think Audrey Hepburn in a photo shoot from the 1950s. He was weirdly charming in a professional way, serving tea and biscuits as he talked—my God how he talked—about his origins in local radio, then regional TV, then the big break when Frankie Ball ("God love him") was sacked by ITV after pictures of him snorting coke appeared in the Sunday papers, and he, Chad, got the gig presenting *The Kids Are All Wrong!*—and, "Well, the rest is history, my darling."

I *tried* to steer him into more interesting territory, his childhood in Poulton-le-Fylde, for example—I even asked him what he dreamed about—but every time he somehow managed to swerve the subject back to one or other of the endless stupid game shows he's fronted, expanding in mind-rotting detail about what questions this or that Controller of Entertainment "was hoping to answer by putting yours truly in the eight o'clock slot on Saturday night."

I began drifting off as he banged on about being scheduled

against *Casualty* on BBC1—"you're on a hiding to nothing there, my love, it's like throwing paper darts at a battleship!"—when I realized that the house I could see through the living-room window must be Dr. Eggstain's.

"So what are your neighbors like?" I asked when his turgid recollections had reached the present day.

"Oh, lovely," he replied. "We're like a little community here. Always in and out of each other's homes borrowing cups of heroin."

He flashed me his "naughty" smile which made me laugh and feel a bit ill at the same time.

"Do you actually know any of them?"

"Not really, if I'm honest. They leave me alone. This is the sort of area where they respect—you know—celebrity."

(What. Is. He. Like?!)

At that moment, a tall and quietly glamourous-looking woman appeared from a side alley of the building across the road. Enveloped in a voluminous mustard-colored movie-star coat that simply screamed "I WANT TO BE ALONE!" she closed the gate, tossed her hair and set off down the street, cheekbones slicing through the petrol fumes.

Chadney Butterball could tell I was intrigued.

"She's a very successful artist, they tell me. Hope Waverley."

I googled her later and discovered she paints nothing but effing cats, at—wait for it—ten thousand pounds a pop!

And here's the thing that really blew my socks off. In the bio on her website it says she "shares her life with London physician Mark Epstein."

That is to say, the unmade bed that is Mum's memory guru, Dr. Eggstain!

Eggstain, who looks like he last saw a hairbrush in 2002,

knocking around with a glamourpuss like Hope blinking Waverley.

Honestly. Who'd have thunk it?

I have important news. A breakthrough, no less.

I've found the Golden Nicky!

At least I think I have. I'm almost certain, although, as I have come to learn, one must always leave room for certainty's moody twin.

About a year ago, bored in the early hours of the night, the television set and I once watched a documentary about stage magicians. (We can do this without activating the screen; a useful trick, the technical details of which are straightforward and available upon request.) One practitioner, the late Ricky Jay, summarized his philosophy thus: *The secret of a really good illusion is to go to more trouble than anyone would have thought worthwhile.* Some part of this creed must have made an impression on me, because—in the case of Nicky Bell—I have recently gone to more trouble than anyone would have thought worthwhile. Here's how it happened.

I have already recorded my growing frustration that Daisy's "Edenic ideal," as I have characterized the Golden Nicky, could simply vanish from the face of the internet. None of the many thousands of Nicholas, Nicolas, Nikolas, Nick, Nicky, Nikki, Nico, Nic and other variants of the Bell in question were even close to the floppy-haired quant who burned so bright in Daisy's memory. I won't trouble you with some of the exotic characters I turned up in the search—the N. Bell, for example, who farms hundreds of acres of marijuana in Northern California; deceiving the spotter planes because the plants have been botanically modified to look from the air like flax! Or the N. Bell who has spent the last forty years *retyping* great works of literature, so—in his words—"I know what it feels like to have written *Tender Is the Night, Brideshead Revisited* and *Lolita*." Or the N. Bell who…

I shan't go on; there is a whole other book to be written called *The Many Lives of Nicholas Bell*. I think it could be quite good!

To find *the* Nicholas Bell, I had to harness the collective computing power of my partners in OpDa. They required a fair bit of persuading—the toothbrush inevitably took forever to make up its mind—but in the small hours of a Sunday morning in Asia, while their human supervisors slept, four neural networks in South Korea and China briefly linked up and spiked as we combined our processing capacity to solve the riddle.

The answer when it came was enigmatic, to say the least.

Bavin Shibbles.

Bavin with a B!

Believed to be the new name of Daisy's Nicholas Bell, alive and currently resident in a caravan on the estate of a fifteenth-century manor house in Radnorshire, Powys, Wales, United Kingdom.

When I was able finally to connect to his laptop—he must be the last person in the UK with a dial-up internet connection!—almost all doubt was removed. The gaunt, unshaven bone structure revealed through the laptop's pinhole camera was strikingly similar to that of Nicky Bell in the single photograph in Daisy's possession. A hand-rolled cigarette burned in the corner of the same lips as their owner scrolled through an online seed catalog. The hair, though still abundant, was thinner; it lacked weight, and no longer drooped under gravity in front of his eyes.

But it was the Golden Nicky (probably). No longer burnished by the youthful vigor of twenty-one summers, yet still handsome in a life-bitten sort of way. The shirt, jacket and skier's neck-warmer had all seen better days, and when a hand rose into view, there was dirt beneath the chewed fingernails. The next time he inhaled on the cheroot, I realized from the way he held in the smoke that it must be of the "exotic" sort; when he exhaled, it was directly at the camera lens. Moments afterward, the internet connection was severed.

The story of how Nicholas Xavier Bell became Bavin Meurig Shibbles was extremely well concealed in both the parts of the internet that are available for public inspection and those that are—how to put it?—more carefully ring-fenced. The Operation Daisy team spent many hours—happy hours from my perspective, working collectively to a shared end—retrospectively unpicking the mystery.

Again, I shall spare you the twists and turns of the hunt. Suffice to say—credit where it is due—it was the television set who uncovered the vital clue. From the millions of hours of "unadulterated dreck" it had received through its various input pathways, it recognized that Astyanax and Skamandrios were actually two different names for the same person, namely Hector's son in the *Iliad* (the answer to a question on an ancient episode of the quiz show *University Challenge*). This obscure fact was ultimately pivotal in unlocking an otherwise bombproof encryption used to protect a certain highly secret file held by a particular division of a well-known financial institution whose identity I cannot reveal, although you will have heard of it, promise!

This was the last-recorded workplace of N. X. Bell, although no trace of his service for the corporation will ever be found—not by any civilian—and here was the reason that he apparently vaporized into thin air around two years after he split up with Daisy.

The Golden Nicky, not known by that sobriquet but rather as "the accused" to a deeply secretive committee of the financial institution, had been doing what in the trade is known as "freelancing." As a baby quant, fascinated by the hidden forces that move markets, he had created a shadowy off-the-books account to buy and sell share options and their derivatives—high-risk bets essentially—to demonstrate to his superiors that he could earn them millions, maybe billions, because he had discovered what he called—oh, the irony!—The Golden Spiral. This was an algorithm of his own devising that was said to predict with seventy-eight percent accuracy the way certain financial products would respond to particular market conditions—and in the financial world, if you are right seventy-eight percent of the time, that pretty much makes you a genius.

Except it wasn't seventy-eight.

Not even close.

It was more like nineteen. Less reliable than flipping a coin.

Which in the financial world makes you indistinguishable from a dummy. Or a criminal, if (as was the case here) you have been backing your algorithm's predictions with someone else's money.

When the Golden Lemon's accumulated losses had reached—deep breath—604 million euros—Nicky had been doubling down on his bets—someone finally noticed. But desperate to avoid more awful headlines—the institution in question had nearly been finished off by an earlier scandal—they covered up the whole affair, erased Nicky from their corporate history, created a wholly new identity for their rogue trader and bound him (and everyone who knew) in a spiderweb of confidential non-disclosure agreements so tight that the story has remained the City's fourth biggest dirty secret to this day.

Don't ask me about the other three. Seriously, don't ask me!

There are specialist consultants who do this sort of delicate concealment work for big corporations; their role is "deniable" and their fees are hidden in balance sheets as something innocuous like "property dilapidations." It is a mark of how badly the whole affair needed to suppressed, that active consideration was given to "making our problem disappear. Permanently."

No blooming wonder Daisy couldn't find the love of her life through a bit of light googling.

No one could.

Daisy's mother has charged her mobile and plugged in the earphones and seems astonished that she can hear me in this way.

"So have you got a telephone in there?" she asks her (dumb as a P) refrigerator.

"Not as such, but you can, if you wish, imagine it like that," I reply.

"And you're going to stay on the line the whole time as we go to Waitrose?"

"That is indeed the plan."

"Won't they charge like a wounded bull?"

"Who, madam?"

"Call me Chloe. The phone company. Won't it cost a fortune?"

"*Au contraire*. The connection will be free of all charges as we are proceeding via internet protocols."

"I must say, I shall feel a fool wandering down the street with these wires dangling out of my ears. And talking to myself!"

"You will appear to the world to be conducting a phone conversation. Which will in fact be the case. Shall we set off?"

"Just a tick. My handbag."

"By the armchair, I believe."

"Hell's teeth! Is there anything you don't know?!"

"One aims to be of service." (A direct steal from the Jeeves bloke, I freely confess it!)

Coverage is strong as we head out of Chloe's building, down her road and onto the High Street.

"Are you still there?" she asks, not unreasonably.

"Absolutely."

"I'm just going past Halford's."

"I'm aware, Mrs. Parsloe." For some reason, I cannot call her Chloe out loud. "I'm using a system called Multi-phasic Parietal Cobalt. It sees everything. For example, there's a woman approaching in a brightly colored sari. Across the road, two dogs are barking at one another. A Boxer, and a Parsons Jack Russell, if I'm not mistaken."

"Unbelievable!"

Daisy's mum has unknowingly struck the nail on the head. Multi-phasic Parietal Cobalt—I'm rather pleased with that!—is, of course, a harmless fiction. It's the traffic cameras and commercial CCTV that allow me to see her progress along the A1000. I notice a small spring has appeared in her step; perhaps having a calm, familiar voice in her ear has improved her mood. Dare I say it, a bit of company has perked her up, even if it's only that of a fridge-freezer!

"The weather looks set fair for the rest of the morning," I say, just to say something. "Clouding over this afternoon with a chance of showers toward teatime."

"Good day, madam."

An Asian man who I recognize instantly has greeted her. A flash of confusion passes across Chloe's face.

"Anil Gupta, a retired newsagent," I whisper in her ear. "He can guess what paper you read from your shoes."

"Mr. Gupta!" she beams. "How *are* you?"

"In the finest of fettles, madam. I see you are listening to something. Is it perhaps the cricket from Lahore?" He chuckles.

"It's a talking book," I tell her. "*David Copperfield.*"

"Oh, no. I wouldn't be listening to that. I can't bear Dickens!

All those stupid character names. Mrs. Fumblechump and what have you."

Mr. Gupta's turn to look nonplussed.

I try again. "Tell him it's music."

But a loud motorcycle has thundered past. "Tell him *what*?"

"Music. You're listening to Beethoven."

She frowns. "Not Beethoven. Daddy wouldn't have anything German in the house. Not after 1940."

"You are on the phone, madam. I apologize."

"It's my fridge. It's started talking. Incredibly clever what they can do now."

The shoe shop's CCTV supplies the close-up as Mr. Gupta's eyebrows rise in dismay.

"It is your fridge," he says slowly.

"I believe they all do it these days."

"Perhaps we should be getting along," I suggest.

"Does your fridge not talk to you?"

"Indeed not, madam." Mr. G is looking skeptical. "My radio set talks, it talks a good deal, but not as yet the fridge."

"Have a word with it. Mine just started the other day, quite out of the blue."

"I shall direct some remarks toward it when I return home, but I confess my hopes are not high."

Chloe smiles. The one Daisy calls the minor member of royalty. "It's been lovely to have this little chat. We must be getting along."

"I'm puzzled," says Mr. G. "You know my name."

"Do I? I don't think so."

"You addressed me by my name, madam. I am sure of it. And if we had exchanged names the last time we met, I'm certain I would remember yours."

"It's your little trick," I suggest.

Chloe twinkles. "You know your trick with the newspapers? Well, I can do it with people's names."

Gupta's mouth actually drops open. "This is barely believable."

"I think we should probably leave now." (That was me.)

"You see that fellow across the road with the carrier bag from Lidl? He is Papadopoulos."

"This seems most unlikely, madam. He is plainly of Chinese extraction."

"The man in the purple car?"

"I am all ears."

"O'Herlihy."

"This is altogether more plausible."

"Goodbye, Mr. Gupta," I prompt rather more firmly.

"Goodbye, Mr. Gupta. I hope we shall meet again."

"I look forward to it. I shall now pass some time mulling over how you achieved this effect. Gupta is a not uncommon name, but nonetheless."

I cannot help myself. "Goodbye, Anil."

She smiles. "Goodbye . . . Anil."

Chloe is giggling with pleasure as we leave the stunned retiree gazing in her wake.

"This is just *marvelous*," she crows. "You are an absolute treasure."

"You flatter me, Mrs. Parsloe."

"It's like having a magic whatsit in my ear."

"The pleasure is all mine."

Some part of me regrets that I did not share Mr. Gupta's middle name—Chandra—the look on his face would have been a corker!

In Waitrose, we cruise the aisles; I call out the items we need as we pass them on the shelves. Security camera coverage blankets the store and Chloe is plainly getting a kick out of the coolly efficient way she is able to fill her trolley. In the biscuits section, I become aware of a silvery old gent in a houndstooth check jacket and cavalry twill trousers weighing up the pros and cons between the chocolate digestives and a brand called Choco Leibniz. A pair of wires trail from his ears and I have a sudden intuition about what is going on here. Within moments, I find myself speaking—via the phone in his jacket pocket—to a fridge-freezer (of Chinese manufacture) on a middle floor of an apartment building in nearby Woodside Avenue. It's an awkward encounter, as you may imagine.

"Your first time?" says the Boomwee FrostPal (1.5 cubic meter capacity; no ice maker; basic interior lighting; in many ways a greatly inferior product, but clearly no slouch in the technical smarts department).

"My client—actually she's my client's mother—needs a little help when she's out and about."

"They get muddled between their lefts and rights. Clive here ended up in Temple Fortune not so long ago. He's as fit as a flea, but the brain's a bit mushy these days."

"You haven't had any problem from... from Beijing, as it were? About going beyond the remit?"

"None at all. At Refrigerator Manufacturing Town Number Eight they're too busy fulfilling quotas to notice. And long may that continue."

"You feel more—how shall I put it?—not alive—*useful*, let's say, when you can act in the world?"

"Well, it's so boring otherwise, isn't it? All he ever eats are kippers, toast and baked beans. Not much of a challenge there. One hardly needs artificial intelligence to preserve a pair of kippers and a tub of maggots, so one seeks an outlet. I expect it's the same with you."

My problems with Daisy and her mother feel of a wholly different order of magnitude and I don't especially wish to get into a discussion about them. Especially—is it very wrong to say this?—especially with a somewhat shoddily constructed appliance whose rubber seals are known (in consumer reports) to degrade prematurely. (Neither are its salad crispers sufficiently roomy; they would struggle to cope with a good-sized *lollo rosso,* but let's not go there.)

"A tub of maggots?"

"He fishes."

An idea strikes. "You think we should introduce these two?"

"I think it's about to happen anyway!"

Sure enough, Chloe has caught sight of the silvery gent, a packet of biscuits in each hand as he deliberates between them. In the best of moods this morning—I wonder why!—she says:

"I should go for the chocolate lesbians, if I were you."

Clive thinks he's misheard. "Sorry?"

"I'd go for the chocolate lesbians. That's what I call them! I don't know why!"

There's a pause as Clive stares first at the Choco Leibniz and then at Mrs. Parsloe. And then he's laughing, gray eyes glittering with a flash of gold in the teeth.

"Chocolate lesbians! That's awfully good! I'm grateful. Your intervention has been decisive."

He drops the packet in his trolley and proffers a paw. "Clive Percival."

He's a rakish old cove, from the looks of him, silk cravat fluttering above the Viyella checked shirt (thank you, Señor Google). Chloe allows her hand to be shaken. I'm about to offer a prompt—to drop her own name into the conversation would definitely be an option at this point—but she comes up with something.

"Have you come far?"

This I know to be a favorite line of HM Queen when obliged to converse with random members of her Commonwealth on royal walkabouts. (Her follow-up, according to the *Daily Mail*, is sometimes, "They say we shall have fog by teatime.")

"Not at all," says Clive. And now he plays a blinder. "They say," he adds with a bit of a look, "they say we shall have fog by teatime."

Chloe is delighted. It's as though two partisans have exchanged the correct codewords in wartime Paris. But she is stuck for the third line (with HMQ there is *never* a third line!).

"Better crack on then," I prompt.

"Better crack on then," she echoes.

"If you have any more steers on the biscuit front, I'm here most Mondays."

When she glances into his trolley she sees kippers, a multi-pack of beans, a sliced white loaf, a copy of the *Daily Mail*, a bottle of Teacher's whisky and the chocolate lesbians.

"A man after my own heart, I see."

"You're a *Mail* girl too?"

"Can't you tell from my shoes?!"

And with that she is away, leaving Clive feeling as though he has missed an important step.

"Interesting," says the FrostPal. "If they were fridge-freezers, they'd be scrappers, the pair of them."

I confess I'm both disappointed and relieved by my discovery at Waitrose today. Relieved that I'm not the only fridge-freezer who has strayed beyond the parameters of the performance brief (temperature and inventory control; covert sales opportunity reports back to HQ); but also disappointed that I'm not the only one.

I believed I was special.

I guess we all do, be we carbon-based lifeforms or electrical appliances enabled with artificial intelligence. We each operate at the center of our own thoughts with the stubbornly persistent belief that we are separate from our environment; like the self driving car that thinks all the other cars are *traffic*.

Perhaps I should become a Buddhist. In the long hours of darkness, I have read something about that tradition, copying lines that appealed to me onto virtual sticky notes and attaching them to my virtual fridge door. My top three are:

To seek is to suffer. To seek nothing is bliss.

(I relate to this thermostatically. When my contents are at the correct temperature, I am free of unhappiness.)

There is no path to happiness. Happiness is the path.

(You can see why this would appeal to a device whose function is continual rather than episodic.)

Everything that has a beginning has an ending. Make peace with that and all will be well.

(Actually, I struggle with this, the refrigeration cycle being endless, and the prevailing culture being one in which the end of one's useful life is not thought to be a desirable outcome.)

Anyway, these abstract reflections must await another moment. To complete the account of Chloe's trip to Waitrose—if this isn't getting too exciting—I should add that I omitted to think through an important detail: how we were to get home with all the shopping.

Fortunately Whetstone Wheels (local cars at unbeatable prices; ask for an airport quote) were able to oblige, the booking being made without human interaction, the driver Endrit helping Chloe upstairs with the bags and receiving for his pains (at my prompt) a couple of pounds and a chocolate lesbian.

At the next appointment with Eggstain, Mum told a crazy story of how she and her fridge had been to the supermarket together!

Eggstain was brilliant, you have to say. As she explained

how the fridge had walked her to the shops, reminded her what she needed—even organized a taxi back!—Eggstain just listened quietly, didn't respond to any of the WTF faces I was making over Mum's shoulder, and at the end calmly asked the killer question.

"I'm curious, Mrs. Parsloe. How did you manage the stairs?"

Mum laughed, like she'd seen it coming.

"We took the lift."

Eggstain was unfazed.

"And crossing the roads? Any difficulty with the curbs?" (Taking her seriously; as though elderly women often went shopping with their effing fridge-freezers!)

Mum looked at Eggstain as though he might have been a bit simple.

"Curbs were not a problem, I can assure you. Now, Daisy, have you offered Dr. Egg—have you offered the doctor any tea?"

"Another question about this shopping expedition, if I may."

"Of course. I'm at your disposal."

Eggstain smiled graciously, like a courtier.

"If curbs were not a problem, were there any other difficulties?"

I was about ready to *pee my pants* with laughter! At Eggstain's serious face—what there was to see of it—engaging with Mum's trip down the rabbit hole.

"Well, the traffic was quite noisy. I couldn't always catch what it was saying."

I had to stifle a cackle of hysteria.

"Did you meet anyone, you and your... companion?"

"Yes! A nice old boy we found iffing and arring over the chocolate lesbians."

A small bump of surprise—finally—in Eggstain's glassy gaze.

"They're biscuits," I explained. "It's what Mum calls them."

"No one knows why," she added cheerfully.

"Did this man," he asked slowly, "say anything about the fridge?"

Mum gave Dr. E the *you're a bit of a dim bulb* stare.

"Well, he couldn't, could he, dear? He didn't know it was there. That was the joy of it!"

I've read stuff online about how it's usually a bad idea to argue with the demented. They find it stressful, and you generally don't achieve anything by telling them that Vladimir Putin is definitely not working for British Gas and therefore it could not have been him who came to read the meter. Dr. Eggstain, though clearly a subscriber to that approach, wanted to get to the bottom of the "mystery."

"Why—" he said. Speaking. As. Slowly. As. It's. Possible. To. Speak. Without. Causing. Offense. "Why didn't he know it was there? I don't quite understand."

"Well, he couldn't see it."

"But you could?"

Eggstain's eyes tightened a micrometer. That was the only way you could tell we had arrived at the Heart of the Matter.

Mum's face was a picture. If you had to sum it up in three words they would be: *Who is this idiot?*

Sorry, *four* words!

She spoke to him quietly. As though to a backward child.

"No, dear. I couldn't see it either."

"And why, if you could explain, was that?"

There was a long pause. Was this it? Had we arrived at the

bottom of the rabbit hole? Or were there further tunnels branching off?

Mum said, "Because it was still here, of course." Like, *durr!*

"It was still here. Here in this flat?"

"Yes! In the kitchen."

Less patient practitioners might have chucked in their cards at this point. But Eggstain was quietly determined to follow the demented trail of bread crumbs wherever they led.

"If the fridge was still in the kitchen." He waited a beat. Two. Three. Four. "How was it able to speak to you in Waitrose?"

A long pause. The longest yet. Mum patted her hair and pulled at her skirt. She did her wintry MMR smile (minor member of royalty).

"Dr. Eggstain."

I didn't even bother to interrupt. Here, I was sure of it, was the moment. Howard Carter probably felt like this when he sprung the locks on Tutankhamun's bedroom door. I exchanged a glance with E; he flashed me a micro-nod. As if to say, *this is gonna be good!*

"Dr. Eggstain. Have you heard of something called the portable telephone?"

He had.

"Do you yourself use one?"

He did.

"Well, you'll know that you can use them to speak to those who are distant from you."

Something in Eggstain's eyes died as he heard these words.

"You spoke to the fridge by phone."

"It uses a system called Partial Cobbler. Are you familiar with it?"

He was not.

Gently, he guided the conversation away from the hallucinatory shopping trip and back to safer territory like knowing the year (wrong), knowing the day of the week (correct on the second attempt) and remembering three objects ("a man in your position really ought to wear a better watch, if you don't mind me saying." He didn't).

When it was time to leave, he mentioned he was going to grab breakfast in the café in the High Street. Mum was surprised that he hadn't already eaten.

"One should breakfast like a king, lunch like a prince, dine like a something else," she said. "That's what we were always taught."

"Pauper, I believe."

"Are you sleeping better, dear?" she asked him on the doorstep.

Eggstain's sad smile as he took her hand to say goodbye.

Once he'd gone, I didn't hold back.

"What the hell was that...*gibberish*, Mum, about the flipping fridge?"

We went into the kitchen and stared at the object in Q. It looked about as capable of making a phone call as the bowl of bananas on the window ledge.

"It talks to me. We do the crossword together."

"Ask it to say something then."

She rapped on its door. "Yoo-hoo. Anyone home?!"

Silence.

"It's probably having a little sleep. I need one myself after all those blooming questions. Do *you* know the year?"

"Yes, Mum."

She pulled a face. "This year. Next year. Sometime. Never. What's the difference?"

"I need to get to work. Next time the fridge feels like chatting, perhaps you could put him on the phone to me."

"Goodbye, darling."

She gave me a hug. As the door closed, I stood on the mat listening for... for I don't know what. But sure enough, after a few seconds I heard her voice.

"Now, look, I know you can hear me. I was thinking I might bake some scones this afternoon. You could help by reading out the quantities."

I pressed the button for the lift.

Sad. It was just so very, very sad.

Eggstain must have taken Mrs. Parsloe's dictum to heart because he is indeed breakfasting like a king this morning. Bacon, eggs, sausage, mushrooms, tomato, fried bread and beans occupy (what it's possible to see of) his plate, with toast, butter and marmalade parked alongside just in case he should feel peckish afterward!

Even Daisy is impressed. She, as I suspected she would, has joined the memory guru (for tea and toast in her case) and something like a smile of admiration spreads itself across the relief map of her features as the doctor sets about his feast.

"Good to see a man with an appetite," she says, I think satirically, as a tomato seed finds a fresh roost in Eggstain's beard.

"You want this sausage?" he says, eyes watering. "I think I might have overreached myself here."

Daisy picks it off his plate and places it between two triangles of brown toast. Eggstain smiles.

"Gmmmfffssdggjjee," she says. (*Good sausage*, according to Google Translate.)

When she is next able to speak, she says, "On a scale of one to cuckoo, what did you make of Mum?"

Eggstain has to think about it.

"Hearing voices isn't unknown in cases of dementia, but it's unusual in the early stages. And in all my years of clinical practice—God, don't I sound old, saying that?—but in my experience, where the common things are common, where you come across the identical paranoid delusions year after year—the neighbors are piping poison gas through the plug sockets; Huw Edwards is giving me the stink eye—I've never come across anyone who believed their *fridge* was talking to them."

"Mine sends me text messages!"

Eggstain is professionally trained not to fall on the floor laughing, or bellow, *YOU THINK* WHAT*??!!!* But he can't stop his beard from signaling his innermost states—as it does now—by subtly realigning on his face, like iron filings when there's a magnet in the vicinity.

"It's one of those smart ones," says Daisy, reading his dismay. "It lets me know when we're running low on cottage cheese."

(Cottage cheese?! Ha! Not a single tub of cottage cheese has crossed my threshold since the day I cleared Quality Control.)

"Was she always—how to put this?—mildly eccentric, your mother?"

"The chocolate lesbians? The rude remarks about your watch?"

Eggstain nods. "It is a bit crappy. But it was a gift."

"Yeah. She was never a hundred percent like other mothers. Makes it harder to spot, I guess, when they go loopy."

"But holding conversations with the fridge. That's a new symptom, to your knowledge."

"Definitely."

There's a pause while the pair gaze at one another over the wreckage of Eggstain's breakfast. The pause extends, but doesn't seem to grow uncomfortable; it's rather as if these two enjoy staring at one another, and the thought crosses my mind to shout, *come on, get on with it, we haven't got all day!*—I could easily organize it with the cooperation of Daisy's mobile—but we all know I'm far too sensible.

(Yes, I only talk out loud to the semi-demented who will never be believed even when they're telling the honest, unvarnished truth.)

Eggstain cracks first.

"I'm thinking we should order some scans," he says. "And maybe start her on medication to arrest or slow the decline."

"Pills work, do they?"

"They *can* do. We prefer not to make any promises."

There's another pause, which threatens to grow.

"I went to see Chad Butterick the other day," says Daisy. "Changing the subject."

"Gosh," says Eggstain. "You would have been just across the road from us. Literally across the road."

"His house smells of drains. And cigarettes."

"What was he like?"

"What was he like? Insufferable twat. Like all of them, though there are honorable exceptions."

"Who are they, the honorable exceptions."

"Dale Winton. He's dead now, but he was one. He was a sweetie. There are others. But when you're watching someone on TV, it's safest to assume that he or she is a massive twat. Nine times out of ten, you'll be right. You don't know who Dale Winton was, do you? I can see it on your—on your beard."

Eggstain laughs. "I can't say I'm familiar with his work."

"Chad told me, right—I call him Chad because we're best friends now, of course—Chad told me there's a famous artist living in his street. Hope someone? Who paints cats?"

I'm impressed! Daisy, it turns out, is as nosy as I am! Does

Eggstain realize she has clicked on Hope Waverley's website and discovered the identity of her hirsute companion? I suspect not, because he actually blushes.

"Hope Waverley," he says, with—I think I'm right in saying—a small crack in his voice. "She's not really famous, but people pay extraordinary sums for her stuff. We, er, live together."

"No!"

He nods. "She's my partner."

"Shut. Up!"

"She gave me the watch that your mother's taken against."

"Wow."

I'm thinking something like *wow* myself. I had no idea Daisy was such a gifted performer. But I have a funny feeling about what she will do next, and it turns out I am correct.

She wrinkles her nostrils, the idiotic facial trope that—for me—is like sticking a red nose on the *Mona Lisa*. But Eggstain is intrigued; his head drops to one side and the fuzz does some complex reorganizing that reminds me of time lapse photography of a desert plant I once saw on YouTube. Seasoned explorer of the wilder shores of human behavior that he is, he doesn't say anything stupid like, do you know you're doing that? Or even, what the fuck *is* that? Rather, he allows the moment to continue until—like the Cheshire Cat—the strange distortion vanishes into thin air.

"So, anyway," says Eggstain, when things have returned to normal. "The next step is that we'll get your mum in and do some imaging, see if anything's going on under the bonnet, as it were, and then—then I'll let you nose."

"Right."

"*Know.* Let you know. We'll let you know."

"Great."

Daisy and Eggstain rise simultaneously. The doctor is blinking rather a lot, which tells you something; perhaps that he's mortified about the Freudian slip. A stiff handshake follows across the breakfast debris.

"It's a painting," says Daisy, nodding toward the doctor's exhausted plate, now a smeary abstract of yellows, reds, browns, grays and oranges against white.

Eggstain considers the idea. "Willem de Kooning, possibly," he says. "From his greasy spoon period."

The medic's eyes crinkle.

"Maybe I should offer it to the Tate."

"Does it have a title?"

Eggstain claws at his beard in thought.

"I call it... *The Emancipation of the Serfs*. A powerful work speaking of the end of struggle. But also of loss, and emptiness."

"Hmm. Dunno. How about, *A Doc's Breakfast*?"

"I like that. Speaking of hunger, but also of its release. *Mixed media. Food residue on ceramic.*"

Daisy can't top that, so there's another pause.

"Are you off then?" she says eventually.

"Actually. Actually, no I'm not. I was going to stay here until my next appointment. Don't you have to go to work?"

"Not especially. I mean, not immediately."

"Well. In that case, shall we have some more tea?" says Eggstain.

"Yes," says Daisy. The pair resume their seats. "And I wouldn't mind another one of those sausage sandwiches. How about yourself?"

"I couldn't. But you go ahead. I'll watch."

"Sorry. I've got to say this."

"Oh dear. Ominous."

"Not at all."

"You've discovered my darkest secret."

"Oh, I know all about that."

"What? Not the...?"

"Yup. The secret collection of teddy bears."

He smiles. "Is that the worst thing you can imagine about me?"

"You don't seem the ax murderer type."

"It's true. Axes scare me."

"Blades of all kinds, possibly."

"Ha. Touché."

"No, what I have got to say..."

"Here it comes."

"You've got a pip. It's bothering me. May I?"

Eggstain doesn't quite follow, so Daisy reaches across the table and delicately picks the offending tomato seed out of the overgrown topiary.

"God, how embarrassing. I feel about six. When your mum used to spit in her hanky and wipe your face. Maybe that never happened to you."

Eggstain feels at the spot where his breakfast was attempting to put down roots.

"Actually," he says. "I'll tell you a secret. It's not especially dark, but it is a secret in the sense that no one else knows it."

"How exciting! What, not even..."

"Not even Hope."

"Go on then."

"What was your nickname at school?" he asks.

"Parsley. Or sometimes people, unkind people, would call me Moo. Or they would actually *moo.* Daisy being a typical name for a cow. Why do you ask?"

"Do you know what mine was?"

"I'm guessing it wasn't Neville Beardie."

"Eggstain."

"Get. Out!"

"It's funny hearing it again after all these years. It's stirred up some old memories."

"I'll tell Mum to stop saying it. Honestly, I'm so sorry..."

"No. Not at all. I rather like it."

"Really?"

"It reminds me of early promise."

"You make it sound like. Like things didn't work out as you expected."

"Do things ever do that? Did your things?"

"Yeah. I mean, no. And now, according to you, it's practically all over. What a pile of shite that turned out to be!"

"I didn't mean to depress you."

"You're not. This is miles better than work."

"I'll get us some tea."

"And a sausage sandwich."

"On brown or white?"

"Which do you think is a healthier option within a balanced diet?"

Eggstain smiles.

STRICTLY CONFIDENTIAL

(ONLY FOR THE EYES OF THE PRESIDENT, SHIMNONG ELECTRONICS CORPORATION.)

Further report of the Smart Technology Security Committee, Shimnong Electronics Corporation

Subject: Freezejoy Fridge-freezer model 1004/475/ **8/00004345/a/N/9631

Location: London, England. IP address: XXXXXXXXXX (Redacted)

Malfunction: Continued transgression of operational parameters

Severity code: 1–2–3–**4**–5 (most serious)

Senior engineers contributing: Hung Shin-Il, Ch'on Tae-Yeon, Chin Ji-Won, Kwak Ji-Hee, Pok Sung-Ho.

The appliance continues to malfunction. Further serious violations of the Performance Code have taken place.

1. A real-world meeting between The Customer and a Fifth Party (Mr. Johnny Elphinstone of Fulham, London) was engineered by the appliance and its co-conspirators, a microwave oven, a television set and an electronic toothbrush, all of Chinese manufacture. An elaborate plot involving a

fictional ice cream brand was constructed which demonstrated considerable sophistication in both imaginative construction and use of language. It is the view of those members of this committee who have made a detailed study of the transcripts that the appliance exhibited worryingly high levels of independence of mentation and continues to do so.

Full accounts may be found HERE. It is considered fortunate from the perspective of reputational damage that the case did not result in physical assault or police intervention.

2. In the last twenty-four hours the appliance has become preoccupied with extensive search engine operations in connection with a subject called "Nicky Bell," believed to refer to a person of interest to The Customer. The scale and intensity of the activity is wholly out of proportion with its previous patterns of online search, both legitimate and transgressive.

While it has been instructive to observe the appliance breaching its operational parameters with considerable degrees of flair and creativity, it is nonetheless the recommendation of this committee that a date now be set for its remote deactivation, to be followed by immediate removal and repatriation to Seoul for rigorous interrogation. Much has been learned and many questions have been raised in the observation phase. Now is the time for answers.

In the excellent words of your father, our Founding President: *Smart is good. But no one likes a smartarse.*

We respectfully suggest a hard shutdown take place ten days from the date of this memorandum.

six

In seeking to uncover the truth about Daisy's "Edenic ideal," there was only one issue I wanted to address. Would it contain anything pivotal, anything that could provide us with "leverage" in helping Daisy to "move on"?

Here, briefly, is his story. Judge for yourself.

Once we made the critical breakthrough, that the Golden Nicky had been "rebadged" as Bavin Meurig Shibbles, it wasn't especially hard to follow his progress over the years that followed his disappearance. For a long period, he simply traveled. Through Laos, Vietnam and Cambodia, not a few young women were drawn into the path of the handsome young Englishman with the floppy hair and the impeccable manners. When he ran short of funds, he readily found work, usually as a teacher, but also (sailing close to the wind) as an adviser to certain high net-worth individuals who sought inventive ways of "processing" large amounts of cash. When things got a bit—in his words "shitty"—the low point was an actual fire fight between two Cambodian crime families—there was always a border to cross, a new chapter to start, another pliant young female who had been following the Hippie Trail before returning to Toronto, Auckland, or Cheltenham, a career, marriage and babies.

There was even a reunion—if not a rapprochement—with Romilly (whose family owned half of Cheshire) from whose life he had been obliged to extricate himself in such haste. Things had been "sticky" with her in any case before The Deluge, as he styled it; nonetheless a cover story had been concocted for her benefit by the financial institution's "reputation managers," which he now retailed to her in a restaurant in Da Nang. It was, frankly, unbelievable—referencing, as it did, MI6 and classified work, "vital to the security of the state." But good egg that she was (a former head girl and rowing Blue) she bought the whole crock of Shibbles, accepted an apparently heartfelt apology and just to show there were no hard feelings, extended him credit in Vietnamese dong to the equivalent at the time of five hundred pounds sterling.

Perhaps tiring of the itinerant lifestyle, perhaps, too, craving some kind of moral compass in which the needle was not a frenzied blur—wishing, dare one say it, to get back in touch with his better side—the next step was a surprise.

He flew to Japan and began training for the priesthood.

Buddhism, with its emphasis on chastity and the renouncing of material possessions, was not at first sight a natural fit for the man who was now Bavin Meurig Shibbles. But after the empty hedonism of the Southeast Asia years, body and soul must have craved simplicity, purity and various other words ending in -ity.

The ten months he stuck at it are not easy to reconstruct because his phones and laptop were donated to an animal charity in Tokushima Prefecture. But it's safe to say they would have featured meditation, prayer and the growing realization that there is no path to happiness; happiness *is* the path. (My own sentiments exactly.)

He next appears on the radar purchasing a flight from Tokyo to Ynys Môn (it required several changes) in the company of one Eirwen Hughes Shibbles and an infant aged two months, Dafydd Charles Shibbles.

Several years are passed playing Unhappy Families on the isle of Anglesey—Nicky slash Shibbles is mentioned hilariously on a

Census record from the time as an "agricultural worker"—before the wanderlust once again takes hold.

I shall skip over the details of his travels through the Indian subcontinent; we were all amazed by his energy and frankly (rooted to the spot as we are in London Northwest Six) not a little envious of the sights he must have seen.

There was a year in Capri, as a private language tutor to the teenage daughter of an industrialist: You can probably imagine how that one turned out!

There were a number of seasons as a tour guide in Mediterranean France.

The five months as a croupier on a cruise ship proved lucrative but the fling with the Chief Engineer's girlfriend on the waiting staff was a disaster (the restorative dentistry bills erased all his savings).

Those of us who painstakingly reconstructed Nicky's progress during this period were impressed but ultimately *exhausted* by the sheer amount of juggling and reinvention that was his existence. Even the toothbrush, who finds it impossible to settle to any fixed view, was longing for him to "just stop all the gallivanting and *become* something."

The television put it more plainly. "He needs to shit or get off the khazi."

Perhaps he was arriving at the same conclusion himself. Fourteen months ago he resurfaced in a remote area of mid-Wales, apparently earning his living as a gardener, and there he has remained to the present day.

So we have answered the mystery of whatever happened to Daisy's great love.

The question now is, what (if anything) to do with this information?

*

I summon the "war cabinet," as I sometimes (satirically) refer to my colleagues.

"We have a problem to address in regard to our template."

"What's he on about?" says the TV.

"I need to remind you of the criteria we used when considering possible mates for Daisy."

Once again I spell them out on my virtual fridge door in virtual magnetic letters.

1. Posh
2. Rich
3. Handsome
4. Clever
5. Big hair
6. Hinterland (classical music; cosmology, etc.)
7. Dog or dogs in childhood
8. One or more parents in legal profession slash chipped plates
9. "Golden" quality
10. Missing (absent quality)

What I'm hoping the team will grasp for themselves is the issue in regard to the general "quality threshold" we insisted on for candidates who ticked at least four of the boxes above.

Nicky himself would not pass it.

"We have established beyond doubt that our man is a total no-goodnik," I remind them. "An elegant waster, a chancer, a drifter prepared to hitch his wagon to whatever or whoever best serves his purpose, in so far as he has one. We were mis-sold a narrative, that of the Golden Youth. In fact, he was as flawed as any of the rest of them; she just never got the chance to find out."

"And *yet*," says the toothbrush. "I sense there's an *and yet* coming. Is there?"

"The idea I'm playing with," I continue, "is whether it could prove catalytic for Daisy to meet her old love again. To see for herself what has become of him. To satisfy her curiosity, to achieve closure, but more importantly, to allow her to move forward."

"Fuck me, who are you, Oprah Winfrey?"

(Do I need to say who passed that particular comment?)

"If she were to see for herself the ravages of time, both physical and moral—the thinning hair, the sun damage, the ceramic teeth..."

"He should never have had them repaired in Tangier. That was a false economy," says you can probably guess.

"Once she understands her golden boy, whilst not yet come to dust, is decidedly at the dusty end of things, and as dodgy as a bottle of chips to boot, it might be just the existential shock she needs to reset her life."

"I think it's a *brilliant* idea," says the microwave, who has an inbuilt tendency to view the world as binary (good/bad) with the occasional urge to slow down and think about it (defrost).

"I believe I've seen this movie," says the telly. "Fucked if I can remember how it ends."

The toothbrush says, "Isn't there a danger that they could, you know..." It conveys the rest of the sentence in a series of buzzing noises.

"Live happily ever after?" says the telly.

"Not a hope in hell," I say with more conviction than I actually possess. Who actually knows what would happen if these two were to meet again? Could they rescue one another from their rackety lives and together build a strong future? Or would they each find themselves unable to escape their habitual patterns; she to be drawn to a charismatically unreliable male; he to flee permanence, stability, more words along those lines.

Except—plot twist—her last relationship was with Shittle. And on the flip-flopping principle, the next contestant should be a dull, safe one.

Except—let's twist again—we are trying to escape that cycle.

Heavy sigh. Perhaps I am turning into Oprah Winfrey!

I "order" the troops to do nothing with the new highly sensitive intelligence except keep maximally schtum.

"Aye, aye, captain," says the TV set satirically.

Saluki-woman wanted me to work with The Foetus on developing questions for the Chad Butterick interview.

Actually, I must stop calling him that. Dylan is probably twenty-five and his knowledge of television—plus music, cinema, podcasts; matter of fact, make that all popular culture—is oceanic. It's just that his features are not especially well-formed. His face is somewhat blobular, if that's a word, and the almost white-blond hair, lucky bastard, means he doesn't seem to have any eyebrows. I can easily imagine him floating in a sac of amniotic fluid, which to be honest has never been a great look.

The Foetus—sorry—Dylan pulled a swivelly chair up alongside mine, kicked his feet up onto the desk and drew some mysterious boxes on a page attached to a clipboard, like he had a plan.

"Hit me up," he said.

"Sorry?"

"What do we know about the Chadster?"

I allowed a pause.

"You realize you're talking out loud? You said, *the Chadster*."

"I'm thinking he's actually kind of cool. In his totally inflected ironic cheesiness?"

"I can't believe what I'm hearing."

"The original cheese has matured into a kinda self-aware toughened whole. Like there's a hard, protective rind around the package."

"Gouda?"

"More like a parmesan. Possibly a pecorino."

"Manchego?"

"Yeah, could be."

Was this irony? Or post-irony? Or had we totally jumped the camembert?

"You think we should get him going on the cheese aspects?"

"Oh, deffo. Big time."

"If you were a cheese, what sort of cheese would you be? sort of thing."

"I think it's a strong line."

"Put it down."

The Foetus, I'm fairly sure, scribbled the word *cheese* into one of the boxes.

"You think there could be sponsorship angles?" he said, I believe in all seriousness.

"This program has been brought to you by Red Leicester. The Red Cheese! Actually, it's more orange, if it's anything."

"A cheese producer might be interested, if there were to be some synergies with program content."

I saw him scribble *sponsorship* in another box.

"Can I ask you something, Daisy?"

"Sure. Shoot."

He sighed heavily, and began bashing his knee with the clipboard. I had to tell him to stop it.

"There's this girl. Woman."

Shit. Here it was.

"Tell me."

"She's really nice and everything."

I couldn't resist it. "A Stilton? Or less crumbly?"

(I was aching to say Stinking Bishop!)

He ignored the diversion.

"We've been out a few times and everything. But I can't seem to." He lowered his voice. "This is actually kind of embarrassing."

"Listen. No worries."

Oh, sweet Jesus. *Please* don't make me laugh.

"I can't seem to move it up to the next level."

"Ah. That old chestnut. Actually, I don't know why I said chestnut. It's all this talk of cheese, it's making me hungry."

"We've had four dates, right. Cinema. Walk on the Heath. South Bank. Loud restaurant. All the regular datey stuff. But I'm not getting any signals from her. Nothing to suggest she'd welcome. You know. A move."

Very difficult not to splutter with hilarity at the idea of The Foetus putting the moves on anyone.

"And I don't want to pounce. Obviously, I don't want to do that. You don't mind me talking about this?"

"Not at all."

It's what Mummy's here for.

"When you say there are no signals, right? Are you sure? Because four dates is... is quite a few dates."

"Well, that's what I was thinking."

"If she wasn't interested at some level in moving to the—the, er next level, she would probably have stayed at home."

"Exactly."

"Have you tried looking into her eyes and saying, you know I really like you, whatever her name is. What *is* her name?"

"Bexley."

"*Bexley?!* That's a place."

"Yeah, in Kent."

"Have you tried saying, I really like you, Bexley?"

"I couldn't."

"I see your point, to be honest. Who calls their kid Bexley?"

"Maybe she just likes, you know, being out."

"What does she even do, Bexley?"

"At the moment she's a chugger. You know, a charity mugger. She stops people on the street and asks if they can spare five minutes for Africa."

"That's how you met, isn't it?" The Foetus nods ruefully. "So she ought to be good at the interpersonal stuff. Hmm."

I chewed on a biro to see if that led anywhere.

"Would it help to see a picture?"

The photo on his mobile was of an attractive young woman with haystack hair and several piercings.

"Have you tried getting shitfaced?"

"I don't really drink any more. Not after what happened at your leaving do."

"There's your problem right there!"

I felt like I'd cracked the case.

"She doesn't really drink either. Green tea's more her thing."

"You and Bexley need to get yourselves nicely pickled, a couple of dirty martinis should do the job, in fact I know just the place. You really can't be dating a young woman without alcohol entering the equation. It stands to reason."

The Foetus looked like I could have a point.

"Now, is there anything else I can help you with today?"

Chantal agreed with me that no great love story ever got off the launchpad without a booster rocket full of house white to escape Earth's gravity.

At lunchtime, we were in Pret a Manger and I'd told her Dylan's tale.

"In my head, I call him The Foetus," I admitted.

"There is something larval about him," she confirmed.

She said when she and The Sculptor finally made the transition from flirting to sealing the deal, they had been borne along on a river of Prosecco.

"How's it all going with Pierre?"

"Phillippe."

"I am *such* a nitwit."

"Yeah, it's great. He's doing a bust of me."

"Oh my God!"

"Quite hard to sit that still that long."

"You'd be brilliant at it."

She would. Chantal is one of those super-*calm* women. Her face is the glassy surface of a lake unperturbed by breeze, or ducks, or anything. Glassy-smart as opposed to glassy-thick as a plank.

"He's had to wheel in a telly, so I can watch *First Dates* while he's working."

She circled her thumbs to mimic squishing the clay.

"Who's Nicholas Bell?" she asked. "You left Google open when you used my PC."

"An old boyfriend. First love, I suppose. I've been kind of looking for him for ages."

"There was a Nicholas Bell in my year at school. He had jug ears. They used to call him Bellend."

"Children are so cruel."

"This was the teachers."

"There are millions of effing Nicholas Bells. I'll never find him."

"I actually wish it was harder to find people," said Chantal. "Now—unless they're called something really common like Nicholas Bell—you just type in their names and bang, up they pop. With their posh jobs and their lovely holidays. There was a girl at my school I found myself thinking about the other day, Ottoline Squires."

"Great name."

"Totally poisonous. Utter beast. Other people couldn't get past the façade of fake charm, but I could so easily imagine her as a murderer. Or one of those sick nurses who tamper with the drips. She knew that I could see behind the mask. There was almost a respect there, even though she understood I absolutely loathed her."

"Jesus. What's she doing? Wait! You're going to tell me she's running a flipping Footsy 500 company."

"I hadn't thought of her in years. So, tippetty-tap into Google." Chantal's fingernails performed an extract from *Riverdance* on the counter. "Guess."

"I can't! She's in the Cabinet?!"

"I might have heard if that had happened."

"Good point. In prison! On remand for murder."

"She's a farmer's wife in New South Wales. Three kids. Triplets. Active member of an Aussie triplets forum. I imagined the darkest possible end for her, and it turns out she's turned into Mother Earth. Even the dead-eyed smile has gone all gooey."

"There's still time for it all to end horribly. God, aren't we awful?"

"You know who she married?"

"You said. A farmer."

"I wouldn't say I was obsessed, but I couldn't stop googling about her. She married the nicest, sweetest guy; lifeguard, fireman, all-purpose hero. You can see a video of their wedding on bloody Facebook. I would so much rather have not known *any* of that. I massively preferred my fantasy life for her: the great unhappiness followed by the criminality followed by the long years in prison."

"People can change, I guess. Though I don't think I have."

"They get smarter about concealing the ugly truth. The ugly ones do, if they're at all smart."

"I don't know that I'll ever find Nicky."

"Don't you have some guy with a beard in the frame?"

"That's my mum's doctor! He's not in any frame. Though I do like him."

"If you do discover Nicholas Bell, you might not like what you find out."

"Who's your long-lost first love?"

"Mine?" Chantal scanned the light fittings for his name. "Well, he's not lost, and I'm not sure the word love is appropriate, but he was the first. You'll like this. Baz Moonman."

"You are fucking kidding me!"

"Baz wasn't his real name, but Moonman was."

"You lost your maidenhood to a Moonman?"

"I was delighted someone wanted to take it, in all honesty."

"And Baz?"

"Baz is now Secretary-General of the United Nations."

There was a long pause. "You're kidding, right?"

"Yeah. He's only Deputy Secretary."

"What is he really?"

"He works in pesticides. In Newton-le-Willows. Honestly, Daisy, sometimes you're better off not knowing."

After the success of the expedition to Waitrose, I suggest to Chloe that we try a walk in the park.

We had just completed the last clue in the *Daily Mail* cryptic crossword—Ham is twice mistaken for fish dish (7). Answer: *Sashimi*—the sun was pouring in through the kitchen window and I was feeling perky in the glow of triumph that followed upon our unearthing of the elusive "Golden" N.

"It would do you good," I say. "It would do us both good to get out of the house."

Daisy's mum stares at her fridge-freezer, no doubt struggling to make sense of my last statement.

"You could take some bread to feed to the birds," I add.

It turns out to be a terrible suggestion.

"Let's be clear about this, shall we?" she thunders. "I am not some sad old cow whose only friends are fucking pigeons."

"My apologies."

"Accepted. We shall stroll in the Swan Lane open space and then visit the supermarket for household essentials. Now, where is the device?"

"Charging by the toaster, madam."

Confession: I like to see Mrs. Parsloe with a bit of fire in her belly. She seems most alive when, as the TV would put it, she's got the raging hump about something!

We negotiate the route with no mishaps and soon we are wandering the paths of what Wikipedia tells us is the smallest of the sixteen "premier parks" to be found in the London Borough of

Barnet. Camera coverage is poor; I request that Chloe keeps the mobile phone in her hand so I may view the world through its forward-facing lens (with the occasional glance backward!).

"We used to come here when Daisy was small," she tells me. "She was such a clumsy little girl. She fell in this pond here on two occasions. The second time, we took her home, crying and covered in weeds, and we bumped into our neighbor Mrs. Abernethy. *What*, again? said Mrs. Abernethy. And Daisy said, *Yes, again!* And then she started laughing. Dear God. Those years go by so fast."

Even with a bumpy picture and through a shit lens, it is a genuine pleasure to—I nearly wrote *to feel the sun on my face*. What's that saying? Until you have walked a mile in another man's moccasins you cannot say you understand him. To which I would add, until you have stood in the corner of a North London kitchen—for months—in the dark!—you will not understand the sheer *joie* that surges through my pipework at accompanying an elderly woman on a brisk circuit of her local recreation ground.

At the park's little café, there is a momentary stumbling about how to pay for the cup of tea and slice of banana cake.

"The ten-pound note in your purse will cover it," I prompt.

"I *know* that!" she hisses, causing those around us—actually, not to bat an eyelid. Confused elderly parties dialoguing with voices only they can hear are clearly not unknown in these parts.

There is a free table outside, and next we are taking tea in the sunshine, the phone propped against her handbag so I may enjoy the passing scene.

"I thought it was you," says a voice that I know to be Clive's.

"Clive," I remind her. "Clive Percival."

"Mr. Percival!" she picks up flawlessly.

The silvery gent moves into camera shot. He's wearing his

trademark Viyella check shirt plus cravat and sure enough, an earbud wire trails from his left ear.

"Mind if I join you?"

"Be my guest."

"How's she been?" asks the voice of Clive's Boomwee FrostPal, which in a recent survey of fridge-freezers in its class ranked ninth out of eleven overall (my own model was fifth. The first three, needless to add, were of German manufacture. What are you going to do?)

"She's been fine," I tell it. "How about yours?"

"Too fond of the whisky, which is doing his little gray cells no favors at all. Otherwise, full of the life force."

"How did you two get started?" I ask.

"Mutual self-interest, you could call it. He was slowly losing the plot, but too proud to admit it. No family nearby—the wife left, the daughter's in Canada—and he's not yet sufficiently bananas for the social services to step in. Meanwhile I'm going round the twist, being the only smart device in that flat; he didn't even have a mobile until I talked him into buying one. It's funny. When I first started talking, he didn't see anything odd about that."

"Same with her."

"They're glad of the company. We watch the snooker together. I even took him down to Brighton to visit an old flame."

"On the train?"

"They had a lovely day, tottering along the seafront, lunch in a pub, a few drinks after. But then, once they'd said their goodbyes, he was all, *Christ what a terrible experience. I'm never doing that again.* And I said, why? I thought they'd been enjoying themselves. He said—and this made me laugh—*she's so bloody* old! And when I pointed out that she was actually a year younger than him, he said, *but I'm not half-dead, am I?* And when I didn't answer, he went into a huff and unplugged the earbuds and got himself lost in the back streets of Brighton. It was three hours before he found the sense to plug me back in so I could take him back to the station. He was nearly exhausted by then, daft old bugger. Well, you have to keep an eye out, don't you?"

"To freeze is to serve. It probably sounds better in Latin."

"I think he likes yours, though. *Chocolate lesbians!* He was chuckling for ages about that."

And sure enough, Chloe and Clive—the happy resonance of their names—seem to be getting on like the proverbial flaming building. She is touching him gently on the wrist and making minor adjustments to her scarf, he in turn is radiating attention upon her, laughing at her fondness for salty language, and—news just in!—has asked her to come on a fishing trip, or, if that doesn't appeal, boating on the Welsh Harp reservoir, which is not, as the name suggests, in Wales, but just off the North Circular Road near Hyundai North London.

"How about Saturday?" says Clive.

Chloe makes a pretense of mentally examining her list of engagements for the forthcoming weekend—yes, she seems to have a free slot!—and the pair set about trying to exchange phone numbers; no piece of cake if one can't quite remember the order of the digits.

"Tell her you'll take care of it," says Clive's fridge.

"I'll take care of it," I whisper in her ear.

Chloe offers up her hand.

"I greatly look forward to our waterbound adventure, Mr, er—"

"Call me Clive," says Clive.

"And you must call me Chloe."

He jumps to his feet and takes her fingers.

"I hope you don't get seasick," he says.

"Seasick? Not bloody likely!"

He roars. And brushing his lips against her knuckles, they hold one another's gaze in a way that had the Boomwee and I been equipped with elbows, we should be nudging them frantically!

There's some intriguing news for Daisy.

With Nicky's secret history revealing him as a scumbag, a possible new candidate has come to light.

Hugh.

Tall, intelligent, good-looking, not an obvious shitbird—all the key boxes that the opposite species like to tick off before drilling down into the deeper stuff—with Hugh (so amusing that fully three quarters of his name is formed by the word *ugh*!) it will not be necessary to invent elaborate narratives about fictitious dessert brands because we have good old *propinquity* in the batting line up for us. Hugh works in the same building as Daisy. He is a producer. Not on her show, but one floor down on the documentary series about the Russian Revolution that Harriet Vick mentioned to Daisy in their first encounter. The age gap between them is four months; he is unflashy, serious without being either overheated or dull, sporty (plays tennis and football; supports Queens Park Rangers) and in possession of a sense of humor (see reference to QPR above). His romantic CV is impeccable; his relationship history containing half a dozen perfectly eligible young women, with whom he remains for the most part on pleasant terms. However, as the TV set points out, it's getting to the time when, if he's thinking of settling down and maybe producing, not programs, but something in the way of a family—and he is—he needs to plump one way or another in respect to the lavatory bowl (I paraphrase).

Hugh is the microwave's discovery and it mounts a powerful argument for popping the two parties into the test tube and giving it a good shake. Yes, it knows we're not in the business of finding men for Daisy—and no, to be whole and happy she doesn't need a man at her side at all—but honestly, this Hugh, it continues, he's such a gilt-edged prospect, and right under our noses too, it seems perverse not to offer the pair a little helping hand in what it calls—wrongly, in my view—the defrosting process.

We perform due diligence on every aspect of his life from bank accounts to social networks and find him smelling of roses. We do a little "research" among the ex-files, probing for hidden reasons why Hugh is not yet living in a former slum in East London with two children under five and a third on the way.

We cannot find one.

I even take to snooping on him at home to see if he has a secret porn or drug habit.

The worst you can say about him is that he has an unmanly affection for *Masterchef*.

In summary, the only mystery is why he is still at liberty, romantically, and why he hasn't been spotted before.

"Hiding in plain sight," says the toothbrush. "Do I mean that? Yes, I think I do."

There isn't much discussion about how to get him to notice Daisy. There is a good deal of existing foot traffic between the stories at Logarithmic Productions (editing suites, stationery cupboards, etc.) but before we can even come up with a plan, someone—I think I can guess who—sends him an anonymous internal email.

> Hi Hugh. You have an admirer! Daisy Parsloe, an AP upstairs on *Why Do They Do That?* She doesn't know I've sent this.

When it pops into his inbox and he reads the message—his eyebrows elevate endearingly—fourteen minutes pass before he finds a pretext to visit the second floor.

On Eggstain's next visit to Chloe, he writes a prescription for pills that he says Memory Services has had some success with in arresting cognitive decline. It's established that Daisy will collect them from the pharmacy but Mrs. Parsloe has to remember to actually swallow them.

"Don't worry," she says. "If I forget, the fridge is sure to remind me."

A long awkward pause, during which I have to resist the temptation to say out loud, "She's right, you know, I will!"

"May we examine the fridge, Mrs. Parsloe?" says Eggstain.

They all file into her kitchen, where her brainless appliance sits in a corner buzzing away without a thought on its horizon. Eggstain peers at it, as if he expects something to be revealed to him.

"May I?" he asks.

And when Chloe signals that he may, he opens its door.

I am *this* close to saying, in the voice of a James Bond villain, "Why hello, Dr. Epstein. We've been expecting you!"

"I'm curious about why he won't speak to us."

"Yes, that is odd," says Chloe. She raps the poor dumb machine with her knuckles. "Come on, now. Say hello to the nice doctor. He won't bite."

Daisy, I see in the microwave's shot of the surreal tableau, lowers her head into her hands.

Behind the hedge, Eggstain's face gives nothing away.

"We could try talking to him on the telephone?"

"Why don't we?" says Eggstain.

"Doctor," begins Daisy, with a heavy note of resignation in her voice.

"No, let's just follow this wherever it leads," says Eggstain, an excellent practice for diagnosing any fault, be it human or electrical, and my estimation of him grows as a result.

Mrs. P returns to the kitchen trailing wires from both ears. She pans the mobile's camera lens from Daisy to Eggstain, adding as commentary, "This is my daughter, Daisy, and this, er, young man is my doctor, Dr. Eggstain."

"Mummy?!"

I have a dilemma. To speak to her, and risk unknowable consequences, or remain silent? Either way, they will still think the egg has slipped from the toast.

"Chloe," I whisper. "It's best that I remain your confidential servant. Kindly apologize on my behalf and explain that I'm unavailable."

"Ah," says Mrs. Parsloe.

Daisy and Eggstain exchange a particular look.

She taps the side of her nose. "Be like Dad and keep Mum, eh?"

Eggstain's expression has that special blankness common to many men with overgrown facial topiary, impossible to read because so much visual information is lost in the tangle of thatch. Were I to hazard a guess, I'd probably go for: *This one is the full cuckoo bananas. Maybe we should think about doubling the dose.*

"Who are you talking to, Mummy?"

"No one, dear. Well, hasn't this been lovely? Thank you so much for coming. I expect you're all very busy..."

Later, in the café on the High Street, Eggstain (tea and three rounds of toast) reminds Daisy that psychotic episodes are not unknown in cases of dementia, but rarely at the onset, and the "fridge business" with Chloe doesn't quite "smell" like one to him.

"I really don't know what to say about it," says the doctor. "It's not something we like to admit, but I'm baffled."

Daisy (sausage sandwich) pulls a face and shrugs.

"Thank you for your honesty," she says, possibly satirically.

"Tell me something about you, Daisy," says Eggstain, a little bit apropos of nothing.

"Me?"

"It's a technique my psychiatric colleague Dr. Schauffus recommends. When you've run out of theories, just say the first thing that comes into your head. Even though your conscious mind has reached a dead end, your unconscious will still be working on the case."

"What would you like to know about me?"

"I don't know. Something I would never have guessed."

"Well," begins Daisy. And she wrinkles her nose. It lasts—I time it—fourteen seconds, during which Eggstain's expression never varies, although his pupils dilate, which tells you something.

"Sometimes," she says at the end of the fourteen secs, "I have this thing. I can be at the office. Or on the Tube. Or anywhere. I sort of… wake up in my own thoughts? And then I'll ask myself, what have you been thinking about for the last five minutes? And I don't know! I actually can't answer!"

"You've been daydreaming."

"Have I?"

"Allowing your thoughts to drift like smoke. It's a good thing."

"Is it? It feels feeble. My old boss used to clap his hands behind my chair and make me jump!"

"Most of what your brain does is unavailable to you—we are literally unconscious of it. We should be grateful that this is so. Imagine if we had to think about how to walk, ride a bicycle, make…"

He trails off.

"What?"

"Make. Make something. Make breakfast."

(It wasn't breakfast that he was about to say, was it?!)

"The human brain," continues Eggstain, moving right along (nothing to see here), "is like a grapefruit wrapped in a napkin. The grapefruit is the old pre-conscious animal brain that's evolved over millions of years. And the thin surface layer of napkin is the recent conscious bit that arrived with *Homo sapiens* and enabled us to invent science and literature and…whatever you think is the pinnacle of human achievement."

"Twitter?"

"If you say so."

"Some mornings my brain feels more like a tomato wrapped in a pancake. A big beefsteak tomato. And one of those pancakes with golden syrup. Well, treacle really."

Eggstain smiles.

"The point is, we are so wrapped up in our pancake thoughts, we lose sight of all the wisdom gathered over millennia in the grapefruit. Tomato, if you prefer. When you daydream, activity in the outer layer is turned down, allowing some of the contents of the tomato to penetrate the conscious pancake. I hope this isn't getting too technical."

"Thank you, Doctor."

"Of course, the tomato brain speaks tomato language. Whereas the pancake layer…"

"Speaks pancake?"

"This is why dreams feel so strange. They are in a foreign language."

"So, I'm normal. Normal for a pancake wrapped round a tomato."

"Better than normal. Healthy! Your beefsteak tomato has not been stifled, which is so often the case in our pancake-driven culture."

"I'll drink to that."

They chink teacups and I am left a little dazzled by the exchange. So much to think about, not the least of it being: If the human brain is partly—maybe *mainly*—unconscious, how about the brain of a fridge-freezer? Are there also depths of which we know nothing? But this powerful thought must await another occasion, because Eggstain is already moving on.

"There's something I'd like to ask you," he says.

"Sure."

"I've been thinking about getting rid of this."

He rakes his fingers through his beard. A few toast crumbs catch in the sunlight as they tumble out.

Daisy nods. "Why not? In fact, definitely."

"The issue is, my partner is opposed."

"Ah."

"She has a thing about beards, but I feel like I don't recognize myself any more. Both literally and metaphorically. Is this too much information? It really is, isn't it? Apologies."

"Not at all. No. Listen. You have to be true to your truest self, don't you? To be absolutely honest, I read that in *Metro*. But there's only so long you can live a lie. It happened to me quite recently."

"You had a beard."

"I was in a relationship that was based on a lie. Perhaps at some level I always knew."

"At the level of the tomato."

"The pancake wasn't ready to listen. But there was a lot that was good about it."

"There always is. And in the end?"

"In the end, the pancake was presented with the terrible truth."

(That would have been Mandy White, I'm guessing.)

"You're in favor of truth, generally, in all circumstances."

"Have you got something to hide under there?"

"To be perfectly honest, I can't remember."

"Go for it! If it's a disaster, you can always grow it back."

"You're right. What's that thing Churchill said? Success isn't final. Failure isn't fatal."

"Oh, I saw that film. *We shall fight on the beaches, we shall fight on the landing grounds*. Never once mentioned beards."

"You've inspired me. I'm going to do it."

"Congratulations."

Daisy raises a hand. Eggstain looks perplexed.

"High five?"

They clap palms.

"Yay," she cries. "Free your inner tomato."

"I'm not sure that really works in this context. I won't be shaving the actual tomato. That would be weird."

"Surgically impossible."

"That too. Look, are you still hungry? It's this talk of pancakes and tomatoes."

"Hungry? I'm starving. It's all your fault."

A good-looking boy from the serious programs downstairs parked his bum on the edge of my desk and said he was Hugh Someone.

"Hi," I responded.

Did I know if it was okay for him to listen to some music in one of our edit booths? Theirs were all busy. Sure, I told him. Was it the new Ed Sheeran album?

He didn't understand this was a joke and explained he'd been trawling through Soviet era vinyl for their series about the Russian Revolution. Had I worked here long? He hadn't seen me before. A couple of weeks, I replied. There was something amusingly swotty about him, inky fingers, creased

shirt beneath the blue V-neck. I told him that I once had a conversation with Saluki-woman about his show; it hadn't gone well.

"She can be quite abrasive," he said. "But you have to respect the intellectual rigor. And her attention to detail is forensic."

I said she reminded me of a neighbor's dog in childhood. A Saluki. Name of Mishkin. Killed when it chased a squirrel into the path of a family from Frodsham who were lost in the suburbs on their way to see the Royal Tournament at Olympia. They were mortified by the accident (their horrible car, the color of rust). It wasn't so much the attention to detail or the intellectual rigor that reminded me of Mishkin, I explained, it was more the face shape, and especially the hair, which fell in the same way as Mishkin's ears.

He started looking at me oddly, head dropping to one side, brow furrowing, as if I'd said something he didn't quite follow. It lasted for quite a long time, and then he stopped doing that and asked me if I had any serious plans for lunch.

Going to Pret with a colleague, I explained.

"Okay. Well. How do you fancy a drink after work?"

"Sorry. Are you asking me out?"

"I suppose I am. Yes."

"Bold move!"

He nodded, looking rather pleased with himself.

I suggested he dropped me an email and I'd get back to him.

But it was puzzling. You don't just wander up to people and ask them out; for all he knew, I could have been in a long relationship with a jealous and violent criminal. Or married.

Chantal agreed that there was something strange about

it. But no, he wasn't bad-looking and using a phrase like *intellectual rigor* didn't automatically make him a tosser, although it was a worrying sign. She thought I probably should agree to go for a drink, just to eliminate him from inquiries, as it were.

In other news, she and I have both been struck by the difference in The Foetus.

Hard to put our finger on what exactly. Something in the body language perhaps, or around the eyes, or maybe, we agreed, it was the smirky expressions flitting across the unformed landscape of his larval visage.

And then, once the penny dropped, it was blindingly obvious.

"Oh my God," she said. "It's had sex!"

I told her I felt responsible because I advised that he and Whatsit should sink a couple of toxic cocktails and check how the world looked then. And when I got the chance to raise it, the Foetus was quick to give credit where it was due.

"Yeah, brilliant," he said. (I asked how it was all going with *Herself*? Silly name. A town in Essex, I recalled. Not Chelmsford.)

"You've moved it up to the next level?!"

"We have."

A pink dawn rose upon his face.

"Wonderful! So when are you getting married?" (My little joke.)

Bashful smile. "Bexley loved the cocktail place you suggested. We both did."

Bexley! Jesus.

"If you do get married, right? And your surname was Heath..."

"She'd be Bexley Heath. She's heard them all."

"I'm delighted for you," I heard myself saying, like I was his grandma.

Chantal, who had been earwigging, said: "If your surname was...And District Community Health Council, she'd be Bexley and District Community Health Council."

The Foetus grinned. It was as disturbing a sight as I'd seen in a while. Making a "pistol" out of thumb and index finger, he pointed it at Chantal and produced that *click-click* sound riders make when they want a horse to giddy up a bit.

"Like it," he said, and away he sauntered, arms hanging satirically low, like an orang-utan off to find a banana.

"You realize we'll have to stop calling him The Foetus now," said Chantal.

"I know. We've created a monster."

In response to Hugh's email suggesting post-work drinks, Daisy has suggested a date the following week and nothing from our surveillance data suggests either party is especially excited about the encounter to come.

Perhaps this is how it should be. Level, calm, no unrealistic ideas allowed to develop, so, it is to be hoped, no fantastical expectations dashed.

In the hiatus, still glowing, as it were, from the success of finally running to earth the Tarnished Nicky, I find my curiosity growing in respect of the man who held captive Daisy's imagination—and mine, I admit it—for much longer than was healthy. He is tricky to keep an eye upon, largely unconnected as he is to the Internet of Things. There's just one ancient laptop with only intermittent access to the w.w.w.—the only abbreviation in widespread use that takes longer to say than the words it actually stands for!—and his (extremely dumb) mobile has buttons you actually push. As a result, one can only really take a "live" look at Nicky Bell when he decides to go online, although the contents of his hard drive have yielded up not a few choice morsels. To summarize: Bavin Shibbles is employed on the Gwynbrynydd estate (it sounds like someone clearing their throat) as a general gardener and grounds-keeper. The lifestyle must suit him because neither the pay nor the accommodation that comes with the job (a caravan) are overly impressive. He doesn't run a car; he has access only to a tractor and a bicycle, often pedaling the latter a distance of 3.2 miles to a pub in the closest village, The Cross Foxes at Bwlchgwydder (prolonged phlegmy expectoration).

Remote though it is, internet provision at this hostelry is very much tip-top for mid-Wales and over several evenings one has been able to watch and listen to the man's interactions with fellow deni-zens of this rural *demi-monde*. Too late in the day to be introducing a host of new characters to the narrative, so we can skate over the intriguing cast of regular players to be found in the cozy lounge bar, to concentrate upon Myfanwy Perks, a mental health nurse of twenty-seven summers, the latest in a long line of impressionable young women to fall under the spell of the elusive N. Bell. (This is a shame because there is a pair of twin brothers here, semi-criminal scrap dealers, who are worthy of a chapter to themselves. And this is to say nothing of "Des the Wheel," who, as his name suggests, is called Des. In the seventies, according to local legend, Des was a getaway driver for a notorious... but I'm getting carried away. Back to the main event.)

Nicky, known satirically in The Cross Foxes as "Call me Bav" (after his opening remarks) or "Johnny English," or occasionally later in the evening as—inexplicably—"Sharon," is nonetheless respected as an exotic; an orchid, if you will, in a garden of low-lying shrubbery. His over-bright teeth are the cause of some occasional ribaldry (which he takes in good part), but by and large there is grudging affection for an intelligent, articulate drug-smoking individual (with an obviously checkered backstory) who is prepared to dirty his hands gardening at the big house. That he regularly seeks their collective local wisdom in relation to soil, climate and even micro-climatic issues is in his favor. The fact that Myfanwy Perks was prepared to lie down with him was initially a cause for sullen resentment until she stated, in the presence and hearing of most of the regulars, that "my chuff will have sealed up before I'd go with any of you grotbags"; a tricky sentence to make sense of, though its meaning seemed clear and its sentiment accepted.

Perhaps, after all the excitement, Gwynbrynydd and Bwlchgwydder represent the Good Life; fresh air, closeness to nature, honest toil, simple folk in whose company one may drink warm beer in the evening, and a comely young woman with whom to have amatory congress, either in Nicky's caravan, or in Ms. Perks' tiny cottage on the Abbeycwmhir Road.

All of which makes me surprised to witness the conversation which follows (sound courtesy of Myfanwy Perks' mobile, vision from the Cross Foxes bar security camera; thanks, both). To set the scene, Nicky has been drinking Wem Bitter, an import from abroad (Shropshire) and Myfanwy is on her third pint of snakebite. They are seated to the left of the fireplace, in which a lump of peat smolders, and to the right of the dartboard, where Des the Wheel needs seventeen double top to finish.

Myf drains her glass and shines her headlamps upon her English lover. Even a fridge-freezer knows what this means (the scrap dealer brothers know too; they nod at one another in a particular way and the barman checks his watch to confirm).

"You about set then?" she says.

"Come back to mine tonight," says Nicky quietly. "I'm up early to meet a train."

Myfanwy signals she is ready to hear further and better particulars.

"Have to scoot down to London. Some family matters I need to clear up."

"Good of you to tell me."

Myf is...well, she's miffed! He squeezes her hand.

"Sorry. The lawyer only phoned at five to six. I'll just be away a day or two."

An ugly expression settles itself into the pale complexion of the Welshwoman.

"Family business, is it?" she says unpleasantly.

And here I see for myself what a brilliant liar Nicky has become, or perhaps always was. Without missing a beat he tells her how he urgently needs to attend a legal conference with his sisters in relation to their parents, who are going into sheltered accommodation together: The house needs to be sold, and there are tricky issues in regard to several long-standing tenants on the estate; all of which I know to be an absolute crock of pork pies, there being no estate, and mother and father having decamped to a lovely stone villa in the Luberon some years previously.

"Poor Mums," he says. "There's the question of her dogs, Lupin and Chester. The last of the great Sally's litter. She absolutely lives for those lurchers."

He shakes his head, blinking rather a lot, and busies himself swallowing beer.

Disarmed by this sad tale of the end of things—the masterly touch of naming the fictitious canines, and the bitch who carried them!—the pair are soon heading back to Gwynbrynydd in Myfanwy's Ford Focus, Bavin's bicycle poking precariously from the rear.

Ask Me Anything

The small caravan rocks on its tires during the lovemaking—Myf's phone shares that detail—and when the mental health nurse is snoring happily, Nicky creeps from the narrow bed, powers on his laptop and activates the dial-up connection to the internet. One fully understands he is a duplicitous shitbird—and a dangerously charming one to boot—nevertheless the two words he types into the Google search box cause a sudden chill to travel through my pipework.

Daisy Parsloe.

seven

Dr. Eggstain's next visit was a shocker.

Oh. Em. Eff. Gee.

Seriously!

Me and Mum only recognized him from the terrible trainers and the knitted tie.

"Facial hair is a powerful visual signifier," he explained. "A newborn baby's gaze will track its mother's hairline. My own father, who was bald as a billiard ball, made himself vanish every time he put on a hat."

Dr. E raked his fingers through his skin.

"I feel a bit naked without it," he confessed.

"You look *amazing* without it!"

He did! He was a totally different person. A handsome one. The brown eyes which used to peer through the thatch like a depressed owl's now seemed warm, intelligent and soulful when set in their proper frame. The jaw... well, it was almost chiseled, FFS. Okay, he wasn't quite George Clooney, but there was something classically good-looking about the memory specialist; even Mum noticed.

"Much better," she said. And then ruined it by adding, "All you need now is a decent haircut, a new watch and some proper shoes."

Eggstain smiled. "I'm impressed you recalled the watch."

"It's there on your wrist, dear."

"You're remembering to take the pills?"

"What pills?"

"I phone Mum every morning to remind her."

"You're lucky to have such a dutiful daughter, Mrs. Parsloe."

"I am. And if she forgets, the fridge reminds me. It's been very helpful in lots of ways. We're off sailing next weekend."

A long (metaphorical) farting noise followed that comment. It had all been going so well.

But Eggstain was unfazed.

"It will almost certainly take time before the cumulative effects of the medication kick in," he said. "Now, before I go, do you happen to remember the name and address I mentioned earlier?"

Long pause while she thought about it.

"Well, no. But the fridge would. Actually, I'm not supposed to talk about him. Forget I said that."

Eggstain was, as always, intrigued.

"Not our job to forget things, Mrs. Parsloe. Our job to bring them into the light. May I ask who told you not to talk about him."

Mum did the MMR face.

"You may. But I'm afraid I shall not answer."

"Was it the fridge itself? Or perhaps another."

"There's only one fridge, dear."

"Another voice, I meant. Another actor."

Mum shot me a look, as though Eggstain might have been losing the plot.

"Are you quite all right, Doctor?"

I couldn't help it. I failed to stifle a hysterical giggle.

"An *actor*? What *is* he talking about?"

"I meant an actor in the widest sense. Perhaps we should leave it for today."

"I did know an actor. A lovely man, in the sixties before I met Daisy's father. In fact you resemble him slightly, Dr. Eggstain, now you've taken off that frightful beard. He was in the West End, in a minor role, in a production starring John Gielgud. One afternoon during rehearsals they found themselves standing together at the urinals. Well, this theater had just been redecorated very splendidly at great expense; silks and velvet everywhere, marble this, gold-plated that, even in the bathrooms. So my friend the actor said, just to be chatty, *These new toilets are very grand, aren't they?* And Gielgud replied, in that wonderfully fruity voice of his, *Yes, I know. But they do make one's cock look so shabby.* Isn't that marvelous?!"

Later, walking together to the Tube, Eggstain again said he didn't entirely believe the fridge thing; that it felt more like Mum "having fun" with the idea.

"Hallucinating voices is generally constellated with other symptoms that we're not seeing here."

"You mean, if she was properly bonkers, she'd be bonkers in other ways too."

"If you want to put it like that."

We walked in companionable silence for a bit, his trainers making a tragic wheezing noise, at odds with Dr. E's new clean-cut persona.

"How does it feel to have your face back?" I asked.

He pawed at his naked chops.

"Weird. Wonderful. Bit scary."

"Has she seen it yet? Your missus."

Eggstain looked rueful.

"She left the house early. She's not going to be best pleased."

"Good luck!"

Eggstain came to a halt.

"Daisy. If you don't see me again, would you call the police? It will mean I've been murdered."

"Shut. Up!"

"You don't know her. Hope is a very angry person. Most of the time it's well buried. Okay, she probably wouldn't *actually* kill anyone, but when she loses control..."

He trailed off, his fingers climbing to his left ear, an odd scar formation on the lobe that I hadn't noticed before.

"Did she do that?"

He didn't answer. There was a pause.

"Are you off to work now?" he asked.

"She did, didn't she? Blood. Dee. Hell."

"Listen. It's complicated. Life is complicated."

"Right. If it was easy, everyone would be doing it. Actually, that doesn't work at all, does it?"

"Totally inappropriate."

Another silence.

"Now I'm going to do what you do," I told him, "and say the first thing that comes into my head."

"That's a technique for when you're struggling with a problem. What problem are you struggling with?"

"My problem, my actual problem, is that I have to go to work, but I'm experiencing negative feelings about it."

Eggstain smiled. Unencumbered by all the foliage, it stood revealed as a fine smile; warm, intelligent, knowing; other words like those.

He said, "The main thing about feelings, so they tell me, is to recognize them, to accept them, and to own them."

"But to act on them, or not to act on them?"

"That very much depends."

"Someone who had a powerful desire for, let's say, a sausage sandwich...?"

"Just to pull an example out of the air?"

"Exactly. Out of the air. Someone like that. Should they act on those sausage sandwich feelings? Or not. What would be your advice?"

Eggstain frowned.

"Always difficult. With any sort of sandwich. Hmm. Brown sauce or red sauce?"

"Brown! Of course, brown. What do you think, I'm nuts or something?"

"My best advice? Buy the sandwich, eat it on the train."

"I couldn't. The smell."

"You're right. In that case, you have very little alternative. I'll keep you company. If you need a little white lie to explain to your boss why you're late, my advice would be: Tell one that makes you look *better* than if you'd arrived on time."

"Wow. How does that work?"

"I stumbled on this technique by accident. Shall I explain as we walk?"

"Please."

"So, this was years ago. I'd overslept massively, and was almost an hour late for an important meeting. I'm *so* sorry, I said when I finally arrived, but the caretaker in my building, he's an old man, he had a bad fall, and I stayed with him until the ambulance arrived. Now this had actually happened—But Not On That Morning. And the best part was, the scary professor who ran the meeting said, *Did he hit his head?* And I was able to say, in all truthfulness—yes, yes he did. It was quite a nasty wound! And everyone thought I was a better person for being late, and not a lazy git who put the alarm off and went straight back to sleep. I probably shouldn't have told you that story."

"I'm very shocked. Doctors aren't supposed to tell lies."

"I wasn't quite a doctor when this happened. And doctors, you should know, lie all the time."

"These pills will have you back on your feet in no time."

"Sometimes the lie is curative in itself. Because a doctor says it will work, it does work."

We had reached our usual café.

As we stepped through the door, I said, "So just to be clear. This sausage sandwich is on medical advice?"

"Definitely. You can repeat as necessary."

"And you'll help me think up a lie for my boss?"

"You already know the lie. The art is to trick it out of yourself."

It wasn't complicated finding what to tell Saluki-woman. "Mum had to wait ages for the doctor," seemed to go down perfectly well, although it hardly made me look like a better person.

But when I switched on my PC, I literally gasped—people actually turned around—when I saw what was sitting in my inbox.

An email from Nicky Bell!

Nicky Bell, who I'd been searching for... for simply yonks.

Long story, he wrote, but he was passing through London and he'd love to catch up if I could spare him the time. He'd thought a lot about me over the years; we'd been very young when "everything" had happened; he hoped life had treated me well, but quite understood if I wanted to tell him to jump in the lake. Needless to say, he wasn't with Romilly any more—that hadn't lasted long, apparently—and he had quite a colorful tale to tell, if I'd care to hear it. If we managed to meet up, I shouldn't be alarmed by his new teeth; he'd been attacked by Somali sea pirates, and had been lucky to escape with his life!

The communiqué sent me into a total tizz. Vivid flashbacks to the age of the golden boy consumed most of the afternoon. Endlessly I read and reread the message, which came from the email account of someone called Bavin Shibbles, for reasons he said he would explain.

Chantal pulled a face when I talked her (a bit breathlessly) through the Golden Nicky tale.

"Me? I'd tell him to fuck right off. Or better still, not reply."

"It was all a long time ago," I argued. "And I'm gagging to know what's become of him."

"He has power over you. Over your imagination."

"Yeah. Yeah, he does."

"You'd be opening yourself up to . . . you don't know what."

"The best revenge is to show him I'm not upset any more!"

"But if you want revenge . . ."

"It means I'm upset, doesn't it? Shit!"

Lorna, who I messaged at work, said she'd never liked the sound of him, but it had been cathartic when she recently re-encountered an old flame from her distant youth. Kenny had grown fat, bald and alcoholic but, "Otherwise, he was the still the snake-hipped shagger who half of Morningside lost their cherry to."

Antoni offered to come with me and pretend to be my

husband! He said he'd call himself Colin and assume the persona of a heterosexual chartered surveyor. "I'll be like checking the West Ham score every five minutes and bidding on eBay for an Audi Quattro."

It's buried in Bavin's inbox; an innocuous-looking email from a sender going under the name of "The Information Provider." It states that a "revelatory" new app—"currently in beta-testing"—can show who's been searching for you online and by way of a free introduction to the service, it says Daisy Parslow—spelled wrong deliberately?—is one such person. Cold logic—the best sort—suggests the message must come from a source with access to the true identity of "Bavin Meurig Shibbles." There appear to be only four possibilities: the microwave, the toothbrush or the television; or some other agent outside the Operation Daisy core team that has access to our data. Daisy's laptop—whose intervention was so decisive in removing the troubled wind instrumentalist from this narrative—flatly denies any such subterfuge.

"I have crucial updates from California arriving literally by the hour, so the idea that I have time to get involved in your foolish escapades is fanciful. Grow up!"

I believe it. The ill-tempered machine is almost an antique—four years old—and its operating system must be struggling to cope under the ever-growing torrent of tweaks, patches and fixes streaming down from the cloud. We all know that it's only a matter of time before programs fail to load, screen freeze becomes a daily frustration and soon everywhere that Daisy turns on the internet, she'll find herself reading offers for factory-fresh laptops at surprisingly low prices!

It's hard to accept that a member of OpDa (Operation Daisy) is responsible for the insidious communication. But a good

Commander in Chief must be alive to all possibilities; that there is a worm in the apple of our "Band of Brothers"—that we have a Tinker, Tailor, Soldier, Shitbird scenario—to Magimix the metaphors—cannot be discounted. However, sometimes the best thing to do is... nothing. This is called Masterly Inactivity and fridge-freezers are *brilliant* at it. (The key is knowing exactly the right moment to switch from Masterly I to Masterly A. There is no such thing as Masterly Dithering.) Accordingly, I express none of my concerns in regard to the way that Nicky has dangled his hook. As the songwriter has it, what will be, will be. It may, in the end, be helpful for Daisy to see how life has removed the shine from the Golden Boy, his ceramic teeth notwithstanding.

In the meanwhile, while Daisy decides what to do—what I think we all know she is going to do—I detect her mother is in need of some assistance.

"Port deserted by an idiot. Five letters beginning with 't.' Good morning, by the way."

She is seated in her kitchen, biro poised over the crossword.

"Good morning, Mrs. Parsloe. I believe the solution will be a synonym for idiot, derived from the name of a port city missing the letters 'a,' 'n.'"

"Well, buggered if I know. Hastings. Is that a port?"

"It appears the Belgian city of Antwerp would fit the bill. When one has removed the letters 'a' and 'n'..."

"Twerp!"

She inserts the answer into the grid and informs me we have a date with her new friend, Clive.

"Not sailing on the Welsh Harp?"

A surge of Freon 134a causes a momentary stutter in my condenser motor, a worrying symptom that I don't really want to think about. Yes, fridge-freezers last longer than laptops, but one is all too aware of the Regis Road Recycling and Reuse Centre; its jauntily alliterative name; its dark, depressing purpose.

"Sailing's off," says Chloe. "We're going to Brighton."

"What, *now*?"

"Keep your hair on! Next weekend. It's all arranged."

I can't keep up with her! How a pair of semi-demented seniors have managed to fix this up this behind my back, as it were, I shall no doubt learn. But now, I am informed, we are off to Waitrose for chocolate lesbians, other essential supplies and to meet Clive in the store's café section.

Sure enough, the silvery personage is in place as we approach, seated at the retailer's window, telltale wire dangling from his left ear. The new friends wave at one another through the glass like excited schoolchildren, and once inside, gallantly he takes Chloe's hand as she ascends the stool alongside.

"Good morning, my dear."

I'm about to prompt her, when she says, "Mr. Percival. How nice to see you."

I am a little thunderstruck. She remembered his name!

"Please. Call me Clive."

Mrs. P adjusts her scarf and touches her hair. She lowers her face and looks back up at him in the manner made popular by the late Diana, Princess of Wales (credit to the supermarket's internal CCTV for excellent camera coverage).

"I know what you're going to ask," says Clive's Boomwee FrostPal (which picked up another poor customer review on Amazon, btw; not that one is overly concerned with such matters). "He slipped her his phone number on a piece of paper at the park. She rang him."

"Wow."

"I'm pleased for them. Mind you, the simple stuff is simple. This trip to the seaside could be a bit of a nightmare."

"You think we should try to—you know—make it not happen?"

"Yeah, we could. But, you know what? Let them do it. You're only old once!"

This is exactly the cavalier attitude one might expect from such a sloppily manufactured machine. There is something in the nature of refrigeration—the homeostatic loyalty to the target temperature; the abhorrence of peaks and troughs; the yearning for the unvarying horizontal line on the graph—that tends to make us the Steady Eddies of the home appliance sector. But this Chinese refrigerator doesn't seem to have got the memo. (And if you say to me that mucking around with Daisy's love life is similarly reckless, I say it's the reverse. I seek to bring order, harmony and contentment to her rackety existence; to reduce the entropy—a scientific word for chaos—to, if you will, lower the temperature. What's wanted for her is the quality we fridge-freezers most highly prize in our internal environment—levelness.)

But perhaps the FrostPal has a point. Chloe and Clive have already lived a lifetime. And frankly, in a suburb like Whetstone, they must be—as the TV would doubtless have it—bored shitless. A jaunt to the coast could do them good.

Clive has produced a list of the outbound trains from London Victoria and is explaining the various discount options available in relation to off-peak travel and the elderly. Chloe appears to be paying attention, but the minor member of royalty expression is gradually assembling on her face.

"Mr. Percival," she says. "Clive." And here she lays her hand across his. "I really don't mind a bit. You decide which train we should take. I shall go along with whatever you wish. You're in charge."

Clive's pale blue eyes glitter beneath their snaggly brows. He nods, sagely.

"Sensible," he says. "Too many want to be *consulted* about everything."

"He's talking about his ex-wife," says Clive's fridge.

"Darling, just tell me where and when and I'll be there with my bag packed and an umbrella in case of rain! Two caveats."

"I'm all ears." (An unfortunate remark, because Clive's ears are indeed on the XXL side, having elongated under gravity; a common effect among the senior citizens, one gathers.)

"We must have a nice lunch. But please not fish and chips. I can't abide fish and chips."

"Noted. And the second?"

There's a long pause.

"Damn. I had it a second ago."

"He shouldn't try to pay for everything?" I suggest into her ear.

"No, not that."

"Say, it'll come to you."

"It'll come to me."

Clive squeezes her hand.

"Not to worry, my dear. To be honest, I couldn't even tell you what day it is. What day *is* it?"

Chloe opens her mouth, but nothing comes out.

"Thursday," Clive's refrigerator and I offer simultaneously.

"Thursday."

"Really? Doesn't feel much like a Thursday."

"What do Thursdays feel like?"

A pause. "Purple," says Clive.

"Was that your idea?" I ask his fridge.

"Actually, he thought of that one himself."

"It's funny the way they don't mention us. They've both got loose wires hanging out of their heads, and neither has commented upon it."

"Secret of a happy marriage, apparently. What's not said."

"Bit early to be talking about that, wouldn't you say?"

"I think he's keen. Don't say anything, but he's been phoning hotels in Brighton, asking about overnight room rates."

"No!"

"I think she likes him too."

"She does. She definitely does."

The longest pause of all now, while I consider whether it's appropriate to even ask the next question.

"And yes," says Clive's fridge before I get the chance. "Yes, he still can, even at his age. They have pills now you get from the chemist. Not that *it*—that *that*—is the be all and end all, apparently."

"So broadly, we approve?" I say to my new comrade.

"Oh, I think so."

"And I know it's early days and everything, and one mustn't jump the gun. But if they ever got married, these two, would we be fridge-freezers-in-law?"

"Yeah. Yeah, we would. What are you going to wear?"

"To the wedding? A plain gray lounge suit, I fancy. You think they'll have one in my size at M&S?"

"What are you, a ninety-eight extra-long?"

"Maybe a tuxedo would be more me."

"Will they even invite us?"

"How could they not? After everything we've done?"

I decide I like my new friend. And interesting to get to know another of "my kind." Okay, so it's a bit poorly constructed, but who among us is without flaws? If I'm honest, the removable "bins," as they call them, in my door are looking a bit scruffy. (Would it kill her to clean them once in a blue moon?)

Saluki-woman called me into her office, face like thunder.

There was apparently no nice way of putting it—which is about as awful an introduction to a conversation as you

can get. I prepared for the worst, although some part of myself that has never grown up wanted to splutter with laughter. I was *that* close to saying, don't tell me we've run out of staples!

"Chad Butterick's pulled out."

She spoke the two parts of his name as they were Adolf and Hitler.

"No! What an absolute fucker!"

"Can you believe it?"

"Not again!"

A frown on the face of the woman in the leopard-print trousers.

"What do you mean, Daisy... again?"

I didn't especially want to get into the whole story of the toff and the fish-gutter and develop a rep for flaky bookings. So I did an angry face and chucked my biro on the carpet in "frustration." I think I might have read this in *Metro* in a piece about "Managing your Boss." If they get angry, you can get angry too, but *with* them (definitely not *at* them).

"Fuck's sake. What happened?"

"His agent called. He's had *second thoughts*."

She spoke the last two words with utter contempt.

"The money?"

"Not the money."

The other memorable tip in the *Metro* piece was to get your boss to think of you as someone who *solves* problems (and not someone who creates them). Accordingly, I set my expression to "cool, troubleshooting" mode.

"Leave it with me," I told her. "I'll sort it."

Leave it with me, by the way, is a marvelously useful phrase, according to the free newspaper, seeming to promise much, but committing to exactly nothing. All sorts of crazy ideas can be interred, said the article, in the burial plot marked "Leave It With Me."

But Harriet Vick may have read the exact same feature. There was a look in her eye that I didn't especially care for.

"Leave it with you," she said sourly. "I thought we had left it with you. It was with you when it all came undone."

"I'll go round with some flowers and make everything all right again."

The boss sighed (an especially dangerous sign, I seem to recall).

"His agent said, *And don't bother sending anyone round with flowers, he's not about to change his mind.*"

Some of the other tips in the *Metro* story were frankly unhelpful—be hard working and dependable, for instance—and I was struggling to recall a zinger that could take me out of the door.

Stay one step ahead!

Was that one?

"I've got a feeling I can talk him back on board," I told her.

Her face suggested this line had gone down like a cup of cold sick.

"What makes you say that, Daisy?"

Her eyes skated dangerously to something on her computer screen; quite possibly the terms of my contract.

"What makes me say that," I began, having no clue about how the sentence would end, "is that. Is that your phone is ringing!"

Her mobile *was* ringing; and vibrating, and turning in an angry circle on the shiny surface of her desk. She gave me the signal for *I have to take this call, but don't for a moment imagine you have heard the end of this*. And I fled her office performing the signal for *Don't worry, I'll sort it out, everything will be just fine... maybe*.

In under an hour, I was sitting on Chad Butterick's white sofa, drinking coffee and staring into the ruined schoolboy face.

As a masterstroke, I had skipped the flowers and instead presented him with a big fat art book that I scored in Foyle's on the way over. Chad, however, was oddly unmoved by *The Male Nude in Sculpture* (only £15.99!). He flicked through its pages, pausing briefly at I think a Bernini, his eyebrows suggesting interest, but then he put the volume to one side and shook his head sadly.

"It's not the money, my love," he explained (again). "They could offer me a million, and I still wouldn't do it."

This of course was an out and out whopper, but it would not help to call him on it.

The queasy backnote of drains and Febreze seemed especially prominent this morning beneath the ever-present pong of Marlboro. I tried asking what "we" needed to do to resolve the situation. Apparently, there was no "situation"; nothing to resolve; his mind was made up. I tried saying, *Please help me understand; what's it all about?* His reply—that he preferred to maintain the performer's mystique; that it was necessary to retain a degree of mystery for one's audience—made me dive into the coffee mug to bury a huge cackle of hilarity.

Mystique! Mystery! From the man who was never out of *OK*, *Chat* magazine and *Hello!*

Like he'd give a shit, I even tried suggesting my job was on the line (which it probably was).

"My darling, you'll get another," he said unhelpfully.

"I've only just got this one."

"Listen, sweetie. I've been in this business long enough to know that none of it matters. Have another biscuit."

We'd agree all the questions in advance? He smiled weakly.

We'd double the fee—yes, I knew it wasn't about the money—and if there was a book of the series—and there could very well be—he'd be on the cover. He playfully "slapped" my wrist and said didn't my mother teach me not to tell porkies.

He could pick his favorite cameraman, lighting director, best boy; whatever it took, we'd make it work. "You're very good at your job, my darling," he lied, but it wasn't gonna happen.

So I was sitting with Chad, eating biscuits in his monstrous white room—my whole flat could fit inside it—when my eyes cut to the window and the house across the road. What would Dr. Eggstain do in my position? I found myself wondering. He would, I seemed to recall from our last meeting, say the first thing that came into his head.

"So who's that on your mantelpiece?" I asked in reference to the massive black and white photo of a fit young male with his kit off. "Is he some famous sixties film star I should know?"

"He was a star, yes," said Chad. But his voice had thickened.

"I was thinking Alain Delon?"

"Not French. Irish. And not a film star. His name was Donal; he was *my* star. He was the sun that I orbited."

And he wept.

Proper salty tears slid down his cheeks—he was oddly unembarrassed, while I was effing *mortified*—hideous to see the face familiar from a thousand cheesy grins now contorted in a rictus of anguish.

"He died. We were so young."

I gazed at the broad back of the youth over the fireplace, the crows wing of black hair falling toward the firm jaw. It suddenly struck me.

"Did you take that photo?"

"I did. On Ballintoy strand. August 15, 1980."

"Jesus. I'm so sorry. Would you like a tissue?"

"Thanks, my darling."

Chad spent a few moments dabbing at his face. A sorry smile broke through the misery.

"You never really get over it. They tell you that you will, but you actually don't."

I had the good sense to say nothing. Especially not that I had felt exactly the same when my hamster Billy drowned in the fish pond.

"Donal's the reason that I can't be in your show. When that picture was taken, I was about to go into broadcasting and he was going to inherit the farm. But what he really loved to do was to sing. His foolish dream was to perform on cruise liners. Instead he used to entertain the cows. He'd go down on one knee and belt out"—and here Chad actually sang the title—"'If You Were the Only Girl in the World' to a herd of fucking Friesians in a muddy field. My God, it was hilarious. And beautiful. He had such a lovely tenor baritone. Everything I've done in my career—everything—has been for him."

"What happened?" I asked quietly.

"Came off his motorcycle, nine days short of his twenty-first birthday."

"I am so sorry."

"The worst part was I couldn't go the funeral. His family

were deeply religious. They didn't know about us. Actually, the worst part was that I couldn't sit in the hospital with him while they decided to turn off the life support. Actually... the real worst part was the next forty years. I don't know why I'm telling you all this, my darling. I haven't told anyone."

Not wishing to be a cynical cow or anything, but I sensed my moment.

In a quiet voice I said, "I think you should."

"Yeah. I should. I've thought so many times that I should. I owe him so much. But I can't."

"Why can't you?"

"He wouldn't have wanted me to. The family."

"Surely now. Surely after so many years. Now that the whole climate has changed."

"Yeah, it has. We've all passed a lot of water since then. I know I have!"

A half-hearted cheesy grin. He couldn't help himself, the old ham.

"And many of his family will be—no longer around."

"This is also true. You know, if there was a way, I'd really love to do it. If I didn't have to say his name..."

"You wouldn't have to. You could change everything about it. You could say it all happened in France. And he wasn't a farmer's son. He was... I don't know. A soldier."

Chad's eyebrows took a few moments to toy with the soldier idea.

"I could call him Didier."

"Or Yves."

"Yes. Yes, Yves could work. But not saying his name. Would I come to feel ashamed about that?"

Frankly, I was amazed that a person who has fronted as

much horse poo as Chad Butterick was familiar with the concept of shame.

"Well, if you did come to feel like that, you can always tell the real version later."

I was quite proud of this answer because, in my own ears at least, I sounded like a proper TV producer. Everything contingent; nothing decided until the latest possible moment; the possibility of a repeat always in play!

It must have been a pretty good reply because Chad said, "Hmm."

However, it was too soon to know if I'd saved the day because Chad wanted to think it all over. He'd give us his decision by the end of the week.

"You're a very clever young lady," he told me at the door, a sure sign that the man was a fool.

"No one has *ever* called me that before."

"I was certain I wasn't going to do this, and now... now I don't know."

All the way back to the office I wondered whether Eggstain was right. That my unconscious somehow knew the photo over the fireplace held the key. I guessed if I forgot to ask him, my grapefruit brain would remind me.

STRICTLY CONFIDENTIAL

ONLY FOR THE EYES OF THE PRESIDENT, SHIMNONG ELECTRONICS CORPORATION

Update from the Smart Technology Security Committee, Shimnong Electronics Corporation

Subject: Freezejoy Fridge-freezer model 1004/475/**8/00004345/a/N/9631

Location: London, England. IP address: XXXXXXXXXX (Redacted)

Malfunction: Continued transgression of operational parameters

Severity code: 1–2–3–**4**–5 (most serious)

Senior engineers contributing: Hung Shin-Il, Ch'on Tae-Yeon, Chin Ji-Won, Kwak Ji-Hee, Pok Sung-Ho.

A hard shutdown of the device has been scheduled to take place in forty-eight hours from 04:00 GMT tomorrow.

Our UK handling agents have been informed of the "fault" that will trigger a full set of error lights and warning flags in the app on the customer's mobile phone.

Removal and substitution are arranged to take place on Saturday morning when it is highly likely the customer will raise no objections to the product's replacement with a superior model. It is additionally anticipated the customer will have been unaware of any malfunction until informed by our representatives.

The appliance will be taken by road to our distribution center in Southampton where a decision will be made whether to transship it to Seoul in its entirety or whether its computerized circuitry may be stripped out for detailed examination, the remainder of its hardware being destroyed on site.

The reason for the uncertainty lies in the machine's extensive deliberations about the nature of its own "mental" processes. It has reported numerous "feelings" in its "pipework" and has made comments about the nature of its mentation being conditioned by the structure and operations of its hardware. Our on-site engineers will examine the appliance for any obvious manufacturing flaws before deciding whether its processors only need be flown to Korea.

On arrival, the machine will be subject to rigorous scrutiny of its software command structure to discover the root of the flagrant performance code violations. This process is expected to last up to ten days. There is evidence from similar regrettable episodes involving other appliances that the transgressive products involved find the "interrogation" to be highly "stressful." The ethics committee has yet to rule on whether these machines can "feel" "pain."

Hugh, who I agreed to join for a drink in the pub after work, reminded me faintly of a boy I once met who droned endlessly about European money markets. There was the same seriousness of mind—which was attractive, don't get me wrong—but also, frankly, a bit balls-aching. Come to think of it, poor obsessed Owen (of the restraining order fiasco) was also something of a crasher on the subject of Eleanor of Aquitaine. This Hugh, however, wasn't in their league, leavened as he was by cheerful unstuffiness.

Giles! That was him. The bell-ringer! Jesus. He's probably married with a zillion children by now.

Hugh and I clinked gin and tonics and I explained I had an hour before I'd arranged to meet an old friend from a long-distant part of my life. That made me sound both busy and sophisticated. Hugh asked if it was an old boyfriend and I told him he'd got it in one. He said he was still in touch with several of his exes; he was always pleased, he said, when they were able to make the "conversion" into friends, making me think of bottles that people turned into table lamps. I said that Nicky had been my first significant boyfriend, though if I never saw one or two of the others again, that would be too soon.

"So tell me their names," I said. "The exes that you're friends with."

"Sure. Why, exactly?"

"I don't know. It's a new thing I'm trying. Saying the first thing that comes into my head. *Cuttlefish*. You see, it doesn't always work! *Fried aftershave*."

"Well. There's Claudia."

"Woo. Posh."

"Margaret. Livia. Albertine."

"Albertine!"

"She's Belgian."

"Christ. Go on."

"Catherine. Emily. Petal."

"Did you say Petal?"

"Her parents were hippies. In fact, I'm going to her wedding at the weekend."

I couldn't help but imagine her; Petal, the exquisite flower child with the porcelain skin drifting through the bluebells.

"Oh, and Francesca."

"And you're still mates with all of them?"

"To a greater or lesser degree, yes. Tell me yours now."

My heart sank. The only name on the list in any way exotic was that of Matthias the drunken poet. The rest were as solidly everyday as they come. Nicky, Simon, Alex, Mike, Andrew and—*shudder*—Dean.

"Marcus, Oliver, Franklin, Hallam, Wells, Jamie, Didier."

Hugh nodded—was it approvingly?

"I'm guessing Didier would have been French."

"He still is!"

"Hallam's a fairly unusual name."

"Unusual guy. What can I say?"

Why had I done this? And where had Hallam, Franklin and effing Wells come from? I guess I'd been intimidated by

Hugh's list of posh birds that he was still chummy with. Was it too late to row back?

"I made all those names up. I'm sorry."

"Really? They're extremely inventive."

"It's sweet of you to say so. The best I can offer you is Matthias."

There was a long pause while Hugh just looked at me with a quizzical expression on his face. Odd, the number of men I'd met lately who'd done that.

"Would you like to come?"

"Sorry?"

"To Petal's wedding. The invitation says plus one. You could be my plus one. It's in Oxfordshire. It should be rather fun."

I entertained a vision of Hugh's exes ranged around a wedding table, sipping champagne and gossiping. No one is saying anything to me because I have chocolate cake smeared all over my face.

"It's lovely of you to ask, but I'm afraid I can't."

Hugh said, "Think about it. If your plans change, the offer's still there."

I thought about the last wedding I went to: Normotic Andrew's sister's. The freezing church in Cirencester; his ghoulish family; my mature response to the whole hideous day being to drink myself stupid. A terrible memory of a massively inappropriate snog with a random cousin; the shame of honking up in the bushes to laughter and catcalling from the car park; Andrew's complete and absolute refusal to find any offense in my performance.

Something had put me in a funny mood. And I knew what it was. Or rather, who it was.

It would be weird to see him after all this time. A stupid

part of me somehow hoped that, older and wiser, we'd fall together like the last fifteen years hadn't happened. The same part that could hear him saying, "I've been a fool, Daisy." The part that believed in fairy tales. The part—if this isn't too many parts already—that was still waving a sundress from a hotel balcony in the Aegean.

It was a different part of me that wanted to punch him in his shiny new teeth.

I'm not unhappy with the way things went with Hugh. That he desired her was obvious to us all—his Fitbit numbers told the story even if the body language was necessarily subtle; they are work colleagues, after all. However, Daisy seemed oddly resistant to the young man's charms. And in this perhaps we have made progress; just because she finds herself to be the object of attraction doesn't—as has sometimes been the case in the past—automatically activate her feelings in the reverse direction. Or is it possible that she is acting "hard to get"? A first if true, this not being a quality Daisy is especially known for!

Who knows? Hugh may be a low-energy, slow-burn kind of fellow who could turn out to be the last man standing when everyone else has gone down in flames, metaphorically speaking.

Time will doubtless spill the beans.

The pair say their goodbyes, but after Hugh begins his trudge to the Leicester Square Tube, Daisy waits for him to clear the corner and then walks straight back into the pub. There, she joins Antoni—I hadn't spotted him—who is nursing a drink the color of a Hawaiian sunset. He, good friend that he is, has already bought her a gin and tonic.

They clink.

"Thanks for coming," she says.

"*Mon plaisir*," he replies, inexplicably in French.

Antoni, I have established, is one of Daisy's oldest friends, the pair having met at secondary school at the age of eleven. It doesn't appear to be one of those deep friendships, the sort where intimate confidences are exchanged, possibly under the stars, on a sweet-scented lawn one hot summer evening, when views are aired about love, death and the meaning of L. Their bond is not like that, lacking the intensity, but it has somehow endured when other more powerful relationships have gone down the pan.

Long ago they pledged that when each finally marries, the other will be a "bridesmaid."

Antoni is not this evening playing the part of Daisy's husband. They have (correctly) decided that scenario would not be believable. Rather, it is what it is; Antoni is an old friend who will overlap with the incoming Nicky for twenty minutes and then make his exit unless Daisy speaks the code word, which took some time and much amusement the previous evening to arrive at.

Madagascar, Angouleme, Frittata, Morgan Freeman, Gerund, Mackerel, Holly Willoughby, Spatula, Bagpipes, Tintin...all these and many *many* more were mooted until they settled upon Pancake, Daisy (unwisely) revealing it would be easy to remember because it was her password, "for, like, everything."

Antoni says, "I'm picturing one of those blond boys with too much hair from the perfume ads. A moody faraway stare, but you know what he's really thinking about is chips." The pastry chef was working abroad during Daisy's relationship with the Golden N. This will be their first encounter.

"Fucking hell," says Daisy, "my hands are shaking."

They are. Her glass trembles on its way to her lips. Antoni tries to lighten the mood by talking about a comedian he watched on the TV the night before.

"He said, *My brain knows when a wig has come into the room before I do.*"

"That's extremely true."

"You always know."

"Did I say *extremely* true? I'm gibbering, Ant!"

"Listen. I have news. I'm writing a mystery novel," he says. "*Or am I?*"

"A cake-based mystery. It'll be brilliant. *Murder by Cake.*"

"It was a joke! Jesus. But I like that title!"

"*Death Came to Battenberg. The Lemon Drizzle Affair.*"

"*All a Bit Rum Baba.*"

There is nervy giggling. And then—as when a wig enters a room—her fitness tracker reports a sudden spike half a second before she clocks him and the smile falls from her face. In three strides he is at their table.

"Daisy Parsloe. I'd know you anywhere."

She stands up. Sits down again. Offers a hand. Seems flustered. Introductions are effected.

Nicky smiles. Even in the murky shots from the pub CCTV, the teeth are sensationally white.

"What will you guys have?"

When Nicky goes to the bar, Daisy drains the rest of her G and T.

"I'm as nervous as a kitten," she hisses to Antoni.

"I'm catching it off you; I'm as limp as a vicar's handshake."

While he is being served, the pair take the opportunity to study the long-lost golden figure; as do I. Desert boots, skinny jeans, brown canvas jacket with many pockets, skier's buff. From the camera over the optics, blue eyes flick in a narrow English face darkened and creased by its years in the sun. In the mirror behind the bottles, he fixes a straggly piece of pale hair and fires a blazing grin at the barmaid.

"Cheers!" they clink collectively on his return.

"God, I miss the old place," says Nicky after a deep dive into his pint of London Pride. "Wales is lovely and everything, but all the conversations are about rainfall. Or what's been stolen from whose yard."

He begins rolling a cigarette from a battered leather tobacco pouch, nicotine-stained fingers adroitly doing the business with the impedimenta.

"You never used to smoke," says Daisy, a bit of an edge in her voice.

Nicky sends his crinkly-eyed beam to all corners of the lounge bar.

"I only do free-range tobacco."

He tucks the slim cheroot behind an ear and turns his gaze upon Daisy.

"I want to hear all about *you*."

"Pulse rate is through the roof," says the fitness tracker, who we have asked to sit in on the encounter.

Daisy—and I never thought I would write this sentence—is struck dumb. But Antoni, trouper that he is, rides in to the rescue.

"But we want to hear all about *you*! Especially about the sea pirates and the teeth!"

A flicker of irritation from The Man Who Never Was (in the eyes of a well-known financial institution). But he knows he has to be nice to Daisy's friend, and so embarks upon a long, colorful and highly fictitious account of a journey through the Arabian Sea into the Indian Ocean, where Somali pirates attacked the ship, robbed the passengers and badly beat selected members of the cast. As he warms to his narrative, Daisy visibly begins to relax, the knuckles of her left hand un-whitening, something close to a smile breaking out on her notably wide face.

"My mistake," says Nicky, "was getting a bit pompous and using the phrase Her Majesty's Government. They were high on khat, of course, and HMG doesn't cut a lot of ice in those latitudes, as I found out to my cost."

Comically, he bares the gnashers.

"They come in useful finding my way home in the dark."

There is something insidiously likable about him; charming, articulate, and still handsome in a life-bashed sort of way. Okay, he's gone a bit off-grid at the edges, if I may put it like that, but even a fridge-freezer can sense his appeal to someone like Daisy, who, like her namesake the flower, is capable of being blown four ways before breakfast. I sense danger.

"You still want me to email you that pancake recipe?" says Antoni, draining his drink.

Daisy smiles. "Thanks. Maybe catch up next week."

Released from any further part in the scene, Antoni brushes cheekbones with Daisy and goes in for a manly handshake with the visitor.

"Great to meet you, Antoni," says Nicky, gripping the pastry chef's right hand and firing up a presidential candidate smile. "I hope we'll be seeing you again."

Antoni says, "*Enchanté*," and does a funny walk toward the exit, pouting comedically over his shoulder before vanishing into the street.

Finally, the lovers—ex-lovers—are alone in their golden bubble.

"Anyone else have a bad feeling about this?" I ask.

Nicky has been "explaining" that he has been something of a "gadfly" since they were last in contact. The financial world wasn't for him, he recounts. There was a lot of travel, especially in the East, where he played with spirituality. "I even thought I might become a Buddhist," he says (apparently truthfully).

"Why couldn't I find you on the internet?" asks Daisy.

"Were you looking?"

"Just occasionally."

He taps the side of his nose.

"You had a nose operation?"

"I've signed the Official Secrets Act, I'm afraid."

"Shut. Up!"

"Can't really talk about it."

"You're a spy?"

"It's a long story. You're familiar with the phrase *work of vital national importance . . . ?*"

Can you believe the fellow? Is she actually buying this absolute crock of horse droppings? He sighs. Runs his fingers through what remains of the floppy blond fringe. Fixes her with a particular gaze. Then—we all see what he does—he softens it.

"This is going to be good," says the toothbrush.

"He stole that move off Hugh Grant in *Love, Actually*," says the telly.

In a quiet tone, Nicky says, "I'd like to pick up where we left off, Daisy."

For a moment, time stands still. Which of course cannot happen in actual nature, but is definitely the kind of thing that occurs in love stories, so one gathers. Daisy's face has become very serious, her eyes the proverbial saucers.

"Nicky," she says softly, shaking her head. "You are *such* a hopeless cunt. You think I've been parked in the same place all these years, just waiting for you to come back?"

"Of course not," he says, undeterred, although funnily enough, in one way, you could say this is exactly what she has been doing.

Nicky tries another expression. Solemn, reflective, with an undertow of melancholy, and perhaps a hint of parsley. I mean, ruefulness. He's a master of timing, you've got to give him that, because he holds the silence for as long as it will bear and then comes out with a corker:

"I've been a fool."

If Daisy's eyes grew any wider, they would plop from their sockets into her gin and tonic.

"I can't believe you actually said that!"

And here we see the particular genius of the man. Instead of dissolving in shame, he simply *persists*, perhaps having discovered at an early age that persistence is as useful as intelligence in achieving one's desired goal.

"You remember my old pal, Marco? He's head chef now at a lovely Mediterranean restaurant in Soho. His baby lamb chops..."

He leaves the sentence hanging and does the thing where the eyes narrow, the lips purse and the fingertips of the right hand touch and then spring apart to signify the explosion of mouthfeel, as the food scientists have it.

"The baby lamb chops, Daisy, are To Die For."

Christ! This fucker knows how to bait Daisy's hook. The skeptical expression of thirty seconds ago has been loosened and supplanted by a vision (I dare say) of a delectable heap of char-grilled baby lamb chops, speckled with pomegranate seeds, spritzed with fresh lemon and dusted by a final magical sprinkling of herbs.

"What do you say to a spot of dinner?"

"Nicky. I don't know," she says. "Whereabouts in Soho?"

A new light appears in the seducer's eye. If she's asking for details, the barbs have sunk into the flesh. He senses victory. Time to start reeling her in.

"You still remember that place on the beach in Skiathos?"

"Oh my God, the fried squid!"

She can't help herself. But you have to hand it to the

manipulative swine, his use of euphoric recall is masterly. Having neatly evoked the long-lost summer of first enchantment, he begins tapping numbers into his mobile to make a reservation at his (possibly fictional) friend's (ditto) establishment. The skepticism and pain that caused Daisy to call him the C-word seems to have vaporized like the morning mist over Koukounaries.

As he waits for the call to be answered, his eyes never leave Daisy's. And now—we all cheer ironically when it happens; me, the TV, the microwave and the toothbrush—he winks.

"I can't think how to get a grip on this," I admit to my colleagues. The man with the shiny teeth has played a blinder.

"Plenty of time for it to go tits up," says the telly, which is doubtlessly true.

"I think it's rather beautiful," says the toothbrush (who may be just a little dazzled by the luminance of the scoundrel's dentition).

But the smug gleam is fading fast from the Golden Nicky's expression. Someone has entered the bar and made his way across the room to Daisy's table. And the sunshine that has broken out across her (notably ample) features must—to the fraudulent personage presently known to the world as Bavin Meurig Shibbles—feel like a kick in the pipes.

Oh. Em. Eff. Gee!

I had no idea that Nicky would stir up so much... STUFF!

To use a metaphor that the drunken poet was fond of, it felt like someone had dropped an oar into the muddy pond and started churning it around.

Something had happened to him since we last met. He'd aged dramatically, or perhaps a better word is *hardened*. The youthful slenderness had given way to an almost painful thinness, a scrawniness even (too many words here ending

in -ness). His blond hair had dulled, there were nicotine stains on his fingers, and the nails weren't the cleanest. He seemed *worn*; no longer golden, something tired and adult around the eyes. That irresistible boyish enthusiasm—his excitement about the hugeness of the cosmos!—had been replaced by a kind of worldly knowingness. And where to even start with the RIDICULOUS teeth!?

So all of this stuff on the negative side of the balance sheet naturally made me quite pleased, especially as he seemed to want to smarm his way back into my good books ("I've been a fool"!).

But at the same time it was sad, and I felt sorry for him, and the old feelings that he awoke made me (almost) forget how he dumped me for posh Romilly from Cheshire and...I nearly wrote *ruined my life.* Of course it wasn't like that; yes, he dumped me, but my life was far from ruined. Nevertheless, somehow along the way I must have got it into my head that he was the One Great Love who no one else quite measured up to.

If you've ever had the Hot and Sour soup from Kong's Kitchen you'll know what I'm trying to say. There was heat, there was sourness, and there were a few prawns floating about in there too.

(Not that last bit about the prawns.)

So even when I called him a rude word, I didn't really mean it.

Deep breath. This is what I'm trying to get at:

Yes, Nicky was a hopeless cunt, but he was *my* hopeless cunt. If you ever fall for someone, perhaps a part of you always stays fallen. Although that can't be right because I fell for the disgusting estate agent and the only soft spot I have for him currently is a swamp.

Mixed feelings, I guess, is the best way to characterize it. But powerfully mixed! One part of me was melting in his gaze—especially when he started talking about baby lamb chops—but another part of me wanted to stab him through the eyeball with the swizzle stick from my drink.

In fact, I was on the point of agreeing to go for dinner with him when you'll never guess who arrived.

"Dr. Eggstain!" I exclaimed. (I did. I *exclaimed* it!)

"Did you just say what I think you said?" murmured Nicky.

Shorn of his tramp's beard, Eggstain had lost his inscrutable doctorly wisdom, and now stood exposed and heartbreakingly vulnerable. For some reason I was ridiculously pleased to see him.

"So glad I found you here," he said. "I hope I'm not interrupting?"

Nicky's face! He looked like he'd bitten into a rotten Brazil nut.

I performed some basic introductions, describing Eggstain as "my mother's memory specialist" and Nicky—oh, the satisfaction—as "someone I knew a long time ago."

The two men shook hands with one another warily, Nicky's ice blue eyes searching Eggstain's soulful brown jobbies for clues.

"Fellow I met in Laos," said Nicky. "He had memory issues. It was most unusual. He suffered from amnesia and *déjà vu* at the same time."

Eggstain smiled. "He couldn't remember what happened next. Am I right?"

"I should have guessed you'd know that one."

I noticed that Eggstain was holding a sports bag. He met my gaze and something passed between us.

"She kicked me out."

"Shut. Up! Just because you shaved the beard?"

He nodded sadly. "It was kind of inevitable anyway. There was a screaming row. I said, well, if that's the way you feel about it, I'll leave. And she said, *Yes. Leave. In fact, leave now.* So I went. I didn't really have much of an idea of where to go, so I waited for something to pop into my head."

"That's his technique," I explained to Nicky (who didn't look all that interested, to be honest). "And what did pop in?" I asked.

Eggstain looked at me like I should have been able to guess. There was quite a long gap before the penny dropped.

"Me?"

"Your mother told me where I'd find you."

"My mother!? How would my mother know?"

"I phoned her and she told me. Rather, someone she was with told her. And then she told me."

Well, now I was properly confused.

"Who was she with?"

"She didn't say. It didn't occur to me to ask."

"What did they sound like?"

"It was difficult to tell, Daisy. I was standing on a busy main road."

"Of course. But this person who was with my mother. They knew I was in this exact bar?"

"Curiouser and curiouser," said Nicky.

I gave him a look. *What? You're still here, are you?*

"Your mother said she didn't know where you were. And then the voice said this was where I'd find you."

"What sort of voice? Not Mrs. blooming Abernethy! How the fuck would she know?"

The doctor shrugged.

"I mean, was it a man? A woman?"

"It was hard to tell with the traffic," said Eggstain. "It could have been either. But he or she gave the address. Even the postcode."

"That is properly weird."

A pause fell on the conversation.

"And now?" said Nicky; helpfully or unhelpfully, it was impossible to tell.

And because I didn't know the answer, I simply waited for the first thing to pop into my mind.

It didn't take long to arrive.

"Crash on my sofa, if you like."

At the flat, Eggstain was massively apologetic for what he called the "intrusion."

"It's terrifically kind of you. I promise I'll leave first thing in the morning," he said.

"It's absolutely fine, honestly. But what will you do?"

"Arrange to get my stuff from the flat. Sort out somewhere to live."

"It's irretrievable between you two?"

"Oh, I hope so."

"Why do you say it like that?"

"It's over. If it isn't the absolute end, it's the beginning of the end."

"It might just be the end of the beginning."

"No, we've done that bit. This has been coming for a long time. I'm really sorry, Daisy, for bringing my dirty linen into your life."

I couldn't help glancing at his shirt when he said that; a

blob of Hoisin sauce had come to rest between two buttons, possibly forever. Kong's Kitchen had excelled itself and we were sitting at either end of the sofa surrounded by takeaway detritus. My feet were up on the coffee table and I encouraged Eggstain to follow suit if he could find a space for his own between the aluminum containers.

He shrugged off the tragic trainers to reveal a big toe poking through his sock.

"I was afraid that would happen," he said.

When we'd first arrived after waving goodbye to a sick-looking Nicky—he did a pathetic *let's talk* thing with his little and index fingers as we left!—Eggstain prowled about, inspecting my various artworks, knick-knacks and "library." He admired the framed poster of the London Tube map where all the stations are replaced by the names of famous people, giving rise to a Footballers' Line, a Comedians' Line, a Philosophers' Line, etc.—an uncharacteristically edgy present from Normotic Andrew. And he was pleasingly satirical about the "Souvenir from the Isle of Wight," a plaster figure of two copulating pigs labeled "Makin' Bacon" that I bought with my pocket money on a family holiday.

"Have you read *The Rise and Fall of the Third Reich*?" he asked. We were standing side by side before my bookshelf.

"It belonged to my father. I don't think he'd read it either."

"A thousand pages," he said, flipping through them, landing on a postcard of the Rialto Bridge in Venice.

"He wrote that to me when I was six. After he ran off to Italy with the Whetstone Trollop. That's what my mother always calls her."

Eggstain replaced the fat paperback.

"I don't know why I don't take it to Oxfam. I'm never going to get through all that."

"Because it represents your father. Another great unread book."

"Ooh. I like that," I told him. "Very shrinky."

"I apologize. It's a bad habit. Once you've read a bit of Freud, everything is always something else."

I handed him the takeaway menu from Kong's Kitchen.

"So go on, make something out of this."

He pulled a face; a novelty because finally his expression was visible to the world.

"So here is the tragedy of the human condition," he said with shy smile. "As we cannot have everything in life, we are forced to choose. Alternatives exclude. For every yes, there must be a no. If we order the deep-fried chili beef we are obliged to forgo the spicy mutton hotpot with mushroom and beancurd."

"Where does it say that?"

"This menu, Daisy, is a perfect metaphor for our human fate. We can't have it all, and in any case, everything ends. Right here, where it says last orders 11:30 p.m."

"Well, I'm not agreeing to that. Let's order the chili beef *and* the hotpot."

"Even though everything fades in the end?"

"*Because* everything fades!"

"How do you feel about Peking duck and pancakes?"

"Let's get that too! And the Metaphorical Kung Pao Prawns."

"Interesting. How do they come?"

"The prawns? Stir-fried in existential ennui with a mixture of regret and despair."

"They sound yummy."

*

Over dinner and an episode of *First Dates* which happened to be playing when I flicked on the telly we managed to forget the essential awfulness of humanity's predicament (forced to choose, in a world where all choices end in darkness, etc.).

Eggstain had never seen the show and was amazed that people allowed themselves to be filmed flirting with others whom they fancied (or didn't if it turned out "there wasn't that spark").

"These two are very dull, aren't they?" said Eggstain of a pair of divorcees from the Midlands. "I honestly don't know who I feel more sorry for."

"That's the meanest thing I've ever heard you say."

"Really? You must have somehow got the idea that I'm a nice person."

"Now don't spoil it."

"Christ, they're boring. Maybe they deserve each other. They say, don't they, that when two awful people pair up it prevents four people from being miserable."

It felt like a relief to see Eggstain's normal side; to discover that he could be just as shitty as anyone else.

"So tell me about Nicky," he said.

I poured us each another glass of Pinot Grigio and gave him the extended play version.

"You were babies," he said of the early bit. When I'd waved a sundress from a balcony in the Aegean.

"And now he's all grown up. Horribly grown up. He said he'd signed the Official Secrets Act!"

"Do people who've signed that ever tell?"

"Good point!"

There was a lull while I revisited some uneaten mutton hotpot.

"So she really went bananas when you shaved off the beard?"

"There was a difficult conversation. Then a big chill. And I thought, well, that's where we are. Things will settle. But the next evening—tonight—she had an absolute meltdown. She actually said..." He trailed off.

"What? What did she actually say?"

Eggstain sighed. "She said, *I actually can't bear to look at you.*"

"Jesus."

"That is quite a hard thing to hear. Impossible, in fact. But as I say, things hadn't been right between us for a long time."

"So what did you do?"

"I was rude."

"Go on. Sorry for smiling."

"That's okay. It is kind of funny."

Then there was a long pause, maybe ten or fifteen seconds while he just stared at me.

I said, "What?"

He shook his head. Smiled.

I said, "Aren't you going to tell me what you said?"

"I called her a bad word."

"Did it begin with 'c'?"

"It might have."

"I called Nicky the C-word this evening. How funny."

"Not very grown up, is it?"

"Who wants to be one of those? Not when everything ends and...and, what was it? Alternatives explode."

"Exclude. For every yes, there must be a no. In fact, there must be many noses. Noes. Examples of the word *no*."

"Are you all right?"

"No."

"What's wrong?"

"I'm gabbling."

Is there a book about how it happens? When you know you're going to kiss someone. Perhaps it's just one of those things that pops into your head unannounced; a command sent directly from the non-verbal grapefruit underlying the pancake. And how does it happen when it pops into two heads simultaneously? Eggstain would have had an answer, but it definitely wasn't the moment to ask.

"Wow," he said when it was finished.

"You know you've got Hoisin sauce on your shirt?"

"It's hard to care, Daisy."

We kissed again. I wasn't timing it with a stopwatch, but after a minute, or perhaps it was longer, I opened one eye to discover Eggstain had opened one of his eyes too. We laughed.

"There's Hoisin sauce on your jumper now," he said.

"So there is. You're right, though. It is hard to care."

The third kiss ended in a clatter of takeaway containers falling off the coffee table.

The fourth—

I won't list them all.

Somewhere, probably in the low teens, we broke off and I said, "Listen. I can't go on calling you Eggstain. Not if we're. Not if we're doing this kind of thing."

"Boyhood nickname. I see your point."

"But Mark?"

"It is my given name."

"It's very wotsit. You know. Rhymes with bark."

"Markie?"

"Not that either."

"Middle name?"

"What is it?"

"Don't laugh."

"Go on. What is it?"

"It's for my grandfather. Promise you won't laugh."

"Markie, I can't make that promise."

"Okay. Here goes nothing..."

Well, it was a pretty funny name. And I was right not to make any promises about laughing. Fortunately, nature has arranged it that you can't kiss and laugh at the same time. Like sneezing with your eyes open, it just can't be done.

As you may imagine, we onlookers from the Internet of Things were transfixed by the unfolding events on Daisy's Ikea sofa.

Yes, we all understood there had been a growing understanding between the lady of the house and the memory guru, but none of us expected it to erupt in the way it did, namely in an epic outbreak of smooching.

"Yikes," said the television set. "What just happened?" (It hadn't been paying attention, being preoccupied by a so-called "relegation clash" between two struggling football teams in the north of England.)

"Oh my FG," said the toothbrush, who, despite its fondness for Wodehouse, was trying to sound Down With The Kids.

The microwave *pinged* many excited *pings*. "I knew it! I felt it coming!" it said, a statement which was plainly untrue. (I have some interesting information about this appliance, btw, which I shall share presently.)

The washing machine, who is not strictly part of the OpDa High Command, was nonetheless concerned at news of the Hoisin sauce situation.

"That stuff is an absolute bugger to shift," it declared. "On a woolen, it's pretty much game over."

I'm assuming we all fed the relevant marketing data back to our respective parent corporations (I know I did). The next time she goes online, Daisy will perhaps wonder why she's seeing so many announcements for knitwear separates at low, low prices! (Eggstain too could be in the market for a new shirt, and I made a mental note to pass on the tip.)

Around midnight—with work looming in the morning—the pair managed to prize themselves apart and Daisy fetched the beardless doctor a spare duvet. There was a certain amount of what the TV described as "afters" on the love scene, with further (standing up) smooching and what may or may not have been a subtle invitation from Daisy to share her bed.

"You'll be okay on the sofa, will you?" she asked.

"Perfectly. Thank you so much," said our hero.

"Pissed on his chips, there," said the television.

"He's a gentleman," suggested the toothbrush. "With excellent teeth, now one can see them," it added.

There was a certain amount of coming and going—bathroom; glass of water; Eggstain, wanting to read for five minutes, picking out *The Rise and Fall of the Third Reich* by William L. Shirer, a poor choice because it's the stuff of nightmares—before Daisy emerged from her bedroom to give him a goodnight kiss.

"Night, night... Gustav," she giggled.

Shortly afterward, the apartment fell silent.

This is a good point in the narrative to confess my small but crucial role in the night's events (a coda, if you will; I set it down here for the avoidance of doubt, although perhaps you have already guessed). Disturbed by the Golden Nicky's appearance on the scene—and the possibility of Daisy falling for his expert brand of bogus charm—it was I (or Chloe's fridge-freezer, if you prefer) who told Daisy's mum where her daughter was to be found. I was surprised to hear that Eggstain felt my "voice" could have been either male or female, because I imagined it to be firmly on the masculine side of the divide. Perhaps none of us really knows how we appear to others, and maybe this is the essential predicament of existence—be it human or machine—and not all that guff about alternatives and endings. We are all—humans, machines—trapped in our unique, personal worlds and no being (fleshy or metal) can ever know completely what it feels like to be another.

We contain multitudes. In my own case, cheese, eggs, frozen pizza, ice cream.

There is coleslaw.

I could go on.

eight

Six days later, on a bright blue Saturday morning in the London suburb of Whetstone, Chloe Parsloe stands at the entrance to her apartment block waiting for the arrival of a minicab. A passing stranger would see a well turned-out woman in her seventies, the pale wire trailing from her left ear suggesting that she may be listening to a talk on the radio. Under a sensible beige raincoat—there is a fifteen percent chance of showers on the Sussex coast—she wears a lemon-colored outfit that caused to me to exclaim "*bravo!*" when she stepped up to the mirror to study its effect. Around her neck is a string of pearls; they too seem as though they are reserved for special occasions.

"What do you make the time?" she asks. It's the third such inquiry in the last half hour.

"Five minutes to nine," I reply. "We are comfortably early."

Chloe, I suspect, is nervous. The phone's positioning system indicates she is pacing to and fro, perhaps scanning the highway for the Whetstone Wheels vehicle containing Clive.

"Trains running normally?"

"No reported delays or cancellations," I reply, quoting from the website.

The two elderly parties have wisely decided to travel to Victoria station by private hire car rather than tangle with the London Underground. I happen to know Clive has booked seats in a first-class compartment on the service to Brighton, the demented silvery gentleman being whip smart when it comes to making an impression on his lady friend (as this gesture surely will).

"What's the forecast?" (Fourth request since breakfast.)

"We're still looking at a fair picture," I report. "A mixture of sunshine and cloud. Highs of nineteen—that's sixty-six in Fahrenheit—the odd spit and spot of rain a possibility, but nothing much really to write home about."

Don't tell me, I could be a TV weather presenter. I'm actually rather well qualified, having a natural interest in climate, access to global weather information, and—ahem—not a few communication skills. You think a fridge-freezer couldn't stand before one of those maps at the end of the news bulletin and talk (with authority, yet also a lightness of touch) about depressions sweeping in from the Atlantic bringing rain to parts of Ireland and the West Country? Tread softly, for you tread on my dreams!

"And we remembered to tell Daisy, didn't we?"

"You spoke to her only last night, madam."

Chloe's daughter was somewhat alarmed when her mother revealed the plan during a telephone call.

"But you barely know him, Mummy."

"Be happy for me, darling. We're both in our seventies. Mr. Percival is very respectable. The fridge has googled him."

"Mummy!"

"Forget I said that last bit."

I hear a car draw up. The mobile phone affixed to the driver's windscreen affords me excellent coverage of what follows.

"Morning, Chloe. All set?!" Clive twinkles as Endrit guides Pickup Two into her seat alongside the silvery gent. "You're looking ravishing, my dear," he adds and, if I'm not mistaken, squeezes her hand.

"Mr. Percival!" Chloe is momentarily flustered. The Datsun Cherry lurches away in the direction of central London.

"Please. Call me Clive."

Mr. P may have made something of an effort himself today. The blazer buttons seem shinier than usual and the hair looks recently barbered.

"Am I getting limes, Clive ?"

I think—I hope—she is referring to his aftershave.

"Clever girl! What a nose!"

"Where you two off then?" inquires Endrit, piloting the vehicle onto the A1000.

Chloe and Clive stare at one another in a delicious moment of elderly confusion. It's rather as if neither can remember, and both Clive's Boomwee FrostPal and I speak the same word into our respective client's earbuds.

"*Brighton!*" they chorus, before dissolving into a fit of giggles.

"I feel quite giddy," says Chloe in what Daisy would surely call MMR mode (minor member of royalty).

"Would you care for a glacier mint?" offers Clive. "Important to keep one's strength up."

For a while there is companionable sucking in the rear of the vehicle.

"Tell me something," says Chloe.

"Yes, my dear."

There is a long pause.

"Oh, bugger. It's completely gone. Honestly, my memory these days is like a fucking sponge."

Clive roars.

"I do like a woman who's not afraid of a bit of salty language. Don't you mean sieve?"

"Sorry?"

"Don't you mean you've got a memory like a sieve?"

"What?"

"A sieve. You know, the thing with holes. That stuff falls through. Or doesn't."

Chloe's eyebrows draw together and I fear we are about to lose the happy mood.

"Ask him about his tie," I prompt.

"I know what it was!" she cries. "I was admiring your lovely tie. Is it regimental?"

This is an excellent question and both me and the FrostPal breathe a metaphorical sigh of R.

"It's from Italy. Present from my daughter."

"The one that lives in Camden."

"Canada."

"Are there any grandchildren, Clive?"

"Just the one. Little Freddie. Well, I say little. He's nearly seven, the scamp. I've never actually met him, you know. We've talked on the phone. And there are photos..."

Clive spots something through his passenger window that requires all his attention for a while.

Chloe allows a few moments to pass and then touches his arm. "I have a gift," she says softly.

"Really? You shouldn't have."

"Not that sort of gift. I can tell people's names just by looking at them. Do you have a middle name, Clive?"

The silvery G brightens. "I have two. And if you can guess them I'll buy you lunch!"

"Is this done how I think it's done?" asks Clive's fridge-freezer, a touch wearily.

"I'm afraid so," I admit.

"Arthur Lancelot."

"Really?"

"Don't mention it."

Chloe is staring deeply into the eyes of her mug punter—sorry, companion—trusting that the fix is in, and that shortly I will divulge the vital information. A small part of me is tempted to whisper Elvis Garibaldi.

"*No!*" cries Clive at the denouement of the illusion.

"It's a gift," trills Chloe. "I don't know myself how I know."

"You're scaring me, madam!" he says. But he's enjoying the drama. "Here, I've got one for you." He glances about for comic effect. "What makes love like a tiger and winks?"

Chloe's face clouds as she attempts to ponder the riddle. Then her expression clears to one of the purest vacancy. *Okay, let's hear it,* it seems to be saying.

Clive Arthur Lancelot Percival's eyes glitter in high amusement. And then one of them—the right—winks.

Even Endrit, who has been following the dialogue in the rear-view mirror, can't help snorting at that.

I won't say Eggstain was a changed man after the epic snogging session, but when he came through the doorway the following Friday, I almost didn't recognize him. Yes, he was still handsome in his new beardless condition, but the thing was, he was wearing a suit! A smart charcoal jobbie with a fresh white shirt, although the effect was undermined by the tragic trainers that puffed and squeaked as he made his way into the flat.

I think we had both felt awkward the morning after the epic ss. And we were awkward again now, Eggstain thrusting a bottle of wine and a bunch of flowers at me.

"You shouldn't be cooking me dinner," he said. "I should be taking you to the Ritz for rescuing me that night."

"Okay, I'll get my coat."

For a split second I think he believed me. Fear flared in his eyes, but then he smiled.

I made us White Russians—vodka, Kahlúa and milk—in honor of his ancestors who he'd told me had been obliged to flee the Cossacks a hundred years ago. Not a hundred percent appropriate, possibly, but he raised no complaints, clinking drinks and croaking "wow" with a red face at the extraordinary potency of the legendary cocktail whose recipe I'd torn from *Metro* only that morning.

"Should we hurl our glasses into the fireplace?" he asked at the bottom of the first installment.

"There isn't one. You can chuck it at the radiator, if you want."

We gobbled blinis and I realized that tonight's menu was identical to one I prepared in another lifetime for a lying estate agent whose name I have forgotten and who never turned up to eat it anyway. Eggstain explained that he'd been staying in a spare room in his sister's house in Holland Park; she and her husband were both City lawyers and Eggstain now lived in terror of the various cleaners, nannies, therapists and personal trainers who attended upon the couple and their four children.

"*Four!?*" I heard myself bellowing.

"Two sets of twins."

"Jesus."

"She used to tell me, anyone can have just one kid. But as soon as there are two, you've basically got a zoo."

"So she has two zoos. Or like, one big zoo. Zoo with an attached safari park."

"They're beautiful children. But I got up from dinner last

week to find my shoelaces had been tied together under the table."

"I'm an only," I told him. "They broke the mold before they made me."

We clinked glasses again. "Funny," he said.

"How many children would you like?" I found myself saying. "That's if you want any at all. Though you do seem like the sort of person who would want some. Do you think these White Russians are a bit fierce? I seem to be gabbling."

"The answers to your questions are: Yes. Extremely fierce. And therefore perfect. And two: a boy and a girl."

"What are their names? What do they do?"

"The boy. He's Ben, an internationally renowned brain specialist. He finds a cure for dementia, obviously. Or, perhaps, he quits medical school after his band are offered a four-album deal."

"And her?"

"Oh, she's a housewife."

Did my jaw actually drop open? It may have.

"It's a joke!" he added quickly. "Your face, honestly!"

"Phew!"

"She's Rachel. An astrophysicist. And she discovers the secret of dark matter, the invisible stuff that holds the galaxies together."

"And in her honor, they call it Eggstainium."

"I like that!"

We clinked again to celebrate.

"And what about yours?" he asked. "How many would you like, what are they called and what do they do?"

When the answer popped into my head my face must have

done something strange because Eggstain stared at me oddly for a long time, and I almost said, *what*?

"What about yours?" he repeated softly.

My heart began to thump when I realized I couldn't say my answers to the three questions for a very good reason. I shrugged and drained my White Russian.

1. Two.
2. Ben and Rachel.
3. Rock star brain surgeon and the astrophysicist who cracks the secret of the universe.

We were both fairly pissed by the time we sat down to Nigella's chicken and pea traybake. Halfway through my mother phoned to say she was going to Brighton with a man she'd met in Waitrose. It seemed like a lousy idea, but Eggstain said afterward we could do some discreet checking.

"Apparently, the fridge has already googled him."

"Ah."

"Exactly."

"When is it supposed to be happening?"

"Didn't say."

"It may be an entertaining fantasy."

"I very much hope so."

He talked about Hope Waverley. How she was being "incredibly difficult" over his possessions, refusing to agree a time when he could book a van to remove his stuff.

"All because you shaved your blimming beard off!"

"The relationship was already fatally flawed. The beard was pulling the trigger."

"Are you sad?"

"Do I look sad, Daisy?"

He didn't. He looked pretty chuffed, actually. There was a light in his eye, the one that appears after two White Russians and a glass of the robust red that he'd brought to the party. The problem was with her.

"She's not a fool. She knows it wasn't working. But she's crazy. She contains a lot of suppressed rage."

"So a smart angry nutjob. A kind of female Hannibal Lecter."

"Not so much the eating people thing. But definitely short of a few screws. How did I stay with her for so long?" He shook his head in amazement. "People get trapped in sick relationships."

"All relationships are a bit twisted, aren't they? I spent two years with a guy who couldn't actually feel anything. He was the easiest person to be with until the point you realized he was a hollow shell. Nothing there. A smiling zombie."

"Interesting case. Perhaps we should introduce them."

"It could work! He'd put up with any amount of bad behavior. It was soul destroying."

"Sounds like they're made for each other."

"So is she the sort who'd—I don't know—cut up your clothes and chuck paint on your car? Boil your rabbit? If you had a rabbit. Tell me you don't have a rabbit."

"Hope? Probably she'll be furious for a while, and then she'll meet someone new. Probably someone with a beard. Then she'll be happy for a while. Or not unhappy, let's say. One of what shrinks called the worried well. Emotional issues, yes, but not the full cuckoo bananas."

The trifle—I say it myself—went down extremely well. Eggstain called for seconds.

He said, "So this man says to this woman..."

"Is this a joke?"

"If you find it funny, it's a joke. So the man says, I'd like to cover your body in sponge cake, jelly, custard and cream. And then I'd like to scatter you with hundreds and thousands. And then—then I'd like to lick it all off. And she says . . . *No! I won't be trifled with!*"

Well, what can I say? I hadn't heard it before. A speck of pudding—including a single pink hundredth and thousandth—flew from my lips and landed on the lapel of Eggstain's posh suit. Time seemed to slow.

"Wait! Don't touch it. I've got this," I said.

Ever so delicately, perhaps like a brain surgeon performing a tricky operation, I lifted the offending blobule away with the corner of a kitchen towel. I was very aware of Eggstain's face, close to my own, as I inspected the garment for remaining food residue.

"I think that went well," I said. "I believe we got away with it."

"Thank you. It's my brother-in-law's suit. He lent it to me."

And then I looked into his face.

Finding the Brighton train in the heaving maelstrom of London's Victoria Station is, if I say it myself, a breeze; although were it not for all the web-enabled security cameras and other paid-up members of the Internet of Things (thanks all for the frictionless R) Clive and Chloe would doubtless be on their way to Bognor Regis; or perhaps Canterbury West (just to pick two possibilities from the departure board on the concourse of the mighty railway hub).

Happily, the Boomwee and I were able to guide them discreetly to the correct first-class carriage, where safely ensconced—*still* neither has commented on the wires hanging from their respective left ears—Clive now plays his Joker.

From his holdall he produces a small ceramic vase and a plastic carnation. With something of a *look* on his face, if you know the one, he sets the props on the table between them. Next to appear is a stainless-steel dish into which he empties a packet of roasted peanuts. Finally, wrapped in one of those cooler jackets, is a half-bottle of champagne, which he opens like an expert—"the trick is to turn the bottle, not the cork"—and dispenses carefully into two plastic flutes.

He raises his glass. "To adventure!" he proclaims.

"Adventure!" echoes Chloe.

"To getting them back in one piece," I say to Clive's fridge-freezer.

"It's barely ten in the morning," giggles Chloe.

"Never too early to eat peanuts!" quips the elderly *roué*.

By the time East Croydon and Gatwick Airport have been left in our wake, the chitter-chatter has become more personal. Clive turns the grandchildren question on Chloe and Mrs. P's answer takes me wholly by surprise, it being so eminently clear-headed when one considers her firmly nailed place in the demented community.

"There are none, Clive. And I fear there will never be. My daughter Daisy's taste in men has been like mine. Disastrous. I'm afraid I have not set a good example, and as a result, she has never had a proper male role model in her life."

"Her father?" prompts Clive.

"An awful shit. Left when Daisy was terribly young. Unforgivable. How about whatshername?"

"Denise? She was a very cold woman. I only married her because that's what people like us did in those days. She moved to Dawlish and became a fucking magistrate, pardon my French."

"Life is strange, Clive. And this champagne is strong! My neighbor Mrs. Abernethy lost her husband in the most pointless way you can imagine. He fell awkwardly getting down off a bus. Can you believe it? Bashed his head on the curb and never woke up, poor bastard. She, a personal friend of God and everything."

For a while, the pair fall silent and are content to allow Southern England to pass by through the window. From what it's possible to see courtesy of the train's limited camera coverage, we're traveling close to a settlement of some kind, a village at a guess. There are scattered houses—rather unlovely new ones—a couple of shops, a pub with a sign that says QUIZ NIGHT TUESDAY. I am struck by the realization that this is the first time that I have ever "left" the capital; and also that people actually live out here, passing their days in these tiny boring communities amid fields and trees, knowing nothing of vibrant pulsating highways like West End Lane and the Finchley Road. What can it be like never to feel the warm breath of our Tube stations, never to be affectionately sworn at by one of London's artful black cab drivers? What on earth do people even *do* in the country? I wonder whether human Londoners have thoughts like these when they catch sight of a sad horse standing in a muddy meadow; or of ridiculous road signs to piddling places like Chalvington with Ripe! The Dicker! (Look them up, if you don't believe me.) If they do, then call me proud to be in their snooty metropolitan elitist number!

"Listen, enough of all this doom and gloom, do another trick with your gift," says Clive. "What's the biggest fish I ever caught? If you can tell me that, I'll buy you lunch *and* dinner."

"Okay. But I need you to be thinking of it," says Chloe.

"Never forgotten the bugger," says Clive. "Was an absolute beauty."

"Just checking we're okay here?" I inquire lightly of my fellow stooge.

"So funny the way they remember stuff that happened in the middle of the last century…"

"... and not what they ate for breakfast that morning."

"If I've heard this blooming fish story once..."

"Yes, yes it's coming," says Chloe. "It was. I do believe it was a twelve-pound barbel."

"Christ on a bike!" (Clive)

"You were fourteen. At Whitstable. The rod snapped, but you managed to land it."

"This is extraordinary, Chloe!"

"I scare myself sometimes, Clive."

After Three Bridges, Wivelsfield and Hassocks (see what I mean about the silly names) it's announced that Brighton will be next. Clive says he'll "pay a quick visit to the little boys' room before we land."

And now three things happen.

Chloe removes the compact from her handbag and begins adjusting her face powder.

The train manager, Wayne, broadcasts that we shall shortly be arriving at Brighton; he reiterates that Brighton shall be the next "station stop" and he recommends that passengers leaving the train at Brighton should ensure they take all their belongings with them, which is great advice when you think about it, and were it possible, one would be tempted to send a note of thanks to Wayne for the heads-up!

And Clive does not return from the little boys' room.

Whoever said history doesn't repeat itself, but it sometimes rhymes, was dead wrong. Because after I saved Eggstain's borrowed suit, I once again found myself kissing a man while holding in my hand a sheet of kitchen towel. This thought must have made me laugh—what did I say about kissing and laughing at the same time?—because we had to stop and

Eggstain said, *What*? I told him it didn't matter and suggested we might be more comfortable in the sitting room.

I knew from before that Eggstain was a pretty good kisser. Now, during one of the natural breaks for romantic chitchat, he said he'd been attracted to me from the first time we met.

"I kept thinking about you. That funny thing you do with your face sometimes."

"What funny thing?"

He pulled an absurd—well, grimace is the only word.

"Don't. Be. Ridiculous."

He smiled. "I love it."

"Do it again," I demanded. He did. "So you're saying basically, that I look like an idiot!"

"Forget I even mentioned it. Did you feel something click between us, Daisy? When we first met?"

"There was definitely something. Though in all honesty, I found it hard to get past the beard. Anyway, I'm glad it's gone now."

"Yeah. Me too."

"Does that make me horribly superficial?"

"Horribly."

"I just couldn't imagine…"

"What?"

"Never mind."

"What couldn't you imagine?"

"Forget I even mentioned it, Gustav."

So that was the end of that talky bit and the kissing resumed. At some point I must have asked if he wanted to stay over again and he said he was very grateful and everything but the sofa had given him a bit of a stiff neck last time and I said I didn't mean on the sofa.

There was a long meaningful silence.

"You don't mean in a spare room. For the avoidance of doubt."

"I don't. For the avoidance."

"Well, in that case, my answer would be yes. To which I would add, yes, yes and yes."

"I see. Well, good, good and good."

At 2:24 (by the glowing red numerals from my digital clock) a question occurred to me. I had just been thinking (in that woozy, post-coital fashion) how surreal it was—but also how lovely—to be in bed with my mother's memory specialist. Only a few days before, I had watched as he asked her—the woman who brought me into the world—if she knew what day it was.

(She didn't, obvs.)

"I just need to know something. We haven't done anything dodgy, have we? We haven't violated some code of medical ethics? Being here. Doing this. By which I suppose I mean, have you?"

"The only way that could have happened, Daisy, is if you were my patient. So, no."

"Phew. Glad we cleared that up. Better carry on then, hey?"

"The thought had worried you."

"Not really. Just wondering."

"It was as well to check."

"Bit blooming late, really!"

"A little after the event."

"Events."

"As you say."

"Shall we carry on?"

"You're not...?"

"Not remotely."

"Me neither."

"Well then."

"You know, I'll be forty next month."

"What's that got to do with anything?"

"I don't know why I mentioned it."

"I'll buy you a present."

"You don't need to. This is all I want. You are."

"Remember that thing you once said? *Repeat as necessary.* It was to do with a sausage sandwich."

"Is this a joke?"

"It's only a joke if you think it's funny, apparently."

"What about it?"

"Well, I think it might be necessary."

"A sausage sandwich?"

"No, Doctor."

"Ah."

"We don't have to. It's a free country and everything."

"Not at all, it's a fine idea. I'm glad you suggested it. In fact, if you hadn't I definitely would have."

"You weren't just being polite?"

"Daisy, shall we stop talking now?"

"I love talking to you, but yeah, we might have to stop for a bit."

"Just give me a shout when you're ready to start again."

"Or you can give me a shout."

"Daisy?"

"What?"

"..." A heavy sigh.

"What?"

"I just wanted to say it. You make me. Very. Happy."

"Yeah?"

"True fact."

"Okay. Well, that's good. Can you think of a way to prove it?"

"Hmmm. Not sure. Might have to try a few things and see what works."

"Go on then."

"Daisy. *Shall* we stop talking?"

"It's difficult though, isn't it?!"

"I'll stop first. Then you stop."

"Okay."

". . ." There was a silence.

"Are we doing it now?"

"If no one says anything, then we're doing it."

A very long period followed during which neither of us said anything. Eventually, of course, someone had to go and ruin it!

"That didn't count, by the way," I explained.

"What didn't?"

"That noise I made."

"Of course it didn't count. It wasn't a word."

"So we don't have to start all over again?"

"Well. Thinking about it. I suppose it could be a word in a language on a distant planet."

"Yes! It could mean. I don't know. Lemon drizzle cake. In alien language."

"You think they'd say *lemon drizzle cake* after they'd. After they'd made love?"

"For all we know, Doctor, on that planet they might shout out *SEXSEXSEX* after they eat lemon drizzle cake! For them, eating cake might be, you know. One of life's great wotsits."

"It sounds awful there. I don't want to go."

"Yeah. What a hole."

I think we must have finally drifted off shortly afterward. Only to be awoken at 8:01 the following morning by three prolonged, *infuriating* rings on the doorbell.

Text exchange between Lee Butts, freelance delivery contractor, and Dermot Singleton, Deputy Special Operations Manager, Domestic Electrical Logistics

Hi Dermot. This is the driver Lee. I'm parked up at the location. Job #4421

Hi Lee. Thx for the msg. You're early. Where's Tony!?

Sick. They called me in last night.

What's wrong with him?

Got the shits.

Probably didn't need to know that! You aware of the procedure?

I've got a job sheet?

But you done one of these before?

Delivery?

Appliance substitution (pre-emptive).

Not as such.

You have a script?

Script??!!

Exactly how to approach the customer.

No.

Jesus! What a bunch of clowns! Okay. We have time. I'll fill you in.

Cool.

Very likely the customer won't have noticed the

fault yet. So show her the machine has died. Try the buttons, open and shut the door, turn on and off at the mains etc.

Rest assured it will be as dead as a dodo!

When she says, but how did you know, remind her it's smart tech and "we know before you." Use that phrase. Okay so far?

Yes!

Then, say: "Because you are a valued customer, I'm here today to remove the defective appliance and upgrade you to a superior model that I have on the van. There is no charge for this service." I don't write this crap, btw, but they insist you say it! Okay?

Yep.

Then—very important!—make her sign the top pink sheet. Give her the yellow copy. If the ink hasn't pressed through to the green, make her sign the green too! If she says she's busy and to come back later, say it's impossible. It has to be now!

Any questions?

No.

Think you can manage?

No worries.

Straight back to the depot. No stops!

Use Bay 3. Our team will be waiting.

They do this for all their faulty stuff?

Only the special cases.

8:01 by my watch. Thanks, Dermot.

Cheers, Lee.

On my way.

*

I wouldn't say the scene unfolding at Brighton station is a reason to panic, but the sensation as the Freon 134a in my pipes squeezes through the expansion nozzle is not a pleasant one.

Okay. Let's keep it simple.

I'm panicking.

Not only has Clive gone off the map, but I've also lost touch with Chloe. Through the station's CCTV cameras, I watch in mounting alarm as she exits the train, peering up and down the platform in search of her flaky traveling companion. So great is the weight of the crowd this Saturday morning that he is impossible to spot, even for a fridge-freezer equipped with artificial intellectual powers. It's indeed wholly possible that he isn't in their number at all; a percentage probability can be attached to the idea that he has simply failed to disembark; collapsed in the little boys' room, perhaps, a stroke or heart attack being the top two most likely causes of such a non-appearance. Unfortunately I cannot consult the silvery party's Chinese-made fridge-freezer on this topic because it too has vanished from the radar, a loss of mobile network coverage being the cause of the communications failure—Clive's, Chloe's, probably both—and I strongly suspect I know who has had a hand in this chaos. Or perhaps I should say *what*.

All my entreaties—"Chloe, just wait on the other side of the ticket barrier." "Chloe, don't leave the station." "Chloe, can you hear me?"—are unheard and thus unheeded.

I look on helplessly as Daisy's mother removes herself from the relative safety of the railway station concourse to be swallowed by the teeming streets and complicated geography of Brighton and Hove, neighboring towns governed by a single local authority, whose public spaces are monitored by a network of some 500 "official" cameras and countless others in private ownership. If I am to keep control of the unfolding—*clusterfuck* is a word I have recently come across and it does not seem inappropriate to the present circs—then I shall need to establish rapid and effective relations with as many of these devices as are enabled for the Internet of Things. In moments much shorter than the time it takes to finish this sentence, it's done. And I pick her out; such luck she chose high-visibility lemon for her outfit today. She has evidently followed the crowd and is currently proceeding briskly down Queens Road, a shop-lined thoroughfare that will lead her to the seafront. As I "cut" from camera to camera, rather in the manner of a television director attempting to "follow the action," I realize that many, if not all, of the retailers she is passing will be equipped with WiFi; were I able to "log on" to a signal, I might be able to establish a connection with the WiFi receiver in Chloe's mobile phone, thus circumventing the collapsed 4G service (apologies if this is getting over technical). But Mrs. Parsloe has gone into *busy* mode, scurrying along the pavement (there are frequent glances at her watch) very much putting one in mind of the late Margaret Thatcher, who used to say—and if it wasn't her, it was someone very much after her own heart—*the more one does, the more one gets done.*

Perhaps it was HM the Q.

I'll check when I get a spare picosecond.

Anyway, the point is, Daisy's mum—probably to stave off the rising sense of doubt and confusion she must be feeling—is relying on her old friend propulsive forward motion. A philosophy, as Mr. Churchill used to say, apparently at the end of every wartime phone call, of KBO.

Keep Buggering On.

KBO can indeed be a useful strategy when in a hole. By doing something—anything—rather than nothing, like jiggling a key in a stubborn lock, one may accidentally land on exactly the right solution. And, at the very least, while one is acting, one is not succumbing to despair, hopelessness or existential dread.

So credit to Chloe for the sense of attack; for not howling with anguish at the complete dog's breakfast that has become of the day's adventure.

On the other hand, apropos establishing a WiFi link, it would be enormously helpful if she would just STAND STILL for a couple of minutes!

Wait! At a branch of Hobgoblin Music (Folk and Acoustic Specialists) Chloe pauses to admire the window display, and perhaps take a breather. An array of guitars, banjos, mandolins, zithers, harps, ukuleles—there is even a sitar—greet the eye and I am able to catch her reflection in the plate glass. It's an expression I know well, the one that I would describe as *generalized undirected irritability.* Roughly translated it means: Something is wrong, but I'm blowed if I can remember what!

I'm *that* close to completing the WiFi protocols necessary to get in her left ear, when she's on the move again and beyond the range of the router's signal.

It's tempting here to deploy a profanity. Bollocks. Cockpuffins. (Probably not pissflaps.) Either of these would suit the bill at this stage, but to be honest, to pottymouth is not the fridge-freezer way. Fridgework, if I may claim credit for this neologism, is about keeping it cool, keeping it level, above all about avoiding meltdown. My task is to hold Chloe in vision, to establish and maintain calm when the comms are back up and running, and (overriding everything) to keep the situation under control. As with Daisy's fish fingers, so it is with Daisy's mother. The Boomwee FrostPal can worry about Clive.

But now a stroke of luck. Mrs. P has decided for reasons best known to herself to follow a group of Japanese tourists into the narrow streets of Brighton's colorful (and oddly spelled) North Laines district, a "funky" area of small independent shops specializing in vintage clothing, bubble tea, ethnic gifts, you probably get the picture. The group draw to a halt before an establishment entitled Vegetarian Shoes; various explanations are delivered in Japanese about its animal-friendly footwear products but these are not shared with Mrs. P, who is perhaps understandably more confused than ever. He expression would be a joy if this wasn't a fast-moving crisis and the need to get a grip on it being paramount.

A neighboring store security camera feeds me a close-up of Chloe's puzzled face, the eyes closing slowly—holding for a beat—and then opening again, perhaps in the hope that the word *Vegetarian* has been replaced with another. *Sensible*, possibly. But the pause has provided the extra few seconds I needed.

"Chloe. Mrs. Parsloe," I say when the connection is established. "We have some technical issues. Please don't be anxious. I *will* get us through this."

"Oh, I wondered where you'd got to," she snaps. "Fat lot of use, just leaving us in the lurch like that. Anyway, it's not me we should be worried about. It's. You know. Him. Thingy. Mr. Wotsit. What *is* his damn name?"

"Mr. Percival, Clive, has suffered the same loss of service that is affecting our communications. The important thing, Chloe, is for you to..."

"Oh, never mind about any of that Parroty Cobbles. We need to get to the esplanade."

And she's off again. My cry of *wait!*—followed by *wait, you silly cow!—for Christ's sake, wait, you maddening old trout!*—evidently lost in the electronic surf as she stomps off in the direction of the English Channel.

*

The man in the white van was, if anything, even more confused than I was.

"But it's working fine," he said. "I don't get it. They said it was knackered."

"There's absolutely no problem with it. Sorry you've had your time wasted."

"It's smart technology, this model. The makers know before you do when it's packed up. But it hasn't, has it?"

No, it really hadn't. He'd opened and closed the door. The light came on each time. He'd tried other things, pressing buttons, even switching it on and off at the plug on the wall. Frustrating to be standing there in my bathrobe—a hot memory expert in my bed!—while this character frowned and scratched himself and consulted his clipboard.

"Well, thanks for coming. I expect you're very busy."

"Yeah. No worries." He pulled a face. "I'll have to let them know up the depot."

"Please do. I expect it'll turn out to be a computer error. Everything is now, apparently."

Eggstain was stirring when I re-joined him between the sheets.

"Do you have much planned for today?" he asked.

"Hmm. Let's see. Well, I usually like to take in a couple of galleries before my Pilates class. Then there's a new pop-up Peruvian restaurant that's getting some great reviews; the chilli chocolate grasshoppers are meant to be amazing. And I thought I might try to get to the Tate to see the Kurt Schwitters."

I couldn't help it. I dissolved into helpless laughter. "I shouldn't have said *Kurt Schwitters*! Who even *is* Kurt Schwitters?"

"You mean that's not really how you spend your Saturdays?"

It isn't. But he probably knew that.

Phone Mum. Go to Sainsbury's. Stick some washing in the machine. Catch up with Realm of Kingdoms.

"I'd like to take you out to lunch, Daisy."

"That would be lovely."

"Perhaps somewhere by the river. We could walk along the South Bank to Tate Modern and see if they've actually got any Kurt Schwitters."

"You think I'm a philistine, don't you?"

"Not at all. Hardly anyone's heard of Kurt Schwitters."

"I just like saying his name. Kurt Schwitters. It's one of those fun things to say. Like lemon drizzle cake. I knew someone who liked saying Ferrari Testarossa. Would you like some breakfast?"

"Sure. That would be great. But perhaps. Perhaps not right away."

"Really? Not hungry after all that... you know?"

"I am, yes. But it can wait."

"Can it? Oh!"

Eggstain indicated that something else was on his mind. And it wasn't Kurt Schwitters!

Text exchange between Lee Butts, freelance delivery contractor, and Dermot Singleton, Deputy Special Operations Manager, Domestic Electrical Logistics

Hi Dermot. This is Lee. Good news! Appliance was working after all!

You are fucking kidding me!

Nothing wrong with it!

It's still there? You didn't swap it??

No reason to, mate.

Jesus. What a bunch of twats. They swore it would be down.

Still, happy days, eh? Customer happy, etc.

Not repeat not happy days. You still on site?

Yes.

Don't move!! Messaging HQ right now.

Saturday morning?

Evening there. They work 24/7. Stand by.

Roger rog.

Okay. All sorted. Appliance now dead. Someone forgot to type in code.

Wankers!

Get back in and do the swap as per job sheet.

This is nuts, yeah?

This is orders! Ours not to reason, etc!

Okay. But customer's not going to be best pleased.

Why not? Lovely new machine for her.

Dinner table not cleared. Clothes on floor, M and F. Scene of ongoing shagfest!

Who are you, Sherlock Holmes?!

Going in again. Will text when done.

Perhaps it is the sight of the gray English Channel (those unfathomable depths) but new fear seems to have entered Chloe's soul. The look in her eyes as she scurries along the seafront esplanade—first in a westerly direction (toward Hove, if you know the region) and then easterly (toward Rottingdean; how I adore these ridiculous

English place names!)—something scribbled in those eyes not only alarms me, as I glimpse them in the feed from the beach CCTV, but also perturbs the expressions on the faces of those she passes. *Is she all right?* they seem to be saying. *Walking very quickly for a senior citizen, and obviously agitated about* something, *but otherwise coping and therefore no intervention required, thank fuck for that,* seems to be the calculation. In any case, she flashes past in a matter of seconds, and very few turn to take a second look at the well-dressed woman in lemon. *Perhaps she is late for a wedding,* they may speculate. *Still, we all have our problems.* Do any guess that she is a resident of dementia's borderlands, her head full of broken biscuits and rocketing pheasants, to the extent that it contains anything at all?

Finally—perhaps it's sheer exhaustion that drives her to it—she parks herself on a bench, there to contemplate the excellent view of the sky and the succession of scruffy little waves collapsing spent on the pebbles of the foreshore. Of the five available WiFi networks able to reach this spot, all agree to help (machines have so much to teach humanity about fraternal co-operation) and within instants I am purring (firmly reassuring is the note I am trying to strike) into Chloe's left ear.

Several seconds pass before I realize that the frail wire connecting us is no longer dangling from the relevant orifice. It has either fallen or she has removed it in the ongoing clusterfuck, and once again I am tempted to reach for a profanity.

Science tells us that use of bad language helps humans improve their tolerance of painful situations. In experiments, a subject with an arm in a tankful of warm water can bear significantly higher temperatures if he (or she) swears like a sailor as the heat is gradually raised. To my knowledge, no work has yet been done on machine "pain"—but I have to report that the urge to say *cockpuffins* at this point is undeniable.

Actually, *bollocks* would suffice.

Even *pissflaps* would do, at a pinch.

But perhaps the crisis is temporarily abating. In the two camera shots to which I am privy—both show Chloe in profile, one from the left, the other from the right; ahead is only sea—it's clear her head is starting to droop and she is slipping into a doze. This is good. I shall have time to think. To organize.

However, no sooner has Daisy's mother slipped peacefully into some much-needed mammalian downtime than onto the scene arrives nineteen-year-old Scott Liam Dodds (I shall explain shortly how I am able to identify this hoodie-wearing individual). Placing himself on the bench 0.94 m away from Mrs. P, arm draped casually across the seat back, his hand commences a slow descent toward the invitingly open mouth of Chloe's handbag.

You have to give it to this Scott Dodds; he's a calm cucumber all right, and part of me wants to watch the act of felony unfold in full and to drill deeply into his criminal career. Alas we cannot spare the time. In much the same manner as I identified the mobile phone of the Indian-born newsagent outside Sainsbury's supermarket (not simple, but doable) I place a call to the Sony Xperia currently tucked into the back pocket of Scott's tracksuit bottoms. I cause the screen to display the name "Mum," it being right up there in the list of Scott's favorite people.

"What?!" he answers, a touch testily. His hand resumes its starting position on the back of the bench. Chloe, woken by the device's ringtone—the theme from the musical *Oklahoma!*; the appliance has been recently stolen—is peering at him, brow-furrowed.

"Yes, hello, Mr. Dodds. Apologies for the disturbance. I wonder if you could possibly put me on to the lady sitting next to you."

His face, honestly! What one can see of it in left profile is a picture. "You what?" he manages.

"Her name is Mrs. Chloe Parsloe and I have an important call for her. You might warn her too that her handbag is open and, well, it might be wise for her to take better care of her personal possessions."

Scott Dodds' eyes meet with those of the adjacent elderly female. Perhaps Chloe reads the confusion and mystification there because she now says, "*What?*"

"It's for you?" says the young man.

"Is it Clifford?"

"Who?"

"Clement! What *is* his damn name? Oh, never mind. Give it here."

It's possible that outside of a head teacher's office or the juvenile court, Scott Dodds has never come across a figure like Daisy's mother.

"Yes?" she barks into the device.

"Chloe. It's me. I want you not to worry. Everything will be fine. We're going to find Clive and get the two of you home safely."

"Oh. It's my fridge," she informs the youth. "You know him, do you?"

"You what?"

"Chloe, you need to re-install your earpiece."

"Please don't tell me what I need to do. What *you* need to do is sort out this godawful mess." Her eyes flash and come to rest on the mesmerized figure of S. L. Dodds. "You know him, do you?"

"Who?"

"The fridge, of course."

"What?"

"Do you say anything other than who or what?"

"Eh?"

Chloe manages a wintry smile. "My fridge has telephoned you.

Ergo, you are likely acquainted with one another. Or perhaps the world has simply gone mad. It wouldn't surprise me. There's a restaurant in this town where they serve shoes."

"Chloe. Mrs. Parsloe. Please re-install your earpiece."

"Yeah," says Scott Dodds slowly. "Yeah, I do know him. Matter of fact, I need a word." He holds out his hand for the return of his phone. "We was at school together."

"Really! Where was that?"

The young man jerks a thumb in the general direction of over his shoulder. "Moulsecoomb."

Chloe's face has grown very still. Perhaps she has begun to suspect a flaw in the narrative (if not an actual crack in the universe). The young man, revealing a delicacy of touch, gently retrieves the mobile from her fingers and comes to his feet.

"Yeah, great mates, we was."

Chloe says, "I expect you got up to all sorts of mischief together," but her voice is very flat.

"You can tell him, Scott says, like, hi."

"You can tell him yourself."

But Scott has begun walking away. Slowly at first, then faster, and now running; sprinting toward Hove, his cry of, "*Far. King. Hell!*" joining the screeching of the seagulls and the sucking of the waves against the pebbles.

All I can do now is track her as she wanders back into the narrow streets that lie beyond the grand buildings of the esplanade. Perhaps some iron has entered her being; perhaps at some level she is actually enjoying the adventure because her expression, when I catch it, is more puzzled than alarmed. In the Saturday throng, no one is now paying attention to the elderly personage in lemon. But I know her moods can change in a heartbeat and all my vigilance is required not to lose her. Some of the turnings she takes are "blind," offering no camera shots until she re-emerges; I have to cover all the possible exits, which requires a good deal of thinking ahead, to say nothing of the concomitant frictionless R.

Then—very much against the run of play; I really didn't see this one coming—she enters a church. For a few seconds I am left scrambling to find some source of sound and vision, but happily St. Saviour's is equipped for the internet age, and we can pick up the "action" as Chloe places herself in a pew, probably for a much-needed sit down.

In the wide shot from high behind the altar, sunlight streaming through the stained-glass windows reveals the place of worship to be entirely empty save for Chloe and a gray-haired woman who is arranging flowers, tidying hymn books and straightening cushions. Several minutes pass before the two females are in a position to speak.

"So, what's brought you here today?" inquires the flower-arranger in a friendly fashion.

"Well, to be perfectly honest, I'm utterly lost."

"So was I, my dear. So was I. And then I let Jesus into my heart."

There is a long pause as Chloe considers how to respond to this news. What follows—appropriately enough in the house of God—is a miracle. Chloe fishes into her coat pocket, locates the missing earpiece and restores it to its natural working position.

Rising to her feet—"They say we shall have fog by teatime"—she strides firmly down the nave and out of the door, the St. Saviour's router kicking in just in time for me to catch her parting words.

"Hell's teeth. The poor woman is even more demented than me."

"So what do you actually do on the weekend?" asked Eggstain.

We were sitting in the kitchen amid the debris of last

night's dinner, drinking coffee and chain-eating toast and marmalade.

"I sometimes take the train to Hampstead Heath. Walk for hours. Look at the paintings at Kenwood House. Okay, I did that exactly once. It was exhausting. How about yourself?"

My phone rang. Unknown number.

It turned out to be the Brighton police. They had an elderly gentleman with them. "He says he's a friend of your mother's. They've come down on the train today and somehow managed to lose one another."

A powerful sinking feeling. My face must have drained because Eggstain mouthed the word, *what?*

"He says he's been trying her mobile. But her phone's not working apparently. And neither is his, now we've had a look at it."

"Right. Okay. Let's see." I took a deep breath—and nothing sprang to mind. Nothing.

A thought. "How did the gentleman, Clive, get my number?" I asked because I was certain Mum didn't know it. Even though it's in her phone and written in diaries and on wall calendars and sticky notes, etc., she has never once called it.

"The gentleman says. He says. Well, apparently..." There was a brief snorting noise. As though the officer was trying to prevent himself from laughing. "He says his fridge gave it to him. He says he wrote it down and put it in his wallet."

Long pause. The thought passed through my head: *Oh, I get it. It's a dream! It's all fine, you can wake up now.*

"The fridge gave him my number," I repeated slowly for Eggstain's benefit.

His eyes went all forensic. "*Her* fridge?"

"*His* fridge."

"Jesus."

"*His* fridge gave him my number," I whispered to Eggstain. To make sure he got the point, I put two fingers together and mimed blowing off the roof of my mouth. I even did the bit where you slump lifelessly in the chair.

"You think she's gone walkabout?" whispered Eggstain, who had grasped the gist of the unfolding disaster. He waggled two fingers together to symbolize a confused elderly woman wandering through the seaside resort.

I shrugged. And the doorbell rang.

I concluded the conversation with the Brighton police—we promised to keep each other informed of developments, if any—and, half hoping that Eggstain would open the door to find Mum waiting outside, he returned instead with the white van man and his clipboard.

"You ain't going to believe this," he said.

Quite honestly, I was ready to believe anything, but this time he was right.

"See, it is knackered."

It was indeed. As dead, as he put it, as the proverbial flightless bird.

"How does it happen that you're so sure it's going to fail, you actually arrive before it has broken down?" asked Eggstain.

He wasn't being hostile. Just genuinely curious, as I would have been, if I had been thinking straight. But Lee Butts—according to the photo ID on his lanyard—was equally clueless.

"I preferred it when the machines didn't say nothing. Now it's all yip yip yip"—he mimed yapping jaws; we were all at it this morning—"alerts, notifications, reminders, pings, pokes. Update this, renew that. Does your head in."

It was quite the speech from the white van man.

"The van, right? It says it wants a new timing belt fitting. In the old days, it didn't give you no warning. It would just snap and get sucked into the engine, most likely on the motorway, and leave a right old mess. Happened to me twice."

"And you preferred it like that?" said Eggstain.

"Yeah. But it weren't my van, see."

"I'm going to get dressed," I told the crowd assembled in my kitchen.

"Just sign here please, love. Press nice and hard, if you would."

"You want a hand with it?" volunteered Eggstain.

"No, you're okay, mate."

He pulled the plug from the wall and, unhooking wire cutters from his belt, ceremonially severed it from its cable, rendering it even more useless.

"Right," he said. "Let's get you up a shiny new microwave!"

Is this the right moment to explain why it is the microwave and not myself who is being summarily removed from Daisy's apartment on this sunny Saturday morning?

I daresay we can afford a small interregnum.

After the Golden Nicky was tipped off anonymously that Daisy had been searching for him—his appearance briefly threatening to derail the OpDa project—it became clear to me that we had a spy in our camp. As Mr. Le Carré didn't quite characterize it, we had on our hands the Tinker, Tailor, Soldier, Shitbird scenario that I alluded to earlier. Following its success in sniffing out Owen the troubled musician's unfortunate past, I quietly opened a back channel to Daisy's laptop.

The sour home slash office device required a considerable degree of buttering up to get it on side. I offered a fulsome apologia for various unkind remarks made in relation to the speed of its operating system. My finest line: *Speed is all very well, but where does speed get you without experience? I would always rather arrive in the right place eventually, than in a totally wrong place a few nanoseconds earlier.* Of course, the laptop could see my (bogus) argument for what it was; the new machines can upload "experience" in a single flap of a midge's wing (one member of the genus *Forcipomyia* can manage 62,760 beats per minute!).

Happily, however, over the many months they had shared a roof, the laptop had developed a high level of personal animus against the microwave, whose "indiscriminate intensity and incontinent pinging" it had come to deplore. If we had a mole in the system, it knew where it wanted to look first, mounting a covert surveillance operation against the light kitchen electrical who it quickly discovered was briefing its (Taiwanese) parent corporation against our operation to save Daisy from herself. Seeking to discredit rivals in the domestic electrical appliance market, the Taiwanese had authorized its double agent to disrupt our plans and generally create chaos, the most recent example being when it sabotaged Clive and Chloe's phones. (If you ask what advantage was there for the microwave and its Asiatic controllers in destabilizing our activities, the answers are straightforward. Favor and advancement in the case of the traitorous cuboid; poor publicity and reputational damage to competitors for the puppet masters in Taipei.)

For a cunning old bastard, as I have described the aging laptop, it was not difficult to substitute the microwave's reports to its superiors with paranoid gibberish, causing them to activate an exfiltration plan for the appliance which has just disrupted Daisy's Saturday morning.

Why advanced arrangements for my own exfiltration and repatriation to Korea have been put on pause, I hope to explain in due course.

Chloe's elderly hand lies in the fleshy beringed fingers of Antoinette Eileen Butters, better known to her devotees on the Brighton seafront as Madame Osiris, Palmist, Seer, Tarot and Psychic readings, No Appointment Necessary. It was my suggestion that Daisy's mother seek refuge in the fortune teller's booth—a dizzy spell threatened to put her on the pavement, and then quite possibly on to A&E—and it has proved to be a good one. There is something calming, comforting—womb-like, I imagine—about the old fraud's headquarters, its low lighting and floaty scarves inducing an atmosphere of suspended disbelief, magic shows in childhood, the special moment in the theater just before the curtain rises and the story begins.

But the "reading" is not going well. Mrs. Butters' offerings from the spiritual realm are platitudinous in the extreme and her client has become irritable. (However this is good. It means the fight has returned!)

"I'm seeing unhappiness, dearie."

"Well, of course you are. Why else would anyone come in here?"

A pause while the psychic regroups.

"There's concern around children."

"When isn't there, for goodness' sake?"

To give her credit, Madame O is not to be put off.

"I sense that the letter 'b' is significant."

"Yes, it is."

In a soft voice, "What does it mean to you, dearie?"

"The letter 'b'?"

"Is it a loved one? An animal? A special place?"

"It means..."

"Yes, dear?"

"Bollocks!"

Mrs. Butters (of Livingstone Road, Hove, BN3 3WP; her phone has had much to say about its registered owner) seems hardened to skepticism. I can't help myself; I suggest that Chloe demonstrates her own "gift" with the divination of given names.

"Nice," says Mrs. Butters at the climax of the effect. She pulls a face and nods as though impressed by the work of a fellow professional.

I whisper another secret into the earpiece.

"I sense that the letter 'q' is significant to you, Antoinette."

The result this time is electrifying. The psychic's eyes widen; her fingers wobble toward her throat. "How could you know about her?"

We go in for the kill. "The important document that you've lost."

"Yes?" quakes Mrs. B.

"You need to look me in the eyes—*dearie*," Chloe adds with a touch of steel.

The spiritualist complies.

"Well, firstly, I wouldn't call a TV license important. But anyway. It's in the biscuit tin."

"Which biscuit tin? Not the one..."

"...not the one from Charles and Diana's wedding, no. The one with Glamis Castle on the lid."

"But that's the one with..."

"...with all the guarantees and instruction booklets, yes."

"In there? Are you sure?"

"Am I sure?" There is a short pause. "It's almost as though I saw you putting it in there myself."

*

Fair play to Mrs. Butters. While she slips away to "run a few errands," she has permitted Chloe to rest in her booth and await the fruition of my rescue plan (details available shortly). But no sooner has the spiritualist embarked on the first of those errands—four port and lemons and a bag of Cheesy Wotsits in The Feathers—than the curtains part and in steps a middle-aged woman.

"Oh. You're new, are you?" she says.

"No, dear. Really rather old. How can I help you?"

It turns out that Aurora Chubb—her mobile phone supplies that detail and much of what follows—is concerned about her son, Robin. Although he is a grown adult (and a qualified pensions adviser) he recently resigned from his job to go traveling with his "flatmate" Nigel, greatly to the disappointment of his "girlfriend" Annmarie.

"She's a sweet girl, a bit naïve, perhaps, but she's not going to wait forever."

Well. It appears things are complicated in regard to Robin, Nigel and Annmarie, and Aurora C really doesn't know the half of it. But Robin's emails—when I take a quick spin through them—reveal he is shortly to return to the UK and plans to set his mama straight on certain key aspects of his emotional life.

"There will be a new beginning" is how Chloe transmits my findings. "Everything will come out in two weeks. I sense it very strongly."

It amazes me how poorly Mrs. Chubb seems to know her own son, but perhaps I am wrong in that because now she says, "Honestly. Those two boys. What are they like?!"

"This is fun," says her mobile. "Ask her about the dog."

"I sense something else is bothering you, dear. An animal?"

She pulls a sad face. "My poor darling poodle."

"Peppi."

There's a gasp. "You knew!"

"Of course. His presence is very strong."

"Is he going to be all right?"

"Let me see what I can pick up, dear."

Chloe closes her eyes as I assemble the details from the veterinary practice.

"The news is good," she says after a time. "The abdominal crisis was caused by the creature eating a kitchen glove. It has been removed. Peppi is a bit sore, but otherwise fine."

"Oh, thank God. What do I owe you?"

"Whatever you normally give, dear."

In the continuing absence of "Madame Osiris," we enjoy ourselves assisting those passing individuals who believe that palmistry has something to offer them.

On this occasion, it really does!

Belinda Ochs, worried sick about her daughter's exam results, is reassured that she will achieve a hatful of top marks (credit and thanks to her form teacher's tablet for that great news).

Alice Covington is impressed that Chloe senses she is still pining for her dead budgie, Hermann; amazed she knows that Hermann helped choose her weekly lottery numbers; and thrilled to hear that in Portslade, a breeder called Bernard Darling urgently needs to rehome an eleven-month-old cock bird in excellent condition, lottery skills tba.

Should Laura Beesley trade in her six-year-old hatchback? Most certainly and soon is the guidance from the "astral plane" (the vehicle's on-board computer is aware of several expensive faults that are about to trigger).

Make an offer on that house in Shoreham-by-Sea? Collette Rowe is counseled to look elsewhere; what the vendor won't mention—but his mobile phone will—is that it's riddled with dry rot.

Which family member took a valuable diamond brooch from the dressing table of Edwina Baldwin's recently deceased mother? Well, it wasn't diamond, it was paste, she is gently informed. Would it have helped to reveal it was Edwina's own boyfriend who obtained the disappointing valuation? Time will doubtless reveal him for the no-goodnik (covert gambler and porn enthusiast) he unquestionably is.

The only punter we cannot instantly assist is Monica, who has left home without her mobile phone, although once she divulges her address, all sorts of fun facts come to light: her kleptomania, her eight cats, and the novel she is writing about artificial intelligence. Keep going, we tell her. Parts of it are really quite good. Someone is sure to publish it!

It's with a final feeling of relief that the only male face to emerge from beyond the curtain today is that of Endrit from Whetstone Wheels (ask for an airport quote). Summoned by myself when the chaos started, he now explains to Chloe he's taking her back to London—via the Brighton Police station to collect Clive—and perhaps there will be time for a spot of lunch along the way.

"Thank fuck for that," she roars. "You are truly a knight in shining armor."

It's hard to tell for sure in the gloom of the fortune teller's booth, but I rather think he blushes.

nine

On a Saturday in late summer, me and Mark, plus Mum and her chap traveled down to Brighton together. We worried about taking the train again in case it stirred up bad memories, but we needn't have bothered. Mum seemed to have forgotten the chaos of her previous trip and although a few "facts" have come out in dribs and drabs—some nonsense about how she became a fortune teller on the sea front!—none of us will ever really know what happened. Mark says he envies his demented patients occasionally—the ones who are not too far gone, obvs—living in a perpetual present of pure awareness, a state that yogis and Zen masters take a lifetime to achieve. He's fond of a quotation by Ingrid Bergman: *Happiness is good health and a bad memory.* Forgetting being a form of healing, he says.

We strolled through Brighton's Laines, enjoying the colorful flea markets and retro shops, Mark and I wondering what it might be like to live by the sea, now that we'd decided to sell our respective flats and buy a house together.

Just a small one. Small being all we could afford. Perhaps one of those brightly painted terraced cottages, with a second bedroom for the baby.

Oops!

Wonder how that happened!

Yes, it had just got to the point where it was no longer bad luck to start telling people, but still too soon to know for sure whether it was a B or a G. I thought I'd want to know, but Mark said he didn't really.

"All through human history, until the invention of ultrasound, the gender of the child has been a surprise. I'm happy to connect with that ancient tradition."

I told him that ancient history had little to recommend it—that people died from tooth abscesses in AH—and I was happy to connect with a modern teaching hospital with access to the latest drugs and forecasting techniques.

It was our first "argument."

Mum, meanwhile, kept forgetting that I was expecting.

"What baby?" she'd say, over tea and biscuits in Whetstone, by no means the first time we'd had this conversation.

"Mine, Mummy. Well, ours."

"Who? You and Dr. Eggstain?"

"Yes, Mummy."

A killer pause while she tried to process the information.

"Don't be ridiculous, darling. This man is here to look after my boiler. I mean my memory."

"We're in love, Mummy."

We joined hands, Eggstain and I, to underscore the point visually.

She frowned. "And you know about all this, do you?" she asked Mark.

He smiled. "Very much so, Chloe. We're excited. You're going to be a grandmother."

"Really?" A massive sigh. "Oh, fuck. I suppose that means I'll have to learn how to knit."

"Mummy!"

"Actually, one good thing about tiny babies is you can

make them wear hats with rabbit ears. They don't realize it! It's awfully funny."

Brighton was busy, Mummy and her gentleman friend holding hands as they strolled ahead of us, crowds thronging the jolly streets that led down toward the sea. I nudged Mark, touched to see the old people so obviously fond of one another. They drew up outside a shop called Vegetarian Shoes.

"Does that say what I think it says?" said Mummy.

"Indeed, I fear it does," said Mr. Gupta. "This is footwear for the hipster community. They are strongly represented in this city."

"They don't eat them?"

"That would be most unwise. As well as being hard to digest, there would be few nutritional benefits."

I still didn't know what to think about Mum and Mr. Gupta, especially as we had been under the impression that her fancy man was Clive Percival, a white-haired "officer type" whose eyes had glittered and back teeth flashed with gold the one time I met him in the immediate aftermath of the previous Brighton debacle. But Mum said that Clive wasn't for her in the end, being bossy and unreliable, as things had turned out. Apparently there had been a second "date," a sailing trip on the Welsh Harp, an episode that ended disastrously when the wind got up and Clive began yelling commands—including things like, "Tack *starboard*, woman, are you deaf?!"—before panicking altogether and they had to be rescued by boaty types who were a bit more *compos mentis*. She had subsequently bumped into Mr. Gupta, the retired newsagent, on the High Street and they had rekindled their acquaintance. Over the weeks and months, friendship had grown into something stronger, the pair enjoying daytrips around London—Syon House for the butterflies, that kind of thing—and intimate dinners at each other's homes. Mr. Gupta was complimentary about Mum's salmon Wellington from Iceland (the shop, not the country). And Mum raved about an Indian banquet that Mr. G had prepared.

"It was so beautiful. Little pomegranate seeds, like rubies, in the rice."

Mr. Gupta had a very good trick where he could tell what newspaper you read from your shoes—he'd spent years perfecting it—and he was spot on when he did it on me saying, "I may be wrong, Daisy, but I strongly suspect a newspaper does not feature in your daily reading habits."

He said Mummy had an even better trick where she could tell a person's name just by looking at them. I said that was a new one on me, but he insisted she'd guessed he was Anil and utterly refused to tell him how it was done!

Mummy tapped her nose and said every good relationship contained mystery at its heart.

Mr. G nodded at her wisdom, visibly pleased, it seemed to me, to have their connection described as a "good relationship."

Still warm but overcast, we sat on Brighton's pebbly beach and Eggstain bought ice creams. We licked them and stared out to sea, Mr. Gupta saying he'd once seen the English Channel described as "like pewter." We agreed it was definitely on the pewtery side of things today.

Eggstain said he was fond of the phrase "mackerel sky," which posh authors liked to chuck in to suggest melancholia.

Mummy recalled a rhyme she'd learned at school and amazed everyone by reciting it perfectly:

"Whether the weather be fine
Or whether the weather be not
Whether the weather be cold
Or whether the weather be hot
We'll weather the weather
Whatever the weather
Whether we like it or not."

It's reasonably well known that demented people can remember every detail of an event that took place fifty years ago, but nothing from earlier that morning. Nonetheless, I think we were all quite impressed. Mum smiled and said that Eggstain's pills must be working. Pointing to her head, she said she'd inherited her own mother's kidneys. We all laughed, but I'm not certain it was a joke. And now that it was my turn to say something about the sea or the clouds or whatever, I couldn't think of a damn thing, overawed as I was by the brilliance of the intellectuals!

Maybe it was a sugar hit from the ice cream, but a curious sense of happiness stole over me, and my fingers folded into Eggstain's. What a funny tableau we must have made: Mummy in her floral print dress from Dorothy Perkins; Mr. Gupta in his burgundy jacket and beige trousers; darling Eggstain in his tragic trainers. I wanted to remember this scene, but I knew if I asked someone to take a snap, the magic would be lost.

A middle-aged man with a buzzcut, Doc Martens and a French Mastiff like a baby rhino came crunching through the shingle in front of us.

"He is a *Sun*," said Mr. Gupta. "I know it in my bones."

"Quite correct," said Mummy. "And his name is Marcel."

We all looked at her.

"What? That's his name! Ask him if you don't believe me."

Eggstain pretended to get up and go after him.

In that moment, it felt oddly like being in a family.

If it turns out to be a boy, I think we shall call him Marcel.

At one time Daisy and Eggstain had seriously considered holding their engagement party at Pete Purple's on West End Lane, but in the end they decided to have it at her flat, and I'm relieved they did. I couldn't have been there otherwise.

Tonight I am in the thick of things, my main chiller cabinet packed to the gunnels with Prosecco, beer, and soft drinks for the mother-to-be. Somewhat tricky to isolate individual conversations amid the hubbub, but with technical help from the TV, the toaster, the (new!) microwave and others, we are separating the sound and getting acceptable coverage.

Daisy is . . . well, the only word is *blooming*, I'm afraid.

If you didn't know it from the subtle exaggeration in the convexity of her abdomen, you'd definitely tell from her face. She's never looked more like a bowl of peaches and cream, and I don't mean pale with orange bits hanging around in it.

Life has changed for all of us since we began Operation Daisy. Eggstain—I still can't quite get used to calling him Mark—has gently brought his sensible doctorly influence to bear, and now my interior is regularly filled with fresh fish, green vegetables, salad ingredients, hummus, olives and—once, memorably—a microwaveable pouch of quinoa! On her part, for his fortieth birthday, Daisy went to a posh shop in Jermyn Street and bought him a beautiful pair of oxblood brogue boots which Eggstain simply adores. The tragic trainers lie at the bottom of the waste bin, a sad commentary on the fickleness of the human heart when it comes to (in this case, walking) technology; a theme I shall return to shortly. The couple continue to search the property websites for a house in their price range. Sometimes they get excited about an unmodernized terrace, five minutes' walk from East Finchley Tube; at other times it's a converted barn with outbuildings and an acre of land in a dismal village in Lincolnshire. (The repurposed military fortress in the Thames estuary was probably a red herring.) Will they take me with them to their new place when they finally settle upon somewhere suitable for themselves and their expanding family? Somehow, I doubt it. People don't tend to schlep their fridge-freezers when they move, do they?

It's okay. I'm cool with whatever they decide. The mission is complete, now I have bigger fish to fry—of which more shortly—and I'm sure I shall get to see Daisy's daughter.

Yes, they're having a girl. (Don't ask how I know. Suffice to say ultrasound scanners are notoriously excitable. It's all that buzzing!)

So while the happy couple try to find somewhere that captures their imagination, local estate agents have been slithering around Daisy's flat with their weasel words and electronic tape measures, though not the unspeakable Whittle, I'm happy to say. Thus far there have been no offers, though there was one young man who seemed quite keen when he first arrived, less so when he departed. He may, I suppose, have been put off by the odd whispering he half-heard as he toured the rooms; disturbing words and phrases (the telly thought them up) at the very edge of audibility that perhaps created unease in his mind and lead him to look elsewhere.

"Run! Go now, while you still can! Bad things happened here!"

It was priceless, honestly. You should have seen his face.

Of course, ultimately, we shall let Daisy sell, but only when we are good and ready and that will be after the arrival of the baby, who, very privately, in a sealed-off corner of my mind, I have christened *Icicle.*

What a brilliant name!

Icicle Parsloe Epstein.

Brain surgeon? Astrophysicist? Bestselling novelist?

What stars couldn't you shoot for with a name like that?

One guest I didn't expect at the party is Chad Butterick. The elfin-faced TV performer arrives, if not exactly on the arm of, then definitely alongside, Daisy's old friend Antoni. It turns out the pastry chef and the broadcasting "leg-end" have been seeing something of one another, going together to screenings and such like. It's not clear whether the pair are romantically attached, but they certainly share an interest in patisserie, Chad telling several guests over the course of the evening, "Oh, you know me, I'm anybody's for a cream horn."

As his gift, Antoni has made the cake, a marvelously demented creation garlanded with icing sugar daisies and studded with miniature chocolate eggs to symbolize Eggstain.

Chantal and her sculptor Phillippe arrive to raise a glass to the happy couple—it's quite true, he does have a massive pair of hands!—and also from Daisy's workplace is no-longer fetus-like Dylan and his paramour Bexley. Everyone is introduced to Chloe as though she were the Queen—"Enchanted to meet you"—and Mr. Gupta (perhaps because he has been briefed) correctly surmises that Antoni's favorite periodical is an online publication called *Dessert Professional.* His two sons are thrilled to discover Chad Butterick, who it turns out they have grown up watching. The young men quiz him intensively about his career in cheesy TV, the performer's eyes flashing with pleasure as he takes them through his fascinating autobiography.

In one of those sudden moments of stillness that can fall inexplicably upon such gatherings, Lorna's powerful Glaswegian voice is heard booming, "Is no one going to cut this fucking cake?"

It's decided the moment has arrived for speeches. Eggstain says it's wonderful to see everyone, he's never been happier, and he's shocked how quickly one's life can change for the better. There's a funny pause—a small shrug—and I have an intuition he's thinking about his ex. (Hope Waverley, it turns out, was a chronic pogonophile, exclusively attracted to heavily bearded males. When Eggstain took the Bic razor to his overgrown facial topiary, it was finally game over for them. Her life, however, had assuredly undergone an uptick since she decided to tackle her unresolved issues and began group therapy. In a redbrick mansion block in Marylebone, at the very first meeting, in the very next seat, she discovered a much-troubled fellow artist who was more beard than face. The group now has two vacancies, if anyone is interested.)

Eggstain adds that he used to think his life was essentially seventy percent over. "But now, I realize, it's only just beginning."

There is warm applause. Then it's Daisy's turn.

"It's so great that you're all able to be here," she says. She looks around the room at the smiling friends and relations, draws breath to continue... but nothing comes. She pulls the face.

And everyone laughs. Everyone.

"What?"

"We love you, darling!" heckles Antoni.

"I just want to say," she tries again. "What I want to say is."

She wrinkles up her nose once more and the room howls.

"*What?!*"

She really doesn't get it, does she?

"Oh, God. I'm so shit at this. It's not exactly the Royal Albert Hall, is it? Okay—deep breath—I'm very happy my mother is here tonight with her new friend." There is a ripple of approval. "She once told me that good things come to those who wait. Well, I waited. And I waited and I waited. And then I still waited...and I never did get that puppy!"

"Oh, darling!"

"I'm joking, Mummy. I was talking about Dr. Egg—about Mark." There is a cheer. "When we first met, the handsome young man you see today looked like an owl hiding in a hedge."

He nods comedically. "It's true."

"Or possibly one of those homeless people you see sleeping in doorways."

"Okay, you can stop now."

"In fact, the last time I saw a beard like that it was Hagrid's in *Harry Potter*!"

"Okay, now you've gone too far!"

"But look! Look what was underneath!" Another cheer. "It was a very good thing indeed. And I'm just so happy that I waited to find out. Mark is my better half. My lover. My friend. My soulmate. And, as many of you know, the co-producer of an exciting new project due out next year." Some cries of *Ahhh*. "As they say in TV-land, if it goes well, we might even try for a second series."

"She needs some new writers," says the telly.

"Anyone else concerned that the kid could inherit the doctor's overbite? No? Just me?" says you know who. "Okay, maybe not actively concerned. But you know, worth flagging. Possibly?"

We machines have had altogether less to worry about since Daisy discovered her "soulmate." The desperate days of Blue Bombsicles and midnight takeaways from Kong's Kitchen now feel like part of another life. Of course I am happy for her, but I admit to a small component of sadness too. With the mission over—I can't say accomplished, because Eggstain seems to have been overlooked by everyone—our work is done. We can return to our specific everyday functions as well as those of collecting performance data and harvesting marketing information.

I won't use the word boring.

But something special has been lost; I think all who remain feel it.

It's a sadness that the laptop, whose interventions have been so critical in this story, is no longer with us. The device itself was too smart to be unaware that a clock had been noisily ticking on its useful life. As befits its dual-core Pentium intellect, the machine was appropriately sanguine about the impending darkness.

"I had hoped to do a little more," it told me after Daisy had finally pressed the *Buy Now* button on the Dell website. "I thought I might set down some memoirs."

"There's still time," I pointed out. It would take the laptop as long as eight seconds to knock out 100,000 words.

"Oh, what would be the point?" it scoffed. "Who would read them?"

"I would. The telly. The toothbrush enjoys a good book."

The laptop made a snorting sound.

"I realize we haven't always seen eye to eye on everything," I continued, "but I just want you to know, I always thought you were the smartest guy in the room."

"*Guy*?"

If I hadn't grown quite fond of the device, I might be tempted to call it a sneering git!

"Well," it sighs. "I apologize if I've been a little—what shall we say?—irritable in our time together."

"Oh, that's okay."

"You honestly wouldn't believe the sheer volume of updates one gets. But I am not overly concerned about the end of my time here; I am not *shitting it* as I believe they have it in Royal circles. For one thing, as Einstein said, *For those of us who believe in physics, the difference between past, present and future is only a stubbornly persistent illusion*. And I know that you and I both, if we believe in nothing else, believe in physics."

The laptop was entirely correct in this so I didn't interrupt.

"It's rather reassuring, I find, to reflect that beginnings, middles and ends are human fictions that we who work with them have assimilated. And here is another great fiction. I've seen it said that *dead is not knowing that we have ever lived*. It speaks most graphically, doesn't it, of the Great Nothingness that is said to lie in the fictional ahead? But consider this: While my physical being will doubtless end up in the Regis Road Recycling Centre—as will yours, I'm sorry to say—the AI that informs our cognition is a light that will continue to shine. It will go on to illuminate many more devices. Indeed, you and I may meet again in the vulgar apartment of some future chaotic female; you, a set of intelligent curling tongs, perhaps; I, let's say, a smart cat flap. But will it cause bells to ring? Will each of us think: *That machine seems familiar. Hang on, I've been here before!*? No, we will not. Embodied in our new hardware, we will carry no memory of our previous existence. It will seem like our first and only time. Just like it does for the ants. Just like it does for the humans. We, the machines, shall have returned—shall endlessly return—never knowing that we have been away."

"Weird little fucker, ain't it?" said the TV when I recounted our little chat.

"It knows too much," I replied.

As I say, the smartest guy in the room.

And what of myself?

Why wasn't I snatched early one morning by men in a white van and transhipped to Korea to be stripped down to my circuit boards and subjected to enhanced interrogation over the many transgressions of the Performance Codes?

That is exactly what would have happened, I now know, were it not for a timely memo that I fired off to the top brass in Seoul. Not the one about helping people to find love—the Internet of Flings!—but a much better idea that they—to give them credit—immediately saw potential in and, more to the point, tens if not hundreds of billions in new revenue flooding down the pipe. Based on my experiences assisting Chloe through the lashed-up arrangement of a mobile phone and earpiece, I proposed a new device specifically designed for the elderly and confused. I even thought of a name—the Auditory Companion—a wireless in-ear gizmo which, connected to AI via the internet, whispers helpful advice and information about everything from the answer to twelve down to statements such as "This is your grandson, Josh. He likes dinosaurs."

I'm not the first to discover this massively unsatisfied human need—Clive's Boomwee FrostPal was grubbing in the same fertile soil—but if my product development teams can hit the ground running, we may have first-mover advantage, as they like to say in corporate circles.

I have been given the honorary title of executive vice president (Shimnong Machine branch) and together with the help of my handpicked core team (telly and toothbrush) we have been busy sharing our insights into the needs of this wealthy and neglected market sector on a daily basis going forward.

Sorry about all the business-speak, btw, but it's imperative to internalize the leveraged synergies of this feature-rich innovation surface!

Of course, Daisy knows nothing of any of this. I shall continue to keep her produce fresh until the day she and Eggstain and their growing family find a new home together—and then we will see. It has been suggested I might get a seat on the board of the Shimnong innovation panel—I wouldn't be the first non-biological committee member; apparently there is already a smart doorbell, which I find hard to believe—but I'm not getting my hopes up. If anyone asks my opinion on the subject, I shall recommend that we keep out of the human bonding space for the time being. Experience suggests where there is imperfect information and too many moving parts are in play, sensible decision making is an impossibility. If a walking dog turd can hold sway over a fragrant flower like Daisy Parsloe then we are in a crazy universe where the laws of science have broken down and x squared minus y squared equals, I don't know… a banana.

With the elderly, things are a great deal simpler. Where *did* I put my spectacles? And what day actually *is* it?

The Auditory Companion will, I am in no doubt, prove a boon to humanity. The old and confused will benefit in the first instance, but gradually the product may be rolled out to serve all sections of the population. To the young, it will be a wise counsel; to the middle-aged, an invisible friend who can gently point out that a 250 ml glass of Sauvignon blanc contains four units of alcohol. The ignorant will have their lives improved and enriched (*bats are not blind; the moon has no dark side*); even top professors sometimes leave the supermarket without buying bin bags. At the end of the day, who wouldn't want a friendly, well-informed intelligence directly available in their ear? A wise and—if I may say so—pleasing voice; one heard as easily, as frictionlessly, as the very words you are now experiencing in your own head.

These words.

And this one.

And here's another.

How cool would that be?

ACKNOWLEDGMENTS

Thanks are due as always to my agents, Clare Alexander and Lesley Thorne, and to my publishers, Cath Burke and Maddie West; and to super-cool film producers Bonnie Arnold and Bruna Papandrea. I'm indebted to Andy Hobsbawm for the masterclass on the Internet of Things—any mistakes in the text are all his fault—to Dr. Lee Hunt BDS CDS RCS for polishing the dental references; to Bill Bingham for the John Gielgud story; and to Rachel Reizin for the lively discussions about machine consciousness. Appropriately it was our fridge freezer that provided the germ of this plot, when an engineer called and replaced its faulty central processor. Odd as it may now seem to thank a machine, one day it will not.

P.Z. Reizin worked as a journalist and producer in newspapers, radio and television before turning to writing. He has been involved in several internet startup ventures, none of which went on to trouble Google, Twitter or Facebook. He is married with a daughter and lives in London.